Wildflowers

Wildflowers

Lyah Beth LeFlore

POETRY BY SHIRLEY BRADLEY LeFLORE

Broadway Books
New York

BROADWAY

This book is a work of fiction. Names, characters, businesses, organizations, places, events, and incidents either are the product of the author's imagination or are used fictitiously. Any resemblance to actual persons, living or dead, events, or locales is entirely coincidental.

Published in the United States by Broadway Books, an imprint of the Crown Publishing Group, a division of Random House, Inc., New York.
www.crownpublishing.com

BROADWAY BOOKS and the Broadway Books colophon are trademarks of Random House, Inc.

Library of Congress Cataloging-in-Publication Data available upon request.

ISBN 978-0-7679-2119-0

PRINTED IN THE UNITED STATES OF AMERICA

1   3   5   7   9   10   8   6   4   2

First Edition

During the process of writing this book I underwent a major transformation personally, professionally, and spiritually, and I thank God, first and foremost, for seeing me through.

To the women whose stories and spirits inspired this book: Mom, thank you for blessing these pages with your powerful and prolific poetry, you are my rock and the wind beneath my wings; my sisters, Hope and Jacie, who give me the encouragement to fly even higher; my cousin, Karen, who read draft after draft and pushed me to the finish line; my other big sister, Theresa, for helping me find peace within and not allowing me to give up on myself; and to my cousin Melissa and my niece, Noelle, remember that through great challenges, great women emerge; and Aunt Cynthia for your support. And to the women who laid the foundation for our very special *House of Estrogen*—Annette, Barbara, and Minnie.

Finally, to the men who tolerate *all* that estrogen: Daddy, my cheerleader; my brother-in-law, Drew, for always having my back; Richard and Nick Bohr; my nephews, Jullian and Jordan; Eno, the chosen "one"; baby Zion; and to the memory of John "Poppa" Lindsay Sr. for your legacy through photographs that captured our stories.

THE DAVIS WOMEN

The Mothers	*The Daughters*
Joy Ann Davis Nash-Michaels	Fawn Nash-Moore
	Eve Nash
	Chloe Michaels
Billye Jean Davis Crouthers-Wilcox	Thora Crouthers-Gold
Carol Jane Davis Gibson	Cecilia "Ceci" Gibson

A NOTE TO THE READER

My great-grandmother, MaMaw, was elegant and stately with beautiful, velvety mocha skin and keen features that traced back to our rich African roots. She was well respected in the Joplin community, a small town in Missouri where she and Paw, my great-grandfather, owned their own farm. MaMaw prided herself on that and the fact that she was self-educated and the daughter of a free man, Joseph Nance, an entrepreneur from the North, who purchased her mother—a slave—Vivian's freedom. People would come from all over the area to hear her read her poetry and speak at church gatherings, where she encouraged Negro women to empower themselves. MaMaw and Paw had seven children, five of whom were girls—Honor, Hazel, Elizabeth, Margaret, and Sarah.

Sarah, also known as Muh, was my grandmother and followed in MaMaw's footsteps with her work in the church and the community. Later, when she moved to St. Louis, her home became the centerpiece of family activity, especially on Sundays. The women in our family would gather for a "feeding of the souls and spirit." Growing up, that same tradition evolved, and alternated between Sunday dinner and Saturday night social hour, both of which took place around the kitchen table. The women told stories, shed tears, and shared pieces of their lives through philosophical, comical musings on life. This *was* your initiation into womanhood—a "rite of passage."

Unfortunately, as wonderful as the tales of MaMaw and Muh are, there's a dark side to our family too, filled with secrets and lies. That's the part I had to piece together from half-whispered conversations over the years. So you see I'd much rather hype up all the fabulous things about my family's history, but then I'd be doing like everyone else . . . lying. Well, let me not say that. Truthfully, about 50 percent of it is pride, and the other 50 percent is just plain denial. The only thing no one in this family *can* deny is the fact that the female chromosome dominates the gene pool. Call it a curse or a blessing, but Lord knows we have our share of mood swings, migraines, and menopause. Yet, in spite of it all, love sustains us, and our faith and belief in God is our bond. So, on second thought, since keeping quiet is what we've always done, why shouldn't I keep with tradition?

Sincerely,
Chloe Michaels

PROLOGUE

Wildflowers
A flower grows/beauty wild/seed of nature's soul/wildflowers
grow/heaven's tears and sunstruck rays/wicked winds a breath of
storms under winter's gray or autumn's raspberry clouds/a flower
born/laughs, lives, dances, sings, dies, returns, blossoms/again live
Nurtured by nature
B'tween green weeds and sweet grass/meadows and fields/clover
and brush like a woman tale-spinning her colorful journey swirling
and skirting pinksweets and poppies/primrose and buttercups/
chamomile and chicory/blue flax and baby breath/purple cones,
dandelions and daffodils/catchflies and dragon fly among a basket
of gold
Nurtured by nature
Wild as black-eyed suzies/scarlet yarrows/morning glories/wild blu
iris/johnny jump-ups/ox-eyed daisies soothing as lavender hyssop
and creeping zinnias growing wild along roadsides and byways/
highways/country trails and iron rails
Nurtured by nature
A colorama spray growing/beauty wild like a ladywomanflowergirl/
bending/swaying/face-up/and bowing and standing tall in earthtones
and greens in chaos and calm/growing/
Wildflowers

Wildflowers

For it hath been declared unto me of you, my brethren, by them which are of the house of Chloe, that there are contentions among you . . .

—I CORINTHIANS 1:11

SECRETS

I have known women
Blu/blk/tan/highyella/blu-vein women/rivercrossing women/
Waters deep as the Nile/Mississippi as mudd/seaboard and island
ocean women/who ride the waves and balance the tide/swimming
women/waterwalking women/treading waters/floating going with
the flow women/backstroking/jellyfishing/mudd crawling women/I
know women who drown/sinking women who sleep at the bottom
of the waters . . .

Chloe

A BIBLE AND A GUN

MY HANDS WERE as steady as a surgeon's, precise and meticulous as I flipped out the chamber of my Ladysmith .357. Sweat poured down my trembling body, soaking through my cotton nightgown and terry-cloth robe. I felt as though I had just walked through hell's fire, but had been yanked out by hand of the Lord and baptized in his blood all at once. I closed my eyes tightly, my thoughts battling the deafening throb, pounding between my ears. I could hear Mother's words, *"Don't tell nobody everythin'. You gotta keep the devil guessin'!"*

I'd owned this gun for almost three years and as many times as I'd practiced loading and unloading it I'd never actually shot the damn thing. I figured tonight is just as good as any to break it in. I grabbed a fistful of bullets from a small leather pouch, dumping them into a pile on the floor, and started to load them into the chamber one by one. My brain was running on fumes, but one thought was crystal clear: *The devil has to go.*

I know you shouldn't question God, but this is one of those times I gotta make an exception. What *happened*, God? Was this a test and I failed? I wonder, if a God-fearing person has to make a decision to do something drastic, in this case taking another's life to save two, does that still make it a sin? God, *please* forgive me, but there just ain't no more time to keep contemplating the what-ifs, whys, and how comes. I have to do this for my unborn child.

Crash!

I was jolted by the sound of a wooden chair scraping across the tiled kitchen floor, quickly followed by the loud cracking sound of splintering wood and shattering glass. My heart raced as I slipped the last bullet into the chamber and snapped it closed.

"You owe me money and I want out of this marriage!" His menacing, rage-filled voice echoed through the entire house.

"Stop breaking my things!" I screamed, cupping one hand over my ear.

No weapon that forms against me shall prosper . . .

"Chloe!" Every time he called my name it sent a shock wave throughout my entire body. "Get the fuck out here now! Do you hear me?" He slammed the hall closet door shut. "I used to have a good life!" His shouts faded in and out as he walked from room to room. "You ruined my fuckin' life!"

His expensive Italian loafers made a series of quick dull thuds on the carpet as he barreled down the hallway toward the back bedroom, where I had sought safety.

Clop . . . Clop . . . Clop . . .

His steps stopped just on the other side of the door. He liked expensive things, shoes especially. I had grown sickened by how he made it a point daily to advertise how much he paid for each pair he owned. It was his idea to sell all my large pieces of furniture. He said we were going to start our lives fresh together. The first thing he convinced me to do was clear out the guest bedroom.

He turned the entire room into his personal dressing room. Shoes, some never worn, housed in fancy shoe boxes, stacked in alphabetical order according to designer, lined the walls. I had never met a man who owned more pairs of shoes than I did.

"Chloe!" he shouted as he furiously jiggled the doorknob. "I can't believe you locked the fuckin' door. Open the door!"

Bam! Bam! Bam! Bam!

His fist pounded against the door.

No weapon that forms against me shall prosper . . .

"Get away from my door!" I shouted. With one hand firmly gripping the gun and the other clenching my belly, I scooted across the floor, bracing my back against the base of the bed, and grabbed my bible off the nightstand shelf with my free hand and wedged it in my armpit.

"I fuckin' hate you!" Venom oozed from his words.

Bam! Bam! Bam! His fists sounded again. This time more forcefully, as if they were tearing through the door. "I wanna talk to you!" *Bam! Bam! Bam!*

"You're crazy! What do you want? You don't bang on the door like a lunatic if all you want to do is talk," I firmly replied.

"Look, I just need to talk to you face-to-face." He leaned his head on the door, and let out a deep sigh. This time his voice was calmer and his words, more controlled.

"I'm not opening the door, but I'm listening," I said.

"Listen to me, you need to get an abortion," he said matter-of-factly.

"You are insane!" His shocking demand nearly knocked the wind out of my lungs.

"Don't you realize you and this fuckin' baby are ruining my life?" he exploded, pounding his fist on the door repeatedly, no longer able to contain his anger.

"Your mama should've gotten a damn abortion!" I was furious, releasing the safety on the gun, aiming it at the door. I tightened my sweaty grip on the handle and placed my finger on the trigger.

"I want my life back. Unlock the fucking door!" He kicked the door repeatedly like a madman.

"I'm calling the police!" I yelled, picking up the cordless phone and quickly dialing 911.

"911 operator, may I help you?"

"Yes, I'm in the middle of a domestic situation," I said in a strained whisper. My right hand was shaking. The gun felt like it was weighing my whole body down.

"Are you hurt, ma'am?"

"Well, no. I mean, not yet," I answered, slightly confused. "But I know he's going to hit me. He's kicking the door. Don't you hear him? I don't feel safe." I felt a sharp pain in my stomach. My forehead was sopping wet by now, and a salty mixture of tears and sweat trickled down my face, seeping between my lips. "Look, will this call be logged in?" I frantically asked.

"Yes, ma'am. What's your address, ma'am?"

"Get off the goddamn phone!" he taunted outside the door.

"I'm at 12669 Camarillo Drive!" I said, holding the receiver closer to my mouth. "The police are going to come!" I warned, covering the phone.

His fists slammed against the door. "You bitch!" he shouted, slamming his fists against the door once more, before storming off.

Clip! Clop! Clip! Clop! Clip! Clop! Clip! Clop!

His urgent footsteps were suddenly moving away from the bedroom door, back up the hallway. I heard the front door fly open, then quickly slam shut.

"Did you say you *had* or *hadn't* been hit?"

"Hadn't!" I snapped. "But he was in there breaking up all my things, and threatening me!"

"So you're *just* in an argument?" she asked in a condescending tone. "Well, do you want us to send a unit out?"

She had taken my dilemma about as seriously as a hangnail. I sat, momentarily choked by silence, glancing down at my gun.

"Ma'am, do you want us to send a unit?" she asked again.

His SUV engine revved up, and the tires ripped across the driveway's asphalt.

"Ma'am?"

"No, that's okay."

"Are you sure?"

"Positive," I said, hanging up, distraught and frustrated.

There was an eerie silence in the house. I was still holding the gun, but my hands weren't shaking anymore. I scanned the dimly lit bedroom, catching my reflection in the dresser mirror. I was no longer certain of anything, and I didn't even recognize myself. All the good times, girlfriend gatherings, barbecues, house parties, laughter, and joy were frozen. The stench of lies lingered in the air, and ugliness loomed in each room. It wasn't supposed to be like this.

My pastor, Reverend Ward, had blessed this house when I bought it four years ago. Mother even flew out here to anoint each room with sacred oil. She told me my ancestors' spirits would always watch over me. My home was supposed to be *my* little piece of peace, but now fear and pain covered these walls.

When I was a little girl, my mother told me I could be whatever I wanted to be. She also told me I'd grow up and meet a man who would love me like he loved his own mama. Daddy told me I was a princess, that I deserved the best. He never laid a hand on me or my sisters, and I'll be damned if a man not worthy to have air in his lungs is gonna do that now. Mother taught me how to pray good prayers just like her mother and hers before that, but I couldn't muster the words tonight. God, just make this all go away.

Tonight, I imagined my mother stroking my hair, putting her arms around me. "Let Mama hug you up and make it all better." I could almost hear her soothing whisper. For a moment I found comfort in the thought, wrapping my arms around my bloated, warm belly. Don't worry, little one, Mama's gonna take care of us.

No weapon that forms against me shall prosper . . .

I should've called home sooner. I should've told Mother the truth all the times she called, asking was I *really* okay. I thought I could make it work. I thought the baby would make it right. I had even convinced myself that I could live with things. I squeezed my eyes shut even tighter. So hard I almost blinked myself into another time, space, life.

No weapon that forms against me shall prosper . . .

I kept rubbing my belly, remembering how when I was a little girl, my mother would make warm milk and honey at night to settle my stomach and help me dream about the "happy things," like bright colors, butterflies, and being tickled until you laughed yourself to sleep. We would sit at the kitchen table for what seemed like hours. Mother would tell wonderful stories about my grandmother, Sarah, affectionately called Muh, and my great-grandmother, MaMaw. Strong women who loved their men, but loved themselves first and always protected their children.

"You know we been blessed with many gifts, Chloe. Our ancestors saw to that," she would whisper, turning the eye on the stove off as the milk began to bubble and steam over. My eyes, ears, and breath would hang on to her every word.

"What kind of gifts, Mother?" I asked with wonderment.

"The gift of sight, child," she said, slowly stirring a small teaspoon of honey into the milk, carefully pouring the steamy, frothy white liquid into two teacups, without spilling a drop. My favorite part was listening to the quiet sizzle of the milk against the sides of the saucepan, and how the aroma of warm sweetness teased my nostrils and made me drowsy, soon to be followed by sweet dreams of those happy things she always talked about. "You come from mystical, spiritual women of past generations," she'd say.

I didn't understand for a long time what she meant by "sight." Later I learned it meant they could see things in their dreams. Things like the birth of a child, even premonitions of death. Others could perform powerful rituals that could heal the sick, or cast spells on bad people. Muh and MaMaw could even speak in tongues, pray so good the devil knew better than to come crossing their paths. I was calling on them tonight, in need of some of those good fighting prayers right now.

I had been evasive for weeks, smiling when I was on the verge of crying, laughing when I felt like dying. A prisoner in my own home, my every move watched. Trips to the grocery store timed. My own money rationed out. I had only been married to Gregorry Marion Robinson III for four months, but it felt like I had been robbed of the best years I had to offer.

Mother's words carried the same power as Muh and MaMaw's. As much as I had dreaded spilling my guts about the mess I had gotten myself into, I knew it was time to call home. I grabbed the phone, quickly scrolling down to MOM, still keeping a good hold on the gun. I checked the clock. It was after 1:00 A.M. back home. I changed my mind, and closed the phone.

I climbed onto the bed, put the safety back on the gun, and slid it underneath the pillow. I opened my bible to the Twenty-third Psalm and began to read. *The Lord is my shepherd, I shall not want. He maketh me to lie down in green pastures. He leadeth me beside the still waters.* I yawned, resting my head on the coolness of the pillow. I curled up into the fetal position and gently caressed my stomach.

God keep us safe. My eyelids felt like weighted fingers were pulling them down. I yawned again, fighting back the temptation to just close my eyes for a second or two. I needed to stay alert in case Gregorry came back. I ran my fingers through my damp hair. My scalp was warm, tight, and tender, too many thoughts and worries fighting to get out.

I could hear my ancestors whispering, *Rest sweet, Chloe. No weapon that forms against you shall prosper. No weapon that forms against you shall prosper . . .* They were watching over. Calmness encircled me. I could feel the presence of God's angels, Mercy and Grace. I closed my eyes, giving in to the battle, and drifted off to a place that was safe. My bible kept guard over the gun. *Vengeance is not mine . . .*

Joy Ann

SOMETHIN' IN MY BONES

To my girls: I wanna dream you a special place. I wanna take whatever's hurting you away . . .

I NEVER WORRIED SO much about my girls 'til recent years. I guess I'm no different than any other mother in the sense that by instinct you want to wrap your arms around your children, hug 'em up good, protect 'em. I know they grow up and you have to set 'em free, but they're still mine, and I can feel in every inch of my body when somethin's not right with one of them, too.

I've been sick for a week and I wasn't sugar sick or heart sick. I can't really describe it either, but I ain't been able to paint in days. Somethin's blockin' my creative flow. I feel stifled. I ain't even been dreamin' lately. I need a breakthrough, Lord. So I woke up early this mornin' and burned some sage. I placed fresh lemon water on every windowsill in the house, and opened the Bible to the Seventieth Psalm. Then I got down on my knees and prayed real hard.

Lord, you've blessed me with three daughters. I would've done more for 'em if I had it to give 'em. But I think they turned out pretty good. Just like the song says, "Never woulda made it, never coulda made it without you," Lord have mercy, that's my testimony. Thank you,

Jesus! Without you, God, I would've gone stark, ravin' crazy tryin'
to protect each one of 'em.

I've had to cover up a lot of the truth about life, especially the
truth about their daddies. Some things you just don't need to tell your
children. But I'm tired. I'm tired of holdin' it all together, tired of being
the cleanup woman. At sixty-eight, I deserve me some kind of life, too.
I still ain't gave up on the hope of my art being seen all over the world
and even finding me some piece of love. I still got dreams and I know
you ain't through with me yet. Thank you, Jesus! Amen.

When I was finished with my morning prayers, I gathered my
brush bucket and paints and headed out into the yard. I stretched a
piece of canvas over an old wooden frame I had out back. This damn
arthritis in my hands has been creepin' up on me for the last few days,
but I put a little of my green Chinese oil on it and was able to get it on
there pretty good.

I put my easel out in the yard. The sunshine is healing. They say the
temperature's gonna start heatin' up good. Probably gonna be a long
hot summer. Those tornadoes been hittin' around the area seem like
every other day. I guess with all this damage to the environment, the
seasons are confused, too. I made me a cup of fresh mint tea. Somethin' was tellin' me that I was gonna conjure up a masterpiece.

Purple would be the color. Purple was healing. I sat down on my
stool and picked up my brush, but somethin' made me stop before
I could dip it in the paint. That troubled feelin' came back over me
as I stared into the vacant white canvas. The warm summer breeze
shot a strange chill up my back. My eyes welled up with tears and I
began to cry. Most people don't understand these kinds of feelin's, but
I know what I've been taught, what I've seen with my own eyes when
I watched women like my grandmother.

MaMaw's body would give her a warnin'. Sometimes you just know
when somethin's wrong with one of your kids. I know one thing, this feelin' I got *is* my warnin'. I gots to suit up in God's armor. I got to stomp the
devil down. Whatever's goin' on will make its way to the light, but I will
not let Satan come up and try to lay claims on none of my children!

Chloe

TICK . . . TOCK

(TEN MONTHS AGO)

JULY . . .
My best friend, Deborah, surprised me with a celebratory champagne lunch at The Ivy, one of L.A.'s notorious "in" spots, and one of my favorite Beverly Hills eateries. I had been swamped for weeks, preparing for the launch of my new publicity firm, the Bloomberg-Michaels Group.

We were far from a full roster of clients, and the money had barely started coming in, but we had made noise with a ton of publicity. To top it off we had just scored our first A-list client. All in all, I was starting to see the fruits of my labor. The money was on the horizon. Mother was right when she said leaving the corporate public relations world was the best thing I could've done. It was time, as she said, to "follow my divine path."

That's what I did when I approached my good friend and former college roommate, Christy Bloomberg, and suggested starting our own business. I was the nuts and bolts, Christy, the flash and schmooze expert. Now we were making our assault on Hollywood, going after the who's who of young, hot Hollywood—thanks to Christy's father, who started the powerful Bloomberg Agency in Hollywood. His name was our calling card.

Our table on the outdoor patio was prime real estate, overlooking the buzzing, popular strip of Robertson Boulevard, known for its cool and hip boutiques, where all the young, thin, famous (mostly white), and rich romped and shopped. Deborah motioned for the waitress to pop the cork on the bubbly so we could make it known, loud and clear, just how fly, fierce, and fabulous the brown girls be!

"Chloe, I'm so proud of you taking the leap of faith to go for dreams," Deborah proclaimed, dramatically crossing her shapely legs. She was petite, but curvy, and girlfriend was one of the most stylish sistas I had ever met. Deborah removed her large Gucci shades that overpowered her perfectly round, cinnamon-cocoa-colored face. "You're young and now I can live vicariously through your career and love life!"

"Cheers!" I said as we tapped our glasses.

"I swear, I've faced reality. I'm ten years from sixty and shit, I'm tired. I wish I even had a man in my life to help balance the load. Do you know I was so depressed the other day I thought about flinging myself into the pool and drowning myself?" My eyes went wide as she took a big sip of champagne. "Don't panic. I'm Catholic and suicide is a sin, plus what would my babies do? Look at them," she said, pointing to her Range Rover that was parked in front of the restaurant.

Deborah always made the valet park her car where she could see it whenever she had her dogs with her. "Hi, babies!" she called out, waving. "Yes, Mommy loves you! Oh, yes she does!" she chirped, making a series of *goo-goo-ga-ga* noises toward the car. Her hyperactive cocker spaniels were going wild at her antics. "Baby, those dogs are a lot more dependable and supportive than any man I've ever had," she said as we both continued sipping on champagne.

"Hello, can we just go there! Girl, I am so exhausted with commitment-phobic brothas in the entertainment industry," I said.

"Uh, yeah, that's because you only date the same kind of men. Bling bling, flossy, flossy!"

"Deb, I'm offended!"

"Be offended, but be honest. What was Kwame? Record industry executive, jet-setter, baby mama drama. The Negro was undependable and uninterested in supporting your career. And then let's talk about Jerrod, can we? NBA superstar, amazing in bed, you'd go strong for three, maybe four months, and then he'd disappear. Next thing you know you'd see him in the gossip pages hugged up with the latest Hollywood black starlet. Blah, blah, blah. Should I go on?"

"Enough!"

"But I don't know what you have to complain about. You've always got your old standard. Mr. Edward Gentry?"

"I'll always love Edward, but I faced that reality a long time ago. He can never be the one for real. But remember, we don't talk about him. It's complicated. I think I'm ready for a change."

"No, way! He's the love of your life!"

"I'm getting tired of playing by his rules. I'm over it! Do you hear me? O-V-A-H it! I've got to think about a new plan. The first step is to do like I've always done in business. I isolate the problem, focus on the issue at hand, and go about solving it. I'm about to be thirty-five, no more games. I've got to get a husband!" I said, taking a hearty sip.

"I'm supposed to be the depressed, desperate bitch, not you! Just promise you won't do anything rash!"

We let out a rousing round of laughter and downed that entire bottle of champagne that afternoon. Perhaps there was some truth to what Deborah was saying about me needing to slow down. Mother and my sisters Eve and Fawn—heck, damn near the whole family— had been telling me that for years. The last thing I wanted to do was come off desperate.

At the same time, I knew what I wanted, and when you know what you want, you have to go after it. Make it happen, right? I guess that's the alpha personality thing my oldest sister, Fawn, is always referring to. But I didn't care. I was going to make myself happy, damn it! Even if it kills me!

That night I prayed:

> *Dear God,*
> *Thank you for giving me a nice house, a car, and a great career.*
> *I know I'm always trying to be in control. Forgive me, Father, I just*

get anxious, sort of like I am right now. I've been feeling restless with myself a lot lately. Basically, God, I don't want to look up at forty and still be single and childless. My clock is ticking and I need a husband! Amen!

Mother said you should ask God for what you want and you'll receive it. Bloomberg-Michaels was definitely a manifestation of my prayers and dreams. It was evidence of the power of prayer. So I wasn't ashamed to be praying in secret for God to bring me a man. And just like that, *he* came . . .

Well, sort of. Not really *him* per se, but *his* phone call. Just a couple of weeks after I had laid down that powerful prayer.

"Chloe, you've got a call on line one!" my assistant, Deja, shouted over her cubicle wall. I picked up and before I could even speak, I heard *his* voice.

"Hi, Chloe Michaels? This is Gregorry Robinson from Atlanta." He was articulate, corporate, like a friendly bill collector.

"Uh-huh," I replied suspiciously.

"Well, I'm actually from Los Angeles, but I went to school at Morehouse. I was friends with your friend Chuck Lewis."

"Uh-huh." I was still clueless.

"You don't remember me, do you?" he asked.

"I remember Chuck, of course," I answered abruptly. "He's one of my closest childhood friends, but I'm sorry, I really don't remember you. And I don't mean to be rude, but why are you calling me and how did you get my number?"

"Look, I know you're busy. I've been seeing all the newspaper write-ups on you and your company and just wanted to call and say congrats from an old friend. I got your number from information. I'm a financial consultant with a large firm, Boiyt and Nushe, and I just moved back to Los Angeles not too long ago. I don't know many people in town. I thought this was a good idea, but I guess not."

Okay, so I let the guy off the hook on getting my number and all. You didn't have to be in the Hollywood circles to have heard or seen all the media buzz about the Bloomberg-Michaels Group.

"Honestly, this is just not a good time." I was not only uneasy with this "Gregorry" person's call, but preoccupied with working on a publicity proposal.

"Can I just give you my number?"

"Sure," I said flatly. I could tell this guy wasn't taking no for an answer. I figured getting his number wouldn't hurt. I casually jotted it down on a Post-it, slapping it on a page inside my daily planner, and that was that.

Eve

THAT MAN

I'VE BEEN HAVING the same dream for over a month now . . .

The water swells. My body becomes paralyzed, heavy and limp. I can't feel my limbs. I try to call out for help, but the current is too strong and pulls me under. I swallow mouthfuls of water and begin to choke. If I could just swim to the surface. It's only a few feet above, but it's useless. Suddenly, something or someone is forcing me down, but I can't see what or who it is. The feeling starts to come back in my arms and legs. I begin kicking, treading furiously to no avail. My lungs give . . .

I awoke in a panic, my heart beating like I'd just run a ten-mile race. I was half asleep and still coming out of my dream state, feeling around, grabbing the covers on the bed before realizing I was still on dry land.

"Damn, girl! Stop movin' so much. You know I gotta be at the office early in the morning!" my boyfriend, Dale, groggily snapped as he rolled over. He yawned, farted loudly, then flopped his arm across my chest, practically cutting off my airflow. His former All-City high school football star physique had seen better days, and I didn't help the matter.

I had spoiled him with daily home-cooked meals, from pancake breakfasts to my famous fried chicken, and Sunday dinners that were more like holiday meals. I had spoiled this man so terribly that I couldn't get away without at least baking a cake or his favorite, peach cobbler, once a week. Dale had to have dessert with every meal. Four years and forty pounds later, I had my nerve talking about his gut. Humph!

"It was that dream again. It spooks me every time," I said, adjusting his arm and letting out a harbored sigh.

"I told your ass not to have that damn Mexican food. Go back to sleep, baby."

"I'm tryin'," I said, closing my eyes tightly.

"You want me to give you somethin' to go back to sleep," he mumbled, grabbing my hand, pushing it toward his crotch, subtly forcing me to massage his penis. The thought of sex seemed to automatically give Dale an erection.

"Get on top, girl. You know I'm tired!" Dale demanded. "C'mon, give me all that good stuff," he growled, pushing himself inside of me. There was no foreplay, no setup, just give it here, girl. I faked a moan, pressing myself farther down on him. The more I pressed, the harder he shoved himself in and out of me. Dale's approach was simply to, as he calls it, "punish that pussy." It was almost like he was mad at it and had no choice *but* to take it out on me.

I had given up my grand dreams of romance, or Dale passionately making love to me on some remote desert island, six months into our relationship. I wasn't head over heels in love, but Dale was decent and, most important, good to my child. Being a single mom and trying to date is scary. My daughter, Christina, was thirteen going on fourteen when Dale and I met and at a crucial time in her postadolescent life. I couldn't just be bringing anybody into her life.

When he finished doing his business, I sat there unable to move. Once again he had gotten his and I stared blankly into the darkness, naked and numb.

"I bet you won't have any bad dreams again. Damn girl, your ass is heavy. Get on off a brotha!" he said, pushing me off. "Baby, you really need to back up on that Mexican." He chuckled. "I like you thick but damn!" Lately, I had become, literally, the butt of all his jokes. He turned on his side, grunted, and farted loudly once again. "You feel better now, baby?" He yawned, quickly falling into a deep snore.

"Yeah," I whispered back.

Sitting on the toilet always gives me a chance to think. All I seemed to be thinking about lately is about me and Dale. What's next for us?

I remember when we met. Chloe had flown in for Aunt Billye Jean's sixty-eighth birthday. That was a trip in and of itself, because she actually made the family plan her a party that year. She swore she wasn't gonna make it to sixty-nine. Well, she's seventy-two now and swearing she won't see seventy-three, but that's just Aunt Billye Jean. Anyway, we kicked it hard that night. After the family party we went out dancing.

Everybody around town knows when me, Chloe, and Fawn get together, shit, the three sisters turn the party out. I think that night we topped all the other nights. Fawn could never hold her liquor. Me and Chloe could always go the distance. Only problem is that Chloe is always looking for a fight when she drinks. Me, I get mellow and just wanna dance. I'm not too good in the rhythm department, but a little alcohol gives me what my cousin Ceci calls "liquid courage."

"I'm ready to go, y'all!" Fawn whined. She was loopy after two drinks. Her perfectly applied mascara was ruined, and raccoon circles had begun to form around her eyes.

"Oh hell no, her ass always does this crap! I'm ready to get my party on up in here! She'd betta just sit her ass down," Chloe slurred, getting pumped up.

"I want another drink, too!" I chimed in, tripping over my words.

"I don't want nothin' else to drink; I'm sleepy and I wanna go home!"

"Shut up! We ain't leavin' yet, Fawn. I want some champagne!" Chloe barked.

"Look, Fawn, we're gonna have just one more drink! Chloe, one more, that's it, okay?" She waved me off. This is what always happens. I can't even fully enjoy my buzz, because I gotta play mediator between the two of them when we go out and start drinking. "Plus I gotta be at work at six."

"Six? In the morning?" Chloe quipped. "Now see, that's some bullshit. The three sisters are partying tonight. I never get to party like this in L.A.!"

"Yeah, that's 'cause they don't know your ass is ghetto out there," Fawn said, rolling her eyes before laying her head down on the bar.

"Everybody ain't high rollers, Chloe. I got a child to feed and rent to pay!" I snapped. Chloe always easily forgets how good she's got it— no kids, makin' money, and datin' a man who's rich.

"Um, hello! We want another round. No, make that a bottle. Do you have Veuve Clicquot?" Chloe slurred as she slapped her gold AmEx on the bar counter.

Baby sis, aka Miss Hollywood, was also *always* quick to buy a bottle when she was drunk. Thank God our cousin Ceci wasn't there or they'd really be clownin'. She always gets mad the next day when she looks at the bill. But what the hell, tonight we were having a good time. We hadn't all been at home at the same time in four or five months. Chloe had been so busy with work. I was even enjoying our little arguments.

"Naw, we ain't got that." The bartender frowned, and curled her top lip, revealing a gleaming, gold tooth.

"Well, what do you have?" Chloe said, cocking her head to the side. I could see where this was going and quickly intervened.

"Okay, I'm sorry, Miss, can we just get whatever champagne you have. I mean, what do you have?"

"Moët," the bartender said, rolling her eyes.

"Okay, we'll take that," I said, pulling Chloe to the side. "Chloe, you need to quit trippin', you are back home, not . . ." and that's when I saw Dale at the other end of the bar eyeing me.

He was well dressed, somewhat conservative, clean-cut; only thing, he was a bit too yellow for my taste. You know what I mean?

The brotha was in need of a tan. I generally like my men on the brown side. He smiled. And I was taken, girlishly batting my eyes.

"Whassup, y'all!" My cousin Ceci had made her grand entrance and she was on full tilt. "How y'all gonna go out without me?"

"Hey, cuz! We're poppin' bottles tonight!" Chloe called out.

"Oh, no, I just wanna go home!" Fawn had rejoined the party.

I tuned the three of them out as the man from the end of the bar approached. He extended his hand and I blushed.

"I'm Daleton. Daleton Mitchell. But everybody calls me Dale. I hope you don't think this is really corny, but I think you are beautiful."

"I'm Eve, and thank you," I gushed.

"Are you here with someone?"

"No. Well, just my sisters."

"Where's your husband?

"I'm not married, and you ain't slick," I said, coyly turning away.

"I hope you don't have a fiancé or a boyfriend either, because I really want to get to know you."

He never took his eyes off me. I got ready to respond when all of a sudden Chloe and Ceci busted between us.

"Let's dance, Eve!" Chloe said, grabbing my hands.

Three songs later, Dale had gotten us a table in VIP, and while Chloe and Ceci polished off the last of the champagne, I was stuck with babysitting Fawn, who had quietly passed out. The conversation was light and fun, and honestly, I hadn't smiled that much since Henry and I had been together. Henry was my tired-ass Puerto Rican ex-boyfriend and the father of my daughter. Although for twelve years we pretended like we were married for twelve years, we weren't.

That damn Henry could do the silliest things, like playfully whisper sweet nothings in my ear in Spanish while we were making love. I'd giggle like a giddy schoolgirl. Mmmm, those were some good times, but it ain't worth going back in time. That's the past, and I'm glad. The only downside was that I was so out of practice on the dating scene that my stomach was fluttering a mile a minute. Yet, despite my apparent nervousness, Dale and I clicked.

He slipped his arm around my shoulder. I inhaled. Dale's scent was masculine and inviting, crisp and spicy. I was out way past my bedtime, and our crash course in get-to-know-you-better had sobered me up.

"C'mon, Eve, we gotta go. Fawn's ass done passed the fuck out and the bar done ran outta cognac. This is some for real bullshit," Ceci said as she and Chloe gathered Fawn and headed out to the car. We said our good-byes.

"I do need to go. I have a thirteen-year-old and have to be up for work at FedEx in four and a half hours or ain't nobody gonna get their packages." We shared a laugh.

"I'm a divorced engineer with no children, but I love kids," he said, reaching for my hand. "And I'd really love to see you again."

Yes, God had answered my prayers! I floated out of the club and could still smell him on my blouse. Dale was strong and comforting. He was the kind of man I had been dreaming about for a long time. A professional man, and like me and my girlfriends tease, "one of those men with good teeth and benefits" to match.

The whole ride home I pictured myself sitting in my elegantly furnished suburban home, with a white picket fence and a well-manicured lawn. I'd spend my days ordering from the Home Shopping Network (something I've always wanted to do) and preparing for cocktail parties and holiday gatherings.

I giggled to myself. My Martha Stewart dreams might sound silly to some, but it's what I want. It's who I am. I'm like the polar opposite of my mother. She would never think like I think. Mother and I, as much as I love her because she *is* my mother, well, we're just different in too many ways to count. Maybe it's more like she's different from "normal" mothers.

I like shopping at the mall, getting my nails done, and if I have the money, going to the spa every now and then. I read popular magazines and cut out the recipes, and I love shopping at craft stores and decorating.

On the other hand, when it comes to housekeeping, Mother doesn't believe in throwing anything out. And when it comes to men, I don't know why she's still talking about when she was married to my father.

She talks about it like it was yesterday. Hell, that was forty years ago. If Mother would get herself a man, she could stay out of my business.

We just bump heads, simple as that, and some things are just deeper than I care to get into a lot of times. We get along better than we did when I was growing up, even five years ago. I think I'm getting more patient the older I get, but I will say this, I don't apologize for being who I am. I refuse to be like her at sixty-eight with no man.

My phone rang and the screen flashed his name: DALETON. I smiled as I unlocked my apartment door.

"Did you make it home safely?" he asked.

"Yeah, thank you." I blushed, smiling from ear to ear. This man was thoughtful, too! The whole day at work, all I could think about was how God had finally brought me the right man. The perfect man.

It's going on four years and I'm about to turn forty-five and no ring, no move-in date, no nothing. I guess if I just hang in there a little bit longer, my time is going to pay off. Dale's big on tests. He feels like I haven't proven myself enough. He thinks I'm not responsible enough because I have bad credit, and let him tell it, baby daddy drama.

Henry may be hard to deal with, but that's my problem not his. He loves our daughter. Plus, Dale forgets we were together for twelve years. He's far from just some run-of-the-mill "baby's daddy"! And another thing, I've been breaking my neck to provide for my child and make a good home. How about give me a damn good credit score for raising a straight-A student, who's just finished her freshman year at Spelman and is there on the Presidential Scholarship!

I'm trying to be more fiscally responsible, but, hell, I'm a single mother doing the best I can. Dale doesn't understand, because he don't have no damn kids. Maybe if I'd gotten pregnant before now we'd be married. But I know deep down I've gotten too old.

I definitely think worrying about what's going to happen with us has got me down. I do need to lose some damn weight too. Shit, I was a cute size ten when he met me, but this fourteen creeped up on a sista.

I know I gotta lose some damn weight. I love Dale, and do you know how hard it is to find a man who cares about your child?

I'm happy Chloe has found someone to love her. I really am happy. However, I can't help but feel as though it should've been me at that altar. I think I cried every day leading up to her wedding. My whole New Year's Eve was ruined when she called to tell me she was getting married.

"Eve!" she screeched. "Gregorry asked me to marry him! And it was so romantic. He took me to San Francisco and proposed. He wanted to fly to Vegas right away and make it official at the Little Wedding Chapel, but I said hell no! My family would have a fit. My ring is beautiful. Not quite as big as I would've liked it, but it's maybe two carats. Can you believe after just two months of dating he wants to marry me?"

Chloe was yapping away like some wind-up toy. Here I am the big sister and I'm supposed to be the one getting married next, not the baby. She barely knew Gregorry and said yes. Plus we don't even know him. But Chloe's the kind once she makes up her mind ain't no turning back. Wait, let me take that other part back. It didn't actually ruin my night, but I was coming into the new year and maybe I was a little envious that I didn't have anything sparkly on my hand to ring it in with.

I quietly climbed back into bed and stared at Dale. I closed my eyes and said a little prayer:

> *Dear God,*
> *I try to pray, but sometimes I just can't. It's like I'm feeling around in the dark trying to find who I am. I just can't do it alone anymore. If I get one more bill, I'm gonna lose it. Things have to work this time. I just want this man to love me. Please, God, make this man marry me, Amen.*

Chloe

HE CAME

O CTOBER...
   They say things come in threes, and here I sit, *three* months to the day of that *strange* man calling my office, and I'm doing what I told myself I'd never do . . . going on a blind date. I didn't dare tell any of my girlfriends, especially Deborah. How would I even explain, "Oh, by the way, he's a guy I met at Freaknic 1989"? First off, she'd want to know what the hell a Freaknic was!

Perhaps this was fate. The other day when I was going through some old photographs from college, there *he* was! In a picture with with me and my girls commemorating what I like to call the best road trip in collegiate history. He was a preppy chocolate brotha with scrawny legs. I chuckled. The caption read: "Chloe and Crew with Morehouse Cutie A.K.A. Gregorry 'The Date from Hell' Robinson."

It's actually quite amusing that on, get this, page *three* of my day planner I found the Post-it I had buried with his number scrawled on it. More amusing was listening to me backpedal on the phone for never returning any of the numerous messages he left at the office after that first call. After several weeks, he finally gave up. I'll give it to him for patience, though. I agreed to join him for dinner. I figured that was the least I could do.

"Chloe?" A warm and inviting voice called out. I swiveled around on my barstool in the direction it was coming from.

"Gregorry?" I said, coyly tilting my head to the side. I extended my hand. He shook it gently, holding on to it for a few extra seconds. Okay, can a sista say F-I-N-E?! He looked like that old picture, but better. The added ten or fifteen pounds after nearly twenty years agreed with him.

"Wow, you look great," he said, helping me off the stool. I caught a whiff of his cologne and thought, *Wow, you smell great!* His scent was yummy and intoxicating. We were getting off to a fabulous start. Gregorry was impeccably dressed in a freshly starched and pressed white dress shirt that looked custom-made. His polished and gleaming sterling silver cuff links were complemented by the stainless Rolex peeking from beneath the monogrammed "GMR" initialed on his left cuff.

The waitress seated us at, oh my God, table *three!* It overlooked an Asian garden. We wasted no time ordering.

"Your area code is 818. Where do you live in the Valley?" he asked, taking a forkful of salad.

Being a single woman, I wasn't eager to give up my street address. "Near Ventura," I guardedly replied, wiping my mouth with a napkin.

"That's a great area. I've been looking at a house on Winnetka," he added, gobbling down another bite. I looked at him incredulously. Strangely, it's a street in my neighborhood. I shook it off as coincidence.

"I'm surprised you suggested this place," I said, taking a sip of wine.

"Why?" he asked, pushing his plate to the side.

"No reason." I shifted, uncrossing and recrossing my legs, then fiddling with my napkin, pushing my plate to the side, too. There was an awkward silence. Hey, maybe it was also just some silly coincidence that the Garden Café was near my neighborhood, only a few miles from my house.

I quickly dismissed the twinge of paranoia that attempted a tug on the back of my brain. I never told him my address or even gave him my home number. I made it a point to suggest we meet at the restaurant. Anyway, I had my pepper spray handy just in case. I reached in my purse, pulling out the old college photo from 1989.

"Bam! Remember this?" I screeched.

"That was a serious high-top fade. I was cold!"

"Yeah, cold, as in *ice* cold. My girlfriends and I thought you were a big jerk when we all hung out that night," I said, taking a sip from my glass of wine, as the waitress slid our entrées in front of us.

"I don't remember all that," he said, flashing a sexy grin. His pearly whites were framed by soft, full, inviting lips, and a perfectly trimmed mustache that I found distinguishing.

"You seem to have a case of amnesia," I said as he took the picture from my hand and turned it over, gently placing it facedown on the table.

"That was the past, and I never look back on the past," he said with piercing eyes, curling his top lip under, pressing it against his teeth, then biting down on his bottom lip.

"Well, I don't either, but I certainly believe one should know the past in order to know what not to do in the future," I pointed out, taking a bite of pasta.

For the remainder of the evening I listened to this handsome stranger's intriguing tales of traveling all over the world as an international businessman. He talked about how he had spent most of his time in Malaysia, Brazil, and China. I was fascinated by his stories. I wanted to hear more. I even imagined traveling the world with him. I could see myself with a guy like this. We could be the next black power couple. It was like we'd known each other all our lives.

I let my defenses down . . .

For our second date, I let Gregorry pick me up from my house for a regular, old-fashioned date. I didn't want to get too excited about this guy. Before we headed into the restaurant, I had to ask the burning question. "Okay, so do you have a girlfriend? Or, maybe I should say, where's your baby mama?" I sarcastically added. Okay, so I guess at this age I'm a bit cynical.

"Chloe, honey, I told you I don't like talking about the past, but, yes, I *was* married. I got divorced about two years ago. And"—he paused and swallowed hard—"I have a five-year-old." I tried to hold back my look of disappointment, but I guess the sigh gave it away. "But listen, I don't have any drama, I can assure you," he quickly stated, picking up on my deflated reaction.

"My daughter would adore you. Her mother is nice, but simple, you know, just a country girl I met in Houston. You know when she got pregnant I wanted to do the right thing. Her father was a preacher and married us. Satisfied? Let's eat!"

Just like that, Gregorry made all my worries go away, and away we went. Each date seemed to get better and better from that point on.

In just a matter of weeks, Gregorry and I had become inseperable. I was falling so hard that I took one of the biggest steps in my life. "Are you sure?" Gregorry asked, as I slipped a set of gleaming silver keys into his hand.

"Absolutely," I replied, my stomach doing a series of cartwheels and backflips. I was both nervous and excited by the fact that entrusting Gregorry with keys to my house was a serious step toward a potential future with him.

The keys were actually Gregorry's idea. He had a new client whose offices were just five miles from my house. He thought since we were spending so much time together he should just start going to work from my place. Gregorry even waited up for me on late work nights, and he understood my culinary limits. He found humor in the fact that my specialties were peanut butter and jelly sandwiches and scrambled eggs.

And then *it* happened . . .

"You're twenty minutes late!" Gregorry's cold-as-steel words ripped through his clenched teeth, as he sharply jerked his face away when I went to offer him a kiss. I was confused and embarrassed by his icy greeting. My girl Deborah's eyes went wide in awe. *It* was our first argument, and Gregorry was showing me a side of him I had never seen before.

"It's humiliating when I'm standing outside waiting like this!" He folded his arms and let out an angry sigh.

"Gregorry, this is completely unnecessary. I was late, but you were here with my friend. It's not like you were alone with some stranger."

"If I wanted to talk to your friend, I would've asked her out!" Gregorry cut his eyes at me again, then spun on his heels, flinging open the restaurant door, leaving Deborah and I standing at the valet.

"What's up with your man, girl?" Deborah whispered.

"I've never seen him act like this."

"All over you being a few minutes late? He'd better get used to it, 'cause, honey, he don't know, *you* and clocks don't get along." Deborah patted me on the back. I let out a nervous giggle, not sure what to make of Gregorry's outburst. Dinner was an even bigger disaster. Gregorry barely opened his mouth the entire time, and when he did, it was to attack me with smart remarks.

"So what's up with the girl who won *America's Next Top Model* dating that rapper, Deborah?" I said, making lighthearted small talk at the table.

"You know, all you do is gossip," Gregorry rudely snapped. "Sometimes you just need to practice shutting your mouth." He wiped his mouth and tossed his napkin on the table. "I'm outta here!" Gregorry jumped up, tossed a few twenties on the table, and stormed out of the restaurant.

"Girl, you can't let him talk to you like that. You don't need or deserve that," Deborah said, reaching across the table and touching my hand.

"I've been kissing his ass all night. You're right, I don't deserve this." I sat in dismay, hoping that something or someone could explain the verbal smackdown I had just received.

By the time I pulled up in my driveway, I was even more furious to find Gregorry's car parked and to see him standing with a bouquet of flowers.

"Fuck you and your flowers, Gregorry," I said, slamming my car door and clicking the alarm. *Chirp! Chirp!* "I want my keys back and you out of my driveway!"

"Chloe, babe, I'm sorry. I feel terrible," he said, looking at me with remorseful eyes. "I was an asshole and an idiot, and I'm sorry I hurt you. I'm under a lot of pressure at work. There's a merger going on and I've been offered a job overseas. I want the job in Seoul, but I know that I want you to be with me more. I'm just really irritated and stressed out." He gently wrapped his arms around me.

"That's no damn excuse to talk to me the way you did. And in front of my friend? Have you lost your mind? I've never been spoken to like that. My father would never—"

"I know, shhhh," he said, putting his lips over mine. "I promise to take you and Deborah out again and apologize in front of the whole place. I just wanna make up." He planted a romantic kiss on me. "Plus, I'm frustrated. You've been holding out on me for too long. I want you." He kissed me again.

"Tonight?"

"Yes, now!" It was like his kiss, his caress, the way his body felt against mine forced me to surrender. What was this strange power he had over me?

He slipped under the sheets, pulling me with him, sliding me on top of him. When he reached for a condom, I stopped him. Tonight, I was sure. I trusted him. I imagined our union creating the perfect baby I longed for. I reached for his erect penis, holding it firmly in my hand. His manhood throbbed and pulsated as I shimmied down on top of it.

The heat from our bodies soared. In a back-clawing-buttocks-gripping moment, Gregorry reached his climax. Beads of sweat gathered between us and rested on our skin like fresh morning dew.

It was the first time I had been with another man since Edward. I didn't know if anyone would ever be able to make love to me like him. Edward had mastered my body, memorizing every secret spot, always generously waiting until I came, at least two or three times. In time, Gregorry would learn mine, too. Things were good enough for now. Good enough to help me put Edward Gentry out of my mind for good.

Please, God don't let this be a dream. Could Gregorry really be the one? I asked myself as Gregorry held me in his arms, my face snuggled in the fuzzy warmth of his chest as we lay in the euphoric afterglow of lovemaking. Gregorry ran his fingers through my hair, softly gripping a handful, then releasing it. I felt safe. I kissed his chest. His smell had become a part of me.

"I need you, Chloe. You are the best thing that's ever happened to me. I don't wanna be without you, and Korea is so far away."

"Nowadays, people run their business in the States from overseas," I hinted.

"You'd do that for me?"

"If we were together, married, of course!"

"I just get scared, because I'm not like the famous people you hang around." He pulled me closer.

"Honey, I just want someone who's in my corner. I don't live that life. I just work with those people."

"That's why I love you. Rub my head, please, baby," he said, rolling me over on my back, before closing his eyes and resting his head on my breasts. I began to slowly stroke his soft waves. "You know, I had decided that if I didn't find the right woman this time, I was going to leave the country, maybe go to Brazil, start a whole new life," he said with a laugh.

"That's the craziest thing I've ever heard!" I said, sitting up and leaning back on my elbows.

"They have how-to books and there are lots of tricks and ways to walk around anonymously. But I don't have to do any of that now." He lifted up and looked deeply into my eyes. "I have you. A successful, beautiful, amazing woman," he said, kissing me softly on the lips, placing his head back on my chest and moving my hand back on top of his head.

Fawn

THE PERFECT NERVOUS BREAKDOWN

I'VE BEEN STANDING in this same department looking at the same polka-dot blouse for thirty minutes. It's giving me a headache. I feel nauseous, like I could just throw up all over this ugly-ass blouse. I swear I could just walk up in that boring-ass gala butt-ass naked, maybe then my husband would notice me.

I've dedicated the last fifteen years of my life to raising a child and running a household, but what about me? What about my desires, and passions, and dreams? I put my life on pause, and now the button seems to be stuck. All of them, Mother, Chloe, Eve, they all think my life is so great. Chloe was *so* anxious to get married and have a damn child—huh, she'll see. I could've done all the things she's doing too if I was single.

"Hello?" I answered my cell flatly, still flipping through the rack of blouses that ranged from mundane to hideous. "Oh, yes, errum, hello Pastor Gibbs." I cleared my throat again and felt a smile creep across my face at the sound of his voice.

"Yes, Pastor Gibbs, I would love to meet with you about our Women's Day program. Tuesday? Sure, one o'clock is fine. Oh, and I look forward to seeing you Sunday morning too. Oh yes, praise the Lord, and God bless you too, Pastor." I hung up, my heart still beating fast, sort of like that feeling you get when you're sixteen and you just got finished talking on the phone to the boy you've had a crush on all year. I was already writing "Fawn ♥ Pastor Gibbs" on my notebook.

Pastor Gibbs was the pastor of a new church I started attending about three months ago. I just wasn't getting anything out of that tired sermon Rev. Yancy was always delivering at Mother's church. First A.M.E. had been our family church for three generations, ever since my great-grandmother moved up to St. Louis from the county. My spirit needed something fresh and exciting.

Pastor Gibbs has that spark. He gives my spirit a jolt. But I'll be honest, Pastor Gibbs jolts a little more than just my spirit. I caught myself giggling aloud. Ooh, I know it sounds terrible, but I can't help myself. Now that's the kind of man I could see myself married to. He's commanding, and his presence is powerful.

I used to be mad that Cliff didn't go to church with me, but, hell, I'm happy now. His ass don't ever have to go. I heard about Faithful Temple House of Prayer from a woman in my cousin Ceci's beauty shop. She was going on and on about this new young pastor who was a widower who'd just moved to town from Kentucky.

She said the church was still growing but how this man of God had changed her life. After hearing her rave about Rev. Theodore James Gibbs V from Louisville, Kentucky, one too many times, she caught my curiosity. I even checked out the church's website.

I remember walking into that tiny storefront church on the south side of town and quietly sitting down. It didn't even bother me that the small congregation was mostly made up of women. A blind woman by the name of Mother Rose played the piano, how sweet, and we all just sang along since there's no formal choir.

Pastor Gibbs came forth to deliver a message so powerful, I felt like the Holy Spirit had jumped into my body. He was talking about making changes and trying new things in life. I wanted to get up and shout, run all over that room.

"It's time to let go, people, of the chains and restraints that have been holding you back. God wants you to free your mind and the rest will follow. Get your shine on, saints! Let it go and let it flow!"

"Hallelujah!" and "Thank you Jesus!" erupted all over the room. His words felt familiar, but I connected with this man of God. I couldn't take my eyes off him in the pulpit. He was mesmerizing the way his tailored suit complemented his svelte physique, and his face had a boyish charm to it.

"I, I, I wanna tell y'all a story about a woman who had just been searchin' and searchin' for the answer, ya feel me. Searchin' but the answer was right in her bible. I don't think y'all heard me." He smiled, oozing southern charm. When he was at the peak of delivering his sermon, he removed his round wire-rimmed glasses and wiped his brow. I was swept into his words, imagining I was that freshly dry cleaned white handkerchief that he used to dab the sweat from his face.

"Hey, Fawn!" A perky voice startled me from behind. I whipped around.

"Oh, my, Angie, you scared me." I put on my best phony act, as if I was happy to see her.

"You look like you were lost in thought, girl."

"Not really," I answered halfheartedly. Angie Lewis got on my last nerve. She was nosy in high school and worse now that we were older. Angie was the wife of one of Cliff's golf buddies and tired-ass frat brother, Vernell Lewis. He has got to be the most obnoxious lawyer I've ever met. He talks as loud as the suits he wears.

"So are you and Cliff coming to the gala Saturday?"

She was talking about the Black and White Ball the local black doctors' and lawyers' association was having. "We'll be there," I said, hiding my disgust. Damn right, my husband was a member before hers was. I was so *over* seeing the same tired people at these stuffy parties.

"Well, girl, it was good talking to you. I've got a hair appointment. See you Saturday!" I grabbed the first thing my hand landed on, a yellow-and-white-striped blouse, and made a dash to the register, my AmEx in hand. I hated yellow!

"Ma'am, where's your nearest restroom?" I asked the sales clerk as she handed me my bag.

My feet couldn't move fast enough. When I made it inside, I rushed to the nearest stall and locked the door. I felt faint and braced my back against the door. I was sick of all of it. Planning what to eat for dinner, what activities Lola should sign up for during spring and summer break. I was sick of being Dr. Cliff Moore's dutiful, perfectly coiffed and well-behaved wife. I held my man down for four years of medical school and sacrificed my own career. It was the right thing to do. But I deserved more, and I'd made up my mind that I wanted it.

I'm tired of making sure my handbag matches my shoes; I don't think anybody in my damn house cares about the difference between periwinkle and baby blue. Somebody else is screaming to break free. I don't know who she is. I closed my eyes tightly and began to pray . . .

> *God,*
> *Everybody thinks the grass is always greener on the other side. Please tell me how does perfect become soiled and stained with silent tears? How do you find your way back to happy or is there such a thing? Sometimes I imagine walking out of the front door and never coming back. God, I hope I'm not losing my mind. Thanks for listening, God.*

Ten minutes later I found myself across the Saks parking lot in a cute French bistro at the bar ordering the most amazing dirty martini in history. I took a gulp and closed my eyes, washing all the frustration and exhaustion with Fawn Moore right down the drain.

Chloe

STRANGER IN MY HOUSE

(THE PRESENT)

MOTHER'S WORDS HOVERED like a protective hawk. *The eyes are the windows to a person's soul.*

I sensed an uncomfortable presence. *Get on your guard, sweet baby!* The ancestors softly alerted me, waking me out of my dream state. My eyes popped open and my body stiffened. Gregorry's empty, narrow eyes were staring back at me, his face just inches from mine. My bible was still clutched tightly in my arms, my heart beating though my chest. The clock read 6:30 A.M. I wondered how long he had been watching me.

I suddenly remembered the gun was under the pillow and inconspicuously pushed it farther underneath, keeping my hand hidden near it just in case. I covered my belly with the other one, guarding my unborn child.

"I'm sorry, Chloe," his voice sorrowfully pleaded as he sat down on the edge of the bed, his torso exposed with a towel wrapped around his waist. Gregorry dropped his head, and tears streamed down his face. Gregorry had transformed from a venom-spitting madman to this innocent, blubbering mound of flesh in less than twenty-four hours? "I'm just scared for you and the baby. I wanted us to make it," he said, turning to me with lost eyes.

Mother's words came to me again. *The eyes are the windows to a person's soul.*

"I've gotta, um, go into the office early, big project, but I wanted to, um, apologize," he said, this time curling his top lip under, pressing it against his teeth, then biting his bottom lip. He was doing that "thing" again. I hadn't learned much about Gregorry during our brief courtship and marriage, but after noticing his peculiar twitch on various occasions, I made a mental note of it. Whenever he told a lie, got nervous, or his temper flared, he did that "thing" with his lip.

"I'm sorry I scared you last night, but I was angry that you locked the door." Gregorry had a choppy cadence to his voice. "You forgot about the other door." He offered a half smile, pointing to the bedroom door leading to the pool and yard. He gently touched my leg. I flinched, pulling it away.

"I love you, Chloe," he said, standing up. "But I just don't want this marriage anymore." He did that "thing" with his lips once more. A hint of evil flashed in his eyes. He stood as if he ruled the world. "This marriage is a disaster." Gregorry was alarmingly calm, slowly unlocking the deadbolt. "I'm going to take a shower," he said, backing out of the room into the hallway.

I had held my breath the entire time he was in the room. I exhaled. I wasn't sure what to do first, but I had to figure *something* out. I was eight weeks pregnant and my husband had just announced he was leaving me. My head throbbed. I scooted to the edge of the bed and didn't move until I heard the shower in the master bedroom down the hall turn on.

Gregorry's morning ritual was long and arduous. He showered at least twenty minutes, followed by several minutes of exfoliating the skin, before another thirty or so minutes concentrating on his face, where he spent the most time. He'd pick, prod, and primp, choosing from a variety of exclusive facial products—visage un deux battre *this* and masque écailler *that*. Words that even the most sophisticated would struggle to pronounce. Finally, after all that, he'd shave, leaving the sink and floor covered with tiny black specks and wet towels strewn everywhere.

He would dress in front of a fan to avoid perspiring. When he was done, Gregorry would stand in front of the full-length mirror, admiring himself, fussing over things like the crease in his pant leg, or the stiffness of his collar. I was in awe, not only of his glowing appearance, but also of the fact that I had never known or seen a man be that particular about how he looked in all my life.

When I entered the kitchen, I was filled with fury and disgust at the sight of a broken kitchen chair. I've spent many a morning at this table, alone, peaceful, sipping tea, gazing out of the large kitchen bay window at the trees, birds, and brightly planted flowers. But sometimes I guess you just have to let it go. I opened the door leading to the garage and tossed the broken remnants out like week-old garbage.

I began clearing the table. Last night's dinner was still sitting— cold, grease-soaked French fries, and a hunk of steak, untouched. I dropped the entire plate into the garbage pail and slowly picked up the other plate that was sitting in front of what used to be *my* chair. A flash of how it had all exploded just before the start of dinner came across my mind.

"Hi honey!" I called out from the kitchen when I heard Gregorry slam the front door. No reply. There was a loud *clomp* from his shoes dropping on the marble foyer's floor. I peeked around the corner, catching his backside walking toward the living room. He plopped down in a large easy chair, turned the television on, and propped his feet up on the ottoman.

This type of behavior had been going on for almost two months straight. No kiss good-bye in the morning, no *sweetheart* greeting or hug in the evening when he returned, and our sex life was almost nonexistent. Gregorry was more interested in *CSI: Miami* and the Internet. Not the blissful life of a newlywed I had imagined.

"Dinner's ready, Gregorry!" Gregorry made it clear after we got married that he could no longer eat food that wasn't piping hot out of the skillet, and also that there could never be leftovers in our house— although he called my attempts at cooking an "embarrassment" and "awful." Cooking was a dreaded task. Lately, I had been struggling with vengeful and vindictive thoughts.

I contemplated adding a dash of Clorox or a sprinkle of boric acid to give his meal a little extra kick on days like this when he came home ornery for no reason. Instead, I opted for adding extra heaping spoonfuls of butter and salt. Secretly praying he'd have a heart attack and die. (God forgive me!)

"What's wrong, Gregorry?" I asked.

"Do I have to hear your mouth every fuckin' time I walk in the front door?" he shouted, jumping up and storming past me into the kitchen. I closed my eyes and counted to ten. When I reopen them, maybe he will have changed back into the man I thought I married. "This is bullshit!" he said, looking down at his plate and suddenly throwing his fork across the table. "This food is terrible and look at you. Your hair isn't fixed and you're fat!" He glared.

"I'm tired and pregnant. You know, with the *baby* you haven't even asked about!"

"Maybe you're not even pregnant. This could be one of those phantom pregnancies," he said with flaring nostrils.

I burst into tears, running to the refrigerator and snatching a three-by-five Polaroid off the door. "Here!" I said, holding the photo from my ultrasound in front of his face. He slapped the picture out of my hand and proceeded to walk away.

"Where are you going? We need to talk!" I said, grabbing the back of his shirt.

"None of your goddamn business. You'd better let go of me or I'll . . ." He balled his fists and whipped around, raising his arm in the air. I flinched, covering my face to protect myself from the blow. "You're pushing me!" His lips were quivering as he lurched toward me, grabbing me by the arm.

"Let go of me!" I said, struggling to pull away. "Get out of my house, Gregorry," I shouted. The grip of his hand was strong, and as he squeezed it tighter and tighter I became more and more fearful.

"Oh, your house? Your house?" His anger was pulsating through his veins, ready to explode. "I'm not going anyplace. This is community property under California fuckin' law, bitch!" I yanked away from him, running into the back bedroom where I had been sleeping for the past three nights. I slammed the bedroom door in his face just as he was racing toward me and turned the deadbolt. My legs collapsed and I slid down the door, burying my head in my tear-filled hands.

I placed my foot on the garbage pail again pedal and began scraping the plate, staring blankly out of the kitchen window. Screw it! I slammed the entire plate into the garbage. *Crack!* It broke in half. The two broken pieces represented my life at this very moment. The container was too full to close, and the garbage bag was overflowing. I lifted the bag out and noticed a ripped piece of paper stuck to the bottom of it. It fell off and slid across the floor.

It appeared to be a piece of a billing statement. The paper was sticky and greasy, but I grabbed a napkin and curiously began wiping away the old food residue. It read: −85,000.00. I heard Gregorry's footsteps coming down the hallway and nervously stuffed the stub into my bathrobe pocket.

"Chloe!" His booming voice made my stomach flutter. I put my hand over my belly. My instinct was to calm the baby. "Aren't you going to make me breakfast?" he asked, leaning into my neck and patting me on the back. Gregorry's words had suddenly turned syrupy sweet, but I could smell the sourness of dishonesty on his breath.

Ding! The toast popped up.

I set a small plate of bacon and toast soaked in pure butter in front of him. I poured him a small glass of juice, then poured myself one too, sipping it while standing at the sink since now we only had *one* kitchen chair.

"Since you plan on leaving, I need to know if that money you suggested we take out of the equity in my house is still in the bank," I asked.

"Yeah, why?" he snapped, midbite. There was a tinge of nervousness in his voice. He curled his upper lip under and bit down on his bottom lip. He was doing that "thing" again.

"I was just making sure."

He gobbled down the last of his breakfast and stood up abruptly, snatching his jacket off the back of the chair, and stormed out.

"Hello?" I held the phone for several seconds then burst into tears. "Mother, Gregorry told me he's leaving me, but I have a gun and I'm gonna kill him if he puts his hands on me or tries to hurt this baby. I have to protect us!" I said, wringing my hands.

"Lord! A gun! Chloe, please don't do anything crazy, baby!"

"I'm scared."

"It'll take me too long to get there. Can you get to one of your friends' houses, Chloe? What about Thora's? Can you get there?" Mother was rambling.

"Yes, I can," I sobbed, bracing myself against the kitchen counter with my hands.

"Just promise you won't touch that gun!"

I couldn't promise my mama something like that. These were desperate times. I silently asked God to forgive me, then lied. "I promise, Mother. I'll be fine. I just need you to pray for me."

Mother told me to concentrate on the words of that Seventieth Psalm: *Make haste O God to deliver Chloe. Make haste O God!*

I unfolded the torn piece of paper that I had found and dialed the toll-free number that was smudged and barely readable.

"Hi, my name is Chloe Michaels and I'm calling to find out why I have a bill that says I owe you eighty-five thousand dollars. I think this is a mistake." I rattled off my social security number, tapping my foot impatiently while she searched her computer records.

"Ms. Michaels, we are so happy you contacted us. We've been trying to reach you for several weeks now about your delinquent payments and the payments on the line of credit you took out. We tried to call you several times, Ms. Michaels, and each time your husband insisted we talk to him."

I sat in a daze as the woman ran down a series of dates and times of those recorded conversations they had had with Gregorry. He had told lie after lie about my whereabouts. The only number they had been given was Gregorry's cell number. He had purposely kept me in the dark and had taken the money, and now I was being held liable. Tears began to slowly cascade down my face.

"Ms. Michaels, I'm sorry, but since you are the sole owner of the property, *you* owe us the money."

I had never added Gregorry's name to the deed, or legally changed my name. However, I allowed my life to be an open book. All Gregorry offered me were his swift, slick, grandiose promises of unconditional, eternal love, and financial stability. I was fucked, superfucked, *intergalactically* fucked! *I didn't see the tsunami coming . . .*

Thora

INSULATED

"**I** LOVE YOU TOO, Billye Jean." I smiled and pressed OFF, placing the phone down on the patio table, propping my feet up on a nearby chair. I could really get used to hearing her say that *and* saying those words back to her. We talk every day around this time, but our last four conversations have been good, I think, for both of us.

I miss Billye Jean and everybody else in the family back home real bad some days, but moving away across the country was the smartest decision I could've made all those years ago. As much as I love everybody, they got too much stress and drama. Vegas has been my home for the past thirty years, and I intend to stay right here. My kids are happy, and after all these years of marriage, David and I still enjoy each other's company. Plus, there are lots of other mixed couples our age in our community.

I wish, though, that Erin and Davis could've grown up around their cousins on my side of the family. I know this sounds terrible, but Erin has always been my "black" child and Davis, my "white" one. They love them some Billye Jean, though, and I made it a point to send them to stay with her every summer. She was really happy that I kept the family name alive, making Davis my son's first name.

When it's all said and done, marrying David was the best thing that could've ever happened to me. I never saw fireworks or felt the earth move when he kissed me, but he was my friend and I always felt safe with him. We both grew up in St. Louis. He was the product of liberal Jewish parents, a father who was a known civil rights attorney, and a mother who was a homemaker. We met in a nondemonina-tional missionary group. David was a young professor of religion, and I was teaching music to underprivileged kids in the inner city.

"You wastin' a perfectly good college education! When you gonna get a real job?" Billye Jean sure had some choice words for me. "And I cain't believe you done got yourself a damn white boy!" She had upset herself so much she was sweating, ready to blow a gasket. David was actually fine. He even brought her a cold towel for her forehead. I was so embarrassed and angered by her behavior.

David has really grown on her, though. And that woman is crazy about her grandkids. She tries to give Erin and Davis the world. She and Davis can talk about those damn Cardinals for hours, and every summer he still flies back to St. Louis to take her to a ball game. I think she's just partial to boys. Just like I think she always loved Junior more, but she'd never admit it.

Life sure is funny. I remember the old Billye Jean better than she does. The *mean* Billye Jean. She was just a child raising children, four-teen when she had her first child. So I don't hold any of it against her. Even though Junior was the the oldest, I had to make sure the floors were clean enough to eat off, and that the furniture, what few pieces we had, could pass the white-glove test. I had to make sure Junior didn't make noise when Billye Jean was taking a nap. And there was no excuse for doing poorly in school.

Some things I can block out; others are there with me every day, just like being black or a mother. I remember things she tries to forget. Like how tired I was that night. I had done my homework and helped get Junior ready for bed. Billye Jean was working the evening shift at the hospital. I washed all the dishes and dried them, and all I wanted was to taste Muh's banana pudding one more time. Just a bite.

I didn't even need a plate. I took a forkful, not even a heaping one; that pudding was so good I even licked the fork. It was three in the morning when I was shaken awake by Billye Jean. "Thora, get yo li'l behind up!" She whipped that fork out and put it close to my face. "I work too goddamn hard, and I'm too goddamn tired, to have to come home to a dirty kitchen."

"But I did do the dishes. I washed and dried all of them." I was terrified, trying to collect my words.

"All except for this! You're just gonna have to wash 'em all again."

When I got downstairs, my eyes couldn't believe the sight. Billye Jean had pulled every stitch of dish out of the cabinets, and all the silverware out of the drawers. "You'd betta not even think about sleepin'. You gonna learn to mind me, Thora. You think I'm out here working for my health?" I was speechless. My eyes filled up with tears. "Huh? Answer me! And you'd better not cry neither, or make a whole bunch of noise. I got a headache."

She left me standing in disbelief when she stormed out of the kitchen, mumbling more curse words under her breath. I wanted to run down the street to Muh's house. She would take me in her arms and rock me. Then she'd make me some fried butter and bread. But Billye Jean would have three more fits if I told Muh about tonight.

Instead, always the obedient child, I ran the dishwater and I washed and dried each dish, placing it quietly back in the cabinet. I was eight years old. I would never make that mistake again.

"Coming to bed, honey?" David asked, cracking the patio door.

"Be right in!" I checked my watch. It was nine o'clock, time for a quick shower. I'd catch the news by ten and be fast asleep by eleven. This was our nightly routine. I took a deep breath. The deep dark sky was like a blanket of peace. I closed my eyes . . .

> *Lord,*
>
> *Thank you for what you started the other day. My mother told me she loved me, and she hasn't been able to stop. In fifty years, I don't ever recall her saying those words. Of course I knew she loved me, she's my mother, but to hear her say it brought tears to my eyes.*

*I haven't cried in many years. What for? Crying never changed any-
thing. The even stranger twist was after she said those words, I said
'I love you too, Mom.' I've called her Billye Jean, but saying Mom felt
so good I may do it again. Oh, and one more thing. Please, help me
to forgive Earl. Amen.*

I like my life. No surprises, nothing out of the ordinary, everything has an order.

Chloe

WHAT HAPPENS IN VEGAS . . .

THE CORDLESS PHONE dangled from my hand. My ears were still stinging from the words: *eighty-five thousand dollars.*

I couldn't panic. Gregorry told me initially he was going to put the money from the line of credit into our joint savings account. It had to still be there. Plus, I know there's money in our checking account.

I felt unsafe, though, and first I needed to get out of this house. I needed some solid advice, and sometimes when you can't call on family, a good friend is the next best thing. I had four close girlfriends, my business partner Christy, Deborah, Tracey, and Deja, who was my assistant, but I treated her more like a little sister.

Deborah was easily excitable. She didn't know whether to be my best friend or mother half the time. I didn't need a lecture. Hell, I'm the one who needs consolation right about now. On the other hand, Deja was a different story. Her attitude: Fuck asking questions, let's just set this whole damn house on fire!

Now, with Christy, it wasn't just the money issue, this was life or death. She wasn't a viable option, because frankly she'd have that frantic-white-lady-from-Malibu, let's-just-have-a-cocktail-and-talk-about-this-like-reasonable-adults approach. Bottom line, what I was dealing with required sista girl handling. You can't negotiate with a mean-ass Negro who's trying to kick your ass. You got to be ready to fight back, not reason. I quickly concluded Tracey was the best one to call.

We hadn't been friends long, only about a year, but ours was one of those relationships where right away spiritually we knew God had aligned the planets in just the perfect order. We thought alike and had the same kind of aggressive energy when it came to tackling business issues and our personal lives.

Tracey was one of a handful of women in the top brass at a major record company. But what most people didn't know was that before her rise to corporate stardom, Tracey had lived in the shadow of terror for five years, married to an abusive man. He was supposed to be the next black Steven Spielberg. He beat her for breakfast, lunch, *and* dinner.

She had escaped with practically nothing but her name, but the best thing that came out of a near-death experience was her daughter, Emmie. With her newfound freedom and endless hours of therapy she started over, reinvented herself, and left that fool she had married sitting in a puff of crack pipe smoke.

"Hey girl, you up?" I asked, pacing the kitchen floor. I found myself slipping into paranoia, checking the window every three or four seconds. "Listen, I just wanted to know what you knew about community property law?" I said, rubbing my belly.

"That's easy, just ask my asshole ex-husband!" She chuckled. "Community property got his crackhead ass a house in the hills worth a half a million. But that's okay, God don't like ugly, and that's why his ass lost it all in foreclosure. Raggedy-ass son of a bitch. Humph!"

All it took was one thing to get Tracey going about her ex. She had to take ten deep breaths, do a yoga pose, and say a Buddhist chant before she was able to continue. "Girl, I'm sorry I just went all off on a damn tangent. What's up?"

"I'm scared and need help!" I broke down sobbing.

"Baby, you're pregnant and you need to grab whatever you can fast and get the hell up outta there. You saw all that Scott Peterson shit. I don't trust a Negro as far as he shits. He's gonna try to hurt you bad."

"I've got a cousin in Vegas, but I don't have any cash on me," I said, blowing my nose into a napkin.

"Park your car at the airport. I'll make all the arrangements and call you in the car. When you get to Vegas, there will be money wait-ing for you at Western Union."

"But what if he tries to find me and comes to your house?"

"Oh, he can come to my house if he wants. My new man, Jacque, and all three of his big-ass firefighter brothers will have a good ass whoopin' waitin' for him!" We shared a laugh.

An invisible clock ticked away as I stuffed one item after the next— toothbrush, comb, bible, yesterday's mail—into an overnight bag. Then I went to my jewelry box and dumped everything into a pouch inside the bag—my diamond earrings, two of my grandmother's rings, my Cartier watch and love bracelets, and finally the only three items he had ever given me, my wedding ring, band, and a new Rolex he had purchased for me as a one-week anniversary gift.

My brain was on hyperspeed. When I reached the car, I hopped in, gunned the engine, and zipped out of the driveway with desperation, never looking back. I made it to the airport with fifteen minutes to spare. Drenched with sweat, struggling to catch my breath, I made my way down the narrow airplane aisle to the last open seat on the plane. I think God was saving it for me.

I didn't know if I wanted to laugh or cry. Laugh, because God had foiled the devil once again. Cry, because of the uncertainty that lay ahead.

As the plane made its ascent, I watched the earth move farther and farther away, and closed my eyes and imagined tossing my problems out into the vastness of the open, blue sky. I yawned, exhausted from waking up to the morning that would forever change my life. The one thing I did know was that I had some serious figuring out to do for me and this baby.

"Oh, my God! Look at that baby bump! It's all going straight to your butt!" Thora called out as she pointed to my belly, waving from the driver's seat of her brand-spankin'-new Cadillac GTS. She reached over to unlock the passenger door and I got in the car, still out of breath from the walk from the plane. "Girl, you are sweatin' like a runaway slave!" Thora teased with her usual playful humor.

"Shoot, the way I ran up outta L.A., I feel damn near like Harriet Tubman just led me through the Underground Railroad!" I said, giving her a hug. I'd made it to Vegas in one piece and was a million light-years away from my troubles. I let out a big breath of elation as Thora started the engine and a gush of cold air shot through the vent. I leaned my pounding head back on the headrest. Thora had her strange ways, but she had come to my rescue without hesitation when I called frantically while speed-walking through the Los Angeles Airport terminal. That's what family is about.

"You like my new baby?" she asked, referring to the car. "My husband said I needed a new Caddy and bought it for me for my fifty-sixth this year. Chile, you know David spoils me!" she boasted with a giggle.

"That's what I'm talkin' about!" I said, as we high-fived.

Her husband, David, treated her like a queen. Thora was one of those plain Jane types. If it weren't for her striking, steel-gray eyes, she would probably just fade into the woodwork. David's always buying her expensive dresses and offering her trips to the beauty salon, but she's not interested, and those dresses never get worn.

Personally, I think she purposely covers up her beauty for whatever reason—baggy khakis, clunky shoes, and no makeup, including that same ponytail she's been wearing ever since I can remember. David doesn't mind one bit. Maybe I should've gotten me one of those white men from the Good White Man department store; then maybe I wouldn't be smack-dab in the middle of a scene straight out of *Escape from L.A.* right now.

After the Western Union pickup, we raced to the bank.

"I'm sorry, I didn't hear you correctly. Did you just say twenty-three dollars and eleven cents?" I sputtered, offering an awkward laugh. I shifted uncomfortably in my chair, across from the pregnant assistant bank manager's desk. "You must be joking. Can you please check again?"

"Ms. Michaels, I've checked twice. Your checking account balance is twenty-three dollars and eleven cents," she said, as if it hurt her to speak the words.

"I need you to check my savings account, please," I said.

"The balance is thirty-two dollars and twenty-three cents," she painfully replied.

Three, two, one . . .

My polite smile slowly crumbled into a million pieces, and my body lost all feeling. I fumbled for words, mouth agape, barely breathing. "That can't be!" I said, shaking my head in disbelief. "Between both accounts there was almost a hundred thousand dollars."

"When was the last time you checked these accounts, Ms. Michaels?" she asked.

"I don't know." I struggled to put my thoughts together. "Ma'am, I'm pregnant and my husband just told me he was leaving me. What the *hell* am I supposed to do?" I cried out.

"I'm so sorry," the woman said, handing me a mound of tissue.

"Listen, ma'am, please just check my husband's account then. His name is Gregorry Robinson III. Marion is his middle name. Just please check his full name," I asked in desperation. "I fear for not only *my* life, but for my baby's life!" She glanced down at my stomach, then at her own, taking a deep breath before quickly typing a few strokes into the computer. Her eyes went wide at the screen.

"Ms. Michaels, why don't I walk you out to your car," she said, giving me an inconspicuous nod and logging off her screen.

Thora picked up on the signal. "Meet me in front," she said, grabbing her keys off the desk and walking away.

The assistant manager calmly led me to Thora's waiting car. The June Vegas sun was beating overhead like a drum. I was nauseated and faint. She inconspicuously jerked me by the arm, looking me in the eye.

"Ms. Michaels, I'm five months pregnant and my boyfriend just skipped out on me. Didn't leave me any money, won't call, nothin'. I feel your pain. So I want to help even though I could lose my job." I perked up and wiped my tears. "Your husband has a sizable balance, and I noticed he recently made a lot of purchases at a place called Ben Bridge Jewelers."

Her eyes suddenly got as big as quarters. "And, I saw on his account he paid for a membership to Match.com with his bankcard. He logs on to it frequently and was on the site as recent as this morning!" She opened the car door for me and nervously looked around. "I have your information and I'm going to get in touch with you," she said, slamming the door. My head began to swell like a balloon.

The mountains quietly rested behind the palatial estates and glistening lake, nestled in the middle of Thora's gated community. I couldn't have picked a better hideout. I was like a fugitive on the run and there was no turning back. The woman at the bank had given me hope, but not enough to keep me from practically wearing grooves into Thora's stone tiled kitchen floor.

"Chloe, if you don't sit and calm yourself down, you're gonna make me dizzy," Thora said, putting the cordless phone back on the charger. "You need to get some sleep."

"Thora, I can't sleep!" I said, waving the torn statement from the home equity line of credit company in the air. Just then my cell phone rang. Gregorry's name flashed across the caller ID. "It's him. What should I do?" I asked Thora in a panic.

"Answer it, but play it cool, and don't say anything about the money or anything else until you get a lawyer," she said.

"Chloe?" I just held the phone. "Chloe, where are you?" Gregorry demanded.

"I'm at a friend's. I needed a minute to think."

"What friend's? Where are you? When are you coming home? It's late and I need to eat dinner," he barked. I had to bite my tongue to hold back the razor-sharp words that were slicing their way through my teeth.

"You're going to have to get your own dinner, tonight," I said, stone-faced.

"I hope you don't involve your family in our business," he said suspiciously. "You're not planning on divorcing me? Are you?"

"You told me you were leaving *me*, Gregorry!"

"I made a mistake. We have a child on the way and I want to be a father to my child."

"You told me to get an abortion!"

"I didn't mean it. I decided I want us to be a family. I'll make it up to you. I want to go to church with you, too."

"I don't think we should talk about this right now."

"What?" Gregorry was infuriated. "Do I have to remind you about community property? I will take everything you have!"

"That is my house!" I had worked myself up to a sweat. I needed to get myself centered. I began to chant softly into the phone, "No weapon that forms against me shall prosper! No weapon that forms against me shall prosper! No weapon that forms against me shall prosper!"

"What the fuck are you saying?" he taunted.

"No weapon that forms against me shall prosper! No weapon that forms against me shall prosper!" I chanted, louder and louder. "God, I call on you, right now in the name of the Holy Spirit!" Be stern with the devil, Mother says.

"Fuck you *and* your God!" he spewed. I felt a surge of heat shoot through my veins.

"Gregorry Marion Robinson, you *are* a demon and no good is going to come to you!" I felt my body fill up with fiery strength. "You will never come near my child!" I screamed. My blood boiled. I dropped the phone, bursting into tears. All that fighting made me dizzy. I had to lie down quickly or else I was going to pass out.

I was still lying on my back in the guest room bed as Thora placed a cold rag on my head. My fever had returned. I closed my eyes and tried to imagine "happy things"—bright colors and running through fresh country grass after a summer shower, butterflies tickling my toes. I rubbed my belly, falling into a light slumber, but my spirit was uneasy.

Gregorry's temper and deceptive ways scared me. I thought Gregorry was the gift I had been praying for. He was supposed to be my Prince

Charming. I was his *honey, darling, baby,* and *love of his life.* Gregorry said everything a woman wanted *and* needed to hear.

"After I graduated from Morehouse, I moved around a lot, Atlanta, Houston, Phoenix; my position with Boiyt has even sent me to Seoul, Korea, for several months." He held my hand tightly as we strolled along the beach in Malibu. When he mentioned Korea, my ears perked up. Come to think of it, the "supposed" job offer he mentioned the first night we made love never materialized. Gregorry's words were so promising.

"I can't wait for you to see my art collection," he said as we gazed off into the sunset. Gregorry was a regular guy who was successful, and when I was with him, I forgot about Hollywood and the next deal. I turned off my BlackBerry and cell. All my attention was on him.

In just a month, he had even started saying the *big* three words, I love you. I was used to Edward. I knew he loved me, but he never said the words to me. To him a man's actions, not "empty words," as he called them, proved his intentions. I tucked Edward away in the furthest corners of my mind.

"You could be *it* for me, Chloe," Gregorry said, touching my face. He swallowed hard, grabbing my hand and squeezing it tightly. "I want another chance at marriage, Chloe. I don't care what you've done or who you've been with, and nothing about me before you should matter," he said, kissing me.

I didn't see the tsunami coming . . .

Ceci

LET-LONE

THE SHOP IS jumpin' today! I'm normally up in here by eight. I'm runnin' two hours late, damn! That Henny put a serious hurtin' on my ass this mornin'. I guess I kicked it too hard last night. I can tell right now, I'mma be on my feet doin' heads for at least four or five hours straight. That's why on days like this I gots to have me a li'l somethin' somethin' to kick it off and keep my engine runnin'. You know what I mean?

"Hey, Trina, hey, Nikki, whassup, Peaches!" I waved, greeting the other beauticians as I entered the shop. Those are my girls, but they can only do weaves or perms. Me, I can do all that shit, color, cut, press, roller set, and I'll slap a piece of weave up in your shit too if you need it. Ain't no sense of nobody walkin' around without some hair these days. Hell, it's yours if you pay for it! Feel me?

"Hey, Miss Angie, gimme a minute. Let me get my eat on right quick and then I got you, boo," I said, pointing to my customer who was already waiting in my chair. I quickly made my way toward the back of the shop. "Nikki, since you ain't got nobody right now, can you put Angie in the bowl, please? Girl, I owe you. I just gotta pee and eat, then I'm cool!"

"I got you, Ceci. Long as you got me a round later tonight!" Nikki winked.

"Girl, you ain't said nothin' but a word. We hittin' that new spot

57

across the river tonight. It's s'posed to be off the hook." I was just about to put my things down and go in the bathroom when Verdine, the shop owner, came in.

"Ceci, Angie been here for almost an hour. Where have you been?" She was standin' there poppin' her gum, with her hands on her hips like she was the damn president or some damn body. "Somebody gonna take your li'l clients if you don't start comin' in on time." Verdine put the ghetto in fabulous with them old tired 1985 crimps in her hair. She was the most hatin'ess-ass heifer I ever met. She lucky she run the shop or I'd slap her into next week. She was always on my back about my schedule.

"Verdine, you need to quit worryin' about me and what time I come up in here. Last time I checked, Carol Jane Gibson lived at 7925 Purdue." I dropped my purse on a nearby chair and put my Chinese takeout on the table, placing my hands on my hips. "Don't you get your booth money on time? I'm the best stylist up in here. I gots this!" Verdine rolled her eyes. "I thought so. What you need to do is let me give you a real hairstyle," I said, slammin' the bathroom door in her face. I ain't even 'bout to let her get on my nerves. I got a hangover and I need me somethin' to eat and a pick-me-up and then I'm good to go. I pulled a small foil envelope out of my jean pocket and opened it carefully. *Sniff! Sniff! Sniiiiif!*

That's what I mean about needin' that "li'l somethin' somethin' " on days like this. A li'l bit will do you every time. I carefully closed the packet up and placed it back in my pocket. Sometimes you just need a jump start. Shit, I could do hair all night now. I ate that fried rice like it was runnin' off the plate, downed me a Red Bull, checked my nose in the bathroom mirror, and was ready to face the night.

When I opened the door, The Gap Band's "Outstanding" was blastin' over the sound system. "Ooh, that's my jam! Peaches, you need to turn that up!"

"C'mon, Miss Angie, let's turn that hair out," I said, draping a cape around her neck and whirlin' her around in my chair.

Within a few short minutes I had made up time for runnin' late, had the blow-dryer goin', and the flat iron was sizzlin' hot. I carefully parted her hair in sections, delicately spritzin' each piece lightly with my special mixture of sheen and holding spray. *Sssssssssssssss!* Angie's hair flowed and felt like silky silk! If I cain't do nothin' else, I can do me some hair. I be readin' all those magazines from L.A. and New York. If I didn't have so many bills and a daughter who liked shoppin' at the damn mall all the time, I would have me enough money to open my own shop. One day, one day I'mma get my own shop.

"Girl, you got that good hair, but you sure be knowin' how to turn my hair out!" Angie gave a girlfriend snap in the air.

"Girl, it's all about conditioning your hair, and I don't put all that unnecessary heat on your head neither," I said, gently combing and styling her hair. Some beauticians around here be puttin' too many heavy products on folks' head. The one thing my mama says is that her grandmother, MaMaw, always taught her and her cousins, Joy Ann and Billye Jean, how to take care of their hair, and they passed that on to me and my cousins. We got all types of hair in my family too: straight, curly, coarse, and *kinky. Hello!* We not only come in all shades, but our hair comes in all grades. Shoot, that's the beauty of being a black woman!

By ten o'clock at night I was countin' up all my money. I had done ten heads at fifty dollars a pop. *Shiiiiiiiiiit!* I had five hundred dollars; I was gonna get my drink on tonight fo sho!

"Ceci, here you go; Peaches did a liquor store run," Trina said, handing me a pint of Hennessy.

"Thank you, boo," I handed her a ten-dollar bill. "I'm just gonna change real quick and then I'll be ready.

I went into the bathroom, quickly slippin' into a short black dress and black pumps and checkin' my makeup in the mirror. I pulled my tiny foil envelope out of my purse, opened it, and took two short sniffs and then one long one. *Sniiiiiiiiiiif!* Sniffin' one last time to make sure

I got it. I wiped the white powder residue from my nose, rubbin' the excess on my gums, and fluffed my hair. It was on tonight.

"Ceci, Twain is here!" Peaches called out.

"I'm comin'!"

Twain is my new man. My young and tasty on the side. My real man is Stanley, but his ass is old and tired. I needed me a young brotha to turn it out in the bed. Twain is thirty, and I be havin' to let him know what that forty-seven can still put a hurt on that ass! Oh, and he a roller too. Drives a brand-new car, sittin' on dubs. He work out at GM on the assembly line, but he got his side hustle too. I know what he be doin', but hell I don't care it's all about that almighty dolla, that paper, that dinero, yeah, mucho dinero! What Stanley's ass don't know won't hurt him.

"Ceci!" Peaches yelled again.

"Damn! I heard you and I'm comin'!"

Hey! It's on and crackin'! Club Regal is my spot and me and my girls is ready to turn it out. I took a long swig from my bottle of Hennessy. My phone vibrated, alerting me that I had a message. The screen flashed: MAMA. Urgh! I ain't tryin' to talk to Mama. She be workin' the hell outta my nerves, askin' me too much about my damn business. I decided to go on 'head and check the message.

Cecilia, this is Mama, you need to call me. I've been worried about you and Satin. I know you got upset when I asked you about that man you been seein'. I just think you shouldn't be treatin' Stanley badly. He's a good man to you and your daughter. Well, are you eatin'? I hope you're okay and not hangin' out in them bars across the river too much. Please just call me. I haven't been feelin' too good. I'm prayin' for you, Cecilia.

I didn't need this from Mama right now. Sometimes a person need some let-lone, just to be left the hell alone! I took two quick sniffs. I gave myself one last check in the mirror, but couldn't help thinkin' about Mama. I closed my eyes . . .

God, I know we don't talk much, but I wanna do right, but shit . . .
Excuse me, stuff is just hard. I got a lot of my own, as Mama would
call it, "demons" I'm fightin'. I don't mean to upset her, but Mama
just don't understand my pain.

I opened my eyes and took a long sip of Hennessy, recapped the
bottle, and turned off the bathroom light. Oh, hell yeah it's on, and
nobody betta say shit to Cecilia Gibson tonight!

Chloe

LOST ANGELS

TRACEY'S SUV SLOWLY crept up the driveway. There were no lights on, and I started to feel a tinge of nervousness. I rubbed my belly, taking a few deep breaths.

"You cool, girl? 'Cause, if that crazy motherfucker tries anything, we got something for him," Tracey said, reaching into the glove compartment and retrieving a small handgun. I guess you could say firearm ownership was the single female prerequisite around these parts.

"I'm cool. I just wanna get this over with," I said, rummaging through my purse for my house keys. My abrupt departure four days ago hadn't set well with Gregorry, and only God knows what's on the other side of that door. I braced myself.

The porch light and all the lights inside the house were off. I didn't recognize the place I used to call home. I unlocked the door. Like Siamese twins, conjoined at the hip, we made our way inside and over to the wall where the alarm keypad flashed. Tracey was still holding the gun steady. I quickly punched in the four-digit code and hit the light switch in the foyer.

"Where are you, motherfucka?!" I shouted. The house was silent. We scurried over to the hall light switch and flicked it on, still linked side by side. We entered the back guest room where I had barricaded myself in just four nights earlier. Gregorry's tirade vividly came back to me and sent a series of chills up and down my spine.

I flung the closet door open, yanking back a hanging row of dresses, relieved to find my gun case, and the gun still inside where I had left it. I grabbed it, quickly stuffing it in my purse. We opened the door to the third bedroom, also known as Gregorry's boudoir, and turned the lights on, only to find complete emptiness.

Where were the expensive shoe boxes or racks of custom shirts? The closet was empty too. I flew into a frenzy, running down the hallway, frantically flipping on the remaining light switches in the house. The brand-new flat-screen television had been removed from the living-room wall. I bolted into the new master suite and discovered the other flat-screen television was gone too.

I immediately went to the master bedroom closet. I entered and turned on the light. All my clothes were hung neatly like always, my shoes still stacked on the racks. However, when my eyes panned to the other side of the massive walk-in closet, it looked as if in one clean sweep, a giant hand had removed all of Gregorry's things. I felt like one of those Looney Toons characters who had been flattened by a steamroller. Except this was real life, and I couldn't just magically pop back into shape like the cartoons.

I hobbled my way, with Tracey holding me up, into the master bath. I began to hyperventilate as I opened and closed drawer after drawer, including the cabinets underneath the large double sink. Empty! I ripped back the shower curtain and all his fancy shower products were gone too. I blinked several times in further disbelief. Had it all been some horrible nightmare and now I was being violently shaken awake?

I sat down to regroup on the new suede sofa that had arrived just a week ago. I began replaying all the bizarre things I tolerated with Gregorry. Like the fact that Gregorry moved in with nothing but two metal footlockers, those racks and racks of clothing, enough shoes to stock Macy's men's shoe department, and the two missing televisions. When I questioned where all the beautiful furniture displayed in his Silver Lake home was, he claimed he sold it with the house.

While he had convinced me that it was all part of his mission to start fresh, I never demanded sales receipt of any such sales. I guess I never demanded proof or reason for anything. I simply took his word.

The biggest mystery by far was his connection to the metal footlockers he kept stacked in the corner of my living room.

I glanced over at the empty spot in the corner, where they used to sit, and remembered how he kept a hawkeye protective watch of them.

"What did you just do?" Gregorry once shouted, hurriedly walking toward me. He practically choked midsip on his Capri Sun drink. "Did you just try to open my property?" he said, placing his drink down on the coffee table, frantically examining the untouched trunks.

"I was looking for the remote control." I frowned, waving the television remote in the air. It had dropped next to the trunks. "Why are you so paranoid?" I asked, shaking my head. Gregorry got so incensed that he puffed up and stomped off to the bedroom with his kiddie attitude and kiddie drink, to surf the Net.

I should've taken a hammer and busted them open. It was as if I had conditioned myself to just act like they didn't exist. What *was* he hiding? Now I'd never know. They'd vanished, just like him. *Poof!* Right into thin air.

I pounded the sofa cushion with my fist out of anger, only to be reminded of the fact that my American Express card had paid for it—all five thousand dollars. Humph, must've been imported cows! Gregorry always had to have the best. Oh, and let's not forget the purchase of other new household items that had recently arrived, like the two-thousand-dollar mahogany California King sleighbed. Or what about the deluxe three-thousand-dollar pillow-top mattress and box spring.

Gregorry convinced me to charge everything to *my* card, never mind the fact that he had a wallet full of his own credit cards. Now neither he nor the money was here, and the bill would be in the mail any day. I was numb.

"Do you know that I don't even know the name of the barbershop where he gets his hair cut on Saturdays? I'm an idiot, Tracey!" I said, swelling up with emotion.

"C'mon, Chloe, now is not the time to beat yourself up. This whole place is creepy. You're coming to my house," she said, pulling me up. "Shake it off," she said sternly, grabbing me by the shoulders. "Girl, there have been days when I didn't know whether I was coming or going when it came to Emmie's crazy-ass daddy. You kept me from giving up a long time ago. You're strong, Chloe, and we can get through this, but we've got to get out of here before some more shit jumps off." Tracey gave me a reassuring nod.

There was no time to change the locks, so we began gathering random items, from clothing to computers, and tossing them into the back of her SUV. As long as Gregorry had a key to my house I needed to get my valuables out. As we drove away from the house I didn't bother looking back.

I woke up bright and early, a woman on a mission—my first stop, the Post Office, then on to the wireless store to change all my numbers, and finally, an appointment with the divorce attorney. I had practiced saying the word *divorce* several times in the mirror this morning, quietly in denial that I was going to go through with filing legal paperwork to end my marriage of barely four months.

Tracey had a friend, who had a friend, who's *other* friend's *cousin* knew about a divorce attorney. "Now I don't know how good she is, girl, but, shit, you ain't lookin' for Gloria Allred, you just trying to get free from a crazy fool!" Tracey rattled off, moving at mind-numbing, lightning speed as she maneuvered making a pot of coffee, putting frozen waffles in the toaster, checking homework, *and* tossing a peanut butter and jelly sandwich, apple, and chips in her daughter's lunchbox, *all* in one swift move. I wondered if I'd be able to do what she does as a single mom.

I didn't have the luxury of turning up my nose when I heard the name—NaKeisha Adderly. Sure, the name didn't have the ring of a Hollywood superstar lawyer, but I was broke and desperate. I didn't have much of a choice.

NaKeisha Adderly entered the cramped conference room that was buried on the fifth floor, inside a dingy Chinatown building, disheveled and distracted. She dropped a stack of files on the table and a blank notepad, stained with yesterday's coffee. I noticed NaKeisha was in dire need of a manicure and hairbrush. "I'm sorry to keep you waiting, but I got stuck in traffic." She was panting and sweating as if she had sprinted all the way to the office.

I spent the first twenty minutes in tears, before bracing myself for more dreaded news.

"Because of California's stringent community property laws, your husband may have a chance at getting your house, and although he may have acted with criminal intent, both of your names were on that bank account, and he withdrew the money legally. However, I'll do my best."

I didn't have anything but her best to count on, and even though I had emphatically explained that Gregorry's name wasn't on my property, it didn't matter. "Then let's get the asshole served!" I exclaimed. "I just want him out of my life and out of my child's life!" There was one small catch. NaKeisha had to be paid five thousand dollars to get started.

Gregorry had cleaned me out for the most part. Yes, I had been fool-*ish,* but my mother told me God always protects babies and fools. That's right, Gregorry hadn't entirely gotten the last laugh. See, Joy Ann Davis Nash-Michaels always told me and my sisters that a married woman should keep herself a stash. Mine was a secret bank account holding twenty thousand dollars in it. Now, that might be okay in a small town, but for Los Angeles that wasn't a drop in the bucket.

I had a mortgage, a car note on a luxury vehicle, and bills, but those things would have to wait. Right now NaKeisha Adderly had to be paid, because she was the best legal thing I could pin my hopes on. The rest I had to leave up to God. I raced out of her office having just enough time for one more stop before my ultrasound.

"But he showed me the appraisal papers on the ring!" I could feel a migrane coming on as the jeweler, Mr. Abib, delicately explained. Turns out my two point five, princess-cut engagement ring was practically worthless, barely five thousand dollars. That price tag was a far cry from the twenty thousand Gregorry had bragged about.

When I handed him the band, a delicate ring of diamonds, Mr. Abib simply shook his head as if he was ashamed for me. Thankfully, when I pulled out the Rolex Gregorry had given me to celebrate our one-week anniversary, I wasn't told it was a swap-meet special. Mr. Abib handed me seven thousand dollars in cash for the whole ball of wax. I tossed my wedding band in the garbage on the way out. Anything having to do with Gregorry or *that* marriage could consider itself history.

As I lay on the exam table in the dimly lit examination room, I began to daydream about baby names. I thought about the name Grace if it was a girl. It was nothing but God's grace that had been getting me through the last several days. I rubbed my swollen and warm belly. The sonogram technician, who barely looked legal, entered quietly and barely said a word.

"Put your feet in the stirrups, please," she said flatly.

"I hope it's a girl." I beamed as she quietly probed and prodded my belly and insides for several minutes.

"I'm having trouble finding a heartbeat," she said.

"What's going on?" She didn't respond. I began to quietly panic and puddles welled up in my eyes. My heart rate quickened. I was clammy and my face was flushed. "Ma'am, answer me!" I demanded.

"You really have to talk to your doctor. I could get in trouble," she nervously replied.

"Then get me a doctor!" I shouted. "Now, dammit!"

"Okay, hold this," she said, handing me the ultrasound wand that was still stuck inside my vagina, turning the monitor screen away from me while she fetched an emergency room doctor, because it was after hours. I was terrified, sitting in a strange place, alone, with my legs spread open.

A tall, lanky, bearded man, who looked more like a Woodstock leftover than a doctor, casually returned a few minutes later. He walked over to the exam table, pulled up a stool, and took the wand from my hands. After a few moments of moving the wand around, a row of wrinkles formed across his forehead.

"So you say you *are* pregnant?"

"Yes, eight weeks! Why would I be here if I wasn't? What is wrong!" My voice had escalated to a high-pitched crackle as the tears streamed down my face.

"Ma'am, I'm sorry, there's no life here," he replied. I opened my mouth, but only the faint sound of *what* floated out.

"Looks like the fetus expired, I'd say about a week or so ago." He lowered his eyes. "You can get dressed now." He got up, turned off the equipment, and began washing his hands. Nothing made sense.

"So that's it. You just tell me my baby's dead and that's it," I said, feeling as though my my lungs were about to collapse. He had just delivered the most devastating news I'd ever heard. "What do I do now?!" I shouted.

"You'll pass it at some point, I suggest you call your regular OB/GYN in the morning," he replied. "Again, I'm very sorry." He turned and exited the room.

I rushed to the sink on the other side of the room and began to heave. The vomit curdled and swelled inside my throat until I purged my afternoon lunch. There was a bitter taste in my mouth and beads of sweat poured down my face, as the bile oozed down my chin and onto the examination room floor.

I stumbled out of the hospital in a zombielike state. A burst of wind sent me into an emotional tailspin. I collapsed to the ground and began screaming and crying hysterically. People walked by sporadically, but no one came to my aid. I crawled to a nearby bench and managed to press Send on my cell, redialing the last call. Mother answered. "There's no life!" I shouted, shaking uncontrollably. "My baby's dead!"

"Chloe, oh God! God! No, God! Where are you, Chloe? Chloe, answer me!"

Mother's voice was frozen. I blacked out momentarily, awakening to Tracey standing over me, frantically screaming my name. Placing my left arm around her shoulder, we limped into the emergency room entrance. "Somebody help us! Somebody help us!" she cried out.

Tracey held me tightly, and we both cried as a nurse rushed us into a cubicle and assisted me onto a hospital bed. I curled up in the fetal position and began rocking back and forth, holding my stomach. "My baby! Why me? Why my baby?" I was still babbling and crying hysterically. The nurse softly tapped me. "Ms. Robinson?"

"Her name ain't Robinson. It's Michaels!" Tracey shouted.

"I'm sorry, it says Robinson on her insurance card," she apologized.

"Not for long!" Tracey barked like a protective guard dog, rolling her eyes.

"Ms. Michaels, we're going to give you some morphine to relax you and take away any pain you might be having," she said, sticking the IV in my arm. "The doctor and our staff social worker will see you once we calm you down," she said. I winced from the sting of the needle and quick burning sensation of the morphine going into my vein. As it seeped into my bloodstream, my eyes got heavy. I slipped deeper and deeper into a catatonic state, fading, but it was all starting to come back to me . . .

Five, four, three, two, one, Happy New Year!

"Happy New Year, my love!" Gregorry got down on one knee. "Chloe, will you marry me?" Gregorry said, reaching for my hand.

After three months of a whirlwind courtship, I had turned thirty-five and had finally found my "real" new beginning. The diamond sitting in the middle of my dessert plate glistened. The San Francisco Bay surrounding the restaurant shimmered under the moonlight sky. Gregorry had surprised me yet again with a romantic drive up the California coast to ring in the New Year. Tonight I was living a real-life fairy tale. Gregorry believed in "seizing the moment."

I remember one day Mother called the house and he answered the phone. I had already been hinting to her that Gregorry wanted to marry me. Well, Mother was so bold that she flat out asked him "Young man, why do you want to marry my daughter so fast?" He answered confidently, "Because I love her and can't live without her!"

So on this glorious night I didn't want to hear what Mother, Eve, or Fawn had to say, and Daddy would never understand how a woman could fall in love so quickly. I would just have to surprise them all. Sometimes you have to ignore family and do what you feel in your heart is best for you. I also knew that by accepting his proposal I was permanently walking away from what some would say was everything, but it wasn't.

Not even the millions that Edward Gentry had was enough. I'm reminded of that even more when I think about the last time I saw him. Honestly, if he had said the word, I would've dumped Gregorry.

"Edward, I need to talk to you." I had been sitting on the edge of the hotel suite couch wringing my hands.

"After this call, baby," he said, flipping out his cell phone. As he started to dial I don't know what came over me, but I reached out and closed it.

"Please, Edward!" My eyes begged.

"Chloe, what's wrong, baby?"

"Edward, I love you, but . . ." I stared at him for several seconds, then broke into gigantic sobs. He put his arms around me. "I need something more in my life. I need what you can't and will never be able to give me . . . you. I want a chance to find the right man, get married, have a child."

"I gotta tell you, Chloe, you have these dreams of some knight in shining armor, riding in on a big white horse to whisk you away, but it's not real," he sharply replied.

"Maybe it's not real for you, Edward, but for me it is."

"Chloe, if this is what you want, then I support your decision."

He asked me to stay one last night, but I couldn't. I couldn't lie in the bed with him and feel his skin melt into mine and not turn back on the promise I made to myself. Wasn't "I" the most important person here? Didn't I have to care more about myself and what *I* wanted, and, most important, needed to be happy? I could see if I was in my forties, past childbearing years, or even never wanted a child, but that wasn't the case. No, not this time.

Edward had been getting what he wanted for eleven years. It was time I got what I wanted. I had to show Edward that I could stand on my own and that, although he wouldn't commit to "us" 100 percent or give me the life I longed for, the life I deserved, someone *was* willing to do that and more.

Gregorry said he loved the same music I loved. He said he'd traveled the world and showed me computer printouts as proof of his financial stability, and it didn't hurt that we looked damn good together. No, I hadn't met one friend or any other relatives outside of his father, uncle, and stern-faced grandmother. He had a good explanation. He said he just didn't get out much socially, because he worked and traveled too much. I know it's fast but sometimes you can know a person your whole life and *still* not know them.

"Yes! Yes, I'll marry you, Gregorry Marion Robinson III!" I screamed as the tears of joy poured down my face.

He came into my life without warning, just like the knight in shining armor who saves the princess that I dreamed about as a little girl. *He* told me he was secure with my lifestyle in the limelight. *He* said he had my back. I trusted and believed Gregorry Marion Robinson III and now I, Chloe Michaels, was going to be his wife. He told my mama that he couldn't live without me. I was a brotha's life support, for Christsakes. You can't get any better than that!

Tonight I just wanted my mother. Mother could fix it all. I had to get home. You see, Mother never wanted me to move to the city of

Lost Angels. My little baby, Grace, was supposed to save me and now she was just a lost angel like millions in this city. God, please give her wings to fly. I drifted off, but the morphine could only mask the devastation of not carrying my baby full term. Now I lay, semisedated, somewhere between catastrophe and the abyss, my spirit bruised, broken, and stolen.

SACRIFICES

I have known women
Flying women/hawkeye and eaglewing who spread/stir the nest/
strike the wind and soar/women who strap mercury around their
ankles/making airborne feet/flying women who fly off the handle
up against brick walls and break wing/women who fly non-stop w/
earlobes/elbows/toenails and tongues like flying saucers/fly by night
women swiftwing and blind as a bat at high noon/Straighten up and
fly right women/women with magic underwing/I know women of
wonder with moon eyes . . .

Joy Ann

AIN'T NO MOUNTAIN

HELPLESS . . .

That's the only way to describe the feelin' that has worked its way up my legs and into my stomach and head. I'm paralyzed, hundreds of miles away from my child who the wolves done got to. I reach out to grab her, but she slips through my arms like time. My emotions bounce between anger, guilt, and confusion. A mother's instincts are never wrong. All those sleepless nights I never told Chloe about. I could hear the strain in her voice every time I called that house. It was wrong for her to have to tolerate so much to try to make her marriage work.

I sat on the sidelines and watched, silently, as this *man* gradually stripped my daughter spiritually, and come to find out financially— everything in the name of being a wife. She begged me not to tell anybody in the family and I have to honor this "secrecy." But is it worth the price of her life? Why is it a secret? No one can help if they don't know.

I get up and begin to walk up and down the floors in my tiny apartment. Sit down. Get up. Lay down. Roll over. Cry. Stomp my feet. Fall on my knees. *Help me, God!* I just keep hearin' her cries through the phone. Echoing cries from the bowels of pain, "Why, Mama? Why me, Mama? Why my baby?"

I got to keep movin', so I grab my cigarettes stashed in the back of the refrigerator and head toward the front door, on a mission. I just needed to get outside for a minute, walk this off, or this anger is gonna bust a hole right through my gut.

One foot in front of the other, one foot in front of the other . . .

I ball up my fists. This ain't happenin', I tell myself, shakin' my head back and forth. My tears slowly run down my face. The blood rushes to my head as I furiously punch and kick the air. I got to beat the devil's ass for sure this time 'cause he's done gone too far. This body may be old, but it's stronger than most would think. I been through many storms in my life. I been where I had no choice *but* to make it 'til the mornin' 'cause I had babies that had to eat.

I open my mouth to scream, but I only make a tiny sound. I don't want my neighbors to hear me. My body shakes. Do you know how hard it is to choke back the sound of a scream? If I could, I'd snap my fingers right now and be there with her. I don't like California. Too many cars, strange, wayward folk with no history, folk livin' in a dream instead of makin' dreams a reality. Everybody knows somebody, who knows somebody, who knows somebody else. But don't nobody really know nobody or nothin'!

I screamed again, this time to the top of my lungs until all the air had escaped and there was no more sound. I'm damn angry and I don't care who hears me. I had to smoke a cigarette. Smoked three to calm my nerves.

Peace be still . . .

My bare feet had made tracks in the grass that was still soaking wet from the bad storm we had earlier today. My tracks had formed a complete circle. A circle of life. A light drizzle started up.

Peace be still . . .

One after the other I watched the raindrops come down heavier. The rain was soberin' and shook me back to my senses. I cain't break into pieces like I want to. I have to be a strong mother now more than ever. I took a series of deep breaths. First thing is to get a plane ticket. Thank God my check from the school board came today for that last workshop I did with the Arts Program.

It was supposed to last me through the summer months, but I can't worry about that. God blessed me with that li'l check, and I gotta have faith that he'll open up another door for me. God, I'm tellin' you to bind us up; give me your armor and a righteous shield.

"Mother!" Chloe jumped out the passenger side of a big SUV, and for the first time in what has felt like the worst days of our lives, I could hear a smile in her voice. I dropped everything I was holdin' in my hands and threw my arms around her. I wanted to fold her up and tuck her away in my bosom, close to my heart.

Thank God Chloe's li'l friend, Tracey, had this extra bedroom at her house. She has been a blessin'. "These things that happen to us that make our lives go in a direction we didn't plan are sometimes necessary, Chloe," I said, placing my hand over hers. "The Lord put you in a safe place until I could get to you."

"Why did it happen to me? I tried. I was trying so hard," she said as her words began to knot up in her throat.

"Stop it, Chloe! I don't understand it all myself right now. But as your mother, and as a prayin' woman first and foremost, I know that God blessed my womb when I carried you, and from the time you took your first breath, I knew you were special. We don't know what God's plans are, but I got to believe there is a reason. I got to believe that boy had to be removed from your life. That baby was your guardian angel."

"I just feel so angry. I should've killed him, Mother."

"Why, so I coulda been comin' out here to see you in jail? Oh, no, God knew what he was doing."

"I just want tomorrow to come and be over," she said, doubling over.

"First of all, we cain't get to tomorrow until tomorrow!" I said, rubbing her back. "I've got to be stern with you, Chloe, because I will not allow you to lose your mind! Do you hear me?"

"Yes, Mother," she whimpered.

"In order to do that, you gotta rest. My heart aches about you losing a child, knowin' how bad you wanted this. But God's plan is not always our plan. Ecclesiastes says, 'To everything there is a season and a time to every purpose under the sun.' You hear me?" I said, cupping her face gently in my hands.

I was so happy to finally be here to see my daughter with my own eyes I had almost forgotten it was time to take my insulin until Chloe reminded me as she climbed into the bed in our room.

"You're gonna be just fine, Chloe. I'm takin' you back home where you can heal and get you some strength to fight this battle so we can put this situation behind us," I said, inserting the needle of the syringe into a vial of insulin, and slowly drawing the murky liquid out. I lifted my blouse, wiped off a small area on the side of my stomach, and injected the needle, releasing the insulin. I let out a long sigh.

"What about my house, and my bills? Where do you think Gregorry is?"

"Baby," I said, sitting down on the edge of the bed, pulling out a small bottle from my pocketbook, and unscrewing the top. "We don't care where he is, because what Gregorry is going to have to face is something I wouldn't wish on my worst enemy! I speak his name with fury and boldness, because the scriptures tell us to be bold with the devil. And don't worry about your money. What God has in store for you is gonna bring more money than you could imagine."

I poured some of the blessed oil in the palm of my hand and began rubbing Chloe's belly. I had to transfer positive, healin' energy into her body. I also had to work on thinkin' positively myself because I was grapplin' with so much anger. My anger not only was coming from the place of being a protective parent, but I was also mad at myself. I knew better as a mother.

That young man had a troubled soul and I could see it in his rigid jawline, in his eyes when I sat up in my daughter's house and talked to him. "Young man, you have a temper, don't you?" I asked, never taking my eyes off him.

"No, no, Ms. Michaels. Why would you ask me that?" he answered with one of those nervous laughs.

See, what he didn't know was that I got what my mother and grandmother called "the third eye." I can see straight through your eyes and clean out your asshole. When I visited Chloe right before the wedding, I watched him closely. The way my daughter jumped at the sound of his car pullin' in the driveway. The way he snapped at her in that nasty-cute tone of his.

"Honey, my mother was going to make dinner tonight."

"What!" He looked at her as if she had just said something so stupid it didn't dignify a response. I could tell Chloe was embarrassed. "Look, I'm taking us out to dinner," he said, fanning her off, giving her one of those whiplash responses.

I didn't need his black ass takin' me nowhere. He knew I didn't like how he talked to her. For the most part Gregorry avoided me. My spirit is strong. Even when I would call the house to speak to Chloe, he was always in a rush to get off the phone. No, I didn't like it, and I'm mad I didn't say how I felt. Humph! Sometimes a mother has to know when to be quiet and when to be as loud as the fierce and proud lioness who guards her cubs. Well, I'm done bein' quiet. Now, I've got to roar like a raging sea.

"Chloe," I said, stroking her hair that had grown to the middle of her back just during this brief pregnancy. "Courage is the key to life. We have to just look at all this as temporary." I kissed her on her forehead and pulled the covers over her as she closed her eyes and sunk into a deep slumber. Then I got down on my knees and prayed in silence.

After the D and C procedure the next morning, I let her have a real good breakdown right there in the recovery room. I wish I could wave my hand and make it all go away, but I can't so I gotta hold on to my faith even tighter. I whispered in her ear, *"Yea though I walk through the valley of the shadow of death I will fear no evil!"* I felt relief knowing the baby *is* gone. She didn't need nothin' that was part of him.

Our flight back to St. Louis wasn't for several hours and that was good 'cause I wasn't gonna leave California without goin' to that house. Sometimes a mother gotta take matters into her own hands. I entered

Chloe's house and could hear the walls weeping. Somebody had come up in here and tried like hell to steal my child's joy. So, after the locksmith changed all the locks, I got to work.

I opened all the blinds and windows in the house. Then, I carefully pulled a bunch of dried sage leaves, which were bound together by a rubber band and wrapped in a soft cloth, out of my suitcase and placed it on the kitchen table. I went over to the cabinet and removed the carton of kosher salt. I lit a match and let the flame engulf the tips of the sage leaves, slowly fanning them to extinguish the flames.

I walked through the entire house chanting Psalm 70 while burning white candles. The white symbolized purity. I took the box of kosher salt and sprinkled it on the front steps and then swept it away with all the bad energy.

Too much evil had been allowed to set up shop and settle, but now there was peace. As the smoke from the freshly burned sage left a thin cloud that lingered in each room, we gathered our belongings, said one last prayer of thanks, and prepared to depart. The alarm had been activated, the last lock locked, and the timers set on all the lights, sprinklers, and anything else that had a switch.

Chloe had even made arrangements for her car to be parked in a garage facility. I knew my child was going to worry herself to death about this li'l ol' house. It's funny, she just don't see it yet, but this house is just like any other "thing." Things come and go. People are just like things too. "Things" can be gone in the twinklin' of an eye.

Chloe

WELCOME HOME, HOLLYWOOD

"**I** FEEL LIKE a thousand eyes are on me," I'd whispered to Mother as we exited the plane and made our way through the Lambert-St. Louis Airport terminal to the baggage carousel.

"Chloe, stop being paranoid," she said, gripping my hand tightly. "Baby, no one is looking at you." Unfortunately, her words gave me no comfort. I could still hear the silent chatter and laughter behind my back. *Did you hear about what happened to her?*

I told Mother I wasn't ready to talk about things with my sisters, or the rest of the family, yet. That must've gone in one ear and out the other, because she planned a big "welcome home" dinner. Didn't she get it that talking about Gregorry and the baby would only make me feel worse and more embarrassed. How in the world was I going to hold myself together?

As we exited the main terminal, I was suddenly reminded of my summers growing up in the Midwest. I wiped my forehead with a tissue. Right away, my hair started to curl and rise at the root, soaking up the thick, soggy mid-June St. Louis humidity. This kind of weather is a beautician's wet dream. I bet my cousin Ceci was cleanin' up at her shop.

"Where is Eve?" Mother huffed, wiping her brow.

"That's why I suggested taking a cab."

"Chloe, that's over twenty dollars!" Mother let out a frustrated sigh. "My hands are starting to tingle. You know when it's time for me to eat, I get the shakes. I need to find my candy," she said, digging in her purse.

I love my mother to death, but Eve had to hurry. I didn't have the mental capacity to listen to Mother complain about her sugar for the next thirty minutes. This was just another example of just how selfish Eve is.

Fifteen minutes later . . .

Eve pulled up to the passenger pick-up area honking her horn like she had lost her mind. She was carrying on like *we* were the ones who were almost forty minutes late.

"Hurry up, Hollywood!" Eve shouted, opening the car door and frantically waving her arm in the air. "C'mon, Mother! C'mon, Chloe! I'm not tryin' to get no ticket!" Eve got out and popped the trunk.

Lord, my sister, Miss Fashionista, was wearing a pair of hot-pink capris with a matching top, high-heeled bejeweled sandals, her hair was whipping in the wind, and she wore large aviator sunglasses. Eve was always crying broke, but she never left the house without hair and nails done, and full makeup. I mean, the works—eye shadow, blush, lipliner, eyeliner, lipstick. All I could do was shake my head.

Mother scooted along, sliding into the backseat.

"Girl, c'mon! It's hot and I don't want to sweat my hair out. I just did it," Eve yelled again, as I pushed the cart carrying my luggage over to the curb.

"You got nerve rushin' us when you're late, and aren't those my earrings?"

"Girl, you left them the last time you were here. I'll give 'em back before you go home!"

"Chloe, don't you lift anything! You just had that D and C. You need a girdle on!" Mother shouted in a panic from the backseat. Great, now the entire Lambert Airport would know all my medical business. Urgh! Some things about home never change.

Eve's car crawled up and around the long driveway that ran alongside a large Tudor home. I let down my window. The evening air was still warm and sticky. The smell of freshly cut grass tickled my nostrils.

The cozy dwelling had a bit of gingerbread house charm, and a yard that looked as if Martha Stewart had done the landscaping herself.

Eve continued past the big house, down a short hill that led to a quaint carriage house, a miniature version of the "big" gingerbread house. This was where Mother lived. We slowed to a stop and parked. My sister Fawn's timing couldn't have been better. She pulled up behind us in her Mercedes.

We all got out of the cars and Fawn quickly trekked her way over to give me a big hug before helping Eve with my bags.

"Chloe, I'm so happy you're home and away from that man! You should've let us come up there, but that's okay, we're still gonna jack him up!" My sister Fawn is the epitome of a midwestern doctor's wife. Her hair was conservatively pinned up, and she was wearing a bright green-and-white polka-dotted sundress and green sandals that tied in a bow.

Fawn is the kind of woman whose shoes always *have to* match her bag, and if you opened the local black paper to the society page, she'd be right there in a full-page color ad. But don't let the prim and proper image fool you. Girlfriend will "cut" you if you get on her bad side.

The four of us shuffled our way up the tiny walkway that led to Mother's door. She moved here a few months ago after her landlord suddenly decided to sell her old apartment building. Her good friend Salvatore, a fellow painter from the West Indies who teaches at one of the colleges in town, owns the property. He offered her this small one-bedroom bungalow for just three hundred dollars a month.

"I like what you've done, Mother. It's exactly how you described it over the phone too, cute and cozy," I said, entering the house.

"Fawn and Eve, just stack those bags in my bedroom," Mother instructed. "I even have a closet for all your stuff like at my other place," she laughed, turning on the air conditioner.

"C'mon, Fawn, help me finish up in the kitchen," Eve said, winking at me.

"Why didn't anybody tell me? I would've made my famous roast," Fawn said. I laughed to myself because Fawn actually made a terrible roast. She thought she was an amazing chef, though, always volunteering to cook at family gatherings.

Mother led me into her bedroom. The same bright green paint, which was the color of grass, that trimmed the exterior of the house also trimmed the borders along the walls inside. Being an artist and all, she had done her usual and transformed this closet of a house into a castle.

Her eye for mixing ethnic and eclectic furnishings, original artwork, African artifacts, and brightly colored walls made the one-bedroom abode come alive. Miss Ozona, our family psychic (or as she likes to refer to herself, our family "spiritual adviser"), had a vision.

She told Mother she should wrap herself in yellow and green. They would bring her prosperity and good creative energy. Mother did just that, and, with Salvatore's help, she had painted the walls yellow and everything else a soft, bright green.

"By the way, Chloe, only your sisters, and of course Thora, know the truth about why you're home. Your grandmother, aunt Billye Jean, and cousins Carol Jane and Ceci just think you're home recuperating after losing the baby. Same with your father. You need to talk to him sooner than later." Keeping secrets was one of the things we did best in this family.

It wasn't long before I could hear everyone piling through the front door. "Hi, everybody!" I shouted, exiting Mother's room. The room returned a round of "hey, Chloes," and "glad you're home, babys." I started making my rounds, heading directly toward Grandmother, who was sitting on the daybed slash couch that was tucked away in an alcove against the far wall.

Miss Millie Michaels was eighty-three, independent, always well coifed and pressed, and still dressed in her Sunday church suit and high-heeled shoes. My grandmother was our honorary family matriarch. Honorary because she's my paternal grandmother. Her only sister, Lady, passed away about ten years ago. So, outside of my father and his sister, we're pretty much all she's got.

Grandmother reached up to hug me and twisted her mouth. "I'm sorry about the baby, Chloe, but now you're home to get all the love you need. And we've gotta get that weight off you, too." She patted me on the behind. I self-consciously ran my hands over my hips and butt. Grandmother's never been too good in the tact department.

"Lola, did you say hello to your aunt Chloe? Girl, Aunt Billye Jean picked her up for me and she's been workin' my nerves ever since she got here." My niece hugged and kissed me. "You know she started her cycle," Fawn said, winking.

"Mom! Urgh!" My niece Lola was tall and thin like a beanpole, with thick crinkly hair that cascaded down her back, like Fawn's when she was little. She got her rich cocoa coloring and full lips from her dad. His family's island roots had come out all over that child.

"Take her with you whenever you go back, *please*, Chloe!" Fawn screeched. "Or, Eve, you take her to live with you!"

"Oh, no, been there done that. I finally got Christina off to college. I love my baby, but I'm happy she's interning this summer in a different state!" My niece Christina had just finished her first year at Spelman, and I hooked her up with a summer internship at CNN in Atlanta. "Please, let me enjoy my peace!" Eve beamed.

I finally made my way to the small kitchen area where Aunt Billye Jean and Cousin Carol Jane were busying themselves, maneuvering between the stove, sink, and refrigerator, putting the final preparations on dinner. Mother had forced a table, chairs, and MaMaw's antique cast-iron stove in there. That's my mama, always trying to fit a square peg in a circle.

"Chloe! Welcome home, baby!" Aunt Billye Jean announced, fanning herself, as she grabbed me and hugged me tightly, before pulling me close and whispering, "Tell yo mama whose greens are betta. Taste this!" Before I could answer, Aunt Billye Jean had shoved a forkful of greens into my mouth. "Go on, tell her," she said, folding her arms. The room erupted in laughter.

Cousin Carol Jane was Mother's first cousin who was raised with her and Aunt Billye Jean like a sister. Her face lit up and she threw her arms around me, giving me one of those squeeze-you-'til-you-can't-breathe, rocking hugs, momentarily cutting off my flow of oxygen. Her large arms felt like two thick down pillows. Carol Jane still gave hugs like she did twenty years ago when she was a hundred pounds lighter. She was all teary-eyed.

"Thank the Lord for a good flight. We prayed for God to circle you in the light, see you through this difficult time, and bring you home safely. And Mark 11:24 tells us that whatever you ask for in prayer, believe that you have received it." I had to fight back my own tears. Carol Jane always got real emotional, especially when she talked about the Lord and the Bible. Both of which she did often.

Just then, my cousin Ceci and her sixteen-year-old daughter, Satin, entered.

"Damn, it's hot as hell out there!" Ceci always knew how to make a grand entrance. A lit cigarette dangled from her bottom lip. Ceci was Carol Jane's daughter. We all called her the wild child because she liked to get her party *on*. She drank sometimes a little too much, and could curse worse than a sailor. However, there was no denying the fact that she loved her family to death.

Whenever I came to town Ceci would stop what she was doing, even if it meant taking off work, call up everybody and have a party for me right there on the spot. It didn't matter if I wanted barbeque, fried catfish, steak, or shrimp, she'd cook it. That girl knows she can burn in the kitchen!

"Chloe!" she rushed over to me and threw her arms around me, hugging me so hard her sandy-blond curls bounced excitedly on top of her head. "You okay? 'Cause you just say the word and we got somethin' for that punk-ass Negro you married!" she whispered. "Hey, Mama! Hi, rest of the family!" she announced loudly.

"Hi, Chloe," Satin said. "Where ya'll want me to put this?" she asked, holding a dish filled with Ceci's famous mac and cheese. Ceci knows she spit that girl out, same powdery fair skin as hers, that brownish-blond hair, and light eyes, except Satin's are green instead of hazel like her mama's.

"Hey, y'all, is that oven still on? My macaroni ain't no good unless it's hot!" Ceci was always in rare form.

"Cecilia, please watch your mouth, and tone it down today!" Carol Jane frowned, taking the pan from her and placing it in the oven. As religious as Carol Jane is, she and Ceci are like day and night. Or should I say heaven and hell. Poor Cousin Carol Jane, she gets so nervous when Ceci's around.

"That girl, ain't big as a minute, is she? And she skinny and tall like Lola," Billye Jean said.

"I don't know where they get all that height from," Carol Jane replied.

"Paw's side! They was tall and looked like a buncha white folks!" Aunt Billye Jean noted.

"Oh, yeah! That's what I want to do next summer, Billye Jean. Take a trip down to where Paw's people lived in South Carolina and do some research," Mother added.

"She finally fillin' out," Carol Jane said.

"No, I ain't, Granny," Satin said defensively.

"Yes, you are! You gettin' thick in the middle," Ceci said loudly, taking a long drag from the last of her cigarette and then extinguishing it.

Carol Jane rolled her eyes, "Lord, please!" Ceci knew that was her cue to chill.

When the meal was ready and each steaming hot dish was placed on the table, we gathered, standing in a circle around the table. Holding hands, all heads bowed and eyes closed, Mother said the blessing.

"Lord, we thank you for this day. We thank you for bringing this family together in the tradition of our ancestors. Father God, we ask that the love that prepared this food nourish our bodies . . ."

"Amen," Carol Jane interjected.

"Praise God," Aunt Billye Jean echoed, waving her hand in the air.

Eve squeezed my hand, then I squeezed Fawn's, who squeezed Ceci's. We gave each other a mutual, here-they-go-again look. Carol Jane finished up thanking MaMaw, Paw, Jesus, Mary, *and* Joseph. Sometimes we'd have church all over again at the dinner table, but you felt good, uplifted. A feast had been prepared, fit for a king, but the queens always ruled at this table.

Plus, being *home* I didn't have to be on my grammar "p's" and "q's." It's true, black folk are born bilingual. We get good and comfortable when we talk amongst ourselves. It's what that rapper Nelly calls "Country Grammar" at its finest.

The food was put away, the kitchen cleaned up, and the house was quiet. I turned on the hot water and let the steam engulf the bathroom as I began to undress, peeling away layer after layer. I stood naked in the shower, rubbing my empty belly as the water poured down my trembling body. I felt more scared than ever, breaking into big gulping sobs.

"Chloe, c'mon on, baby," Mother said, knocking on the door. "C'mon and get out of the shower." Mother pulled back the shower curtain, turned off the water, and handed me my robe. Then she squeezed me like she was hanging on for dear life. Her skin was soft and smelled like honey and sweet oil. "Chloe, right now you just have to be home until you can get things back on track, and you don't have to rush." Mother held me close in her arms and that calmed the uneasiness in my spirit.

After Mother tucked me in, we prayed together. When she left the room, I reached inside my purse that was hanging on the side of the bed and pulled out a small bottle of Tylenol PM pills. I popped two in my mouth. My tears silently crept down my face. The sting of my life being tossed upside down had been less painful for a few hours, but now I was alone with my thoughts and starting to worry about what tomorrow would bring.

Billye Jean

FOOLISH

I ROLLED OVER and sat up 'cause I thought I heard the door unlockin'. The television was flickerin' on mute. "Arnaz, is that you?" I yelled out. I fumbled for my glasses on the night table, put 'em on. It took a coupla minutes for my eyes to focus. The clock read 3:00 A.M. I sucked my teeth in disgust. He shoulda been home hours ago. He said he had to work a double at the movie theater. I don't know what movie in this country last 'til the early mornin'. I know Arnaz is lyin'. He been lyin' for years, but what am I gonna do now?

I got on up and decided to make myself some coffee. Forty years and I'm still puttin' up with the same mess. I thought he woulda got tired by this age. I know I shoulda done somethin' a long time ago, but I got this house, and these cars, and it woulda been too much mess to sort through.

I poured me a cup of pipin' hot coffee and set it down on the dining room table. I got comfortable in my chair. I figure I may as well just stay up and wait for him to get home. Wonder what his tired *old* ass is gonna say this time, and I do mean old. Hell, I'm seventy-two and Arnaz is seventy-five. We ain't had no marriage in too many years to count, but you'd think at this point we could just get along and give companionship to each other.

I reach for my coffee cup and look down at my hands. It's funny lookin' down at old hands. Any way you turn 'em, they just don't look good. I never liked the fact that I got them fat fingers. Got 'em honest from Muh. I'm glad my children had nice hands. That's the one thing they daddy, Earl, my first husband, used to tease me about all the time. "Jeanie"—that's what he called me—"you know you got them swamp clopper hands, girl!" I'd just smack him upside his head. Earl used to tease me like that.

Anyway, Junior and Thora got long fingers from Earl. Them, and them light eyes and straight facial features. You can see Earl an 'nems' genes all in their lips and nose. Junior was my firstborn and when he came out that's the first thing I looked at, his fingers. I did the same thing when Thora was born. MaMaw was worried about the hair, and seein' if their cuticles was dark. Junior had them big locks of curls on his head like me.

Thora was bald like a baby bird for so long, that's what I was worried about. I was, like, Lord, just let her take her hair from me when it do finally grow. That's the only thing Earl and 'nem know they had some rough hair. But Muh was already ready with the pressin' comb. I had to stop her. I was not gonna let her press no li'l baby's hair. But she was a pretty baby. Didn't even hardly cry. Junior's ass cried all the time.

Yes, these hands done been through a lot. Each wrinkle, crease, and callous tells its own story. My hands and my brain are what I've relied on all my life. I had to study double hard and work triple hard to build a decent life with these hands. I didn't have the luxury of pampering my children, pettin' 'em when they did somethin' good at school, or rubbin' their backs at night, like my sister, Joy Ann.

These hands have painted walls, dug holes, scrubbed floors, put up shelves, hammered nails. I did most of the work around this house myself. Arnaz ain't hardly helped wit shit. That's why I don't have no sympathy for Joy Ann. She be all upset if creatively she cain't do nothin'. Now, I think my sister's very talented, but the way I see it, if somethin' ain't bringin' you in a steady check, it ain't a career, it's a hobby.

I remember how I had to do domestic work for all those years until I finished nursing school. I couldn't complain to that white lady and say, "Oh, today I'm just not feelin' creative enough to wash your windows." I couldn't tell my supervisor at the hospital that I wasn't feelin' creative enough to give Mister So-and-So his medication. Joy Ann always had some kinda excuse and even when Muh was livin', she'd say, "Oh, well, you know Joy Ann is doin' this" or "Joy Ann is doin' that."

I ain't never had a minute to think about everything I done had on my mind. I wanted to play the piano, but I had to stop, just like I had to stop goin' to school. I had to be a mother and wife at fourteen years old. I was real smart as a child too. Always smart in the books. I finished elementary school early and they put me in high school at twelve years old, said I was some kind of prodigy.

I was going to the big high school over there on Franklin Avenue and Earl was older than me, but in my same grade. He was scrawny and funny lookin', but had the prettiest green eyes I'd ever seen. He just kept on tryin' to sweet-talk me. We wasn't boyfriend or girlfriend or nuthin'. Muh and Daddy didn't allow none of that, but he kept on and one evenin' I went to take the trash out at the garbage station. He met me there. Ain't no need to say no more.

Back then you couldn't go to regular school if you was pregnant. I was so young when I had Junior, I didn't know no betta. I would take the baby outside and shoot marbles with the otha kids. Muh would have ta come out there and git me. When I went around Joy Ann and Carol Jane, they friends looked at me funny.

It didn't matter, Carol Jane was crazy about her some Junior. She would take him 'round like he was her baby. When it was time for my high school graduation, I went to see the otha kids march. I was depressed for a long time 'cause I had a baby, a husband, and never got to graduate in a ceremony with my friends.

Me and Earl didn't even have no real wedding in a church. Uncle Reverend, my aunt Margaret's husband—his real name was Milton—married us at MaMaw and Paw's house down in Joplin, Missouri, in the parlor. I had a two-piece lime-green dress on. I'll never forget that dress. It was the ugliest thing I ever saw. I was used to being thin, but I was pregnant and fat. I hated the way I looked.

But my marriage to Earl wasn't good. It started off wrong, and when I got pregnant the second time, I didn't know who the father was. I guess the one thing I have noticed about myself, the older I get the more I tell my own business and don't feel a bit bad about it. It wasn't like I was loose or nothin'. It was just that I was young and this boy named Luther got after me. Older boys was always likin' me. Earl was two years older than me hisself.

Anyway, Luther was so nice, and cute too. I was young and I started likin' him. He used to drive trucks for his daddy's truckin' company, but he fell asleep at the wheel and died. I didn't think the baby was Earl's 'cause we had separated for a few months after Junior got to crawlin'. But when they put the baby in my arms, I knew it was. Thora looked just like Earl and 'nem, and I was mad as hell.

She almost died. I felt bad for not wantin' her. She had a real bad respiratory infection. Respiratory problems run in Earl's family, that's why Thora got it bad even to this day. I got into the sanctified church heavy after that. The deeper I got into religion, the further I pushed Earl away.

I didn't wear no makeup, no secular music, no cussin'. Earl started drinkin' real bad around then, too. He would come in drunk and put all my church members out. You sho gotta be careful who you have children wit.

When I think back, I don't think I ever was really in love with Earl. Me and Earl was too young and everything was always a struggle. We split up and kept goin' back and forth. All he did was keep comin' round Muh's beggin', but I ended up leavin' his ass fo good.

Arnaz was just the opposite of Earl. He was a real looker. I liked him most 'cause he reminded me of Daddy and Paw. When I got on staff at the hospital, he was workin' as an orderly. But I remember when they came to get him from the hospital.

"Arnaz, what they doin'?" He couldn't answer me. They was hand-cuffin' him and takin' him away. They finally let me go see him. I dressed up Junior and Thora in their Sunday's best. We rode the bus up to the state penitentiary. It was a long ride. Muh packed us some lunches. "I don't know why you takin' those children up there, Billye Jean." Muh stood on the porch with a worried look on her face.

" 'Cause he's my husband and I love him and these his kids now!"

Arnaz had gotten himself locked up for ten years for sellin' dope to an undercover cop. I waited for him too. For what I don't know. It ain't like we had no kids together. I tried. I had two miscarriages, but I guess God didn't mean for me to have no more babies. Me and Arnaz didn't need none anyway. He already had six by five different women when I met him. All them kids look like him too, even the ones by ugly mamas.

I couldn't finish the rest of my coffee, my stomach was hurtin'. Probably from worryin' about Arnaz. I checked the clock on the microwave. It read 4:00 A.M. Still no Arnaz. I felt my upset lump up in my throat and chest. I rubbed my chest and closed my eyes.

God, I know my days are numbered. I just ask that you bless me with some kinda happiness 'fore I'm called home to glory. I know I got a mean streak and done spent more years actin' hateful to my family than a Christian woman ought to. Truth is, I guess I just hated some things about myself. I know I was too young to be a mother, but I did the best I could. I learned the hard way with both my marriages. Now seem like I'm just stuck with Arnaz.

It's a shame, he ain't never been right by me and my kids. I know he's the reason Junior got bad off like he did. I shoulda left him a long time ago. But now I'm old and just gotta make the best of it. Anyway, what I'm sayin', Lord, is that I know I ain't been the best mother, but I tried to show Thora and Junior how much I loved them by working hard, givin' them a roof over their head, food, and pushing education. Thora never needed me, but Junior, he was weak. I fight the guilt, but I just wanna rectify my wrongs. I'm standin' in the need of prayer! Amen and hallelujah!

Chloe

THE SISTA CAVALRY

*Chloe Michaels is a ghost and she doesn't live in this tattered
and emotionally worn-out body anymore . . .*

I'VE HEARD PEOPLE talk about being depressed, but I guess I never would've thought that I could be one of them. I wasn't sure, but I guessed this is what it feels like. You know when everything is numb, and you open your mouth to speak, but the only thing that comes out is the pitiful whimper of a bleeding, empty soul. You cry, don't want to eat, and only sleep, because sleep is your escape. Sleep is how you forget about living.

I wanted to ball up all my troubles and toss them into Mother's closet, the place where skeletons, scars, and shame seek refuge. My body was too weak to move, but I mustered enough strength to curl up in a ball and hide under the covers. Mother said time would heal everything, but all it seemed to be doing was prolonging the agony. It had been five days since I'd been home, and it had all gotten worse.

"Mother, now you know that ain't normal." I could hear Eve's muffled voice through the closed bedroom door.

"Be quiet! She don't need to hear you say that. Right now it's about understandin' her situation. We have to handle this delicately. She says she needs time," Mother explained.

"Time for what? She's been here for five days and is still in the bed!

I'm sorry, Mother, but time's up! She's home and it's about this family pulling together!" Fawn whispered angrily and loudly. "Ceci said she knows some thugs in the hood, and all we'd have to do is give 'em two hundred dollars and some crack and they'd mess Gregorry up good!"

"Fawn, shut your mouth!" Mother snapped. "First of all, ain't nobody goin' to the hood to get nobody. All you need to do is end up in jail somewhere!"

"Naw, Mother, I'm sorry, but I'm with Fawn, and we need to quit lettin' Chloe make decisions. She ain't thinkin' right," Eve said.

My head began to pound. It was my life that was in shambles, not theirs. Hearing them talk about what I should've done or needed to be doing just made me more stressed out and on edge. I was the one who let some stranger walk up in my life and take over like I didn't have good sense. I lied to my family and friends and pretended that I had history with Gregorry, when in reality I just didn't want anybody asking me nothing!

I'm hiding from the world. Yes, I'm embarrassed because I'm the one who had to have that big fancy wedding, just a month after he proposed. It was bad enough folks thought it was a shotgun wedding. But I wasn't pregnant. I had just always envisioned a winter wonderland extravaganza for my wedding. Waiting until the next winter would be too late. We had to get started on our family!

I even put the pictures in the newspaper, and of all places, *Jet* magazine—the black Bible! I don't *care* how high and mighty you get, every black girl dreams of having her wedding photo in *Jet*. Now that I was back home, the scene of the crime, the whole city would be laughing at me. I'd have to explain what happened a thousand times over!

I shoved a Tylenol PM capsule in my mouth and washed it down with the glass of lukewarm water that had been sitting on the night table from the night before. My only escape had come in the form of a little blue pill. Each time one wore off, I'd pop another in.

Mother wanted me to get out of bed and leave the house to get some life around me. She wanted me to call my father. Mother said Daddy burst into tears at the news about the baby. He was convinced I was having a girl and had already gone out and purchased a dress for her christening. How could I explain anything to him when I didn't understand it all myself? Things like why I jump every time I hear the door slam. Or why my heart races when the phone rings, because I think it's Gregorry calling to harass me and my family. For all I know, he could be watching me right now.

I rolled over and buried my cries in the pillow. Mother had sacrificed her bedroom and a comfortable bed for me and was sleeping in her small living room on the daybed that doubled as a couch. I felt bad about bringing all of my baggage here. My joy had been broken in pieces, and Mother had carefully wrapped, packed, folded, and neatly tucked each piece between my cashmeres, linens, silks, wools, and soft cottons. Everything was quietly packed away inside the two suitcases stacked one on top of the other in the corner.

Mother didn't know how long I'd be here, but we packed enough to last 'til the weather changed. I had a life back in L.A. that I would have to get back to soon, but for now I was frozen in time, my life interrupted. Mother said this was all temporary. She said at some point we have to at least start acting like life is getting back to normal. What is normal?

Moments later, there was a round of soft knocks at the bedroom door. "Chloe, we know how private you are, so cover up, we're comin' in," Fawn said, turning the door handle and entering. Eve shuffled behind her.

I propped myself up against the headboard. "Scoot!" Eve motioned for me to move over. She and Fawn quickly sandwiched me in, then smothered me with hugs.

"Chloe, you can't shut out the people who love you," Fawn said, bracing her back against the headboard.

"Chloe, we got your back and we're not going to let you sleep this away like nothing happened," Eve said.

"It's time to get it together! I just want to know, how did this happen? And then you let that fool run you out of California!" Fawn charged.

"I didn't let anybody run me out of California!" I shouted from beneath the covers, bursting into tears.

"She didn't mean it like that, Chloe," Eve said, peeling back the blanket from my face. She handed me a wad of Kleenex.

"I feel like a failure. I've always been the one who had her shit together," I said, blowing my nose.

"Well, we ain't tryin' to hurt you, but as hard as you are on your own family, I can't get over how you let some *stranger* come in, and have free rein over your house *and* your money! I'm completely outdone." Fawn jumped up and put her hands on her petite hips.

"You? What about me!" I snapped. "Last time I checked *I'm* the one who lost a baby, and it was *my* money that got taken, and *my* life that got screwed over!" I jumped up and shouted angrily. "Thanks for coming over here and beatin' me up!" I was fed up with both of them. "I don't deserve to be interrogated!"

"What's going on in there?" Mother said, knocking loudly on the door.

"Mother, we're fine. We're sisters!" Eve called back, rolling her eyes, letting out a deep sigh. "Damn y'all! Okay, Chloe, calm down. Fawn, you have to realize that she's the one who's in pain!" Eve was typically the one out of the three of us who screamed and hollered the most. Ironically, as we've gotten older, she's become the voice of reason in times of crisis. Unfortunately, Fawn could pummel a dead horse and her "tough love" tactics always rubbed me the wrong way.

"I'm sorry, Chloe," Fawn said. "Okay, so what's up with your lawyer?"

"I don't know. She's not very aggressive," I said, letting out a deep sigh, plopping down on the edge of the bed.

"I gotta be honest, when Mother told me she was black, I wasn't happy. You married the worse kind of snake. You need a white lawyer who can put the fear of God in him. I ain't lying! I bet psycho man's got himself a white lawyer. Don't he?"

"Yep, he does!" I said.

"Oh, and I hope you had an AIDS test, 'cause I'm suspect of that dog!"

"I did at the doctor's office. I'm fine."

"Good, now all you need is a white lawyer," Fawn said.

"I just paid the lawyer five thousand dollars that I didn't have. So I gotta just wait it out."

"Hell, I think you should tell Edward. He's the brotha with all the money and connections," Eve said.

"He's the man you really want," Fawn added.

"I don't wanna talk about Edward, please. I left him and I'm a failure!" I snapped.

"Personally, I'm just glad you didn't have the baby, 'cause that would be a whole other legal headache," Eve said.

"Me too!" Fawn rolled her eyes.

"How can y'all say that?" I said, choking up.

"Chloe, we're not sayin' it how you think. Look, we just didn't want you to have to be tied to that man forever," Fawn said, placing her hand on my shoulder.

"And another thing, you aren't a failure! You did what you thought was the right thing to do because that was your husband," Eve said.

"He preyed on you, and I'm like Mother, I can feel there's something more to all this. But what matters today is that you know how much we love you, and we're going to get through this. And then we're gonna fuck him up!" She laughed as Eve and I joined in.

The three of us clinched hands and sat on the edge of Mother's bed, eyes welled over with tears. We didn't have to speak another word about Gregorry. I realized that I didn't have to wear a mask to cover up my mistakes or pretend to be stronger than I was. I was done explaining. At that moment I knew that our connection as sisters was an intricate patchwork of our mother's struggles and triumphs. We were the fruits of her labor pains. Our tears and blood flowed from the same river.

Carol Jane

STOLEN INNOCENCE

I MADE A WHOLE pot of collards this mornin'. Baked a ham, some potato salad, even threw a cobbler in the oven. I don't know why, ain't nobody here to eat it. I shouldn't say that. Lawrence is here, but most of the time it's like he ain't. I'll probably eat that whole pie by myself. I guess I'll go to Bible study tonight. That always helps me when I'm worried about Ceci.

I know she's doin' some things besides drinkin' that ain't good. I wasn't gonna dare talk about it at Joy Ann's. I keep callin' Ceci, but she either don't answer or if she does, we just argue and then she starts that cussin' and I just have to hang up. I guess if something happens to her at the shop or that bar, the hospital or police will call.

I woke up in the middle of the night 'cause all in my sleep I just felt like callin' out to my daughter. Then I went to the kitchen and heated me up a plate of leftover spaghetti. Well, I had some of the fried catfish too, and some slaw. You can't eat fish and spaghetti without the slaw. And then I had to break up all that salt with somethin' sweet, so I had the last slice of that German chocolate cake I made. I just took some extra insulin so my sugar don't go up.

But tonight eatin' wasn't enough so I went to my altar, got down on my knees, and prayed.

Father God, you've brought me a mighty long way, through pain, tragedy, and fear, the good times and bad, and you still keep on blessin' me. You've brought me too far to leave me. When my enemies encamped around me, you held me close to your bosom. You showed me that I was still a blessed and favored child in your kingdom. I look at my life and simply surrender. I've loved my child as best I could. Just protect her and keep her, Heavenly Father. I am weak and I am tired but like the song says "I won't complain." Oh and Lord, I know gluttony is a sin and I'm tryin' to battle this demon that makes me turn to food. I pray for strength, right now in your sweet and holy name, Jesus! Bless your holy name.

The heaviness of guilt has been on me lately. My mother passed away when she was my age. Perhaps that's why I've been questionin' my own mortality as of late. I've got some things I need to set straight before I go. Mainly some business, as a mother, that I need to handle. Ceci was my only child. The only child I was ever able to have, and I'll never forgive myself if I don't tell her the truth.

I still see *his* face after nearly fifty years. "You gots some sweet-smellin' skin, Carol Jane."

"This ain't right, Jake Spencer." Jake Spencer was the son of Mr. Spencer who owned the general store in town. Everybody said that boy was "slow."

"Look here, nigga gal, you mind yo manners. Don't be tellin' me what's right and what ain't right." He began to touch my face and stroke my hair roughly.

"Please don't touch me like that. My mama just did my hair." I was terrified. I began to pray. "The Lord is my shepherd . . ."

"Y'all think y'all better than us white folk, gal."

"I shall not want . . ."

" 'Cause you educated an' look at you, all highyella."

"He leadeth me beside the still waters," I whispered to myself.

"Yo daddy like white women! Yo momma a nigga lover. I'mma teach yo daddy a lesson!"

"Shut up! My daddy's in heaven and Mama's not white!"

He put his full wet mouth filled with the stench of week-old moonshine over my mouth. His saliva felt like hot lava being runnin' all over my face. I could taste the dirt and sweat in my mouth. I mustered all the strength I had in my body and kicked that man as hard as I could in his crotch and shot off runnin' like lightnin', rippin' the sleeve on my brand-new church dress MaMaw had sewn for me.

"Errrgh! I'mma get you, gal!" he growled.

I ran and ran, until I ran so far that all I could see was darkness around me. I couldn't hear nothin' but the crickets. I thought I was in the clear, so I stopped to catch my breath. I felt queasy still smellin' his smell on my skin.

"I told you, nigga gal, I was gonna get you!" My screams were trapped in the thickness of the night sky, lost in the open field. After a while I just stopped. Wasn't no sense to keep on. Nobody could hear me.

I don't know how I got back home to MaMaw's. Mama 'bout fell out when I came through the door. I heard her say she was gonna be sick. Joy Ann was cryin'. Billye Jean covered her eyes and MaMaw made both of them go upstairs. I saw my reflection in MaMaw's big hall mirror; my bright yellow dress was soiled with blood and dirt. My pretty curls were frizzy and dusty. Jake Spencer was twice my age and had raped me.

The family gathered to discuss what to do. I could hear them all talkin' through the walls. My uncle Frederick—everybody in the family called him Daddy—got his shotgun ready, but MaMaw and Paw put a stop to him goin' out and doin' somethin' crazy.

MaMaw, Mama, and all my other aunts prayed a vigil, burnin' sage, and boilin' all sorts of other roots MaMaw had grown in the back, 'til the wee hours of the mornin'. They even called on Mother Hortense, the old lady in town who was, quietly, a conjure woman. I was stretched out on a table in the front room. One by one, MaMaw and my aunts—Hazel, Elizabeth, Margaret, Honor, and Sarah—each took turns wrappin' me, layer after layer, in gauze that had been soaked in blessed sweet oil and a compound Mother Hortense made with some stuff that looked like mud, but smelled like spices and herbs.

MaMaw gave me strict instructions to lay still. I could hear Mama cryin'. "Now Cora, you got to quiet yourself." MaMaw's soothing voice began to calm Mama. I could see MaMaw's smooth dark skin, her hair, shiny and black like coal with silver strands woven in between the silky curls, draped across the middle of her back. Her long tresses framed those piercing deep-set eyes that could look you in and out and upside down and tell you what only God knew. But as striking and powerful as MaMaw's sharply etched nose and lips were, there was a softness and warmth to her. She was regal and feminine, effortlessly flowin' through the room barefoot, in her starched, crisp white cotton eyelet gown.

"But, MaMaw, look at my baby. How could he do this to my baby?" Mama pleaded with swollen eyes. "She's just a girl!" Her pale pinkish skin was flush. Mama was already what folks called light, bright, and damn near white, and tonight she was so sickened by the sight of what had happened to me, she looked even more white. Her dusty-red hair was limp like a wet mop soaked from tears, sweat, and vomit. "Is my baby gonna be all right, MaMaw?" Mama began to shake uncontrollably.

"Hazel, take Cora and get her cleaned up, and give her summa that warm milk and honey I got on the stove. You go rest now, Cora." MaMaw could always stay calm in the midst of the storm. Mama nodded, and Aunt Hazel wrapped a shawl around her and they both disappeared.

"I'mma kill all them crackers!" Uncle Frederick's boomin' voice nearly shook the whole house. "This is my brother's only child and I know he's fightin' like hell to get outta heaven right now! I gotta do this for him!" I lay still, quietly tremblin' inside.

"Son, I'm not gonna let them put a price on yo head! You my only livin' son. We gotsta be smarter than white folks right now." Paw was a wiry man who, to me, Joy Ann, and Billye Jean, was like a gentle giant. He was red like Indian clay and his hair was always neatly slicked back. Paw believed a colored man should dress appropriately at all times, except for when he was workin'.

Paw was a farmer by occupation and we had hogs and chickens.

He was well respected and had a lot of customers in town. Normally, after workin' in his fields, he'd come in the house and get cleaned up and smell clean and spicy like I remember my daddy smellin' before he died. Paw would dress for dinner, but tonight he never made it out of his soiled work clothes.

"I wanna kill somebody too, but violence is not the answer. Son, give me the gun," he said, reaching out to Uncle Frederick with his steady strong hands.

"Frederick, this is in God's hands!" MaMaw softly warned, and all of a sudden a hush fell over the room, all but the whispered chants coming from Aunt Honor who was speakin' in tongues, as Uncle Frederick handed Paw the shotgun.

By the next morning, MaMaw and Paw had set up a private meeting on the Spencers' property and took the pastor with them. MaMaw and Paw were highly regarded in the community and those white folks didn't want no real colored trouble from the church and the NAACP. It was settled quietly, and I never saw Jake Spencer again.

My cuts and bruises healed up pretty fast. And, instead of givin' the baby up, it was decided and arranged that Lawrence Gibson would marry me. Lawrence had had a crush on me ever since I can remember, and the Gibsons went to church with us. Old Man Gibson, who owned the black funeral parlor in town, was his daddy, and he was a good friend of MaMaw and Paw's.

Lawrence, a nice, smart young man with a promisin' future, was preparin' to attend Lincoln University, the black college in Jefferson City, Missouri. Lawrence knew I was pregnant, but I guess I could love him more because it didn't make him no difference. Most important, Lawrence was the *right*-looking man. He coulda passed for white because he had straight hair and blue eyes. I was already so fair and we knew with a white man the child was sure to look white. The Gibsons were a "good colored family," and Lawrence was what MaMaw called "marrying well."

I gave birth to a blessed baby girl, Cecilia Vivian Gibson, named after my great-grandmother Vivian. Lawrence was so in love with that child he would sit by her crib until all hours of the night. Cecilia was his as far as he was concerned. He loved her like she came from his own blood. MaMaw and Mama and all my aunts helped take care of the baby so that I could go to school and get my degree in social work. Lawrence got his degree and we moved up to St. Louis and made us a nice life.

I always wanted Cecilia to have so much because so much was stolen from me that night. I know Lawrence did too. We probably gave her too much. Lord knows I tried. I wanted more children, but God didn't have it in his plan.

Forty-seven years I've been keepin' this secret. I just didn't have the strength to tell her. I was ashamed. I guess you start to get older and you just wanna clean your soul out before you die. I don't want my child to resent me, but I have to take that chance and hope that by her knowing the sacrifices I had to make, she won't hold anything against me.

I stared at the phone for a long time and thought about callin' her tonight, but I changed my mind. Instead, I decided to scoop out me a saucer of cobbler. I looked at it for a while, thinkin' back to when Ceci was a baby and how I used to hold her in my arms, shieldin' her from harm's way. When did I lose my child, Lord? As a mother you do your best to keep a watchful eye.

You try to give your children a good education, expose them to things. I guess you spoil them sometimes when you should be more stern. Did I give her too much? Lord, have mercy on my child wherever she is tonight, and whatever she's doin'. I had to keep blinking to fight back the tears as I shoved a forkful of cobbler in my mouth.

Chloe

DANCE WITH MY FATHER

I STRUGGLED THIS MORNING, trying to shake off my NyQuil hangover. It's become my latest fix to sleep and escape the realities of a life turned upside down and inside out. How long am I going to be trapped in this bubble? Mother keeps telling me that it's about taking tiny steps every day, but after being home for over a week, I don't feel any different than three days ago, one hour ago, or two minutes ago.

Mother woke me up and said, "Chloe, it's time to start shakin' the blues loose. I will not allow this to take away my beautiful, vibrant daughter!" She said it came to her that I needed to take a sage bath for healing. I took a deep breath, sinking into the tub, and let the hot, sage-infused water suck my body under.

I could feel the nerve endings in my fingers and toes start to come back to life. I pushed myself back up to the surface, letting the spicy herbs trickle down my face. I cupped my hands together, filling them with more water and rinsing my face again. I had found rejuvenation in the healing homemade waters Mother had concocted.

Once dressed, I made my way to the kitchen. My taste buds were even curious, taking in the mouth-watering aroma of fried apples, eggs, biscuits, and sausage. My eyes wandered around the room, looking at Mother's walls, covered with old family photos—great-grandmothers, grand-aunts and -uncles, and cousins once, twice, and three times removed. She likes to call them "heirlooms." I don't know how she's kept up with all this stuff over the years.

"Thank you for making me the bath and making me get myself together," I said, wrapping my arms around Mother's shoulders. She carefully flipped the eggs over in the skillet.

"I'm a mother, that's my job, and that's why it's called home. I made your favorites. There's some tea over there," she said, motioning toward the table. I sat down, picked up my cup and spoon, and stirred in a spoonful of honey. I glanced over at Mother's face again. Age has definitely crept up on her, but you can still see the smatterings of girlish brown freckles sprinkled across her honey-colored face. Her once firm and supple skin now had a sweet sag to it. Her body was fuller and softer. I watched her smooth back her wavy silver strands, and then shake her hands out.

I remember when I was a little girl, Mother's hands could not only cook, but also work up some serious hairstyles. If she happened to be in a pro-black and righteous mood, she'd pick out her hair into a big curly Afro, or wrap her head in elaborate head scarves. Sometimes she'd braid her hair so perfectly that it looked like intricate train tracks. When she undid the braids, she'd comb through her hair with her fingers and it would look like gigantic ocean waves. All that changing up is too much for her now. I guess you get older and little by little you start to let go of things. Give in. Settle.

We said grace.

After a few minutes, I felt the weight of her eyeballs on my forehead.

"What you fishin' for, woman?" I said, looking up from my plate.

"I just wanna know if you gonna call your father today?"

"Yes, Mother. I'm gonna call," I said, slightly agitated.

"Chloe, I know he wasn't the most supportive about you gettin' married, but he is your father and he loves you. Honestly, Ray is not always wrong. He must've seen something in that boy that made him be so strongly against it. In hindsight we all shoulda said somethin'. I didn't like the fact he had li'l ears, I don't trust li'l ears. That means you stingy and mean. Anyway, give Ray more credit than what you're givin' him.

"He's gettin' on my nerves callin' every day. I'm tired of tellin' him you're asleep 'cause then he just wanna talk to me. If I ain't got no money, he's got less! He's lyin'! If I say I'm sick, he's sicker! Maybe I'm just so sick of being in the position where, when there's trouble, I have to deal with him. Y'all are grown now and you need to face your father. That's all I'm sayin'!"

I pressed the last digit of Daddy's number and felt a pull in the pit of my stomach. I was afraid to tell my father about what happened, because the first thing he'd say was "I told you so." Then he'd start talking about how I wasted all that money on a wedding, and that it was a big show for nothing. Doesn't every girl want her father to approve of the man she plans to marry? Doesn't every girl expect her own father to be excited about walking her down the aisle and giving her away? Not mine, as evidenced by the fact that he showed up at the church five minutes before the music started. At the reception he refused to dance with me, then left before it was over. I was humiliated.

Daddy picked up, and hearing his voice made my eyes tear up for some reason. "Hi Daddy, I'm, well . . . I know Mother told you . . ." My stumbling and stuttering trailed off into a pile of meaningless babble, and I felt yet another crying spell building in my throat.

"Hey, hey, hey, just calm down, Sweet Pea. Whatever it is, it's okay." Sweet Pea was my nickname and whenever he called me that I felt instant comfort.

I barely made it past the hostess podium before Daddy was rushing toward me with open arms.

"Sweet Pea!"

"Daddy!"

Daddy had been a small man all his life at barely five eight, but I hadn't seen him in over six months and he seemed even smaller, with a few more wrinkles around the jaw. He wasn't sickly looking or anything, just age settling in. He was still a sharp dresser, in his freshly pressed linen shirt and pants, sporting a new do—tiny, short, salt-and-pepper twisted locks.

"You looking good for an old man, too. Nice hair!"

"Yeah, I waited until I was an old man to take the plunge and dread my hair. But hey, if I start going bald, then I can just do like my buddy Walt. When his started falling out, he just superglued them back in!" We laughed, taking our seats on the patio, and ordered two coffees. Daddy put his arm around me, and I leaned my head on his shoulder.

"I'm sorry about the baby, Sweet Pea." I began to cry, and Daddy's eyes filled up with tears too. "I, um"—he swallowed hard—"I just feel like there's not much I can do or say, except I love you." Daddy grabbed my hand. "I know that you'll get the chance to be a mother again." He reached into his back pocket and handed me a freshly folded hankerchief.

"Wow, you're still carrying these." I wiped my eyes and smiled, holding up the hankerchief.

"Your grandfather carried one every day 'til he died!"

"Daddy, there's also something else." I closed my eyes and took a deep breath. "Gregorry left me." I lowered my head as the tears poured down my face.

"Damn!" Daddy's jawline stiffened and his entire body tensed up. "What do you mean, he left you? Where is he? I want to find the motherfucker!" he shouted, blowing out a puff of air along with a round of obscenities, and began rubbing his chest.

"Where he is doesn't matter! Please, I need you to be calm for me!" I cried out.

"Okay, okay, I'm cool. Just tell me what happened and when." He put his other hand over his mouth.

"A couple of weeks ago."

"And your mother knew all this? I bet your sisters do, too. Damn, I'm always the last to know! I never liked the nigga and he was weird, too. See, that's why, that's exactly why—"

"Stop it, Daddy! That's why I was afraid to tell you. I know you told me never to get married, period, and you even told me not to ever have kids. 'Just focus on your career, Chloe. Make a lotta money, Chloe.' Isn't that what you told me, Daddy? Well, I can't change anything now!" I was sobbing uncontrollably. The café waitress peered over at us.

Daddy's position on marriage and kids was just the opposite of Mother's and the rest of my family. When he and Mother first married, Fawn and Eve were just seven and five. He helped raise them like they were his own until I surprised them all. The catch was, technically they weren't his. He loved them, but in the back of his mind he was probably thinking that if it came down to it, he could take the easy way out. Leave, divorce, cut himself right out of the picture, no strings.

"Okay, okay!" Daddy said, putting up his hands in a gesture of surrender. "I'm sorry." We both took a series of deep breaths to regroup. "None of this is your fault, Sweet Pea, and I didn't mean to explode like that, but I see my daughter hurting and I wanna hurt the motherfucker who did this."

"All I wanna do is get my life back together," I said, blowing my nose again.

"Look, I don't even want to bring any more negativity into this thing. You stay home as long as you need to. You hear me? And, look here, I ain't got much, but I got my retirement payout and I want you to use some of that if you need to." We hugged again. "So, enough of that bullshit for today! Anyway, how are Eve and Fawn? I ain't heard from either of them in a month or so," he said, changing the subject.

"They're good, but you know, Daddy, you don't have to always wait for them to call you," I said, blowing my nose one last time. "The kids are good too. Lola's being a new teenager and Christina's finished her first year and they say she made the dean's list."

"Your mama okay?"

"Yeah, she's good." Daddy thought he was slick easing into asking about Mother. He was just as bad as she.

"Yeah, you know she likes to start mess, tryin' to get all in my business," he said.

It seems like the older I get, the more I feel like a child stuck in the middle of two grown folks acting like children. Both of them need to let go of the past. They haven't been together for over twenty-five years.

"What business do you have, Daddy?" I smirked.

"Well, errrum." He cleared his throat. "I have a friend. I've been meaning to tell you about it."

"Okay? I don't get it. A friend?"

"A *lady* friend," he said, clearing his throat again.

"I see, a *lady* friend." I could feel that same tug in the pit of my stomach.

"Well, I've known her for a while, but, um, see, she's *younger.*" His technique was slick how he let the word *younger* fall off his tongue, out of his mouth.

My eyes went wide. "Just how much *younger,* Daddy?" I demanded. The roles had suddenly reversed. I was the adult, and he was now the child.

"She's actually about Fawn's age," he said, lowering his head. He knew what he was saying was just as ridiculous as it sounded.

"Is that right?" I was starting to get mad as I stared across the table. Now it all made sense. The new twisty dread look, and the earring that I hadn't noticed until RIGHT NOW. This old Negro is going through some sorta *after*-midlife crisis.

What I really wanted to do was reach over and smack some sense into him, and ask him had he lost his damn mind. I took a deep breath and leaned back in my chair, chewing on the side of my tongue to control my words.

"Say something please, Chloe," Daddy pleaded. "I don't want to upset you. Maybe my timing was all wrong, considering what's going on with you."

My father wanted my approval, but I was at a loss. Based on my own set of relationship woes, I was in no position to pass judgment, give advice, or offer criticism.

"Well, do you love her like you loved my mama?"

"Chloe, first of all I ain't looking to be in love with nobody. I'm too damn old. I like her and that's good enough. Second, I could never love anyone like Joy Ann."

"So why are you telling me all this?"

"I'm telling you because you're my daughter. My *adult* daughter and I felt like sharing something in my life with you. I'm not looking to make any major introductions. I just felt you should know."

The way I see it, a man, I don't care how old he is, can run out and find a woman and his choices are wide open. He can go young or he can go old. A woman who starts to get up in age is shit outta luck.

"Oh." I was dumbfounded. "Okay," I said.

"Then, okay," he said.

We sat for several minutes before I broke the silence and ordered another cup of coffee. As we finished up and were about to head out of the café, Daddy put his arm around my shoulder and whispered, "Ah, listen, about my friend, do me a favor and keep this between just you and me for now." Basically, that meant don't get Mother and Fawn and Eve and the rest of the clan all up in arms about his little secret.

I decided to take the long way back to Mother's. Here I was thinking that *I* was the latest breaking news to deliver, but Daddy had his own media alert. Things hadn't turned out quite the way I planned, but lately that's how my life's been. One surprise after the other.

I made a detour through the park and realized the boathouse was a few feet ahead and slowed to a stop. We used to come here as a family when I was younger and rent paddle boats for the afternoon. Then Mother would lay out the best picnic spread when we finished. In the wintertime the Parks Department would make an ice rink over that hill.

I would beg Daddy to bring me out here to go ice skating. Fawn and Eve would brag to their friends that their little sister was going to be the black Peggy Fleming one day. I'd be so excited when we pulled into the rink lot that as soon as Daddy parked, before he could even shut the car engine off, I'd dart out of that car. By the time he got inside, I'd have my skates laced up and be on the ice. Sometimes I'd stay out there so long my feet would freeze up like Popsicles.

Stopping here made me a little sentimental, I guess. I wiped my face with my hands, put the car in Drive, and pulled off. I longed for those days again. Stuff isn't supposed to be this complicated.

Joy Ann

JACKPOT

BILLYE JEAN WORRIED me so bad this mornin' about comin' out to the casino, I finally gave in. My sister's crazy! I wasn't hardly comin' to no casino at no nine o'clock in the mornin'. Besides, Harrah's has the best buffet outta all the casinos, and Crab Leg Tuesdays don't start 'til five.

I prefer comin' out here by myself. Billye Jean spends way too much money if you ask me. I bring my li'l ten dollars, twenty if I have it, and once it's gone it's gone. I saw her play a hundred dollars one time! I know she wins big, too! She got so excited one time she slipped up and said somethin' about "gettin' her thousand dollars to the bank quick!" She ain't gonna offer me none, though.

"Joy Ann, I'm goin' to my lucky machine!" Billye Jean had a sudden burst of energy when she spotted the row of slots that had Wheel of Fortune in bright lights all around them.

"Wait! I'mma go with you!"

"Oh, no! Girl, I need to be focused when I get on my machine, that's how I win. You know that's my favorite show, and I win every time I play on it!" She gave me a high five and high-stepped her way right on over to the one flashin' the most in the middle of the row. All I could do was shake my head. She calls me on the phone soundin' like she's dyin', but as soon as she hits the casino floor, she's movin' so fast on that cane, she's almost knockin' folks down. You'd never know she had cataracts, heart trouble, sugar, or nothin' else.

And I'll tell you another thing. I don't like that outfit she got on. Billye Jean ain't never had too much taste when it came to clothes. Truth is, my sister is country. Look at that purple-and-orange matchin' shorts set. It wouldn't be so bad, but she got that red vest on with all her nursin' pins and buttons with her grandkids' pictures on 'em pinned to it. She says that's her lucky winnin' vest.

I'm just glad she took that sun visor from Sea World off her head. I wish she would try to look betta when she came out with me. If I had me some money, I'd shop for her. See, I get me some good deals at the Scholar Shop. It's a thrift store, but upscale. I volunteer there and get 20 percent off. That's how I got these good sandals. They're Italian made. You could pay over a hundred dollars for these in the store. They were practically new and with my discount I only paid twelve dollars for 'em.

She tickles me, 'cause when she goes to one of her social club functions or an event at her church with the women's group, she really calls herself gettin' dressed up. Billye Jean gets to talkin' "proper" just like when she used to be on that job at the hospital. She was the first black head nurse at the biggest hospital in St. Louis and she knew that job better than any of them white folks.

I'll give it to her, she's always been book smart, and good with some money. Like I said, lucky with it. So I guess I don't mind foolin' with her out here. Maybe some of that luck will rub off on me today.

I found me a nice machine tucked away near the back of the room. I had a good feelin' about it. I like the ones with the diamond designs on 'em. Probably 'cause I've always loved diamonds so much. I just never really had a good diamond ring from either of my husbands. I take that back. Bobby Nash, my first husband, was extravagant, almost too extravagant, that's why we didn't never have no money. He'd go off and buy a new suit with our grocery money.

He bought me a small diamond ring when we got married, but I lost it. Ray, my second husband, gave me some cheap gold band. I look at my life now and the way I see it, my girls are more precious than gemstones and gold. Maybe they'll get to have all the diamonds they can dream of in their own lifetimes.

I slipped my brand-new five-dollar bill in the dollar taker and said me a quick prayer: *Lord, you know I wouldn't ask you if I didn't need it, but please make this li'l bit of money multiply!* I like to start puttin' five dollars into the machine, then I work my way up to ten.

Ding! Ding! Ding!

I slammed the palm of my hand on the double spin button. C'mon, c'mon diamonds! The pictures and numbers stopped flippin' and spinnin' and I was *this* close to gettin' me one of those cherries. I tried my luck again. See, I like it at the casino. I come here because I can escape with all the lights and the different kinds of people. I like people-watchin' and meetin' new people. So many people have great stories written right across their faces. Being an artist, I find that's what is most fascinatin'.

Ding! Ding! Ding! Ding!

Twenty minutes later I hit. A hundred dollars. Thank the Lord! This will get me some gas, a few groceries, and a li'l bit of pocket change. With Chloe being home maybe I can treat her out to dinner. She's always doin' for one of us. I like to do things for her when I have it. I didn't need to play no more. Now, the task is gonna be gettin' Billye Jean outta here.

I know my sister. She's probably winnin' a bunch of money and just don't want me to know. She's like that, thinkin' somebody's gonna ask her for some money. Billye Jean screams broke and the next thing she'll go get a sunporch put on her house or buy some new window treatments.

"Billye Jean, girl, you must be winnin'," I said, walkin' up to her. She slapped her hand on the double spin button.

Ding! Ding! Ding!

"No, I didn't, Joy Ann, you just hear bells and think somebody done won. We waited too late to come. Oh well, I made it to the bonus round twice and won back what I put in. Girl, I just love these Wheel of Fortune machines." Billye Jean slapped her hand on the double spin one more time.

Ding! Ding! Ding! Ding!

"Billye Jean, that's an extra ding, I know you hit that time!"

"Whew! I did."

"Good, let's go to the buffet."

"I'm treatin'!"

We loaded up at Crab Leg Tuesday and made our way to our table, sat down, said grace, and started crackin' those crab legs away.

"Joy Ann! Guess what? I heard *Wheel of Fortune* is gonna be here!" Billye Jean said, tying a plastic bib around her neck.

"You mean here at the casino?" I asked, dippin' my crab leg in butter.

"No, I mean they comin' to the mall out by my house and pickin' folks for the show! This is my chance, Joy Ann, and I want you to go with me."

"I don't know, Billye Jean. We could be wastin' our time."

"Or we could win. At least one of us. Hell, we old! What we got to lose? Shit, I get me a shot I'mma win. I watch that show every day."

"It does sound excitin'. Okay, let's do it!"

"You might win some money to help Chloe out. Seem like some trouble to me."

"Billye Jean, you don't know what you're talkin' about. Pass me that pepper."

"So how long you think Chloe gonna be here?" She put her hand on the pepper, blocking my ability to grab it.

"If you don't give me that damn pepper, you'd betta!"

"What about that boy she married? Kinda strange we ain't heard nuthin' about him since that quick-fast-in-a-hurry weddin'." I snatched the pepper shaker and looked away to avoid eye contact with Billye Jean.

"Joy Ann? I know somethin' ain't right, and you may as well come clean."

I let out a sigh and covered my mouth with my hand. "Billye Jean,

it's bad. That boy left her and disappeared and took some of her money."
The more I told her, the more she kept shakin' her head in disbelief. By
the time I finished, we were both on the verge of tears.

"Well, you know what we gotta do, don't you?" she said. I nodded.
"We got to do what we know how to do best and pray, but we got to
pray some serious prayers on that boy. What's his name, Jeffrey?"

"No, Gregorry."

"Whatever it is, I didn't like him when I saw him up there on that
altar. Somethin' 'bout him just didn't ring true. Did you see the Negro
tryin' to act like he was cryin'?" she huffed.

"Mmmm, huh."

"Did you see his daddy and that uncle standin' up there?"

"Mmmm, huh."

"Yeah, we gotta pray, but in a different kinda way." She looked me
solidly in the eyes. "You know what I'm talkin' about, Joy Ann."

I knew exactly what my sister meant. I just didn't like havin' to
do *those* kinda prayers. "Billye Jean, I thought about it already, 'cause
MaMaw could connect to spirits from the dead or speak in tongues
and pray a bad spirit out of you right before your eyes."

"MaMaw could voodoo you good, if you crossed her or one of her
own. You remember Aunt Margaret's husband, Mr. Tisch?" she asked
with a wink.

"Sure do. He was beating her for breakfast, lunch, and dinner. Then
one morning he just stopped."

"He woke up and couldn't move. Muh said, he got the 'lock joints,'
but we was li'l bitty girls and knew the truth."

"That's right, girl!" I chuckled. "All MaMaw said was, 'I s'pose he
won't be hittin' on nobody else no more, now will he.' Mr. Tisch got a
dose of them serious prayers." She winked again.

Me and Billye Jean didn't say much else about Chloe or that boy
she married. We finished up our meal at Crab Leg Tuesday and got
on to talkin' about some other frivolous stuff, but that was just fine.
We had silently agreed on the matter. We knew what time it was, and
that's all that needs to be said.

We had been taught how to not only chase a bad spirit away, but also how to burn it up for good. I didn't like havin' to, as MaMaw called it, "burn bread" on folks, but it was necessary. She always warned us that burning bread was serious, and not to do it unless you meant to call on the spirits to do "business" on somebody. You cain't play with the spirits!

When we returned to Billye Jean's house, she lit the candles on her altar. We kneeled and began with an opening prayer. *"Let destruction come upon him at unawares; and let his net that he hath hid catch himself: into that very destruction let him fall."* We whispered in unison. Billye Jean reached into her bible and pulled out a photo of Gregorry she had taken at the wedding and handed it to me. *"Let destruction come upon him at unawares; and let his net that he hath hid catch himself: into that very destruction let him fall."* We whispered in unison again.

I placed the photo in a small metal bowl, lit a match, and dropped it into the bowl. I watched the flame slowly eat away at the image of Gregorry flashing a condescendin' smile until it was nothing more than a small pile of charred ashes. Billye Jean carried the bowl outside, and I followed her. I scooped up the ashes and blew them into the wind.

STAGNANT

I have known women
Bold/brave/brass and sassy women/cinnamon breath and whispering
smiles/women with custom-designed life lines that make beauty
a new face/women with struggling wrists/jagged edges/women
with life lines that read like a worn-out road map/I know women
sweetbread and sourdough/rainbow wrapped . . .

Chloe

THE MESSAGE

"LAW OFFICE," the voice on the other end, laced with a heavy Mexican accent, answered.

"Yes, it's Chloe Michaels for NaKeisha Adderly."

"May I take a message?" the woman asked lazily.

"Ma'am, will she be in today?" I felt a knot in my stomach and let out a frustrated breath.

"I'm not sure."

"Okay, does she have an assistant who works directly with her?"

"I'm really not sure."

"Look, I'm one of her clients and I haven't been able to get her on the phone in several days. Can you please leave her an urgent message to call me!" I demanded, losing my patience.

"Um, like I only answer the phones, but you can leave a voice message."

"Fine, please transfer me." I tapped my foot nervously and took several deep breaths to keep myself calm.

Hello, you've reached the law office of NaKeisha Adderly. I'm in court today, but please leave a message.

Beeeeeeeeeeeeeeeeeeep. . . .

"Hi NaKeisha, this is Chloe Michaels, and I've left several messages with the receptionist and on your voice mail. I'm concerned because I paid a five-thousand-dollar retainer to you over a month ago, and I haven't gotten any updates. I don't know what's going on with my annulment or divorce or whatever it is!" I was getting worked up to a slow boil. "Please, I just need to know what is happening. My life is really in limbo and you haven't updated me on Gregorry's response to being served or anything! Please call me!"

I slammed my cell phone shut and put my head in my hands. Mother knocked lightly on the bedroom door. "Come in," I weakly answered.

"You still can't reach her?"

"No," I said, blinking back the tears.

"I'm prayin' on this lawyer, Chloe. You've done what you can do. These things take time."

"I don't have time, Mother! I paid my money, money I didn't have, and I deserve some answers! Gregorry's probably off somewhere living it up with my money!" My lip quivered, and I burst into an all-out ball of tears. Mother put her arms around me and started rubbing my back.

"C'mon, we've got someplace to be. Wash your face and get yourself together!" Mother ordered. I did as she instructed, grabbed my purse, and followed her out to the car.

The small two-story brick house looked vaguely familiar when we pulled into the driveway, but Mother didn't say a word as she led the way up the stairs to the front porch. A small boy with his thumb in his mouth, wearing only a diaper, answered the door. Then a woman's voice called out from a room off to the side, "TyTy, come back in here!" I smiled. It had all come back to me. Miss Ozona, our family psychic, lived here. I hadn't been here with my mother in years. I just remembered how Miss Ozona's house was always full of people, her kids, their kids, her clients, and it always smelled like food cooking—ham hocks, pork chops, apple pie.

"Oh, Lord! Joy Ann, I wasn't expectin' you or I woulda put on a extra pot of somethin'. C'mon in here!" she said, limping to the door and taking the small boy by the hand. Miss Ozona has walked with a limp for as long as I can remember. I don't know why and I don't ask.

Her house is ornately decorated with mirrors and big, gaudy

velvet-upholstered furniture that's too big for the rooms. I think of a funeral parlor, or even worse, a funeral parlor at Christmastime. She was wearing a multicolored house gown and lots of gold bracelets, rings on every finger, and thick tinted glasses. Amazingly, she still looks the same in that big bouffant. I could never figure out if it was a wig or not.

"Ozona, you remember my baby girl, Chloe," Mother said, taking a seat on the sofa.

"Praise God! That's right, Chloe . . . the baby out there in New York," she said.

"No, Miss Ozona, I'm in Los Angeles," I politely corrected.

"That's right, Hollywood! Well, I know they don't eat no good home cookin' out there. Let me fix you a plate."

"I'm fine right now," I said, smelling the aroma of greens and barbecue.

Miss Ozona turned to TyTy, "Go on now, baby, take your bottle and go lay down," Miss Ozona said, patting him lightly on his bottom. "The devil is busy. He's busy on our children," she said. "So we got to hold on and stay armored up in the light!"

"Tell it! I knew we needed to come see you," Mother said.

"Praise him. Lord have mercy!" She threw up her hands like she was about to shout. "The spirit's talkin' to me about *you*," Miss Ozona said, pointing to me.

Miss Ozona took me by the hand and guided me to a small room in the back of the house. An altar was set up next to a small table and two chairs. We sat down.

"The spirit is telling me your heart is heavy, Chloe. You tryin' to take on the world, but right now you just need to be still." She clasped her hands and began to rock slowly back and forth. "Sometimes we runnin' and runnin' and come to find out we runnin' from our own self. Trouble may seem to be all around *you*, but it ain't you, it's somebody else's trouble!"

My ears suddenly perked up. "It's some darkness you battlin'. Ain't you the one who got married?"

"Yes, ma'am, but not really anymore. I'm trying to get divorced, and I lost a baby recently too," I said softly.

"That's hard, I know for myself. But God didn't want no child to come into this world in turmoil. Oooh! Now it's comin' to me!" She closed her eyes and shouted, throwing her hands up in the air. "You cain't give up, baby. You gotta fight and not back down. I see that your husband ain't new to doin' bad stuff to people. You got to be alert about your business, and I mean money.

"He ain't gonna harm nobody 'cause you protected by the blood. He got troubles wit his mama, don't he?"

"Yes, ma'am, she left him when he was a little boy."

"Praise Him! Oh, baby, that's who got the 411. But the mama is sick in da head too. He get it from her! You just be thankful you ain't got no baby that could be sick like them!"

I slipped Miss Ozona her forty dollars (she placed it in her bra), and then I ended up having that plate of barbecue while Mother sipped on a cup of coffee.

That night Mother made us two cups of warm milk just like when I was little.

"Miss Ozona didn't rattle you, did she?" Mother said, sitting two cups on a tiny bamboo end table.

"Nah. I'm glad we saw her."

"Ozona's got the gift. Act on what she said, you hear?"

"Yes." I swallowed hard. "Mother, this is terrible, but I would've really resented that baby."

"No, you wouldn't have. But it wasn't meant to be. And if you had that baby, you woulda met a good man to help take care of both of ya'll."

I went to bed with a clear sense of direction, thanks to Miss Ozona. I made a mental checklist of all the financial aspects of my life and how I needed to protect myself from here on out. I had changed all my account numbers and passwords before leaving California. You can always work hard to get material things back, but getting your sanity back ain't that easy. Miss Ozona was right—it was time to crawl out of the darkness and reclaim my blessing, get my life business in order!

Eve

BILLS, BABY'S DADDY, AND BARBECUE BRISKET

"**H**APPY FUCKIN' Father's Day, or should I say Feliz Dia Padre? Whatever!" I poured me another glass of wine, took a huge gulp, and didn't give a damn about ruining Henry Martinez's night. "Yeah, I'mma month late with these good wishes 'cause your weak-ass excuse for child support just arrived! A month late!"

"Eve, don't start. I'm tryin' to have a *nice* evening with my son and you callin' me with some bullshit!"

"Henry, do you have any idea how much I *didn't* want to make this call on my day off? Do you?"

"I don't need this negativity in my life."

"Negativity? Henry, you are so good at turning things around. I'm bustin' my ass tryin' to raise *our* daughter and put her through college. You barely sent money her last two months of the semester. My child made the honor roll. She's workin' her butt off down there to save money." I took another sip from my glass.

"I just got a final tuition bill for fifteen hundred dollars. I need help. I have no choice but to take things to this level, Mr. Rico Suave!" I drained my glass.

"Eve, are you done? You wanna get real?"

"Yeah, Henry, I wanna keep it *real* fuckin' real!"

"*You* left *me* and moved back to St. Louis."

"And you wanna know why? Let me remind you, you didn't have

a plan for us, for our future. Should I say it *en Español*? La plana! I wasn't gonna keep taking care of your other four kids and not have a ring on my damn finger! Sorry, I wasn't down with the Puerto Rican pretend wifey game no more!" I was on a roll and poured me another glass.

"Well, when I was ready to give you a ring, you didn't want it."

"So just because things don't all of a sudden happen the way *you* want them to, Henry, I gotta give up my life? Hell no!"

"You know what? Fuck it!"

"That's exactly what I said!" I raised my glass, toasting to me. Then I swallowed another huge gulp.

"Look, I'm gonna get you some money, but I can't until next month. I had some things I needed to do for my other kids."

"What about Christina? This girl is making something of herself. She needs a car, but guess what? I don't have no damn money to get it for her! So what's new?"

"What's new?" Henry took a long pause. "What's new is that me and Gabriella are getting married."

"What? You mean just like that, after *just* six months. I gave you twelve years of my life, Henry!"

"We've got one child, and now she's pregnant with twins. I gotta do the right thing."

"You didn't do the right thing when I was pregnant," I huffed.

"I love my daughter, but Christina is eighteen and my other ones are grown, too. I got younger kids to focus on, Eve."

I stopped breathing and my vision went blurry. *Henry is having twins?* I had gotten used to our arguments. Having to chase him down for money because I was too foolish to take him to court. Mother never took Daddy or Daddy Ray to court. I was sympathetic to his situation. I wasn't with Henry anymore, but I didn't want to see him suffer. *Henry is having twins?* I didn't want to see his other children suffer.

I guess that's probably why Mother never got lawyers and all that stuff. She didn't want us to see the ugliness of parents splitting up. A father should just want to do the right thing by his child. *Henry is having twins?* That will make eight kids. So what about my child? What about *our* child? *Henry is having twins?*

"Hello? Hello? Eve, are you there? Hello? Look, I'm sorry I had to break it to you like this. Hello? Hello?"

I slowly put the phone back on the receiver and looked around at the pile of past-due bills I was sitting in the middle of. I felt light-headed. I was so over my life. Every time I tried to take two steps forward, I got knocked back four.

Nobody in my family can even really understand what I deal with. I try to work my ass off and be a good mother. I try not to bad-mouth Henry to Christina, even now. I'm the one who made sure he was in her life as a baby. I'm the one who sacrificed and stayed in the relationship with him, even though Mother and everybody else had something to say about it.

I'm the one! I can't help it that shit didn't work out in the end with me and Henry, but, dammit, I had his back! When I think back to when I met him on my first day on the job at FedEx when I lived in Philadelphia, I would've never in a million years thought that things would've ended up like this.

I ain't gonna lie and say it was love at first sight. But Henry Martinez was special. He was an olive-complexioned fine-ass Puerto Rican brotha. Yeah, it was the physical attraction that caught me. It was crazy how much he looked like my daddy when he was younger. I guess it's true to a certain extent that girls look for their fathers sometimes in the man they date. I used to tell a man to kiss my ass and not think about it. I hate to say it, but I kinda liked how Henry could put me in check.

When we met, he had a side weed hustle. He could provide all the material things, like buying me diamond bracelets and rings. Henry got me a small one-bedroom apartment, furnished it, and made sure my rent was paid every month; after I paid my car note, the rest of my paycheck was spending money. Love had me so blind I overlooked the fact that he already had four kids.

I was so happy when I called to tell Mother I was pregnant, but of course Fawn beat me to it. Fawn was the one who, as usual, opened her big mouth and spread the word in the family. I wanted to surprise everyone. Mother didn't hold back voicing her disapproval. She was pissed because I had gotten hooked up with a man with so much responsibility. Her negative attitude just made me embrace everything Henry was about even more. Hell, this family ain't perfect. Far from it!

Twelve years and we just couldn't make it. I admit, once Henry finally got his "business" in order with his ex-wife and kids, after all those years, maybe I said no because I had cold feet. Or maybe I wanted to get him back for all that time he made me wait.

I was still sitting in the living room when I heard Dale's keys unlocking the front door. I quickly wiped my face and began scooping my bills into a neat pile.

"Aw, damn, I guess you decided not to clean up shit today, baby, huh? You been cryin', Piggly Wiggly?" Dale bent over to kiss me on the forehead. "I woulda kissed you on the lips, but you got snot and shit all on your face!" Dale was bubbly to the credit of after-work cocktails, lots of them. He had cracked himself up so hard he was doubling over with laughter.

"Dale, shut up, please! I have not had a good day!"

"I'm sorry, Piggly." He ruffled my hair. I jerked away. "Ooh, you mad today. I hope that don't mean I can't get me none tonight. You know I got that attitude adjuster right here fo yo ass!" He grabbed his crotch and stood in a vulgar pose.

"Whatever!" I said, not feelin' him at all.

"You know, you and your sisters, and your mama, y'all get too sensitive," he said, loosening his tie as he walked out of the living room toward the bedroom.

"You should think before you open your mouth, Daleton," I called out.

"Eve!" Dale shouted from the bedroom.

"What!" I shouted back.

"Bring me a beer!" Dale shouted again.

I'm about sick of his ass, I thought. "Yes, I will bring the Grinch a beer!" Seconds later, Dale stomped into the living room.

"Eve!" Dale shouted again. "What's up with the beer?"

"Dale, didn't you hear me? Please stop being a baby!"

"I'm sorry. Don't be mad, Piggly Wiggly," he said, sliding his arms around my waist. "That's my Piggly Wiggly." He kissed me on the neck and nibbled on my ear.

"Stop, Dale!" I said, giving into him.

"Baby, you didn't cook tonight?"

"I was kinda tired, babe, and hoping that either we could order or go out. Today has just been really messed up. I had to deal with Christina's father. I'm just stressed 'cause I gotta get her final tuition bill paid. Then I'm thinkin' about books again for next semester. Urgh!"

"See, I told you that's what you get for getting involved with some low-end spic. The problem is you don't have no control over things."

"First of all, don't call my child's father a spic! Thank you very much. And I do have control over the situation."

"No, you don't because if you did, you wouldn't always be chasin' that fool down for money!" he said sarcastically. "But you always wanna bring up marriage. You need to get your business in order first!" Dale smacked me on the butt.

"Shut up, Dale!" I said, pulling away and walking into the kitchen.

"I'm going to ignore your little funky attitude," he said, peeking around the corner into the kitchen. "Just know that in the future, after a long day, I need a hot meal." He winked.

"That's fine. It'll only take a few minutes to thaw some chicken out."

"I had chicken for lunch." He twisted his face before I could even offer it.

"Don't worry, I've got some steak, or salmon, or what about some of that leftover barbecue beef brisket?" I reached in the freezer, pulled out the frozen brisket, and held it in the air

"Whatever, just make the pork chops," Dale said, grabbing a beer and exiting the kitchen.

"Dale, I don't have any pork chops!" I called out. He didn't respond. I was left standing in the middle of the kitchen holding the beef brisket. Once again I had jumped through hoops trying to please Dale, but somehow it never seemed to be enough.

"Eve, never mind, make the steak instead!" Dale called out one last time.

I was so frustrated, I slammed the freezer door closed and dumped the barbecue brisket in the trash can!

Chloe

WHAT'S THE 411?

FAWN'S NEARLY four-thousand-square-foot home sits on an acre of the finest suburbia land a third-generation doctor's salary can buy. Eve pulled up at the same time I did. "Hey, Hollywood!" she called out, walking across the driveway to meet me. Unbelievable—her face was fully painted, and she was fanning her nails and carefully carrying a big plastic bucket of hair rollers.

"Hey!" I said, hugging her. "I don't know how you wear all that makeup every day, girl, especially when it's hot."

"I feel naked without it and you know I gots to have my face, hair, *and* nails right. That's how Dale likes me! I gotta get Fawn to set my hair. I ain't gettin' ready to mess up my nails after spending my last twenty dollars to get my tips filled."

"Why don't you just go to Ceci's shop?"

"Can't nobody afford Ceci, except for you and Fawn. I'll leave that to the rich folks," she said, rolling her neck and sucking her teeth. I decided to stay away from that comment. We were just about to knock on the door when it flew open and Lola came barreling out.

"Hi, Aunt Chloe! Hi, Aunt Eve!" Lola was wearing a leotard and tights, holding one ballet slipper in hand, and her wild mane was bouncing behind. Lola made a two-second pause to give us each a quick peck on the cheek. "I'm late for dance class. Mommy, Aunt Eve and Aunt Chloe are here! Come on, Daddy!" she shouted into the house.

We made our way into the foyer.

My brother-in-law, Cliff, was doing a super speed walk down the staircase, headed toward us with his golf bag slung over his shoulder, his shirt untucked, and his golf shoes untied.

"Look at him. Nice guy, but, girl, he's a mess," Eve said under her breath. "I told you it's too chaotic around here. That's why I don't come over."

"What's up, Chloe and Eve!" He stopped momentarily and gave me a quick hug. "Listen, I'm sorry about things; hang in there, kiddo." In a flash he was grabbing his clubs and headed out the door.

"Cliff! Did you walk on my carpet in those dirty golf shoes?" Fawn yelled from another room. She was regulating all the way from the kitchen.

"It's just carpet, Fawn! It can be cleaned or replaced; damn." His face tightened. "I bought the shit," I heard him mumble under his breath, before storming out.

Cliff fell in love with Fawn the first day she arrived on Hampton's campus. He was handsome, from a good family. When he came to St. Louis to do his residency, Fawn sacrificed her own career plans in New York and moved back home to support him.

Cliff is a good-looking brotha, but if I was a bettin' woman I'd bet that all that gray in his head is the marking of a man worn down by an overbearing wife.

"I told you Fawn was livin' large," Eve said. We made ourselves comfortable in the living room. "She acts an even bigger fool over this house now that she's done all this work to it, and she's obsessed with cleaning. You'll see. When Mother visits, she follows her around with a handful of paper towels in one hand and Windex in the other. And the messed-up part is that I can't even get her to let me hold a hundred dollars until my next payday. Girl, I'm so mad and broke."

"Mornin', sunshines!" Fawn appeared in a bright white terry-cloth short set ensemble, looking like she was off to a yacht in Saint-Tropez.

"It's about time. This is my only day off this week, and I don't have all day to be sittin' up in your house. Plus I need you to roll my hair," Eve complained.

"I love what you've done to the house!" I said.

"Girl, I'm so broke now it's a shame," Fawn said.

"Your broke ain't the same as my broke," Eve said, chiming in.

After Fawn finished the tour and running down how much they'd spent on all the new things in the house—the guest room, Cliff's study, the master suite, Lola's suite, and all four bathrooms—it dawned on me that I had always been the one helping Mother out when both my sisters were off living their lives. Now with my financial state in question, they were going to have to help out. I was just about to break both of my sisters down when Eve excitedly blurted out, "Sister chat! Sister chat! I need y'alls help with something very very important!"

We entered the kitchen and sat down around the table; Fawn placed a platter in front of us that had several small slices of what looked to be a rubbery quiche, surrounded by fresh berries.

"I got the recipe off B. Smith's television show," Fawn stated proudly. I gave Eve a look. She gave me one back.

"Okay, so Christina's about to have two new siblings," Eve said, casually taking a bite of quiche. "Henry just told me he was having twins."

"That'll make eight kids! That man needs to look up the word *vasectomy* in the dictionary and get real familiar with it!" Fawn joked.

"I know, he can't afford the kids he's got," I said, shaking my head.

"Anyway, I was so pissed I had to tell y'all, but I don't even want Mother to know right now. She'll have something to say." She sighed. "On a good note, I'm planning a birthday dinner for Dale, and I want the family to be there!"

Eve's mood had suddenly switched to jovial and happy. Fawn directed her to the sink. Eve stuck her head under the faucet, and Fawn sprayed her hair down with water.

"There's this really cute winery near Dale's house. It's his forty-fifth and I want to make it really special," Eve excitedly continued while Fawn parted her hair in sections, spraying it lightly with setting lotion.

"So how do you expect to pay for this little soiree?" Fawn was always about the money. She continued busying herself on Eve's hair, now skillfully parting Eve's hair in smaller sections and rolling each section on a large plastic roller. Each time she finished rolling the hair, Eve handed her a large bobby pin to hold the roller in place.

"Well, you know I been really working on my candles and soaps."

"Yeah, how's that going?" I asked. Eve was artistic and creative, just like Mother, but every time she seemed to get started working on her stuff, she got sidetracked or broke and couldn't buy supplies, so she'd stop.

"It goes, when I have the extra money to buy my supplies, but when I don't, it doesn't. But I got some overtime the last two checks, made some baskets, and got a woman who works with me to let me put some products in her gift shop and they sold out!"

"See what you can do when you put your mind to it, Eve!" Fawn declared, putting the final roller in Eve's hair.

"Don't patronize me, Fawn!" she said abruptly, turning around to face Fawn. "Nobody would love to have their own line more than me. I might even call it the 'Garden of Eve.' That sounds good, don't it?

"But I repeat, it takes money." Eve sighed again. "Anyway, forget all that dreamin'. This party's gonna kill me, but Dale's worth it."

"Well, if we're done talkin' about parties. I'd like to have a more serious conversation," I said, taking a sip of orange juice to help wash down the rest of my food. "Y'all know my situation. My lawyer isn't returning my calls and I may have to find another one."

"I'm gonna investigate this shit myself and get you a good white lawyer, preferably Jewish! You got to go for the jugular. I watch the E! channel, girl!" Fawn said.

The sister cavalry was at it again, rounded up, and fired up and ready to give Gregorry a beat down.

"I still say you need to call Edward!" Eve added.

"Next subject!" I said, giving her the hand. "On a serious note, can we talk about Mother? As you both know, I've been helping Mother out with her bills for a while, but my financial picture is in the toilet now. I think it's time you all help pick up some of the slack. We should all sit down and figure out a plan."

"All who? Me and you? 'Cause Eve ain't got a dime to offer." Fawn smacked her lips.

"She's right, I'm not the sister who can really be a part of this discussion," Eve said.

Fawn continued, "Look, Chloe, I have a household to run. I'll see about contributing maybe fifty or seventy-five dollars a month. I'm not working. I have to depend on Cliff, and his practice has been slow. We have bills comin' out of our asses, plus Lola's tuition. I've almost depleted my savings too, helping to redo the house."

"I'm a single parent and I don't get any help from my child's father. Fawn's the one who's got a doctor for a husband!"

"She's not just my mother!" I exclaimed.

"You're right, and I'm *not* the only other daughter!" Fawn chirped.

"Excuse you!" Eve chirped with an attitude. "Anyway, I didn't know I was comin' over here for all this," she said, putting a scarf on her head. "Y'all done stressed me out and shit. I gotta go do laundry and clean up my own house. But don't forget the party for Dale," she added with a smile.

Eve blew out of the house like she always does when it's time to talk about something she doesn't want to talk about.

"Chloe, you know what the problem is? You pacify Eve and she takes advantage of you. I've told you that time and time again. And when it comes to Mother, you baby her. Then you expect us to do it! Now, I love Mother, she's my mother too, was mine first! Sometimes you forget that, but Mother is a grown woman. I used to worry about her like you do, but she made a choice to live like she does. Unfortunately it's caught up to her."

"That's just plain cold, Fawn," I said, shaking my head.

"You're taking this all the wrong way. Look at it like this, the good news is that between Medicare and Social Security, it'll all work out." She smiled, and just like that everything was perfect again in Fawn's world.

"So how about some tea!" Fawn announced. "Girl, I've been dying to break in my new Japanese tea set!"

It was like we hadn't even had a discussion about Mother. Fawn placed two empty cups and saucers on the table, then put the teakettle on the stove. The blue flame ignited, making a quick sizzle sound from the water drops on the bottom of the kettle.

"Chloe, I have to tell you something, and you can't tell anybody. I'm so serious," Fawn whispered excitedly.

"Why are you whispering? We're the only two people in the damn house," I joked.

"Girl, I've developed feelings for someone."

"I know you're not telling me you're having an affair."

"Shhhh! Are you crazy, saying that word?" Fawn was looking around like we were under surveillance by the CIA or something.

"I didn't . . ." I said nervously.

"Just shhh!" She cleared her throat and leaned in closer. "I have not *actually* had an affair in the traditional sense."

"Okay, so what is the *untraditional* sense of an affair?"

"Well, I go to a new church, and the pastor is amazing!" Fawn's eyes rolled back into her head and she cracked a smile. "He's just so fine," she said dreamily.

The expression on my face dropped. I was mortified that my sister had the hots for a man of the cloth. "Are you crazy? You can't fool around with a preacher! You shouldn't be tryin' to fool around, period. I thought you were happy, in love, you know, 'til-death-do-you-part type shit!"

"Calm down and be quiet. I do love my husband, but shit, I've been with this man for fifteen years, and it's just *old*."

"Why not try some new stuff? Get some sex toys!"

"The sex is still great. It's just that Cliff gets on my damn nerves and he's boring."

"Fawn, how the hell did this happen with the preacher man?"

"I had a meeting with him to discuss our Women's Day program and sparks just started flyin' all over the place." Fawn was grinning and giggly like a schoolgirl. "He's asked for another meeting. And now, girl, I just can't stop thinking about him. I fantasize about shouting in the church naked and him baptizing me."

"Oh stop! You need to get help, girl. Go to counseling!"

"I know it's bad, isn't it?" she said devilishly. "But you try being married as long as I have. There's no magic. Sometimes we're like two ships passing in this big-ass house."

"Hello? The vow says 'in good times and bad,'" I said.

"And that's exactly what we're doing. *Dying* a slow death. Chloe, you're too idealistic! Just like I told you before you married that dumb-ass boy. Marriage is overrated!"

The teakettle whistled, like an alarm sounding off, saying, Chloe, you foolish girl, there's no such thing as love, marriage, and that baby carriage! Wake up! Have I had it all wrong all along?

Fawn

BAPTIZE ME

BRIGHT AND EARLY I was at Ceci's shop to get my hair done. I had a big day today.

"Whassup, cuz, you know you got that glow this mornin'," Ceci said, cracking open an ice cold Red Bull.

"I've got a really important meeting today and I ain't sayin', but I'll just say it's going to be divine and I need to look *hot!*" I snickered and we high-fived.

"Wait a minute! I know you ain't gettin' no sticky icky icky on the side, cuz. You know you gots to tell me all about it." Ceci slipped on her smock and put a towel around my shoulders and led me over to the sink to wash my hair.

"I think I wanna do some highlights today, Ceci," I said, flipping through a magazine with the latest hairstyles.

"Highlights and curls! Girl, you know you holdin' back on me. By the way, if you really tryin' to be sexy, you need to let me trim these raggedy-ass ends," she said, holding out the ends of my hair in the mirror.

I was envisioning a whole new Fawn and was ready to explore a new look and a new attitude.

"Girl, what done crawled up in your drawers? I'm torn. I like this adventurous side, but don't sound like it got nothin' to do with Cliff, and you know that's my boy now. Talk to me," Ceci said, pulling out a large poster board with sample swatches of hairpieces in various colors.

"I just ain't feelin' it no more, Ceci, and I know my mama don't wanna hear it, not even my sisters."

"First of all, I cain't break nobody down 'cause if I see me a young tender I'm gone get that. My mama don't approve of nothin' I do so who am I to say what you doin' or wantin' to do is right or wrong. I'll just say this, yeah I gots me a play thang, but I like my house and my car, you feel me?

"But I like steak better than I do some damn hot dogs, feel me? Anyway, c'mon girl, let's get this hair turned out! We gonna do some honey highlights on this shit. Ooh, but first lemme go get this fo-dolla soda I done had on ice in the back. Girl, you puttin' me to work today!" Ceci ran off to the back room and I stared at my reflection, thinking about the little lacy secret I was keeping under my clothes.

An hour later, Ceci spun me around in her chair and a new woman was looking back at me. "I love it! I love it, Ceci! I should've done this a long time ago." I shook my head from side to side, watching each highlighted curl shimmer and bounce. I was certain to give Pastor something to shout about!

"You *know* your cuz is fierce when it comes to layin' that hair out!" she said, lighting a cigarette and cracking open a new can of Red Bull.

Just then a stocky brotha wearing frayed cornrows walked past Ceci's booth, displaying an armload of socks and pantyhose. "Whassup, Bootsie? You got somethin' for me today?" she asked, adding the final touches to my hair.

"Ceci, what's he got?" I whispered.

"Girl, he got hot stuff. You know, stuff that by law *belong* to somebody else," she hinted. I nodded, suddenly realizing the items he had for sale were stolen.

"Naw, Ceci, I ain't come across that purse you been lookin' for, but I'mma get it. Aw, here you go." Bootsie reached in his backpack and pulled out an ice cream sandwich and gave it to Ceci, before moving on to display his goods to the next potential client.

"Wait a damn minute, Ceci, did that fool just give you an ice cream sandwich?" I asked, astonished.

"Cuz, I said he was a booster. He just happen to be a low-budget booster!" We fell out laughing.

"On that note, I'm outta here," I said, taking one last look in the mirror before paying her and exiting.

"Sister Fawn, welcome!" Pastor Gibbs said, looking up from his paperwork and removing his glasses. When I walked into his office, he was sitting in a high-backed leather chair behind a large mahogany desk, looking like African royalty on his throne.

"I have to tell you again, that was a beautiful program you planned for Women's Day," Pastor Gibbs said, standing up and removing his suit jacket, suavely draping it over the back of his chair.

"Thank you, Pastor. I was hoping it was to your satisfaction," I said, standing tall with my shoulders back. My nipples perked up as I scanned his opulently furnished office.

"So, Sister Fawn, you said you had some new and exciting ideas," he said, licking his lips, gliding past me, unhooking the ornate velvet curtains, fanning them out to cover the windows.

"Yes, Pastor," I said, clearing my throat. "Okay! I have some new ideas for the Women's Missionary Society in general." I was still standing awkwardly in the middle of his office.

My eyes followed his svelte body as he walked back across the room and picked up a crystal goblet, filling it with ice water. He handed it to me and our fingertips brushed against each other. Then he filled a second crystal goblet for himself. As he slowly drank I imagined his mouth pressed against mine, our tongues swapping lust-filled juices.

"Ahhh, nothing like a cold glass of water to hydrate the soul and the spirit," he said, licking his lips again.

"I agree, Pastor," I said, sipping from my goblet gingerly.

"Why don't you come sit over here on the couch, Sister Fawn," he said, sitting down. He crossed his legs and a glint from the brass buckle on his shiny alligator shoes flashed in my eyes. Cliff would never dress this slick. I wouldn't normally go for flash myself, but Pastor's smooth swagger and flamboyant style of silk shirts and custom-made suits in rich purples and blues gave him an edge, a coolness, a pimped-out sexiness.

I sat down on the opposite end of the couch and pulled out my pink notepad with the matching pen decorated in pink crystals. "I think the Women's Missionary Society needs to come up with a signature event like a women's tea where we celebrate local outstanding women," I said, looking over at Pastor.

"Why don't you scoot a little closer, Sister Fawn," Pastor said with a wink, patting lightly on the couch cusion next to him. I felt myself getting warm all over.

"Eh-hem." I cleared my throat again, making sure to arch my back, keeping my shoulders back. "I think this will really help propel the church's image in the community." I followed his instructions and slid closer to him. "Because, you see, Pastor . . ." My words trailed off as his eyes licked me up and down like a lollipop. An image of me as one of those rap video girls dancing on a pole flashed across my mind.

"Sister Fawn, why don't you give me that lovely paper and pen. I don't think you'll be needing those for this meeting," he whispered seductively in my ear. I felt weightless as Pastor began to nibble on my ear, working his way down to my neck.

"Pastor, what if someone hears us or comes in?" I said between kisses. His mouth now covered mine.

"Why don't you let me worry about that? Now I need you to stand up for me, Sister Fawn," he commanded. I followed his instructions. There was something about a man giving me orders that turned me on. "Take off your panties."

"Huh?" My eyes went wide. "Um, I'm not sure what you mean, Pastor."

"C'mon now, don't make Pastor beg," he said, pulling me toward him by the waist. "Take those panties off for Pastor."

I closed my eyes, completely captivated by his powerful presence, and hiked my skirt up and slowly pulled down my lace panties. He leaned back and watched me as if I were the most desirable woman on earth. Once I removed them, I picked them up off the floor and handed them to Pastor. He took them in his hands and held them to his face and inhaled my scent. After that, he dismissed me.

I sat in the garage several minutes before going into the house, not sure what had just occurred. Part of me was embarrassed, the other part felt wild and free. Later that night, I couldn't stop giggling to myself as I lay in the bed next to Cliff, aka "my boring-ass husband," who had fallen asleep watching *SportsCenter*. Yes, I, Fawn, was a wild woman who had finally unleashed her inhibitions.

Chloe

WILDFLOWER

I OPENED THE MAIL and I was hit with another blow. The elusive husband had struck again. My so-called lawyer forwarded notification that Gregorry has filed a civil suit, accusing me of stealing his, and I quote, "$40,000.00 Rare Watch Collection." This is insane! Apparently, I pay my lawyer *not* to call me, *not* to fight on my behalf, and *not* to be a lawyer! I was so upset I balled the papers up and threw them across the room.

I've dated men who owned *one* freakin' watch that was valued at more than forty thousand dollars! Doesn't anyone see that I'm the victim? I give up. I don't even have it in me to pray anymore. Just keep making bad decision after bad decision, and it all keeps replaying in my head like a broken record.

Life . . . Marriage . . . Money . . . Life . . . Marriage . . . Money . . .

How the hell am I ever going to be able to pick up the pieces when they keep breaking apart? I blame Edward. It's all Edward's fault! He should've put his selfishness aside and just committed. Now look at the hole I'm in. What if this was my only chance at having marriage and a baby and I blew it? I know you can't make other people do what you want them to do, but it doesn't stop me from wishing. I wished and wished and wished for eleven years.

I gave my best to a man who was unattainable, and then I turned around and gave my best to a man who I didn't even know. A man who showed me every sign that he was the "wrong" one and I still went through with it.

"Chloe!" Mother called from the other room.

"What!" I shouted. I was so not in the mood for Mother today. I needed to clear my head, but I didn't even have a private space to do that. I guess I technically did have my own *house* for Godsakes. But no, I was *afraid* to go back to my *real* home. When did Chloe Michaels turn into a coward?

"Chloe, can you come here? I need you!"

Damn, what's new! "Yeah okay, Mother." When I walked out into the living room, she was balancing herself on a stool, trying to hang a picture.

"Mother, let me do that, you're gonna hurt yourself."

"No, I just need you to tell me if this is straight. Is it?"

"That picture is so crooked it's making me drunk. Get down!" I teased. After hanging the picture properly, I sat down on the daybed. Mother could see my sadness.

"I know it's not easy bein' here in this tight space, Chloe."

"That's just part of it. Gregorry's suing me."

"I'm not surprised." Mother chuckled. "I've come to see this whole situation as a test. But what you have to remain is unmovable, Chloe. I know you might think your mother is old-fashioned, but prayer is all I know and it never fails me."

"I'm tired of praying, Mother."

"That's okay, 'cause a mother never gets tired. This lawyer ain't no good for you. So I got to meditate on you gettin' a new one."

"Maybe I just need to be alone."

"Good idea. How 'bout I go out for a while so that'll give you some time, okay? And promise me that you'll just take one day, *one* day, and not give Gregorry, or that lawyer, or the divorce any thought."

"Okay."

When Mother got up and headed to the bathroom to get dressed, I looked at the photographs and paintings on the walls, all the knick-knacks she'd collected and kept over the years. I suddenly thought about when we all lived together as a family—me, Eve, Fawn, Daddy, and Mother. In our house, culture always clashed with the rich fragrances of sandalwood, mint, and chamomile, and it was always bustling with neighbors and cousins, ne'er-do-wells and nomads. *Dig that! Give me five on the black-hand side!* It was all part of my makeup, my foundation.

"Mother, remember when me and you used to move all the time after you and Daddy separated?" I said.

"Sure do. We went through a lot, movin' place to place." She opened the bathroom door as she was putting on her bra. "Shoot, the average person on the outside wouldn't have believed we were living hand to mouth. Your own daddy would purposely not give me any money and we'd still do all right. I'd make a way. Sell some artwork, or get commissioned for a job at the last minute by somebody."

"Mother, you never told me that."

"There are some things you just don't need to tell your children. Chloe, your daddy loved you, and he wasn't a bad father, but he couldn't see past his anger with me to do right by you all the time."

Mother walked over and kissed me on the forehead. "Mother, remember when you made those chairs for the dining table out of tall wooden milk crates and used throw pillows as the seat cushions?"

"Yep, and I painted that big mural of Indian and African women and babies on the dining-room wall in that apartment over on the south side. Those women represented our heritage. It's funny, we made do, even when I couldn't see the light at the end of the tunnel." Mother sighed. "I remember we were in that same apartment and you came home from school, and I told you we were going to imagine we were with our ancestors who were painted on the wall."

"We pretended to be Indians from the South Carolina hills, just like your daddy's people. You let me dress up in all your scarves, and just as it was getting dark you lit all the candles in the room. We danced around and pretended to sing and chant in our native tongue. And we slept right there on the floor on pillows and comforters, like we were around the campfire."

"Girl, I lit them candles and we slept in the living room 'cause our electric had been cut off!" We laughed. "In spite of it all, we made it. I taught and sold my paintings to keep us fed, always keeping my head up high. Ray couldn't stand to see that he couldn't break my stride. The only answer I have is that God has always blessed me, Chloe."

Mother and I reminisced briefly about a few other places we lived during my elementary and high school years. The running punch line in the family back then was, "Where do y'all live now?" But I had no complaints. I learned to look at myself and Mother as unique. Sure it was hard, Mother having to rob Peter to pay Paul, but we made it.

As an adult now, I know how blessed we are. I almost even understand what she means when she talks about feeling sorry for a weak and lost soul like Gregorry. People like him have to resort to hurting others because they have no idea what love is. What my family has, you can't put a price tag on it, and you definitely can't steal it!

Mother kissed me good-bye and for at least the next few hours while she was out, I had that "space" I was yearning for. I turned on my iPod. The O'Jays' version of "Wildflower" took me back in time. The song was speaking to me. The lyrics depicted a woman who epitomized strength and courage even in her weakest hour. *"She's faced the hardest time that you would imagine and many times her eyes fought back the tears . . ."*

A morning in the summer of '78 flashed in my mind and began to play over and over in my head like a broken record. That was the day Mother and Daddy split. When the sweet milk turned sour. Somebody forgot about lettin' the good times roll and swinging me 'til I was too dizzy to stand, and all I could do was fall out laughing 'til my belly ached. It all had unraveled right before my eyes, like a thin piece of thread barely holding a hem in place. My dreams of dancing carousels came to a screeching halt by the sound of screaming voices. I was trying to shake the sand out of my eyes, make it to the toilet to pee, but it was too late.

The next thing I knew, Daddy was in the living room packing his jazz albums in a small cardboard box. Each time Mother passed through the room, she yelled, "Make sure you don't take nothin' that don't belong to you!" She kept going back and forth between the living room and kitchen, Fawn and Eve sticking close by.

I was the traitor sitting quietly on the arm of the couch, cross-legged. Daddy squatted next to me, gently placing a stack of records on the floor.

"Sweet Pea, I'm gonna really miss you, but you be strong for your mother and sisters."

"Don't worry. I will, Daddy." I kept my voice down so Mother wouldn't hear. My tiny, innocent words seemed to reassure him, at least for the time being.

Mother was sitting at the kitchen table drinking a cup of coffee. That's how she liked it. Strong and black. But something that day just made her snap. Fawn was sitting at the table across from her. Eve was standing at the sink drinking a glass of water. Mother jumped up out of her chair, scooped up that hot cup without spilling a drop, and stormed into the living room.

I could feel something bad was about to happen because the house got real still. Like the trees and the wind do right before a tornado. The next thing I remember was hearing Daddy scream. One of those bloodcurdling, grown-man screams too. "Argh! Dammit, Joy Ann!" Eve dropped her glass midair, and pieces of glass splintered across the mosaic kitchen tile. Fawn grabbed her hand and they ran into the living room.

"What the hell is wrong with you!" Daddy yelled, frantically trying to wipe himself off. Mother had given him an Al Green, but instead of hot grits she threw that scalding coffee on him. Then she started smacking Daddy upside his head.

"I'll tell you what I'm doin'. Lettin' you know you're a quitter!" Daddy wouldn't hit her back. He didn't believe in hitting women.

"Stop it, Joy Ann! I'm telling you for the last time!"

"Or else what? Huh? Or else what? You're a coward, Ray!"

Fawn and Eve pulled at Mother's gown and arms, trying to stop her. I covered my ears.

"Mother, no! Daddy, please!" Fawn and Eve begged.

Mother raised her fist, and Daddy lifted his arm to block the blow. He accidentally hit her with an open palm across the mouth. Mother stumbled backward, and a hush fell over the room. Eve and Fawn were frozen with twisted expressions of fear and anguish. Daddy's face dropped, and a tear slowly rolled down his cheek. "Joy Ann, I'm sorry. I would never . . ." he muttered.

Mother looked around in panic. "I think he broke my jaw. Oh, Lord! Jesus!" Mother yanked me by the hand and pushed Fawn and Eve in to the kitchen. I looked back. Daddy had buried his face in his hands. It was an accident! Mother was wrong and me, Fawn, and Eve knew it. Mother knew it. Knew it then and to this day. Daddy had *only* busted her lip. Mother made a big deal, carrying on talking about how she needed an ambulance and the police. Then she did the ultimate . . .

She called Aunt Billye Jean and Carol Jane. Daddy was doomed. Not even Tony Soprano dared to go up against the Davis Mob.

"Let me in! Where's my sister!" Aunt Billye Jean was huffing and puffing when she stormed into the house.

"Is that blood on your mouth, Joy Ann?" Carol Jane gasped. "Oh hell no!" she said, rolling up her sleeves. "The devil is busy up in here! We got to stomp him down!" Carol Ann was supposed to be the more religious of the two, but she was pumped up the most. You didn't know if they were about to perform an exorcism or if a hit had been ordered. Those women got to prayin' and mad-doggin' Daddy so bad they practically ran him out of there. Daddy was gone. Who was gonna tuck me in now? Who was I going to crawl in between at night when I had nightmares?

As the song built to a spine-tingling crescendo, it brought tears to my eyes. Just like the words in the song, Mother was that wildflower sometimes carrying the weight of the world on her shoulders, never breaking her stride or smile. Ironically, I was one of those wildflowers too, free and gentle, growing wild. Mother had survived two broken marriages, and she did it while trying to raise children.

You can't harness a free spirit or forbid a beautiful wildflower to feel the sun. I had to remind myself that I was my mother's child, and Gregorry Marion Robinson III didn't have the heart to be the man I deserved. He could never measure up to men like my daddy or Bobby Nash. Men who respected Mother and were man enough to let go. They would never try to destroy her or put her in harm's way.

I prayed for a tenth of Mother's resilience. I prayed to make it through this mess and that someday, somebody would love me enough to let me feel the sun in my spirit and be that bold, brilliant wildflower I hoped was still somewhere hiding within.

Thora

MIRROR IMAGE

IT WAS **9:55** P.M. when I stepped in the shower.

"Hon, the news will be on in five minutes," David said, knocking softly on the bathroom door. "You okay?"

"I'm fine. I'll be out in a minute." I was running behind schedule tonight. Somehow I didn't think my shower would be that quick. I missed the news altogether. I'd screwed up my whole nightly routine, but I'd gotten enough news already that day. My life was pretty structured and simple, no surprises, nothing out of the ordinary, everything had its order. Until about six hours before . . .

"Just get undressed from the waist up, and Dr. Jones will be in shortly," the nurse said. When she left, I slowly unbuttoned my shirt and removed my bra. I hoisted myself up on the table and slowly laid back. I began to run down the items I needed to pick up from the grocer. I didn't know what would possess Davis and Erin to ask for a soul food dinner that night, but they did.

My kids don't ask for much, and I was happy they were gonna both stop by for dinner. The house feels empty without them. Davis is certainly more independent, but that Erin, she comes over here and goes through our pantry and fridge like Ralph's Supermarket has relocated to our kitchen.

A knock on the examination door interrupted me from making out my mental grocery list.

"Thora, thanks for coming back." Dr. Nancy Jones was one sharp sista. Her presence was as captivating as Michelle Obama's: tall, brown, beautiful, smart. Just the soothing tone of her voice had already put me a little bit more at ease.

"I was a little concerned, because I was just here on Friday. I'm thinkin' if the doc wants to see me on Monday morning it must be serious," I noted lightheartedly.

"Thora, we found a lump in your breast on your mammogram." She placed her cold hands on my left breast and felt around for a few seconds. "Here it is." Her fingertips stayed on one area just above the nipple. "It's about the size of a dime, feel?" I touched my breast lightly and then quickly pulled my hand away. "I want to send you over to get a biopsy right away."

I was always so good at staying calm. I had taught myself as a child to tune out things that made me nervous or upset. Things like Billye Jean screaming and hollering at the top of her lungs when she and Earl fought. I had gotten so good that I could sit in the same room and completely ignore the excitement. I would think about how high the birds flew in the sky.

I was a master at transporting myself to another world. Yet somehow, I couldn't do it today. They went into my breast with a needle, took the biopsy, and it was over just like that. I was expecting more. I got dressed and the next thing you know I was sitting in my driveway. I coasted right through making dinner. Can you believe it? I didn't miss a step on any of my seasonings either. Davis and Erin raved about how my potato salad was just like Billye Jean's.

It was after ten and I didn't give a damn about watching the news tonight. I stood in front of the bathroom mirror, naked, and stared at my reflection. I looked in the mirror long and hard. I couldn't help but think about the fact that the woman staring back was the spitting image of Earl Crouthers. Everybody, family, the folks in the old neighborhood Muh live in, all of them could testify to that.

Billye Jean didn't do nothin' but carry me to term. The flat line of my forehead, my sharp chin, the way my lips protrude slightly, the natural arch of my eyebrows, and my eyes, deep set and ice gray.

That's the reason I don't like mirrors. Never have, 'cause he's there lookin' back at me.

As a child Muh would dress me for church and tell me how pretty I looked after she pressed and curled my hair into Shirley Temple curls. I was all starched and shined like a little brown porcelain doll in a fine antique store. If you touched me, I might break into a zillion pieces. As I stood in front of her, with my back to her big floor-length cherry-wood mirror, she'd say, "Go on Thora, baby, see how pretty you look," but I wouldn't budge.

I didn't want to see the little girl looking back. I was afraid that she would cry. As I got older and became a teenager, I wondered if that girl in the mirror would say I was ugly and tell me I'd never get a boy-friend. I trained myself to look away. But God blessed me with David. He loved me and all my hurt just because. Not for all those superficial things other people marry for.

I forgive Billye Jean for never telling me I looked pretty in my Sunday's best, for not hugging me after a bad dream, or wiping my tears, and for never telling me until I was a grown-ass woman that she loved me. She could be forgiven, but Earl, never! That day fifty-three years ago would *never* be forgotten.

Me, Junior, and Billye Jean had been staying back and forth with Muh, because Billye Jean was threatening to leave Earl every other day because of his drinking. Today, Billye Jean decided to go back home to Earl once again after he had been over to Muh's begging so badly. Billye Jean told him the only way she'd come back home is if he let her have her church meetings and choir rehearsals at the house. Earl agreed without hesitation, and he vowed that he was going to stop drinking for real this time.

Billye Jean's church meeting was in full swing when Earl came back sloppy drunk and started cursing all the church members out and throwing bibles. "I'm sick of all this Jesus shit! You been sleepin' 'round on me! Everybody's laughin' at me." He was mad as "red devil lye," as Muh would say. I was just a toddler, Junior was about five, and Billye Jean snatched me up and sat me on the living-room couch and told me not to move. Junior ran and hid in the corner.

"Earl, I ain't gonna fight like this no more in front of these babies." Billye Jean was trying to quiet Earl down, but he was smelling like a bottle of cheap whiskey and getting more and more belligerent.

"I don't give a damn about no kids that might not even be mine!"

"I told you, Earl, to shut yo mouf in front of these children and my church members!" Billye Jean didn't want them to hear him accuse her of being loose, but Billye Jean was also one not to take much off anybody. She had a short fuse and was a fighter. He called her a whore, and Billye Jean balled up her fist and swung as hard as she could, knocking Earl in the side of his head.

Earl fell into the wall, and when he regained his balance, he lunged for Billye Jean. He grabbed her and started choking her. Billye Jean was always a little bigger than Earl so she had the upper hand to a certain degree. She was able to fight him off with a couple quick stunning jabs to the jaw. But the alcohol had taken over Earl and was making him stronger than usual.

Earl took his open palm and pushed Billye Jean backward and she fell next to me on the couch. Billye Jean had never been one to coddle me or set me on her lap, but she reached for me tonight. But just as I was making my way on all fours over to Billye Jean's arms, Earl had picked up a porcelain vase, and in one fluid movement sent it crashing through the parlor wall mirror behind the couch.

MaMaw's large wall mirror had been in the family for three generations. MaMaw had it in her parlor, then it was in Muh's, and when Billye Jean and Earl got married, Muh passed it on to her for a wedding gift. Billye Jean's natural instinct was to move for cover. She slid off the couch and forgot about MaMaw's mirror and grabbing me.

God must've been watching over me, though. The angels must've whispered in my tiny ears and told me to cover my face. The glass shattered into pieces and shards of glass glided over my back and legs, slicing my skin into fine shreds. My right cheek got the deepest cut, but my eyes were spared. I had seen it all.

I'm sure Earl was very sorry about what he had done. We never talked about much the few times we were around each other, and that day never came up. I certainly didn't bother to ask. It got to a point that I don't think I even cared. Even if he were still alive, would it even matter now? All that matters is that that glass cut deep and I will live with those scars for the rest of my life. When I look at them now, I have to try really hard to see some of them. I hated Earl for so long. I wonder if this is all karma? I wonder what my new scar will look like?

"Hon, you okay?" David peeked in with a worried expression on his face. I slipped my robe on.

"I don't know," I said blankly.

David is normally a pretty reserved kind of guy. He doesn't say much, and our conversations are pretty simple, but always pleasant— what's happening in the news, sports, our next vacation destination, not even too much about politics. Our household is always calm. We never even spanked our kids.

However, tonight something was different that the status quo. David looked into my eyes and I saw that quiet strength, that same reassuring, protective look that he gave me when he asked me to marry him, after I confided in him about my painful childhood. We had a silent understanding that those feelings would be tucked away in a safe place, and I would never ever have to discuss them again.

David was giving me that same look, and I didn't hold back. My legs gave way and David caught me in his arms and held me close as I softly cried. I like my life, no surprises, nothing out of the ordinary, everything has an order. What happened?

Chloe

MAMA'S PRIDE ... MAMA'S LIES

"CHLOE? CHLOE?" The voice sounded familiar. "Chloe?" The voice got closer and I tried to ignore it, until the person it belonged to tapped me on the shoulder. I was frozen in her gaze, panicking on the inside because Eve, Fawn, and I had split up to look for "the" dress, according to Eve, that would rock Dale's world at his big birthday dinner she was planning.

The Galleria was massive. We weren't supposed to hook back up for another hour. But I was suddenly trapped in some bad episode of *This Is Your Life, Chloe Michaels* with no backup, nowhere to run, face-to-face with Lydia James.

Lydia was Gregorry's estranged mother who, coincidentally, lived on the outskirts of St. Louis. However, I didn't expect to see her in a million years. It'd been two months since I fled my life and home, and she was the last person I wanted to run into.

"Well, give me a hug." She was ecstatic about seeing me and showing me off to her girlfriend, who had a stiff expression on her face. "Mable Jackson, this is my daughter-in-law, Chloe Michaels." Lydia was dressed in classic St. John. A plain-looking woman with cropped hair, she was the kind who needed makeup and fine clothing to, as Mother would say, "help her out."

Even when I met her briefly at the wedding and forced Gregorry to take a picture with her, I couldn't dig up the resemblance. Her features were thick and full. His were chiseled, like his father's. She was also light-skinned, and the one thing Aunt Billye Jean just couldn't stop yappin' about was how "dark that boy is."

If she said it once, she said it ten times. "Joy Ann, look at how dark that boy is compared to his mama. She high yellow and funny lookin'. He don't look nothin' like his mama, though. Ya think that's really his mama? Humph!"

Now, I was standing here, awkwardly, while I self-consciously fiddled with my blouse and hair. I smiled politely, but still hadn't been able to speak. Luckily, Lydia was talking enough for everyone present.

"You look great! So how's the little bun in the oven?" She flashed a toothy smile.

I had forgotten that I notified her via e-mail that I was expecting. "We should probably speak away from here," I replied, shooting her a hardened glare.

By the time we reached the women's lounge inside Macy's, I was ready to explode.

"I lost my baby, Lydia. Gregorry is a thief and a liar and he left me." I lit into her like a bolt of lightning.

"I'm so sorry!" she said, covering her mouth with her hand.

"You're his damn mother! Where is he?" I said, putting my hands on my hips.

"I have no idea where he is." She let out a sigh. "Please sit down, Chloe," she said, reaching out to me as she took a seat on the lounge couch.

"That's okay, I'm fine over here," I said, leaning against the wall.

"I hadn't heard from Gregorry in about ten years until I got the call about attending your wedding. The last time I saw him was when we were in Alabama for his other wedding."

"Alabama? You mean Houston?" I said.

"No, Shelly's family lived right outside of Tuskegee. I actually didn't even know about Courtney being my grandchild until your wedding. I only knew about his other daughter, Adrianna, but I've never met her either."

I had to take that seat after all that, because she was tossing out names like some kind of elementary-school roll-call sheet. Two children! I thought he only had one. And what the hell was she talking about, what wedding in Alabama? Mother has taught me well about some things and one of them is "shuttin' up when somebody else is runnin' off at the mouth."

"Chloe, I really hate to hear this news," Lydia went on. "I mean Shelly was a very sweet girl and had a big family, like yours. Gregorry was just so hateful. I was hoping he'd changed after all this time. We've never gotten along well."

"Gregorry told me you left him as a child."

"Look, he was a handful, and I tried to bring Gregorry into my new family once he got older. And quite frankly, my husband, well now ex-husband, didn't care for him," Lydia coldly replied. "He was a problem child, and I wasn't going to jeopardize my family for him. My sister has always kept in touch with him. My mother and Big Greg's parents raised him, and they even sent him off to college. But he screwed that up."

"You mean at Morehouse?"

"Oh God, he couldn't even finish. I feel terrible about all this, and I'm just devastated about your baby, because I really like you, Chloe. I've read all about you, too, on the Internet. You are really quite the successful young lady. You know my daughter Angela just raves about how pretty you are and tells all her friends, 'my sister-in-law knows all the famous people in Hollywood!' "

"I think you should stop using terms like *daughter-in-law* and *sister-in-law* as they relate to me. Gregorry tried to ruin my life!" I turned to walk away, then stopped. "I've got one question, when are you going to take ownership of creating a monster?" I shook my head and walked out.

Lydia was flush with embarrassment, sitting up here in her expensive clothes and designer purse that carried all her baggage. Miss Ozona's vision was right on target. Except, I didn't have to find Lydia, she found me.

I never checked out Gregorry's background or his stories. I never even pressed to visit him at the office. He said he worked from a virtual office and that his cell phone *was* his office number. Hey, I thought that was some sort of "financial consultant" way of doing the business thing. I never saw the deeds on the houses he claimed to own. Why would someone say they owned something that they didn't?

I was so naive and trusting. I thought he knew more about financial matters than me. In the past, whenever I had a question about money I asked Edward. My man was a financial consultant, dammit! I didn't need Edward anymore.

"Baby, you should be taking advantage of the equity in your house. I went ahead and had it appraised and it's worth three times what you paid for it!" he said late one night, between sweet kisses on my neck and lips. The next day he slid a refinancing contract in front of me, and I signed it like a fool. Four days later, the papers for taking out a home equity line of credit arrived. I signed those too. Damn!

Ceci

IN DA CLUB

"**B**ABY, WHY DON'T you just come home tonight at a decent hour?" Stanley had been sittin' his ass up in my face for the past thirty minutes. I was tired as hell, not tryin' to answer all his questions. I had done a shift at the Post Office this mornin', then did five heads at the shop. This was my third job, but at least at the St. Louis Room I could enjoy myself. It was a hood club, but it's all good in tha hood. Hey now!

"Stanley, you gots ta stop sweatin' me like a damn sauna, *shiiiiiit*," I said, pourin' myself a glass of cognac. "I gotta make this extra money 'cause I'm tryin' to open me a shop."

"Ceci, I told you I got your back and I'mma help you get the shop. Ain't anytime you asked me for somethin', I do it? Huh?" Stanley looked at me with them ol' beggin'-ass eyes again. Them was the same eyes that trapped me when we met almost fifteen years ago. I was on the early mornin' shift workin' outta the downtown Post Office.

"Hey, Miss Lady," Stanley would say all early in the mornin' and shit. Them mornin' shifts kicked my ass. But he'd be there with his li'l cute ass all fresh from the cleaners, wearin' some of that good cologne. I think about that time he was into Calvin Klein.

I was young then so I could go straight from the club on the east side to work. I'd still be drunk from the club, but Stanley would have me some hot coffee and a Danish waitin' at my station. When I wanted me a li'l drink, he'd bring it to me. Oh, and a brotha got class. Every

Friday he took me to get either steak or lobster, not at them chain restaurants neither. He still takes me to the best.

"Ceci Gibson, I just wanna make you my woman and give you the best. I know I ain't the richest or the best lookin', but I know what you need," Stanley said, gazin' all in my eyes with them beggin'-ass eyes again. Plus, we was in Jamaica for my fortieth birthday! Aw, he had me fo sho. It's been ten years now. I ain't never said I wasn't gonna keep me some side dick in play, but he gets the "family time," as my cousin Fawn says.

Now, I'm gonna give it to Stanley. He gonna do three things if he ain't gonna do nothin' else. He gonna make some money, he gonna make sure I got some money, and he gonna dress his ass off. I don't play. Don't be comin' all up in my face wit some raggedy shit on. I guess I'm stuck wit him 'cause Mama and Billye Jean and Joy Ann and 'nem like him. Damn, I be tryin' to cut him loose, but I ain't gonna lie, he good to me. His ass just don't understand that I gots ta do me! Ceci gots ta do me!

I spotted my li'l young tender, Twain, walk in the bar at the back entrance lookin' like a sho nuff playa playa. Stanley is like that brotha who gonna always be there. He old school, and the sex is just a'ight. It ain't all that. I need a brotha to rock my world. I'm seventeen years older than Twain, but he loves this good seasoned stuff. Holla!

"Ceci, I ain't gonna keep waitin' on you. Plus, yo mama has been tryin' to reach you and you need to call her. Miss Carol Jane worries all the time!" Stanley tried to catch an attitude.

"Aw hell, so you and my mama in cahoots or somethin'? First of all, Stanley, I'mma be home when I get there, okay? Shit, I gotta make this money. You gonna get me a shop?" I poured myself another drink.

"You need to slow down on all that drinkin'," Stanley huffed.

"You need to go home! I got a damn daddy!" I threw up my hand, lettin' him know I was done talkin' to his ass.

No sooner than Stanley left, I got ready to get my playa playa on and I'm mixin' a drink and I see Arnaz pull up in front of the club in Billye Jean's car and drop some woman off. I felt myself swell up, mad as hell!

"Annie, girl, my cuzin's husband's woman just walked up in here. Take over for me, I'm 'bout to jack her up." I took off my apron and tossed it behind the bar.

I charged into the bathroom behind that Oriental heifer. "Look here you li'l dim sum bitch," I said, grabbin' that heifer by the arm and whippin' her around. "Did Arnaz just drop you off?"

"Who you call bitch!"

"*You*, bitch!"

"I love Arnaz. He my man!"

"He my cuzin's husband!"

"Billye Jean got bad heart. I move in when she die!"

"I will cut yo ass into a million sashimi pieces, bitch!"

"I no Japanese! I Chinese!"

"Don't ever let me catch you with my cuzin's husband again. I don't give a damn about him, but blood is thicker than motherfuckin' water. You tell Arnaz he betta keep his dirt out on the street where it belongs!"

Just then someone opened the door and dim sum squirmed free.

"Crazy lady try kill me! Crazy lady try kill me!" she screamed, runnin' out of the club. Shit, I need a drink!

SOLITUDE

I have known women
Women who see/who lay a third eye on evil/dare it to move and
make it sink in a blink/women who hear/who put an ear to a stone/
X-ray a moan/hear a cry before a tear drops/women with keen
nostrils who smell shit before it stinks/women reminiscing and
ruminating on the rudiments of roots and the source of nature's
remedies/diviners/root women
I have known women . . .

Joy Ann

NO COUNTRY FOR OLD WOMEN

'VE BEEN DOWN here at the Board of Education for almost an hour waitin' on the woman who's supposed to be the new head of Arts Programming and Development for the public school system. It's really amazin' how they can just bring in these folks who are barely outta school and don't know nothin', and I mean nothin', about the arts, but they decidin' what's creative or not.

I was sittin' in the reception area half dozin' when I felt a light tap on my shoulder. "Ms. Michaels, hi, I'm Rochelle Mason, the director of Arts Programming and Development. C'mon back to my office."

I picked up my portfolio that was restin' against the chair next to me and followed her into a small office. She was dressed like one of those typical black women who you see workin' in corporate America, with her sensible shoes, slacks, and a blazer. Her office was pretty basic with a few pamphlets sittin' on a small bookcase. Hell, from the looks of her and this office she coulda worked for the IRS or someplace. There was no connection to the arts, that's for sure.

I sat down and unzipped my portfolio and pulled out my press kit. I didn't have any recent press clippin's but there was enough from my gallery showin's in town as well as in New York several years ago, D.C., and Atlanta. Enough to impress anybody who knew anythin' about the world of art. However, somethin' told me this chile probably didn't know a Romare Bearden from Michael Jackson.

"Thank you for meeting with me, Ms. Michaels."

"No, thank *you*. I've been workin' with the school system, consultin' for many years and my recent work with the elementary-school-aged children has really been wonderful. We did an exhibit at the St. Louis Art Museum. I had them do an experiment with translatin' their feelin's into colors. It was very successful."

"It really sounds like it was great. So how long have you been painting?"

"Oh, dear, probably your entire life. Being an artist is my life." I was a bit taken back by her naïveté. Hadn't she even looked over my résumé? "My work has been seen in many of the major cities and at art festivals around the country. I've had very big showin's in New York too, with artists like the late Emilio Cruz. He was a very, very good friend of mine. I've even done some showin's with contemporary artists like Leroy Campbell."

"Wow, that is really great," she said, restin' her chin on her hand. This chile didn't have a clue.

"I have a copy of my résumé if you need it," I said, pullin' it out of my satchel. "I also have prints of some of my more noted works here in my portfolio." I was gettin' kinda pissed at this girl sittin' across from me who didn't know shit from shinola. It was like I was havin' to prove my credentials.

"No, no, that won't be necessary," she said, takin' my résumé. "The point of me asking you to meet with me is that at the start of the New Year we're gonna have to make some deep cuts in our budgets. The funding for extra *things* like art, and music, and some of the performing arts is just not realistic for us anymore. So, we're going to be reviewing our budgets in the coming weeks and we'll be in touch."

"Let me ask you a question, Ms. Mason. What was the point of me comin' all the way down here? These kids today need outlets like art, and music, and dance, and theater. You think they ain't doin' good now, you wait until they have no way to release that energy in a positive and productive way. I would imagine you aren't cuttin' monies for the basketball or football team? Huh?" I was gettin' in a huff. I leaned back in my chair to calm myself.

"Ms. Michaels, I hear your concerns. I have them too. I remember taking art in school and it was fun." This woman was now tryin' to trivialize my livelihood. I realized it was an uphill battle with her. Why get my blood pressure up? I simply zipped up my portfolio and gathered my tote bag.

"Please understand that it was passed on to me by my predecessor that you were a good friend to the board, and in case we aren't able to fund the workshops I wanted to show you a professional courtesy."

"Young lady," I said, rising to my feet, "I done lived a lot of life, more than you could ever imagine. While I appreciate the professional courtesy, I wanna give you a piece of advice. I'm proud when I see young women comin' up on the road that women like myself helped to pave. I've got three wonderful, talented, educated daughters myself, one who's an entrepreneur. I also have granddaughters.

"So as far as your budgets and all that stuff, just try to remember how we gonna get the next Bearden, or Miles Davis, or Lena Horne, or Chaka Kahn, or even Alicia Keyes if we aren't givin' them the opportunity." I didn't even wait for her response. I may be old, but I got pride. My grandmother taught me that. I held my head up high and walked out of the Board of Education and never looked back. I waited until I got home before I had me one of those good ol'-fashioned Lord-have-mercy-what-in-the-world-am-I-gonna-do breakdowns.

Chloe

BETTER DAYS

VISITING GRANDMOTHER'S HOUSE always gave me peace from the outside world. Her house has a distinct smell. A mixture of lavender sachets and mothballs. Then there's that hint of something freshly fried or simmering in the skillet, like chicken or pork chops. In winter it was warm and snug. In summer it was cool and lazy. Her couch has seen many a hazy carefree day and midday snooze, but it still looks brand-new. Grandmother has kept the plastic on it for at least twenty years.

Every year for spring cleaning she changed the drapes, washed the blinds, scrubbed the walls, and changed the color of her kitchen to something inviting, and bright. Not a speck of dust could be found in Miss Millie Michaels's home. I can't believe that old color console still works, picture perfect. Grandmother has the television repairman come out every year to tune it.

Grandmother insisted on cooking me something to eat. If all this drama don't kill me, the food at home sure will by clogging up my arteries. It's tastes *too* good to be *good* for you. When things get back to normal and I go back to L.A., I'm gonna be working overtime on my morning runs. For now I'm gonna take it all in as part of that mission to "love me up" everyone keeps talking about.

When I was growing up, Grandmother would get me up bright and early Saturday mornings to catch the bus to go to JCPenney. "Come on, sweet Chloe, rise and shine!" She'd shake me awake. "Just five more minutes," I'd whine. There was definitely no rest in this house on Saturday mornings. Saturdays were made for shopping.

In the summertime, the heat and humidity always made the bathroom door swell so it never closed all the way. I could see Grandmother neatly setting out my breakfast through the cracked door—one egg, fried sunny-side up, two pork sausage patties, and white toast with butter. A tiny packet of grape jam set next to my fork. It was from the public school lunches she served on her job.

I bathed slowly and ate just as slowly, because I dreaded the three-block hike to the bus stop. The St. Louis summer heat was stifling, even for that short walk. Grandmother would be fussing with me the whole time at breakfast. "Hurry up, Chloe. We're gonna be late!"

As the bus pulled up, Grandmother whispered to me to be on my best behavior. "Morning, Miss Millie," the bus driver, Miss Donetta, greeted. This was her regular route. I thought Miss Donetta was cool. Instead of a gold tooth, she had a gleaming silver one right in front, and a perfectly rounded and shaped Afro.

"A fine morning it is, Donetta. How's that son of yours?" she asked.

"He doin' real good, Miss Millie. He goin' off to college in the fall. First one in our family. I see yo grandbaby Chloe gettin' prettier and prettier every time I see her," Donetta said, flashing that jackpot-winning smile once again.

Everybody knew us on that Saturday route. We were always the best dressed, better than most folks looked going to church on Sundays. But that's how Grandmother was. She insisted a person have impeccable manners and be freshly pressed at all times.

Grandmother summoned me to the dining table, snapping me out of my walk down memory lane. At least she believed in small portions, not like my mother's side of the family. She thawed out a single pork chop, sliced a fresh tomato and sprinkled salt and pepper on top, and gave me a side of applesauce. She wasn't eating. I noticed during my last few visits home, she hadn't had much of an appetite, but she liked to keep me company at the table while I ate.

"You feelin' all right, Grandmother?" I asked.

"Grandmother's just fine," she said, pausing before clearing her throat. "Chloe, you know your mother and I are a lot alike," she went on, sliding my plate in front of me.

"How you figure?" I asked, stopping to say grace.

"Well, we both know what it's like to struggle and work hard and put our children first, even when their fathers aren't doing what they're supposed to. You know, I think I see more of myself in her than my own daughter."

Grandmother and Mother have gotten very close in the last several years. Strangely, she rarely talks about my aunt Diane who lives worlds away in Iowa with her Canadian husband, Tom, and their children—two dogs and six cats. We'd never say it to Grandmother, but we concluded years ago that Aunt Diane simply has a problem with her blackness. She always seemed uncomfortable around her own. Why else would any clear-thinking black person move to Iowa?

"Chloe, there are some things I want to talk about because I know my days are numbered."

"Grandmother, you're gonna outlive all of us," I said with a smile.

"Chloe, you should never be afraid of death," she said, placing her soft hands on top of mine. Her middle and index fingers were slightly crooked from her arthritis, but she never let it get her down. Her eyes, once vibrant and bright, seemed vacant. "Death makes you stronger. And when it's your time, you have no control over it." Grandmother then folded her hands on her lap and crossed her feet politely.

I don't know what came over her to make her start talking so strangely about death, but I was always taught that when old folks start talking, you'd better listen.

"I always walked around with my head up because I grew up dirt poor," she said, picking at the lace tablecloth. "My mama died from TB, and my father, Solomon, had to raise me and my sister, Lady, alone. I know Lady held it against Solomon that she couldn't go to school because she had to take care of me," she said while clearing my plate. I followed her into the kitchen to clean up the meal dishes.

I remembered hearing stories from Daddy that my great-grandfather, Solomon, was the meanest man you could ever meet. He said Solomon even looked mean standing at a compact but muscular five foot five, hair the color of burnt red bricks, and skin the color of buttermilk. Solomon was small, but they hired him in a heartbeat downtown at the old St. Louis Steel Mill, because he was strong and moved fast.

"Solomon was tough," she sighed. "He'd whip me and Lady good if we got outta line. But I guess it was difficult raising two girls alone." Grandmother handed me a wet plate and a dishcloth for drying. "When he wasn't around, Lady would tell me her dreams of being a famous dancer, dancing all over the world." She handed me another plate and a handful of silverware. She was finishing them faster than I could dry them and put them in the cabinet.

"Lady did domestic work for a wealthy white widow and danced at the Hot Cat Cabaret at night, and what furs or jewelry that old white lady didn't give her and her fella, Mr. Herbert bought." Grandmother chuckled. "Yessiree, your Aunt Lady lived a very glamorous life.

"Solomon made me stop going to school after elementary school to help around the house, but I made a promise to myself that I'd always go back. Just like Lady, I'd show him, too," she said, laughing harder, shutting the water off. I smiled, intrigued by her story, and followed her back into the living room.

"It's very important for a young woman to go to church and have a strong faith in God, Chloe," she said. I nodded, sitting down on the couch next to her. "The Catholic church gave me a place to get involved, helped me find my strength in the Lord, and provided a chance for my children to get a proper education. That's when I met your grandfather and got married. It wasn't easy, but I made a home for myself and my family.

"I worked two jobs, a matron for the public schools by day and cleaning city hall at night. Then I'd come home and see about your father and your Aunt Diane. But every night I'd stop off at the public library to read, because the school board gave me my own library card. Eventually, I got my GED." She smiled, reflecting. I remembered as a little girl seeing her library card sealed in a plastic cover that kept it like new.

"I saved every extra penny after groceries. I was a thinker, a planner, just like Lady. But your grandfather was a scoundrel. Your grandfather would work and come home every day, but come Friday, payday, he was nowhere to be found 'til after the weekend. For three days he'd drink up his paycheck. The last of the Red Hot Papas!

"We didn't have much of a marriage, but being Catholic, I couldn't divorce. We didn't even sleep as husband and wife after a while. I thought I could make your grandfather do right by me when Thomas was born. But Thomas's time was up almost as fast as he came." Grandmother's mood quickly changed. She looked weak. Thomas was her firstborn who died when he was two years old.

"That's why I know what it's like to long for a baby. But, Chloe, nothin' in this world can ever compare to losing a full-grown child, active and happy one minute, gone the next." She put her fist to her mouth. "I don't know what made me decide to hang clothes as cold as it was." She lowered her hand with a glazed look on her face.

"I went out back while Thomas was sleep. I didn't know it, but he woke up and crawled out of his bed. The old black stove was working hard heating up our one-bedroom apartment. He got just close enough to feel the warmth. He used to do all that funny jibber jabber and coo so sweetly, and he had these bright and lively brown eyes. He was so smart, Chloe, and curious, and yessiree, he was fast.

"He reached right out and grabbed that kerosene can. I was still busy hanging clothes on the line. I think I looked up at the sky. You know how cold St. Louis winters are. I was just happy to see the sun." Her words slowed and she closed her eyes like she was trying to picture Thomas's face. "I thought my baby was still asleep. I was just trying to sneak in a little break. Then I heard the most awful sound."

Grandmother's petite, soft body was jolted by Thomas's remembered bloodcurdling screams. "I couldn't get to him fast enough. Thomas was moaning and balled up in pain from the poison. I just kept begging God to let me switch places with my baby. He didn't." Grandmother's face dropped. I could see every year of eighty-three that she had lived. Her cloudy eyes watered up. "To watch your baby, helpless, dying in your arms and you can't do a thing leaves one with unimaginable guilt. Ten thousand confessions wouldn't help me get rid of the pain.

"Tragedy makes you strong," Grandmother said quietly, patting my hand. She slowly got up and headed into her bedroom. "Come on in here," she said, leading me into the bedroom. I joined her in front of her dresser. "You know why I tell you all these things, Chloe?"

"Why?"

"Because I want you to be happy."

"I am happy, Grandmother," I lied.

"My sweet Chloe, I am old and time may not wait much longer for me."

"Stop talking like this!"

"It's true, we all gotta go sometimes." I turned and faced the mirror and looked at our reflections. Although I was more of a Davis girl personality wise, and definitely resembled Mother, there was no denying I was a Michaels. I looked like a young Millie Michaels with her same flat forehead and deep-set slanted eyes. Mother always said Daddy and 'nem had Asian roots, Chinese or something.

"Just don't settle, Chloe, ever again. Promise me that," she said, slowly opening her large crystal jewelry box and reaching inside.

"What are you talkin' about?"

Grandmother pulled out a tiny black velvet box and guided me over to the edge of the bed.

"Sit down next to me." She patted the mattress. I sat down. "I know things aren't right with you and the man you married."

"I told Mother I would tell you and the rest of the family when I was ready."

"Your mother didn't tell me anything, specifically."

"Well, I may as well now. He left me, and I've filed for a divorce."

"It was for the best. I didn't get the impression he was a very nice person, but I just wanted you to be happy. He wasn't the one for you, Chloe. I know you really loved this Edward person." My face dropped in shock. She gave a sly smile. "Everyone thinks Grandmother's just old. I guess old is supposed to mean you don't see with two eyes and hear with two ears. I hear them talkin' at Sunday dinner." I was quiet.

"You don't have to tell Grandmother these things. I know it in my heart, and soul, and mind. I know it in the look in your eyes. If I hadn't been Catholic, I would've gotten divorced. You're doing the right thing. Get out of it and get on with your life. And you don't have to get married again. You don't even have to have kids. No sirree! A husband will drive you out of your mind, and kids worry the hell out of you!"

"Grandmother!"

"No, you'd better listen up. You make sure if and when you get married again, it's right. That he's honest and is a good provider. Life is too much of a burden to have to worry about pennies. What you want is a man who loves you more than you love him. Look at your Aunt Billye Jean. And don't do like your mother and father and break up a home. You gotta put God first. That's the only way I've lived this long.

"Love your children, but when it's time to set them free, let them go. A child can give you a million heartaches and you'll spend your life blaming yourself. You have everything in the world."

"I don't feel like it right now. I'm really struggling to pull it all back together financially."

"Doesn't matter; you're smart, got a good job, you got your family, and you get your good looks from me," she teased. "We all will pitch in until you're back on your feet."

"I love you, Grandmother." I leaned over and hugged her. Her body was fragile, but her arms were strong.

"This is for you," she said, opening the box in her hand.

"Oh, my God! It's beautiful."

"I know. I paid good money for it. Go on, take it out."

I reached in and slowly pulled out her diamond ring.

"Your grandfather never bought me a diamond ring. So I saved for a long time to buy my own. Almost my whole life to get the one I wanted. My fingers just got this darn arthritis and I can't wear the darn thing now. So put it on and get on outta here before I change my mind."

"I love it!" I said, slipping it on my right hand.

"I'm glad you had sense enough to put it on *that* hand. You don't want a man to think you already got all the diamonds you need."

"By the way, while you're in a giving mood. I've had my eye on that mink of yours for a long—"

"What do the kids say?" she said, cutting me off. "Don't even think about it! You'd better stop while you're ahead, child."

I left Grandmother's house smiling from here back to California.

Billye Jean

MAMA'S BOY

"GOOD MORNIN', Miss Virginia." I smiled, wavin' as I dipped my index finger in holy water, makin' the sign of the cross. I greeted a few more folks before buttonin' my coat up. "Mornin', Father Jeff! Church was wonderful this mornin'," I added, shakin' the priest's hand. I've been comin' to St. Bridget's for the last thirty-some-odd years.

Me and Joy Ann grew up right around the corner. For the most part our family is A.M.E., but I just like the Catholic tradition ever since my kids was little goin' to St. Bridget's Elementary School. We got a strong black population here, too, 'cause the church is right here in the center of the black neighborhood. What's really nice is that we got a good gospel choir. Plus, I ain't like Joy Ann and Carol Jane. I ain't 'bout to be sittin' up in church all day.

I wrapped my scarf around my neck and headed out the door. I was in a good mood this mornin' and I'm not gonna let nothin' upset me, not even Arnaz. As I hummed my way down the block to my car, I reached into my purse and pulled my keys out.

"Billye Jean!" I knew that voice anywhere. Lord have mercy, I don't feel like bein' bothered. He ain't gonna do nothin' but get on my nerves.

"Billye Jean, hold up!" he called out again.

I stopped at my car and put one hand on my hip. I was holdin' my bible in the other one. "Yes, Junior?" I said, turnin' around, lettin' out an exhausted breath.

"Hey, how you doin', Billye Jean? I tried callin' the house to check on you." Junior nervously tried to straighten his clothes out. He looked like he had been sleepin' in the gutter somewhere. I ain't gonna lie, I'm heartbroken every time I see Junior. He all worn down.

Junior was such a cute baby with them curls on his head, that big ol' smile, and them eyes. One minute they'd be green, then they'd turn gray. They was even prettier than Thora's. Now he lookin' more like he sixty-eight rather than fifty-eight. His face all sunken in, probably ain't ate in days.

"Well, I got your message, but you ain't leave a number." I pursed my lips.

"I didn't have a phone, but I'm 'posed to be gettin' a cell phone soon. Anyway, you been okay?" Junior was tryin' to talk nice, but I knew right away he was easin' right on into beggin'.

"Yes, Junior, I been fine, just tired mostly. You must need somethin'?" I frowned.

"Naw, Billye Jean, I came by to let you know I'm doin' real good. I got me a lady friend too. We talkin' 'bout gettin' married. She real nice."

"Humph, a lady friend? Well, I ain't got no comment on that. I know you ain't stopped by the church lately, so I figured you must be back drinkin' or druggin' again."

"I'm gettin' my life together, Billye Jean. Look, cain't you be happy fa me?"

"I'll be happy when you stop livin' the life you livin'. I'll be happy when you stop callin' me only when you need some money," I said, foldin' my arms across my chest.

"I ain't even call for all that. I ain't drinkin' or shootin' dope no more. I swear, Billye Jean!"

"Junior, I done heard that a million times. I see how you look!"

"I ain't lyin'! I just ain't had no place to live!"

"Junior, don't be raisin' your voice at me!" I said, turnin' and stickin' my key in the car door lock.

"I'm sorry, Billye Jean," he huffed, reachin' out and puttin' his hand on my arm. "Hold up, I'm lettin' you know I done got in that program over there at the Salvation Army. I'mma have me a place to live in a coupla days. I been even goin' to the shelter's church, and I'm gonna get baptized. Me and my fiancée."

"How you gonna get married and you ain't got no money?" I opened the car door and climbed inside. "Anyway, ain't you still married to that otha woman?"

"I got me a divorce! I'll let you know, maybe y'all can come to see me get baptized and meet Gladys."

"Yeah, okay, Junior. I'll come to see you get baptized." I turned the key in the ignition and hit the button, lettin' the window down, then I closed the door.

"Thank you, Billye Jean. And look I done got me a li'l job over there sweepin' up the floors and stuff down at the convention center," Junior said, leanin' against the car.

"That's good, Junior." My head was hurtin' by now.

"Yeah, I get my first payday in two weeks, but I'm runnin' short until then."

"I knew you was 'bout to beg for some money, Junior," I said, lookin' straight ahead out the windshield.

"Billye Jean, it's my money from disability!"

"Junior, that disability check ain't started comin' yet. Plus, you owe me money 'cause I had to pay off that lease from that otha apartment you had got put out of a year ago. I ain't got no money to give you! If I did, all you gonna do is shoot it up in your arms or drink it up!" I said, lookin' him up and down.

"C'mon, Billye Jean, I need that money. I promise I don't shoot up no more, and I'm workin' on my drinkin'!"

I knew he ain't gonna do no good with no money, but what if he ain't eaten? I didn't want him to go and do nothin' bad to try to get him some money. He still my child and I just hate to see him out here lookin' bad. I reached into my purse and handed him forty dollars out the window. "This is all I got, Junior," I said, lookin' away. It just hurt too bad to see him sometimes.

"Thank you, Billye Jean," he said, quickly snatchin' the money. I put the car in Drive and just before I pulled off, Junior put his hand on my shoulder. "I'mma let you know when I get baptized so ya'll can come."

"Bye, Junior!" I couldn't bring myself to say nothin' else. As I pulled off and made my way down the street, I watched him walkin' the other direction out my rearview mirror. He didn't look good and I felt bad he ain't got no place to live, but I cain't let Junior come to my house no more. He done stole from me too much, too many times.

Stole my liquor and put water in the bottles. Stole my jewelry I got from the dolla store. Stole my Mary Kay stuff I used to sell. That was it. I went to have a Mary Kay party and all my eye shadows and lipsticks was missin'! He don't never steal TVs or nothin'. Junior too petty for that. Lord have mercy!

I said I wasn't gonna let nothin' upset me today. Lord, what do you do when your firstborn done just fell by the wayside? I thought Junior woulda gotten his life together after the accident with Monique.

By the time I got home my head was throbbin' so hard I could barely focus. I reached up on the shelf in the kitchen pantry and grabbed my bottle of Extra Strength Tylenol, popped it open, and shook two pills into the palm of my hand sittin' down at the kitchen chair. I washed them down with a glass of ice water. Lookin' up at the photographs of Monique hanging on the wall, I felt a hard cry comin' on. I closed my eyes, and the tears crawled down my face.

That baby was too young to go, and she went so quickly. Monique was beautiful. She had them light eyes too. Junior was a good daddy. I knew when Jonetta told him she was leavin' him, he wasn't gonna be no more good. He started hangin' down there in them projects with that fool Baby Boy and 'nem. Them was Earl's people, and Arnaz knew Junior was easily influenced. He was impressed by Arnaz.

I turned a blind eye, and I have regrets I'll live with forever. Arnaz was doin' that stuff, shootin' up. I didn't even know it. Arnaz was the one who turned Junior on to heroin. I found out years later. Junior ended up losing his family, his job, all of it. But Monique was gonna make somethin' of herself, despite her daddy.

That chile went all the way out there to California to go to school. She just had one semester left and that child was goin' off to be a doctor. She said she was gonna follow in my footsteps. I told her I was gonna buy her a ticket home, but she insisted on drivin'.

"Grandma, please, don't fuss, I'll be fine. Don't worry," she said. Thora had signed for her to get her first car.

"Baby, you don't need to be makin' a drive that far by yourself." I couldn't stop that chile. Monique was hardheaded.

"I love you, Grandma!"

That would be the last time I heard her voice. I still can hear that smile she always had in her voice. She went clean under that eighteen-wheeler. They say she fell asleep. Thora was livin' in Arizona at the time and was the one who identified her body. She got a strong stomach. She said it was real bad and Monique was almost decapitated.

It happened on a highway somewhere just outside of Arizona. She was gonna stop at Thora's to rest, just twenty miles away. Thora said she probably didn't even feel no pain or nothin' when she died. I got down on my knees and asked Muh to receive her great-grandbaby. She saw her when she was born and now she'd be there to bring her home. "I just hate Daddy sometimes!" Monique shouted and cried the day Junior didn't show up to her high school graduation.

"God got his hand on you," I said, holding her in my arms. "Look, baby, you cain't take this on. Your daddy's problems ain't yours. You are goin' to college and one day you gonna be rich and then you can send me on one of them fancy trips to the islands, and them I'mma get me a new husband!" I always could tease her and make her laugh good.

Sometimes God plucks his young angels up. He got his reasons. What I cain't figure out is the reason Junior went the road he did. Probably 'cause he was my weak child. Thora was always the stronger one. Now, Junior is almost sixty damn years old, and all the drugs he done took and drinkin' he done did and he still here. He my flesh and blood, my firstborn, but sometimes I get real mad that Monique had a chance and had to go. Now, he had all kinda chances and threw 'em out. All I can do is pray for him.

Chloe

RELENTLESS

MOTHER HAD THE television blasting, and it was two in the morning. I don't know how she sleeps with that thing on, but I couldn't take it one more night. I tiptoed into the living room, trying my best not to wake her, gently reaching under her elbow, where the remote was strategically resting against her full bosom. I reached for it, and she grunted. Luckily, I successfully snagged it without waking her. I was just about to turn the television off when the program teaser caught my attention:

She thought her husband was a faithful family man, until one day she discovered he was living two different lives. Next on Relentless.

I sat down on the floor, quickly engrossed in it. The docile-looking woman on the screen began to tell her story of fear and deception. As I watched her fight back the tears in front of the camera I was pulled deeper and deeper into her story. The woman had discovered her husband had a secret life after money started disappearing from their joint bank account.

She found out her husband was living a double life and had stolen all her money. The most gripping part of her TV-land confession was that she decided to disguise herself and follow him one day. She ended up in the parking lot at a small church. When the man went inside the building, she got out to take a closer look and saw his picture on the church billboard, posed with another woman. He was apparently the pastor, and the woman was the first lady of the church. The woman quickly called the county clerk's office in that town and confirmed her husband was in fact married to that other woman.

I had caught the tail end of the program, but a lightbulb went off in my head. I started thinking about Gregorry's tales of living in Houston, Phoenix, and Atlanta. He talked about his lavish lifestyle in each city, the homes he owned, the restaurants he frequented. Also, Lydia's slip of the tongue about Gregorry's wedding in Alabama had been gnawing at my brain since running into her at the mall. Perhaps I'd find my answers the same way the woman on television did, by a simple phone call.

The next morning I was on the phone by 8:00 A.M., with a steady java drip next to me. I had mapped out my plan. I would call the county clerk's office in every city he had lived in, and I wasn't going to stop chasing people down until I got answers. First call was to the county clerk's office in Tuskegee, Alabama. As the operator rattled off several numbers, I scribbled them down. I dialed number after number until I reached a tiny-voiced woman named Gladine McCausley, who sounded as if she'd been sitting behind her desk at the Macon County Clerk's Office for her entire life.

"Yes, ma'am. I'm calling because I'm trying to locate some information on my . . ." My voice began to quiver. "I'm sorry, ma'am. I'm trying to get some information on my husband." I choked back my tears. "His name is Gregorry Marion Robinson III, and I think he was married before. I don't know when, but I know the woman's name was Shelly. I don't have a last name."

"You say you don't know when or a last name? Lawd, have mercy, baby. Well, we ain't too busy so let me see what I can do." The woman must've forgotten to press Hold. I heard her open and close some file cabinets and shuffle through what sounded like an endless stack of papers. I was about to give up on this whole attempt when I heard her shouting to someone else in the office.

"Ezra! Ezra! Come quick! This girl on the phone wanna know about Rosetta Harris's girl, Shelly.

"Lawd, she married that boy who caused all that trouble!" Whoever Ezra was, he knew exactly who Gregorry was.

189

"Hello, Miss?" Ms. McCausley said, returning to the phone. "Yes, we do have a record of that weddin', but it wasn't two years ago, it was ten. He married Shelly Harris."

This was just as Lydia had pointed out, but I wasn't any less confused, because I still had to find out who the hell Courtney's mother was in Houston. However, before I got to Texas I had to make a pit stop in Atlanta, Georgia. Aha! Atlanta revealed wife number two. "Yes, I see that a Gregorry Marion Robinson and Starla Evans were married. He also has an outstanding warrant," the clerk said. I sat in a jaw-dropping stupor.

Gregorry was married to Starla a whopping six months and had racked up several domestic abuse charges. He had even served a short stint in jail. I tried to get contact information on her to no avail. Time was of the essence, and I had at least two more states to tackle.

Bingo! Wife number three, Tamika Norris, was in Houston. So far she had been the only wife Gregorry confessed to having. She was the mother of Courtney. I had never been formally introduced to her. Gregorry didn't allow me to speak with Tamika before the wedding. That was probably our biggest argument. My curiosity got the best of me and I called Houston information, lucking upon Tamika's number. I wrote it down and stared at it for a long time, thinking back to one of those arguments in particular. Two nights before my wedding. I knew *of* his ex-wife, but I never knew her name.

"Why can't I talk to the mother of the child we will soon all be sharing?" I demanded.

"Because this is my business!" he shouted.

"We're going to be husband and wife. Your business is my business! Courtney will be my child, too!"

"No! She will be your *step*child. Her mother is crazy. She won't like you."

"Wait a minute, you said your situation was drama free. What are you hiding? I think once she and I communicate—"

"You always wanna fuckin' communicate! Worry about me and you and this house!" He was so angry he stormed right out of the house.

Thinking back to that night sent a surge through my veins. I couldn't wait another minute. I quickly dialed Tamika's number.

"Hello, is Tamika Norris in?" My heart was racing.

"This is she." The woman's voice was laced with a syrupy sweet twang.

"Tamika, we've never met, but my name is Chloe Michaels and—"

"I know who you are," she said matter-of-factly. "Gregorry told me all about you. Courtney still talkin' about you."

"Well, I recently filed for divorce."

"Divorce?" she asked.

"Yes, we were married in February, but only for a few months. Courtney was *in* my wedding."

"Ooh, I swear he be lyin'," she chuckled. "Every time he opens his mouth he be lyin'," she laughed again. "Gregorry told me he was takin' Courtney to his family reunion. Look, I don't have nothin' to do with what Gregorry be doin'. He good to me and my baby and that's all I gots to say, and all I care about." You could hear the strange emotional mix of woman scorned and protective lover in her voice. Conversation over.

Gregorry had concocted so many lies, but this was one woman who was standing by her man no matter what. I was sure Tamika's next call would be to Gregorry, and I didn't care one bit. I wasn't afraid anymore. Wife number four was next on my hit list: Nicole Anderson of Phoenix, mother of Adrianna.

Her father was the Reverend C. L. Anderson, who married them in a lavish ceremony at their church. I figured it out that Gregorry had combined the various women he married into one composite. Also, Phoenix court records showed a slew of restraining orders against Gregorry. Married to Gregorry in June, Nicole filed for divorce nine months later.

"We need to put Gregorry behind. He destroyed my daughter's career and reputation, and she's now remarried and happy. I must protect Adrianna and ask you not to contact us again!" Reverend Anderson sternly stated, hanging up.

I had heard enough, quite honestly. I was exhausted and just about to throw in the towel when the fax from Alabama came in at Salvatore's house. The good news—not only did Ms. McCausley send a copy of Gregorry and Shelly's marriage license, but she had contacted Shelly's mother, who in turn forwarded Shelly's cell number. After four attempts, I got an answer.

"Shelly Harris, my name is Chloe Michaels and we were both married to Gregorry Marion Robinson III, I think."

Carol Jane

GET GOD!

WEDNESDAYS IS MY night to go out to line dancin' at Studio Blue, that new club over there on Natural Bridge. I like it pretty well 'cause it has an older adult crowd. This Wednesday was Grown and Sexy Night. I knew I'd probably be one of the oldest folks there so I was determined to learn that new cha-cha move before my night at the club. Sometimes you gotta show them youngsters! It's a combination of the Cupid shuffle and the old electric slide.

I told my friends Doris and Gladys that I'd meet them there at eight. I had four hours 'til I had to be there and that was plenty of time to practice. We supposed to wear our blue jeans and sweatshirts with our names in rhinestones on them. But I'll just wear my long blue-jean skirt with the elastic in the waist. I ain't been able to get in my jeans the last few times I tried.

The name of our line dancin' group is the Sophisticated Ladies. Gladys wanted to call us the Sassy Ladies, but we entirely too old to be sassy, I thought. I've been dancin' with my group for about four years. A lot of church folk will try to act like me goin' to the club to dance is a sin, but I tell them God wants us to dance.

I put my boom box on the kitchen table and sat down to lace up my sneakers, tappin' my feet to the beat.

"Mama! Mama!" Ceci stormed through my front door screamin'.

What in God's name? I was midstep tryin' to get that part where you do that dance, the walk-it-out.

"Mama!" She barreled right through the cord stretched across the floor and . . . *Crash!* My boom box toppled to the floor and pieces flew every whicha way.

"Ceci!"

"Mama, this heifer gonna have to move in with you!" Ceci was draggin' Satin behind her. Satin's face was beet red and streaked with tears. Ceci pushed Satin down hard into the kitchen chair, forcin' the kitchen table to move backward. Her nostrils were flarin', and she was practically foamin' at the mouth.

"What is all this ruckus, Cecilia?" I was already startled half to death, but when I saw my grandbaby's face I nearly lost it. "Dear Jesus, what has happened to this girl?" Satin's T-shirt was torn and hangin' off her shoulder and she had large red welts across her face, shoulders, and legs.

"I whooped her ass is what happened. I just found out she done dropped outta school three months ago, and is pregnant! Look at her," she said, lifting up Satin's shirt. Sho nuff that child's belly was poking out. "You see this, Mama? Pregnant!" Cecilia lurched out to smack Satin again, but I was quick to block her aim. Satin screamed and flinched. She was cryin' hysterically.

"You see what she doin' to me, Mama? I work to make sure she got designer clothes, food, a roof over her head. I be workin' double overtime at the shop, and weekends at the club. And her ass been coverin' up her stomach! I guess I'm the damn fool!"

"Calm down, Cecilia. Satin has done wrong, but we got to make sense of this now," I said, placing my hand on Satin's shoulder. "Lord have mercy!"

"You better call God and whoever else," Ceci said, turnin' to Satin and pointin' her finger in her face. "I told you, Satin, not to bring no babies home. Well, you cain't live wit me. You better hope yo granny take you and that bastard baby in!"

I whirled around and threw my hands in the air. "Cecilia, you gonna stop all that cursin' once and for all! Now, I know you upset, I'm just as disappointed, but you not gonna beat this child in my house! She is pregnant for Christsakes!"

I examined Cecilia closely, up and down. She was lit up like a Christmas tree, shifting and jittery. "Are you high?" I asked, but I already knew the answer.

"Damn Mama, hell naw, I ain't high. I ain't got time for all these questions!" Cecilia snatched up her purse and keys that she had dropped on the kitchen floor when she stormed in.

"Cecilia, I'm not askin' no more, I'm tellin' you to stop that filth in my house today!" I began wavin' my arms in the air. "Satan, I rebuke you! I rebuke you in the name of the Lord!"

"Aw, Mama, you ain't got to be callin' on God!"

"Did you hear what I just said, girl! Father, God, I call on you for strength!"

"All this ain't even necessary," Ceci shouted.

"Hananuna! Shatna! Hananuna!" The spirit just came over me and I started shoutin' and speakin' in tongues. Ceci's shifting became more nervous. She was high, but she wasn't that high to keep testin' a prayin' woman.

"Shananuna! I rebuke you, Satan!" I bowed my head and placed my palms on the kitchen table for support, then slowly lowered myself into the chair. Tears began to stream down my face. Satin was so scared, she stopped cryin'. "I have prayed hours upon hours for you, Cecilia. I know it ain't nothin' but the devil that gets in you and makes you so weak that you feel you have to turn to drugs and alcohol instead of God. That's why this child done lost her way. I'm not losing my children to the devil!"

"Mama, this ain't about no damn . . ." Suddenly, before Ceci could finish her sentence, somethin' came over me. Somethin' that never happened to me before. I sprung up out of that kitchen chair and before Cecilia could blink, I had jumped on her. I slapped Ceci across the face with everythin' in me, grabbin' her by the collar and pinnin' her against the refrigerator.

"Lord, I don't want to kill you girl, but I cain't take it no more! You gots to get out of my house. I'm tired, so tired, Cecilia, of you disrespectin' me, disrespectin' this family, and carryin' on drinkin' and takin' that stuff."

"Mama! I cain't believe you jumpin' on me like this." Cecilia looked as if she'd seen a ghost. Her chest was heaving, and she could barely catch her breath.

"I told you to stop it, girl!" I screamed to the top of my lungs, jerkin' Cecilia forward and slammin' her back hard into the refrigerator again. "Get out, Cecilia, and leave this child and don't come back until you get God in your life!"

My eyes were locked on Satin who was standin' in the kitchen entrance with tears in her eyes. I released my choke hold on Cecilia and slowly backed up. I was tremblin' and my heart was poundin' a mile a minute. The sting from my handprint made a large red stain on the side of Cecilia's face.

She wiped the saliva that had started to dribble from the side of her mouth and nervously began wipin' her nose with her forefinger and the palm of her hand. Her bottom lip was quiverin'. She wanted to make sure she wasn't bleedin'. Cecilia ran out and jumped in her car.

I saw Cecilia through the front window, fumblin' for her keys. She got in the car and started to beat the dashboard and steering wheel. She had gone into a fit of rage, rummagin' through her pocketbook, tossin' things out one by one. That chile was desperate! She finally pulled out a bottle of liquor and took a good hard swig of it. She started diggin' in her pocketbook again.

I could barely make out what she was openin' up, and then, do Jesus! I realized it was them drugs. She put what looked to be a small, square corner of paper up to her nose and took a long sniff and leaned her head back on the headrest. I had to hold on to the wall to keep from collapsin'. *This girl is gonna kill herself,* I thought. I was walkin' as fast as I could to the front door, but it was too late. Cecilia had started the car engine, slammed her truck in reverse, and was screechin' out the driveway. Father help me!

Chloe

UNLIKELY STRANGER

I WAS FIDGETY AND my stomach churned as I checked my watch for the third time, looking out the window at Starbucks again. It wasn't the rainstorm outside, or the three lattes with extra shots that had me on edge, it was my anticipation of what, or rather who, was coming. I was about to get a refill, but Mother stopped me.

"You've had enough. Sit down," she ordered.

"Maybe we should go. I don't think she's coming."

"You all agreed on eleven o'clock and it's just ten fifty-five. The poor girl is on the road drivin' from Kentucky. She could be stuck in weather, anything."

"We would pick this nasty day to meet. Maybe this was a bad idea!"

"Stop it, Chloe! Her mama seemed as relieved as I am that at least her daughter ain't alone. We ain't goin' nowhere. This is part of the process to gettin' all the information you need to know about this boy, and having peace of mind."

Just then a white Cadillac Escalade pulled into the parking lot. A petite, cinnamon-skinned woman with shoulder-length hair opened an umbrella and escorted a conservatively dressed, older, silver-haired woman through the rain. Mother and I stood up to greet them.

"Shelly?" I hesitantly asked. My palms were sweaty. I wiped them on my sweatpants and reached out to shake her hand.

"Chloe?" She smiled. "Oh my God, it is so good to finally meet you!" she chirped, shaking my hand vigorously.

"Me too!" I pulled my hand away and immediately opened my arms to give her a girlfriend embrace. For a moment we were in our own world. As our mothers got acquainted, Shelly and I headed off to a quiet four top in the back of the café.

"This is so strange. I'm looking at you, but I feel like I'm looking at myself," I said. Shelly's mother had already excitedly noted over the phone how much we resembled each other after seeing the wedding photo of me and Gregorry in *Jet* magazine.

"Well, at least we can agree that Gregorry had great taste!" Shelly joked. We all agreed, giggling like schoolgirls.

"Thank you for stopping through here," I said, sipping gingerly from my cup. "I'm just trying to put the pieces back together in my life, and as terrible as this whole ordeal has been, at least I have some answers now."

"Chloe, I've been waiting almost ten years to bring closure to this whole mess with Gregorry. Thank you for finding me. When I saw your picture in the magazine, I almost had a heart attack." Shelly shut her eyes, as if the flash of her brief nine-month marriage to Gregorry shot a surge of electricity through her brain. When she reopened her eyes, tears trickled down her face. I reached out and touched her hand and was suddenly overwhelmed with emotion and began to cry too. "I just wanted to be a good wife," she said.

"When we started off he was so sweet to me. He said all the right things, kissed me, hugged me, told me he loved me. We would sit up and dream about building this great life together," I said, breaking down. Mother put her arm around my shoulder to comfort me. "I wasn't as young as you, Shelly," I said, wiping my eyes and clearing my throat. "But I was just as naive and trusting. All I wanted to do was be a good wife. I didn't want to fail. I wanted a family. He said he wanted the same things."

"Girl, Gregorry was adamant with me about having a child, but something told me to keep taking my birth control pills," Shelly recalled.

"He pushed with me too. But the difference is I'm thirty-five and you were in your twenties. I didn't tell you on the phone, but I just lost a baby almost two months ago."

"I'm so sorry."

"It was for the best; otherwise, I'd really be stuck with that fool."

Our mothers excused themselves for refills.

"Girl, before we got married, he would wake me up in the morning to have sex. I couldn't keep him off me, but once we got married I got nada! Nothing!" she said.

"Wait, we had sex all the time, but after the wedding I'd practically have to beg for it. I felt completely undesirable. That's why I was so sure I wasn't pregnant."

"At my wedding his father gave an elaborate speech about how he had never seen his son . . ."

"So much in love before . . ." I chimed in, finishing her sentence. The joy I felt that day flashed before my eyes.

I knew the exact dress I wanted. Cost was no object. Les Habitudes was one of the premier exclusive boutiques in Beverly Hills. Elaborate gowns reminiscent of the Victorian age lined racks throughout the airy and sleek store. I found a delicate beaded gown that seemed to have been molded for my body, crystal-encrusted shoes, and a cathedral-length veil that was something out of a storybook.

Nothing was going to ruin my perfect day, not even the fact that I hadn't met my rambunctious six-year-old stepdaughter, Courtney, until that morning, who by the way had arrived at the airport with her hair all over her head, and a dirty suitcase with dingy clothes and a set of old sheets inside. *Breathe, Chloe, breathe!* Oh, and let's not forget about Daddy, who didn't show up until moments before the orchestra began to play "Here Comes the Bride." It didn't matter, I was Joy Ann Michaels's baby girl and I could handle it! Generations of Davis women had been married at First A.M.E., including my grandmother Sarah.

Gregorry stood at the altar with tears streaming from his eyes. When I approached, he reached out his hand for me. "Stepmama," Courtney whispered loudly. "You look so purdy!" Ahh, my new stepdaughter. Poor thang just had no home training. But there was something about her. Maybe it was her bubbling-over personality. She was country, but smart as a whip. I mean children learn from what they see and hear. I could groom her to be a well-rounded young lady one day. The congregation chuckled and thought her outburst was cute. Gregorry was embarrassed.

The roses, the best imported champagne—the room bubbled over with love.

"I just want to say to Chloe," Gregorry's father, or Big Greg as he called himself, pulled the microphone away from his mouth and put his hand up to his eyes. He was so overwhelmed with emotion that he couldn't hold back his tears. "I've never seen my son so in love before. Congratulations!" He shed a few more tears, then raised his glass of champagne to the sky. There wasn't a dry eye in the dining room of the Crystal Ballroom.

I angrily slammed my fist on the table. Shelly stomped her foot furiously. Our wedding day ceremonies were almost identical, from the speeches, to the wedding party, to the unbalanced guest list. Three hundred people gathered to witness what was supposed to be the most important day of my life. However, two hundred and ninety-two of those people were my friends and family.

Gregorry's guest list consisted of his father, the best man; his uncle, a groomsman; and his estranged mother, Lydia. He called her *Linda*, out of disrespect. Oh and how could I forget Lydia's two teenaged children, her sister, Marion, who looked and acted like she was afraid of her own shadow, and his maternal grandmother, who had Alzheimer's, and of course, baby ghetto-hotmess Courtney, my lovely new stepchild.

"Do Jesus," Ms. Harris gasped.

"Lord!" Mother was equally flabbergasted.

"I can't believe he did this to us." I sat for several minutes in a zombielike state. Shelly continued running down the details from her "big day" that mirrored my own. After a while I was no longer angry or mad. I was emotionless.

"Well, I think the boy has a violent streak in him, too," Mother said, leaning into the table.

"Oh, he *is* dangerous! Shelly, tell them what happened that day I had to come get you from your house 'cause you feared that boy was gonna hurt you."

"Girl, I basically ran away from home," Shelly said.

"You too!" Both of our eyes went wide. "I just knew he was going to do something bad to me, knowing all that Scott Peterson stuff," I said.

"He kept these metal footlockers and threatened me if I opened them. I knew something bad was going on so I opened one while he was at work one day."

"Oh, my God! He kept two locked ones at my house! He went off one day when he thought I touched them," I said, shaking my head.

"Honey, he had all kinds of things, from books on changing your social security number, mix matched linen, photos of naked women, random pieces of china. I even found a woman's wedding ring. I was too scared to open the other one. I just knew I had to get out of there. Mama drove all night to come get me.

"As we were pullin' out the driveway, here Gregorry comes slammin' on his brakes, jumpin' out his car, bangin' on the windshield and the roof. 'Stop this goddamn car!' He was shouting like a crazy man. He demanded my wedding ring back. I kept one of those kid baseball bats in the backseat and Mama grabbed it! I picked up speed, but he wouldn't let go of the car door."

"Chile, I had that bat in my hands and started beatin' his hands with that li'l ol' bat until he screamed like a woman and fell off the car!" Ms. Harris shook her head back and forth.

"It was horrible. I never saw him again, but I had to file bankruptcy, and fight for *my* house," she said, sitting back down. "But that's how it goes down in Texas. It's all about community property."

"Same with California," I noted. "But I never put his name on anything I owned or changed my name. He's not taking my house!"

"Girl, I almost kissed the judge when I got it back. For all these years I've been holding so much inside. I have a wonderful family, but Gregorry Marion Robinson III has always been lurking somewhere deep in the back of my mind. I prayed and asked God to forgive me for hating him like I do, but I couldn't. But when I got your call, a door opened. Behind it there was so much pain, and meeting you here, today, I've been able to let it out.

"I will never forget what he did to me, but I'm thankful my husband had the patience to help me move on, and now those old wounds can finally heal. Please believe me when I say that Gregorry's time is up. He is a sick and sad person, but who are we to judge? That's God's job. Thank you for calling me. Thank you for helping me close that door for good."

Mother and I held hands as we watched Shelly and her mother walk away. I thought about those footlockers. Ain't no tellin' what's inside those things now. But like Shelly said, Gregorry, his locked trunks, his evil ways, is God's job to deal with. Then as sure as I'm living, breathing, and standing in Starbucks right now, we looked up and the sun had pushed its way through, just like the rain had never been there. It was all symbolic of our breakthrough.

As devastating as it all was, I felt a strange sense of relief knowing that I wasn't crazy. That I wasn't the failure. I was a victim. Shelly and I had even found a way to laugh and make light about some things. Ultimately, we were two wounded souls who had connected and found ourselves again. I was sure this wouldn't be the last of our conversations. We had bonded and I sensed a true friendship of unlikely strangers in the making.

Joy Ann
WHEEL OF FORTUNE

A S WE DROVE down the road adjacent to the shopping mall parking lot, Billye Jean's eyes lit up at the sight of the *Wheel of Fortune* sign that was all done up in colorful glitter. Several dozen people had already crowded around the sign and it was just eight in the morning.

"Excuse me, excuse me, excuse me," Billye Jean said, barrelin' her way through the people. "Me and my sista was here first," she said to a frail elderly woman, who looked to be about eighty-five. I didn't mind lettin' the poor woman go in front of us, but Billye Jean wasn't havin' it. That li'l ol' lady was no match for my sister. She gently pushed her to the side and we slid in line. "See, that's what I'm talkin' 'bout, Joy Ann, these folks is just rude," she whispered, clutchin' her chest.

"Girl, you okay?" I asked.

"I'm fine now that we got our spot," she said, catching her breath.

"I just hope we ain't here all day. I know I cain't be out here and not have nothin' to eat. Luckily, I ate breakfast but this line looks like it's movin' slow."

"Stop complainin', Joy Ann. Just think about that money we gonna make when we get on the show!"

An hour later the line had barely moved. Billye Jean had worried the poor man holdin' the walkie-talkie so bad he brought us out some foldin' chairs.

"Joy Ann, I swear I thought after I voted for Obama I could go home to my maker, but this is truly one of those times where you say to yourself, 'Self, if I die today I've done all the things I wanted to do!' You know what I mean?" We laughed.

"I know what you mean about thinkin' about your life," I said, puttin' on my sunglasses. "I been doin' a lot of that lately."

"Muh didn't live as long as us and I know we blessed," she said.

"I want my children to be okay no matter what."

"You know what your problem is, Joy Ann? You don't do enough for yourself." I gave her a confused look. "What I mean is, it's time you realize that your daughters are gonna be just fine. Even Chloe, 'cause we both know that sometimes you gotta go through it to get to the other side of your blessin'. She in some deep mess right now, but it's gonna make her stronger when it's all said and done.

"I'm the one feel bad 'cause look at how Junior turned out. I know I probably never say it, but you a good mother and I'm proud you are my sister. But I tell you, when I worked at the hospital, I'd be tellin' folks, ever'time somethin' come out in the paper about one of your art shows. I would tell all of 'em that you were my sister."

"No, you didn't." I smiled.

"Sure did! My sister was a celebrity!" We laughed and high-fived again.

"Billye Jean, somethin' just been botherin' me."

"What is it?"

"Havin' all my girls home right now, despite the circumstances, makes me happy. Being this age and not knowin' what tomorrow's gonna be like. Don't you miss Thora?" I asked.

"I talk to Thora just 'bout every day, Joy Ann." She was gettin' indignant.

"But there ain't nothin' like seein yo child. That's all I'm sayin'," I added.

Billye Jean began furiously wipin' her face with her sweat rag. "I need me some water." Billye Jean reached in her purse for her half-filled bottle of water, drainin' it and placin' it back down in her purse. "I do wish I could see Thora more often. I guess she just busy with her life," she said, clutchin' her chest as if gettin' out her words pained her heart.

"I just feel like you been sick for God knows how long and outside of poppin' in one day and out the next when you was in the hospital the last coupla times, we ain't seen Thora."

"It don't bother me, I swear. Stop worryin' yourself wit it, Joy Ann."

"I ain't gonna say nothin' else, then. If you happy, I'm happy."

"I'm happy," she replied for the last time.

And that was that. For the next hour we kept the conversation light, reminiscin' about being in the country as kids, and when we'd go back to MaMaw and Paw's farm when we got older. All the stories MaMaw would tell, especially the ghost stories. She'd leave the room after tellin' us a story and pop back around the corner with pancake flour on her face and scare us half to death. Yeah, we been through a lot as a family and as sisters, but the love runs too deep to break our bond. Come hell or high water!

After two and a half hours, we had made it almost to the front of the line. We better had been, 'cause that bond was about to get tested real good.

"Girl, we just five people away, thank God 'cause I'm gettin' hungry and I ain't got no more Glucerna bars in my purse," I said.

"Shoot, I gotta go to the bathroom, but I ain't hardly gettin' outta this line for nothin'."

My cell phone rang. The smile on my face dropped when I heard Carol Jane's panicked voice on the other end. "Calm down, Carol Jane!" I tried to shout over her, but she was too frantic.

"What done happened?" Billye Jean said, clutchin' her chest. I put my hand up to shush her.

"Oh, Lord! Oh, Lord! A baby? You jumped on her yesterday! Do Jesus!"

"What baby? Who had a fight yesterday?" I shushed Billye Jean again.

"Okay, calm down and just head on to my house. There's an extra key under the flowerpot. We'll meet you there!" I hung up and nervously paced in place. "Billye Jean, we gots ta go, right now!" I said, puttin' my purse on my shoulder.

"Wait a minute, we at the front of the line!"

"Lord, have mercy! Somethin' terrible done happened!"

"Shoot! We was almost on *Wheel of Fortune!*" she said, stompin' off like a dejected five-year-old.

Carol Jane was still shakin' like a leaf, lyin' flat across my daybed with a cold rag on her head. I looked at the glucose meter she was holding in her hand and was hoppin' mad.

"Four-twenty! Jesus, Carol Jane, that girl is gonna kill you! You know you have no business gettin' your pressure and your sugar up like this," I said. I cain't believe you waited a whole day to tell us this mess," I said, shaking my head.

"I know, Joy Ann. I don't know what came over me."

"Whatever it was, was long overdue," Billye Jean called out from the bathroom. Carol Jane sat up and removed the rag from her head and started wipin' her face.

"We just gotta decide what we gonna do about this baby now?" I said, fanning myself.

"We gonna have it, that's for certain!" Carol Jane proclaimed. The counsel had come to order and the decision was made. "I don't want Satin goin' back to Cecilia's either."

"I don't think you gotta worry 'bout that," Billye Jean said, suckin' her teeth.

"First thing, we gotta get the child back in school," I added.

"But what about her mama? I think Cecilia is doin' more than drinkin'. I think she's on that stuff again," Billye Jean said, exiting the bathroom, pulling up a seat next to me.

"Jesus! Me and Lawrence rolled out the red carpet for Cecilia." Carol Jane buried her face in her hands.

That they did. Ceci was homecomin' queen, and a debutante. She finished high school and went off to Lincoln University, but midway through her junior year her life took a turn. She started hangin' out with some low-end girls she met up in Jefferson City and dropped out.

"It's like everythin' Cecilia has done is to get back at me or somethin'." By now Carol Jane's tears were uncontrollable.

"I'll tell you what it is. The girl been rebellin' her whole life," I noted.

"You think it's 'cause the way she looks? I looked just like my mama, and she look just like me and I can't help that," Carol Jane said.

"Bingo! We need to just let it all come on out! Betta blame it on MaMaw. All this goes right back to her. You know she used to say that black-skinned people was evil. And she was blue-black herself. That's why she purposely went and got Paw, who was as fair as he was. Your mama, Aunt Cora, was white-lookin'. And then Carol Jane, well you know you ain't have no say." Billye Jean leaned back in her chair and smacked her lips and picked at her nails.

"Shut your mouth, right now, Billye Jean! I mean it!" I jumped out my seat so fast I almost knocked the chair over. "You always openin' your mouth and sayin' the wrong darn thing!"

Billye Jean crossed her legs in a huff. She swears MaMaw married Paw 'cause of color, and Muh did the same with Daddy. Muh was attractive herself. She wasn't thinkin' 'bout light or dark. She knew how to catch the attention of Daddy right away with her bossy tongue, uppity demeanor, and light-spirited humor. Daddy was a good man who *happened* to be light-skinned. He was extremely handsome and, yes, had some straight hair, but that ain't why she married him!

"Billye Jean, you still singin' that same tired song! I think you the one with the color complex! Look how light Arnaz is," I said.

"I wasn't lookin' for no light man, that just happened." Billye Jean was gettin' defensive. She realized she was the one who had done just what she accused Muh of doin'. She quickly turned her probin' back to me. "That ain't the point! The point is, Joy Ann, you know you never went with a dark-skinned person that I knew of. Both your husbands!" She was actin' like she was challengin' me to some kinda showdown.

"All the women in this family did not get no light-skinned man!" I was gettin' highly offended now.

"You *know* I'm right. This family is wrong, wrong, wrong! Carol Jane *is* light enough that somebody, if they weren't lookin' close enough, or maybe at a distance, would mistake her for being white," Billye Jean said.

"You sound like an old fool, Billye Jean!" I said.

"Joy Ann, she ain't said nothin' we don't know. I loved MaMaw, but I hate how this family values color." Now Carol Jane was tearing up some more. "I would've loved for my baby to be browner! I cain't help what happened. I know Cecilia been blaming me her whole life about how she look," Carol Jane said pitifully.

"See, I'm just speakin' the truth about this family!" Billye Jean said.

"Shut up for the last time, Billye Jean," I threatened, turning to Carol Jane. "And Carol Jane, you ain't gotta defend yourself. Billye Jean is crazy," I said, shakin' my head.

"Joy Ann, you'd be lyin' if you sat up here and said you never heard MaMaw say light was better." Billye Jean just kept pressin'.

"Billye Jean, stop being ridiculous!" I was so flustered I jumped up and began pacin' the tiny room.

"No, Joy Ann, I'm just gonna say it! I done held it in for over seventy years!" Billye Jean said, abruptly leaning forward.

"Then say it, dammit, so we can stop hearin' yo mouth!" I stopped pacin' and plopped back down in my chair.

"For one, Muh made a difference in us."

"What are you talkin' about, Billye Jean?" I said.

"Muh was always showin' you off to her friends and people at church 'cause you was half-white lookin'. Muh never paraded me around like that." Billye Jean's voice cracked and her eyes welled up with tears. "It was 'cause I was dark."

"So what I took after Daddy's people, and you took after Muh's side! We are too damn old to still be talkin' about this mess!"

"No, no, Billye Jean, Muh talked about you to everybody. How smart you was in the books, could do this and that. This is just goin' too far. Muh never did any of the things you sayin'. She loved you just as much as Joy Ann and it didn't have nothin' to do with color. I remember!" Carol Jane said, coming to my defense.

"Thank you, Carol Jane! Billye Jean, I sure hope you done diggin' up the untruths of the past, and about our own mother and grandmother, God rest their souls. I know they rollin' over in their graves. And for the record, you are not the darkest person in the family, and nobody has a color complex!"

"Enough!" Carol Jane commanded, clappin' her hands like a teacher does with a room full of unruly children. "None of this is gonna help me get Cecilia to realize she's got to do somethin' about her life and her child. Satin is out there livin' like she's grown, and she ain't even finished high school!"

"You're right," Billye Jean said, suckin' her teeth again, and Carol Jane scooted back in her seat and rubbed the palms of her hands on her chubby thighs. We all got quiet, but the moment was too good to be true. "If you ask me, Ceci just been gettin' away with stuff for too long, humph!" Billye Jean broke the awkward hush, fannin' herself. Me and Carol Jane both shot her a look.

"Hush, Billye Jean!" I swear, sometimes folks in this family don't believe that you shouldn't throw rocks when your own house is made of glass.

SURRENDER

I have known women
Troubled women w/sacks/satchels/bags and bundles of trouble
Women who serve trouble on a platter and chaos for dessert
Women who carry trouble like a bone w/tall tales and who shot
John about other women/lying women/women who sneaky pete at
the backdoor and cheat in the frontroom/seesawin/
hem-hawin/double-tongue lying women/thieving women who steal
your money/your honey and unlaugh your funny.
I have known women
Women peachcheeks/Maybelline/ruby lips/swingin' hips/face in
paint/full of haints/women who sleep in your backpocket/wear you
down to a nub/run you ragged as sauerkraut/women who dare "DO
RIGHT" to come round their stoop and make "GOOD STUFF" tuck
tail and haul ass/I know women who turn peace to piss and put a
hellhound at risk . . .

Chloe

THE STANDOFF

THE STANDOFF BETWEEN Ceci and Carol Jane hit the two-week mark. Mother and Aunt Billye Jean decided it was time to send in the troops. Carol Jane's sugar was so high she was on bed rest. Plus, Satin wasn't a little pregnant, she was more like seven months. That girl was so skinny it looked like she just stuck a volleyball under her shirt. Turns out she had also been camouflaging her bump all these months by wearing big shirts and loose clothing. All hell seemed to be busting loose.

Fawn, Eve, and I were enlisted to go find Ceci and talk some sense into her. Ceci hadn't been to work at the Post Office in days, the shop either, but we knew when all else failed she'd be at her third job. The club. We were here for official family business, but I was actually looking forward to getting out with my sisters. Tonight would be my first time hangin' out since coming home.

The St. Louis Room was a real laid-back, old-school, smoky-air, dark-lights, mirrored-wall, fried-chicken, big-hats type joint. We walked in and a whole row of brothas were seated at a table near the entrance. These brothas gave new meaning to a leisure suit. One brotha had on a cobalt blue suit, shirt, and tie, matching gator dress shoes, and a blue derby to top it off. I ain't mad, though. If nothin' else, folks in St. Louis get dressed to go to the club. It's an event. Shit, damn near a competition.

The DJ was playing Nelly's "Pimp Juice." How appropriate. Suddenly we heard a voice call out, "Hey, cousins!" It was Ceci. We walked over to her. She was standing behind the bar mixing a drink.

"What y'all doin' here? Annie, these my cousins. You remember Eve and Fawn," she called out loudly to another woman mixing drinks behind her.

Annie whipped around. She was a white girl with blond streaks and a mouth full of gold teeth. Damn, even the white folks had gold teeth at home. "Aw, whassup Eve, whassup Fawn," Annie said, wiping her hands on a towel. They waved. "And you that one out thur in Hollywood, right?" Annie said, nodding at me.

"Oh, yeah. That's me." I smiled politely.

"Girl, gon head wit yo family, I'll take over," Annie said, with a blinding smile.

"Give us a bottle of Moët, Annie. Chloe is my baby cuz, and we celebratin' 'cause she done kicked the Negro she was married to, to the curb!" Ceci downed the drink she had already made for herself. "Y'all know I had to get with Arnaz's woman the other night up in here. I was gonna whoop her 'til she rope like okra!"

"I'm in shock! Arnaz has a woman?" I said.

"Been had one. I been hearin' about her for a while. Folks in the streets be talkin'," Ceci said.

"Chloe, we've all known for a while, but it's not somethin' we talk about," Eve said.

"If I was Aunt Billye Jean, I would've left Arnaz a long time ago," Fawn said.

"Once a hustler, always a hustler. His old stankin' ass is seventy plus and still tryin' to hustle. She's some Korean, and Big Fred who work the door said she be boostin' for Arnaz, and he sell that hot shit right out of Aunt Billy Jean's own basement."

"You mean The Store?" Fawn asked. "Oh my God, I bought a pair of golf shoes for Cliff from him. Damn, Ceci, how you know about all these boosters?"

"Girl, hush! Arnaz be lyin' to her ass. I know a lot. Remember

216

when he worked at Six Flags and he would be tellin' her he was wor-kin' double and triple overtime, runnin' rides. Anybody in they right mind know ain't no amusement park open in the wintertime. Shit, somebody'll freeze they ass off tryin' to ride a roller coaster in tha snow." Ceci took a swig of Hennessy. "Yeah, Arnaz is an old dog with old tired tricks."

Just then, a brotha decked out in a yellow-and-black three-piece suit walked in the club. He had a neck full of gold chains instead of a mouthful, and he was wearing a pair of gold-rimmed Gazelle glasses, looking like a big-ass bumblebee pimp. He was sweating so bad I wanted to ask him if he needed a glass of ice water. I *know* he had to be hot in that suit. "My name is Leon, and you are beautiful," he said, walking up to Fawn. Fawn gave him a half smile. "You wanna dance?" She was so choked up, Eve answered for her.

"Yes, she will," she said, nudging Fawn. Fawn mouthed a series of curse words through gritted teeth, before taking a big swig of her champagne and being whisked away by Leon to the dance floor. When Eddie Levert of the O'Jays belted out that first note to "Let Me Make Love to You," I thought every woman in the room was gonna pass out. All I heard was, "That's my jam!" and "Sing it, baby."

I was surprised to see Fawn, as uppity as she acts, out on the dance floor cutting a rug with the bumblebee pimp. She was steppin' so hard I think she broke a sweat. She probably was thinking about that preacher man.

After the song, Fawn rejoined us. We were now seated at a table off to the side of the room. She was soaking wet. "Girl, I haven't stepped in years!" Fawn said, dabbing her face with the palm of her hand.

"We see," Eve said, handing Fawn a napkin. "You sweatin' up a storm."

"Here, girl." Ceci handed Fawn a freshly filled glass.

"You know, I gotta be up early. Plus, we really came here to talk to you," Fawn said.

"If my mama sent you here, y'all wastin' y'all's time," Ceci said, putting her hands on her hips.

"Hey Ceci, I need you for a hot sec. We got a big reunion comin'. I need you to authorize something," Annie interrupted, breaking the tension.

"Okay, Annie, I'm on my way," Ceci said, rushing off.

I turned around to see what all the ruckus at the entrance was about. It was a large group coming in. Three women spotted me out and rushed over to our table.

"Chloe!" I heard one of them call out. The voice was coming from a short, chocolate sista with long, flowing hair, dressed conservatively. She was extremely pregnant, looking like she was going to drop her load any minute.

Next to her was a thicker, hippy sista with a stylish short red cropped hairstyle and freckles. She was dressed expensively, but in an overdone name-brand kind of way. She had definitely seen too many hip-hop videos.

"Oh my God! Moose and LaRonda!" I screeched, jumping up. We gave each other a big group hug. Moose was obviously the larger one. "LaRonda! Look at you all pregnant!"

"All belly! Can you believe it?" LaRonda said with a big grin.

"Ah, excuse me." A falsetto voice belonging to a tall, thin, honey-skinned sista interrupted.

"Chinky!" I threw my arms up and gave her an equally warm hug. Chinky still had the same shape she had in high school. Her shoulder-length hair was streaked with bright red highlights. She got her nickname because of her slanted eyes. Her mother is Filipina and her daddy is black.

Chinky never had much of a sense of style. She dressed borderline tacky and always wore cheap-looking, trendy clothes. However, she was extremely pretty, with the breasts and booty of life. Chinky could drive the boys crazy back in the day with that combination.

Coming to the St. Louis Room was suddenly the best night of my entire visit. This was my old crew from high school, and I felt like I was a teenager all over again. For years LaRonda kept in touch, and kept me up on all the hometown gossip, but between moving cross-country, changing my number a couple of times over the years, starting my business, and just plain differences in lifestyle, we lost communication with each other.

"What are ya'll doin' here?" I asked excitedly.

"Girl, it's our high school reunion weekend, and after the banquet, some of us just wanted to come someplace close for a drink. Why ain't you come?" Moose asked.

"Moose, you know I didn't graduate from West, I graduated from Central," I said. Shoot, I had gone to three different high schools, and sometimes when I ran into old friends I had to stop for a minute to think about what school we met at. I turned to my sisters. "Eve and Fawn, these are my girls Moose, LaRonda, and Chinky. We went to school together. Y'all, these are my sisters."

After the cordials were exchanged, I slid over to the side of the bar to catch up with my girls. Annie brought over a ginger ale for La-Ronda, and two glasses of Hpnotiq for Chinky and Moose.

"So, girl, how's married life? Where's your husband?" LaRonda asked. "We all saw the picture in *Jet*!" I nearly choked on my drink.

"Everything's fine. He's back home in L.A." I coughed once more.

"How you gonna leave a fine brotha like that at home?" Moose said.

"I heard that!" They gave each other hand slaps in the air. "I get my hair done at the shop your cousin Ceci do hair out of and she showed us the pictures," Chinky said. "Personally, I thought you would've married an NBA or NFL player."

I suddenly felt awkward. They didn't know about the "Grand Opening" quickly followed by the "Grand Closing," also known as the wedding fiasco.

"I thought she would've married somebody like Jaheim. Girl, he know he fine! But, speakin' of pro-ballers, remember Lance James? Didn't you go out with him in high school?" Moose asked, polishing off the last drop of her drink.

"Fine-ass Lance James!" I exclaimed.

"Twelve o'clock, there he is," Moose said, pointing to a group of guys entering the front of the club. "He moved back here about two months ago." Moose always had the lowdown on everybody.

"I saw him about six or seven years ago at a party in New York. Isn't he playin' for the Knicks?" I asked curiously.

"*Was* playin'; his daddy died and he just walked away from everything to come be with his mother," she said. "Look at him, lookin' like a Denzel clone!"

"He still looks good," I said, covering my excitement. "So did he get married, too?"

"Widower," LaRonda interjected. "I know, 'cause him and Marcel are boys."

"Hey, Lance! Over here," Moose called out.

"What are you doin', Moose?" My heart quickened.

"Callin' him over. You askin' all these dang 'gon questions," LaRonda said, playfully swatting me.

"Lance, you remember Chloe." Moose thought she was slick.

"Hi, Lance." I smiled.

"Hey, Chloe; wow, I haven't seen you since that time we ran into each other in New York."

"Anyway, Chloe just got married, not too long ago. We gonna go get a table. Chloe, girl, don't leave town without callin' us." LaRonda handed me a piece of paper with all their phone numbers on it. I gave a round of good-bye hugs.

"Oh, I heard about your father. I'm sorry," I said to Lance.

"Thank you. It's been hard, but I'm taking it day by day. Congrats on your marriage."

"Yeah, yeah." I self-consciously pivoted and looked away.

"So is your husband here?" Lance asked.

"Actually, no, he's back, um, in L.A."

Just then Eve interrupted. "Hi, excuse me, Chloe, but we're gonna go in back to the VIP room to talk to Ceci."

"Lance, this is my sister Eve."

"Hi," Lance said with a friendly smile.

"Hi." Eve gave a stale greeting, before rudely turning toward me. "Hurry up!" Then she just stood there with her hands on her hips, screw-faced.

"I gotta go."

"Cool, handle your business."

"Chloe!" Fawn shouted from a distance. I turned and rushed away, joining Eve and Fawn who were waiting at the end of the bar.

"Who was the cute guy?" Eve asked.

"Look, we didn't come here to mack, we came here to handle things," Fawn said, covering her face with her hand. "Lord knows I don't want to run into anybody from my past up in here."

"That boy *was* fine."

"Beyond fine, but, honey, after all this shit with Gregorry, she needs time and that Negro needs a background check!"

"Please, the last thing I'm thinking about is a man. I got a crazy one on my hands who I can't even find. That was just Lance. I went to high school with him. And he played basketball for the Knicks, but just moved back."

"Got cut?" Eve said.

"No, retired. His father died not too long ago, so he came back to be with his mother."

"You know they say those basketball and football players are out there, freaky, on the down-low, everything," Fawn warned as we headed into VIP.

Ceci came into the VIP room with the half-empty bottle of Moët and the still corked second bottle in a bucket. She had a smaller bottle of Hennessy under her arm. She set the bottles and the bucket on the table and lit up a cigarette. "I know y'all here to talk about Mama. Aunt Joy Ann left me a message that she was sick," she said, pouring champagne in our glasses and then pouring herself an additional glass of Hennessy.

"Ceci, you know you need to make peace with your mama," Eve said as she wasted no time getting to the point.

"Mama need to make peace wit me! You shoulda seen how she jumped on me."

"But you were wrong, and she's still your mama. She said you had been drinking and were high and not off no weed. I thought you stopped doing that crap?" Fawn questioned.

"Okay, so I was a little high, but I had a right. Satin said her stomach was hurtin' so I take her to the doctor and find out she's pregnant. Then on the way home, I'm already mad as hell, she gon jus tell me she wasn't goin' back to school. Can you believe that? Sixteen years old tellin' me, her mama, that she droppin' out. Let Mama tell it she'll have ever'body thinkin' I'm on drugs."

"What you put in your body is your business, but Satin can't get anywhere in life without a high school diploma," I said.

"I told her she was stupid. I told her if she was quittin' school, then I was quittin' being her damn mama. Then I commenced to beatin' her ass, right there in the truck!"

"Ceci, I know you're mad, but beatin' the girl is no answer, and it surely ain't gonna help at this point," Fawn said, shaking her head.

"I know, that's why I put her out, to teach her a lesson!" Ceci lit up a fresh cigarette.

"Well, who's the baby's daddy?" Eve asked.

"Some boy named Poo, but she don't know where he is. When she told him she was pregnant, he disappeared. All I know is I'm still gettin' my party on, my drink on, and I cain't stop and help her ass raise no baby. I'm through wit it. Plus, my mama acts so disgusted with me and I'm sick and tired of her, Joy Ann, and Billye Jean trying to compare me to all y'all. I'm sorry, but I got my own life. I'm forty-seven muthafuckin' years old."

"Ceci, you need to lower your voice," Fawn said, looking around the room.

"I ain't gonna never be like y'all asses or they asses. Mama still with Daddy, who ain't slept in the same bed with her in twenty years. They don't talk, they don't even eat together. Y'all see how big mama is? All she do is eat 'cause she unhappy. Aunt Joy Ann ain't much better. What she need is a man. Ray moved on a long time ago with that young piece he got."

"Shut the hell up, Ceci!" I screeched.

"Oops, I forget ya'll get sensitive 'cause you think yo mama and daddies is perfect," Ceci snapped.

"You always runnin' your mouth," I said. "Runnin' it about stuff you don't know nuthin' about!" She was starting to really piss me off.

"I know enough! I can go down the list. My mama, yo mama, Aunt Billye Jean's ass!" Ceci's words were slurring. She finished off the first bottle of Moët and chased the last drop in her glass by downing a glass of Hennessy. Then she popped the cork to the second one and started refilling our glasses. We watched her in awe. Ceci was definitely on something strong. Her eyes were completely ablaze, and her movements were quick and jerky.

"You calm now? 'Cause since you up here talkin' 'bout family and blood being thicker than water, you sure ain't actin' like it. You need to get right with yo mama!" Eve said. Her patience for the situation was getting thinner by the moment.

"Who the hell you think you are, Eve, tellin' me what I need to do about my mama when you don't treat yo own mama worth a shit half the time!" Ceci said.

"First of all, I don't go up in my mama's house drunk, high, cursin' and abusin' her like you do. Me and my mother have gone through a lot, but I love my mother," Eve shouted.

"And now I don't love my mama!" Ceci screamed.

"You sure don't act like it!" Fawn said, jumping in between the face-off. "You need to take a hard look at yourself. Yo mama ain't done nothin' but give you everything. She done practically raised your daughter. She takes all your shit and still gets down on her knees and prays for you every damn night!"

"I'mma say this shit fo the fuckin' record! There are some things that ain't my Mama's business. What I do with my life don't have nothin' to do wit her!" Ceci slammed the palms of her hands on the already wobbly table, causing it to shake back and forth.

"I made up my mind a long time ago that Ceci had to live her life for Ceci, not Carol Jane. This is *my* family up in this here club! *They* know I'm down!" Ceci shouted, then stumbled slightly.

"Look, y'all, we gettin' outta hand!" I interrupted.

"Yeah, everybody does need to calm down," Eve agreed.

"To hell with this! Y'all don't come up in my job, tryin' to call me out. All y'all gangin' up on me, actin' all high and mighty. Eve, you need to check yo'self. You so dependent on a man you act like you gone die if you ain't got one. I run my own show. No man can ever kick me out 'cause it's *my* damn house. Ask Satin daddy. He wasn't shit so I divorced him and put *his* ass out!" Ceci shouted.

"What are you talkin' about? I ain't desperate for no man, and I've always taken care of my child, unlike you. You think you know so much, your own child's belly was swelling and you didn't even know it because you stay so damn drunk and high!" Eve jumped up like she was ready to throw down. Fawn grabbed one arm and I grabbed the other, holding her back, "And for the record, Henry didn't put me out. I left! My child is in college, doin' somethin'. What about yours?"

"Naw, let her go. I used to kick yo ass when we was little. You feel froggy, jump!" Ceci challenged.

"Eve! This is family. She don't know what she's saying, she's on drugs. Let's go. I can't deal with this shit, Chloe! We'll be in the car," Fawn said, turning away and exiting.

"Aw, the kitchen's too hot, Fawn. Take yo ass on, please. You comin' up in here wit yo tight ass always actin' like yo shit don't stink. No wonder yo husband don't never come home. I'mma tell you what you need. You need to get you *some*!"

"And you need to get yourself in check!" Fawn flashed Ceci a look that cut her in half, then grabbed her purse. I reached out my hand and tried to stop her.

"Stop trying to fix every damn thing, Chloe," Eve said, storming out the club.

"I cain't believe this shit! I really cain't believe you, Chloe! I could talk all about yo fake ass, but I ain't got no words for you. You just straight tripped on me," Ceci said with hurt and rage-filled eyes, knocking over the glasses on the table and storming off to the bathroom.

I collected my anger and decided to make one last attempt to talk sense into Ceci. When I walked into the ladies' room, Ceci had just finished taking a hit of coke and was coming out of the bathroom stall, smoking a cigarette. Her nose was red and runny, and she was wiping the powdery residue from the tip. "What do *you* want now?" she said, taking a drag, wiping her nose again with a wad of toilet paper.

"Whatever you think about us ain't all that important, but you owe your mama. And by the way, nobody ganged up on you. We love you. That's why we came here," I said, spinning on my heels and walking out the bathroom. I left Ceci sitting in her own stew of shit, staring in the mirror at what a mess she was.

Eve

MEDDLIN' IN MY BUSINESS

SURPRISE!

Dale's deadpan face was a dead giveaway that my birthday surprise was a fizzle. I was a nervous wreck watching him stand at the head of the table next to his homely looking sister, who was more than a little underdressed in a jean shirt and leggings. Charmaine was expressionless, and her country-ass husband, LeBron, just kept asking how long they were going to be here.

I could hear Mother mumble to Fawn, "Can you believe this man is actin' so ugly?" Fawn shushed her. Chloe rolled her eyes.

"Well, let's all sit down." I motioned for the waiter to give us a few minutes. Dale sat down and you could see he was fuming. I could only imagine what he was going to say after dinner.

"You okay, baby? You want a drink?" He cut his eyes at me and didn't even dignify my question with an answer. Everyone at the table watched in silence. I could feel Mother's energy and ignored her as best as I could, but Mother can just give those looks and you just wanna put a bag over her head or something.

"I'm going to the bathroom," Chloe said as she stood up.

"Me too." Fawn followed.

"I'll be back," I said. Dale blew out a puff of air.

"Yeah, go check on the other two musketeers. I know you can't make a move without them," he said, leaning into my ear. I was glad Mother didn't hear him.

"It'll only take a minute, please, Dale." I quickly adjusted my mood when the waiter handed me a wine list.

"Mother, how about some wine? What about y'all?" I said, nodding at Charmaine, who had an equally displeased smile on her face by now. LeBron at least looked a little friendlier.

"We don't drink, but thank you very much," he said, looking like Mr. Humble Pie. I was over it! How we gonna be at the damn wine bar and they don't drink.

"Sir, can you just start with their orders," I said to the waiter, pointing to Dale and his sister and brother-in-law. Maybe once the food got here Dale would lighten up. Then I said, "Excuse me," getting up and going to the bathroom where Eve and Chloe were. I was torn because I really didn't want to leave Mother alone with Dale. Sometimes she just doesn't know how to keep her mouth closed.

"Why did y'all leave the table like that?" I asked in a panicked tone as I checked my makeup in the bathroom mirror.

"Eve, I'm sorry, but I'm not comfortable. I'm watching Dale and it just reminds me of what I went through," Chloe said.

"First of all, let me stop you right now. Dale and I have a four-year history and I think this is far from Gregorry. I realize you have some issues to work through and it's going to take a while, but I can't control that. Dale has been under a lot of pressure at work, and he was pissed at me from earlier today. Don't worry. Can you all please just come back to the table?" I begged. "I just don't want this night to be ruined. Please?"

"You know what, Eve, I'm just going to have a drink at the bar and then I'll be over there." Chloe brushed past me.

"Eve, you aren't being sensitive to her at all!" Fawn reprimanded.

"I can't even believe I have to deal with other people's emotional baggage when this is *my* boyfriend's birthday. I have him to worry about. Y'all just have to wait!" I walked out.

When it's all said and done, I was not going to have my man break up with me over some temperamental family shit.

"Where are Chloe and Fawn?" Mother frowned when I returned to my seat.

"They're at the bar," I said, sitting down and picking up the menu. "Baby, whatchu think you want to eat?" I asked. He cut his eyes at me again.

"We already ordered the roasted chicken," LeBron answered. Charmaine had an equally hardened scowl on her face.

"I'm going to find them!" Mother scooted her chair away from the table, and just as she was about to get up, Dale had to clown.

"Excuse me." Dale balled his napkin up and threw it on the table. "I'm going to the bathroom, and then we can go, Charmaine and LeBron!"

"Eve, can I talk to you for a minute?" Mother said, giving me that look again.

"Mother, not right now, please," I answered abruptly. It was bad enough Dale was givin' me grief, but this was not a good time for Mother to give me her opinion.

I raced over to meet Dale before he went into the men's bathroom. "Dale, what's wrong? I've been breaking my neck to make your birthday special, but you just aren't happy."

"Back up a few words. You've missed the entire point. Today is my birthday, Eve. But since you asked, this whole day has been handled wrong. Why wasn't your call the first call of the day? Damn, your call wasn't even the second or the third."

"Okay, why are we still stuck on that? I'm sorry, but I went in early so that I could have this party for you tonight, and we got slammed at work. I didn't get a break until after twelve."

"Sometimes it's thinking about your priorities. You still don't get it. By the time you called, my birthday was at the halfway mark. But what's crazy is that my ex-girlfriend even remembered to call me to tell me happy birthday."

"Dale, are you really being fair?"

"You're never going to get it, Eve. And if that wasn't bad enough, I come to dinner with your entire family. Why would I want to spend my birthday with your mama? This should be about me and you. Then you have my sister and her husband up in here, and you know they don't drink. Or did you forget that, too? I'd say you need to think about some things seriously and then we can talk. I'm outta here!" Dale said, storming back to the table.

Dale's words ripped right through me. I struggled to pull myself together, but I was determined not to cry. I sucked up my tears that were on the verge of busting through my eyes and made my way back to the table. By the time I got there all hell was really about to break loose.

"No, I'm not sittin' back on this one. These men are goin' crazy. You owe my daughter an apology for ruinin' this nice dinner."

"Mother, just let it go! We just need to leave!" I said, starting to cry.

By this time Fawn and Chloe were racing over to the table.

"What's happening?"

"What's happening is we are leaving and you need to get your family under control. With all due respect, Ms. Michaels, this is between me and Eve," Dale sternly replied.

"Son, when you hurt my daughter, it's no longer between you and her."

"Eve, I assume you're taking care of this." Dale pointed to the half-touched plates of food that Charmaine and LeBron had ordered. The two of them still hadn't opened their mouths. Dale motioned for them to follow, and the three of them walked out.

My birthday surprise had fizzled.

The water swallows me up again. I slip under, deeper and deeper. And just like always, I'm struggling to swim to the surface. But wait! This time I can see a hand reaching in. Someone's going to rescue me. I try to shout, "Here I am, down here!" But my words are sucked into the current. I look up with pleading eyes and the hand is now on top of my head, and begins to push me down. The bubbles escape my mouth. I see that the person holding me down is a woman, but I can't make out her face. Air bubbles continue to escape. I'm choking. Her hand is forcing me down, deeper and deeper . . .

Chloe
KITCHEN TOO HOT . . . GET OUT!

IT WAS FRIDAY and that meant fish fry Friday at Aunt Billye Jean's. She was finally getting her day to entertain at her house. Aunt Billye Jean's house was always so clean you could eat off the floor. Now, her taste in furnishings and decor is questionable. Her color scheme is a combination of burnt oranges and washed-out browns and greens, and she's got too many pictures on the walls, pictures of folks that aren't even relatives.

We were all seated around the kitchen table. Mother was too mad about what happened at Dale's dinner, and Carol Jane had gone into deep prayer about Ceci, but I didn't see much hope on that one. We were all avoiding Eve's situation like the plague, so Ceci had become the focus.

"I'm tellin' you it's that crack that done got hold of her," Mother said, placing a large serving dish down on the dining table between two other large bowls. It was piled high with golden brown fried catfish. The other two bowls were each filled with coleslaw and spaghetti.

"Humph! Might be that smack," Aunt Billye Jean added, grabbing a piece of fish off the plate, crunching on its crisp fried tail.

"It's gonna take either death or a personal visit from Jesus to set that Ceci straight," Mother said in disgust, sitting down, folding her arms across her full bosom and leaning back in her chair. "We betta do somethin' fore that girl kill her mama and herself. Don't yo church have that program, Billye Jean? The one Junior been in?" Mother asked.

"Y'all know Ceci ain't gone go get in no program, and you see what it's done for Junior!" She chomped down on the crispy fried tail fin she was holding in her hand. "I don't know why y'all foolin' y'all selves," she added, licking her fingers.

"I'm through! From the way she carried on and how she talked to me, she must be on a whole buncha drugs. She had her nerve tryin' to tell me about my husband!" Fawn plopped a dollop of coleslaw on her plate.

"Fawn, Ceci was foul, but kinda had a point," I said, making my rounds sampling each dish.

"Somebody tell me what the chile said," Aunt Billye Jean demanded, holding up her hand, which was glistening with fish grease.

"Basically, *she* said Fawn is runnin' her husband away." Eve had no tact when it came to getting her point across.

"Well now, baby, don't pay no attention to Ceci. But you could soften up a bit. I told you that a long time ago," Mother said, scooping two heaping spoonfuls of coleslaw out of the bowl and dropping them on her plate.

"I ain't thinkin' about Ceci!" Fawn said.

"Well, I just feel bad for Carol Jane. She wanted that girl to love her so much," Mother said, switching subjects. She shook her head and reached for the serving bowl filled with spaghetti. Eve frowned, watching Mother pile an equally manly serving of spaghetti on her plate.

"You know, Mother's appetite is ravenous," Fawn whispered loudly.

"Mother, look at all that food you eatin'!" Eve commented with disdain.

"I don't hardly eat that much. I wish y'all would leave me alone," Mother said, defensively.

"The woman's practically seventy years old. If she wanna have another helpin', let her do it in peace," Aunt Billye Jean said, jumping in, steadily chomping on her catfish bones.

Eve's cell phone interrupted. She checked the caller ID and rolled her eyes.

"I'm so sick of him!" Eve said, rolling her eyes again. Her cell continued to ring.

"Shut that thing up already!" Fawn said, giving Eve an impatient glare.

"Hello!" Attitude immediately jumped all over Eve's face. We could hear Henry's voice booming through the phone all the way across the room. Eve's face tightened up. "Did you send the money? Well, I wouldn't have called her if you had done what you were supposed to do. Handle your business, Henry!" Her contorted expression telegraphed that she had had enough of his mouth. "Oh, oh, oh, no you didn't!"

Click.

Eve hung up on Henry, who was in the middle of giving her an earful of obscenities.

"See what I mean?" Fawn said, with a nod toward Eve. "You need to go in the other room with that mess, Eve," she added, shaking her head.

"Don't tell me what I need to do. This is my business!" Eve snapped.

"Eve, you ought to be tired of all that hollerin' with Dale and Henry," I said, sliding my two cents in.

Just as Eve was about to smart off, her cell rang again. She answered, ready for battle.

"Call me when you wanna talk like an adult!"

"Eve, that's enough!" Mother reprimanded.

"Go outta here with all that!" Aunt Billye Jean ordered, pointing to the side door. Eve got up and went into the garage, slamming the door behind her. We could hear Eve screaming at the top of her lungs, threatening to take Henry to court.

"Now watch she already got an attitude 'cause of Dale, but now she gonna be really actin' ugly 'cause of Henry. I know my child," Mother said.

"I don't know what she'd be takin' him to court for. He ain't got no money. The man has six kids and two more on the way," Fawn said flippantly.

"Whatchu talkin' 'bout?" Aunt Billye Jean said, prying. You could never slip some good gossip past her ears.

"I knew it! I dreamt of fish!" Mother screeched.

"Mother! Eve is not pregnant! Henry got somebody else pregnant and he's supposed to be gettin' married, too!" Fawn's big mouth had done it again. A series of *ooohs* and *aahs* stirred in the room.

"Fawn, maybe you shouldn't be telling all Eve's business," I said through gritted teeth. "You know you are setting things up to be a big argument."

"I can't believe it!" Mother slapped the palm of her hand across her forehead.

"I can," Aunt Billye Jean said, sucking so hard on her catfish bone it whistled.

"I'm sorry, but everybody's gonna know sooner or later anyway." Fawn was trying to justify her slip of the tongue.

Just then Eve reentered the house; she looked like she had been crying. She sat down and resumed eating her fish and spaghetti.

"Is everything okay, baby?" Mother apprehensively asked.

"No, it's not, Mother! I ain't Fawn or Chloe. I don't have nobody takin' care of me and givin' me no money!" Eve was lashing out at Mother as usual.

"Wait a minute! Now I won't have you talkin' to me like a dog. Every time somethin' goes wrong wit you and Henry or that crazy boy Dale, you wanna throw it on me!" Mother got up from the table and walked over to the kitchen sink, dropping her plate in with a loud clank. She dramatically put her fist up to her mouth, tightly closed her eyes, and began shaking her head back and forth as if she were fighting back a dam of tears.

"Don't be talkin' to yo mama like that," Aunt Billye Jean said sternly.

"I don't know why you wastin' breath on her. That's like tryin' to get blood from a turnip," Mother called out, looking up to the heavens.

"I wish we woulda talked ta Muh like that! Cain't nobody help it you gotta man who cain't keep his pants up! Havin' babies all over the place," Aunt Billye Jean wisecracked.

"Who told?" Eve shouted, shooting both Fawn and I a look. "Fawn, I bet it was your big mouth. This is real foul. I would never go tell somethin' that you asked me not to!"

"I don't see what the big deal is. Y'all always actin' like everything is such a big secret!" Fawn said, throwing her hands into the air like she had been victimized.

"Eve, you need to stop takin' stuff out on your family about these men in your life." Mother walked back over to the table.

"Mother! Stay out of this! I'm sick of you always jumpin' in stuff. If I wanted the whole world to know, I would've told everybody!" Eve's voice was building to an unbearable, piercing pitch.

"But when you in trouble, you want me in it! I'm tired of you talkin' to me bad. This will be yo last day raisin' yo voice to me!" Mother stormed out of the kitchen into the back bedroom in tears.

"I want all this hollerin' and mess to stop! Done got my sista all upset!" Aunt Billye Jean rushed to comfort Mother.

"Fawn, I will never trust you again. You put my business in the street!"

"Family is not the street! Get a grip, Eve! I can't be around all this today! I am gettin' my child and leaving!" Fawn shouted, walking over to the French doors that opened up to an upper patio and deck off the kitchen, calling out for Lola to come inside.

"This is so childish!" I said, under my breath.

"Oh, but when it's about your funky little drama, everything is so damn important!" Eve said. "I'm leavin'!"

Eve stormed out and slammed the door. Yes, Eve had done it again. Fish fry Friday was over and the fat lady had even snuck in an encore.

Fawn

SANCTIFIED SLAP

I HAD ANOTHER MEETING scheduled with Pastor Gibbs. It took me two days to figure out the "right" outfit. I wanted to look conservative—after all he was still a preacher—but still give that touch of inner vixen. I picked out a pencil skirt that hugged just so in the perfect places, and my silk blouse still represented a respectable church-going woman. Sensible pumps would be appropriate. I made the final touches to my ensemble by hiding a bit of Vicky's Secret underneath.

I turned into the church parking lot and gave myself the once-over in the rearview mirror, popping an Altoid in my mouth. When I got to the door of the church rectory, I don't know what came over me. I think I got cold feet. I contemplated turning back. I shook it off and decided what the hell, I deserved a little adventure.

I had no idea that when I turned the knob to Pastor's office, I would catch a profile of him anointing Sister Raynell Clark doggy style. I stood in the doorway with my mouth wide open. Pastor didn't even realize I was standing there. I quietly closed the door and took a seat in the hallway, trying desperately to collect myself.

When I got back home, still shell-shocked, I decided to sulk in a hot bubble bath. Cliff was out golfing again and Lola was at a friend's sleepover. I just kept replaying the sight of Pastor and Raynell going at it, swapping sweat and slapping asses. I was even more depressed, sinking deep into the tub and under the water.

Cliff finally came home at about midnight and tiptoed into the bedroom. My back was to him and he thought I was asleep, but I was wide awake. As he climbed into bed I sniffed the air, catching a whiff of a strange scent. It was strong, but sweet and chocolatey. I never wore heavy fragrances, so my senses were extrasensitive.

"What's that smell, Cliff?" I asked, startling him.

"Fawn, you're goin' to give me a heart attack. I thought you were asleep."

"Well, I would've been, but that smell"—I sniffed again—"that's perfume!" I said, rising up.

"Sorry, after golfing, me and my buddies chilled at the clubhouse and ran into some other lawyers at the firm. One of them had a date and she had really strong perfume on. Her sweater was on my chair." Cliff adjusted his pillow and got comfortable.

End of story. Cliff didn't have anything else to say, and although I was suspicious, I lay back down, still exhausted from my traumatic encounter at Pastor's office. I closed my eyes tightly and forced myself to fall off to sleep.

The next morning Mother enlisted me, Chloe, and Eve to go to church. It was Family Day. She was adamant that Eve and I squash our beef. I picked up Eve first, and we barely said two words. By the time we got to Mother's I was so over going to church I just wanted to drop them all off and keep going, right over the edge of the downtown waterfront and into the Mississippi River. I honked my horn impatiently outside in Mother's driveway.

"All right already! We're coming," Chloe yelled out the screen door.

"Good morning," Chloe said, sliding into the backseat. Normally, we'd all hug and kiss, but I guess nobody was feelin' all that.

"Mornin'," I said flatly.

"Mornin'." Eve was equally unenthusiastic.

"Where's Mother?" I said sharply.

"She took her insulin and had to fix something to eat," Chloe said. Eve and I both rolled our eyes.

Fifteen minutes later, Mother scooted into the backseat holding a half bacon, egg, and cheese sandwich wrapped in a greasy napkin.

"The peace of the Lord be with all of you this morning." She smiled, taking a large bite of her sandwich. Egg and bacon clumsily slipped out of the bread and landed on her skirt. Mother paid it no mind. Eve and I both greeted her back, making poor attempts to sound jovial.

"Oh, Fawn, you should've told Cliff to come with us this mornin'. And where's my granddaughter? It's Family Day." Mother frowned.

"Lola did a sleepover, and I don't know what Cliff has planned today," I said with a tight jaw.

"Ain't he yo husband," Eve joked.

"He's my husband, but I don't keep a leash on him. I have my own life!"

"Maybe you should," I heard Eve mumble. I was so not in the mood. I turned the gospel station up and bit my tongue.

"Stop it! I want some peace in this family!" Mother ordered.

By the time we got to the church there were no parking spaces.

"You know we're gonna be late and I hate being late. There are never any seats at your church." I was clearly agitated.

"Fawn, I couldn't move any faster than I was movin'," Mother said.

"But you know what time church starts, Mother," I said.

"Mother, why would you wait to when we was leavin' to fix breakfast?" Eve chimed in, letting out a sigh.

"Just let me out. I'm not havin' y'all mess up my Sunday mornin'. Pull over!" Mother was adamant. She jumped out and instructed Lola to come with her.

"Now was that even necessary. Y'all both jumpin' down Mother's throat," Chloe said.

"You always jumpin' to Mother's defense, Chloe," I grimaced.

"Whatever! I do not!"

"Yes, you do, like you have to protect her or somethin'. That makes me sick," Eve added. I finally found a parking spot two blocks away. Mother was out of her mind to think all of us going to church was gonna help us get along.

Okay, so I was wrong. Something about what Reverend Yancy was saying hit home. I know it's a cliché, but doesn't it feel like sometimes when you're going through stuff, you go to church and the message is for you?

"Ephesians talks about the core of family. Scripture says, 'Yield to obey each other, because you respect Christ. Wives yield to your husbands as you do the Lord. The man who loves his wife loves himself.' Now, I don't know about y'all, but I know about me and my wife," Reverend Yancy jokes. Laughter trickled throughout the church.

"I know we're all challenged in our relationships and households, but understanding one another, patience, and the Church as your centerpiece is essential to healing our families."

As I listened, I suddenly felt so guilty about what had been happening with me and Pastor Gibbs. I was so taken by the spirit I was led to the Altar Call. I just wanted hands to be laid on me. Not unclean ones, not ones that had been touching all over every other woman in town. I just wanted safe hands on me. Sometimes I just feel like I'm at a breaking point, but no one in my own household, or my family, not even Mother understands. Not even me.

Chloe

GRANDMA'S HANDS

"HEY, SWEET PEA . . ." Daddy's voice trailed off weakly. Something about his tone gave me a bad feeling instantly.

"What's going on, Daddy?" My hand tightened around the phone.

"Hey look here"—he took a deep breath—"Mama passed this mornin'." He held the rest of his words in a choke hold. I knew it was bad, but not this. Not her.

"What? What? No, no, no, Daddy!"

"Yes, baby. She's gone, Chloe. Oh, God!" Daddy broke down. His wail turned into a deep, agonizing howl. I was speechless, paralyzed. I needed Mother, but she was out running errands. I was disoriented and my motor skills weren't allowing me to think or move any faster. I had to get to Daddy. I wanted to be with him. Be his little Sweet Pea, make it okay.

I grabbed my purse and ran out of the house in my pajamas and sneakers. I ran as fast as I could up to Salvatore's. My vision was blurry and my face was soaking wet with tears.

"Salvatore! Salvatore!" I was shouting frantically by the time he opened the door. "She's dead! Please, my grandmother!" My words were jumbled, but Salvatore pieced them together and wasted no time rushing me to his car.

We ran every red light and in light-speed time Salvatore had gotten me to Grandmother's. The front door was wide open and when

I walked into her apartment, the coffee table was pushed back at an angle, the dining room chairs were clustered in a corner.

"Daddy?" I called out, making my way through her apartment. Daddy was in her bedroom, sitting on the bed staring out the window. I leaned over and wrapped my arms around his neck, and we both cried until there were no more tears.

Mother, Eve, and Fawn arrived. Thank God. I was sitting on the couch, and Daddy was seated at the dining table. "Oh, Daddy, I'm so sorry!" Fawn's face was swollen from crying as she rushed over to hug him. Eve appeared to be in a state of shock. She was so overcome with emotion her eyes filled up with puddles of tears like potholes after a hard rain. She kept blinking to hold them in place.

Mother took my face in her hands and kissed my forehead, then walked over to Daddy. She gently put her hands on his shoulders when he looked up and began to cry again. He bowed his head, and Mother pulled him in to her bosom. Eve and Fawn sat down on both sides of me. They both started talking fast at the same time, apologizing about all the fighting that had been going on. It was okay. It was all okay.

I was glad they were there, but I wanted *her*. I wanted to sit at the breakfast table where we would have our Saturday meals when I was growing up. I wanted to see her, touch her, but she wasn't there anymore. I would have to pack my memories away in my "hurt-up" chest that was already almost full.

"Ray, you've gotta call Diane and tell her about Millie," Mother said.

"I know, Joy Ann, I'm just so angry right now. Why wasn't she ever a real daughter to Mama? I don't wanna call and tell her nothin'!" Daddy pounded his fist on the wall and began pacing.

"You have got to let go of your anger and call your sister and tell her," Mother said, putting her hand on Daddy's shoulder and looking him squarely in the eye. It didn't matter that they weren't together anymore. Daddy listened to Mother. She handed him the phone.

Diane sat quietly in the back of the room alone, clutching the hem of her dress. As the wake was ending, I walked up to Diane and tried to hug her, but she vehemently pushed me away. Carol Jane grabbed me and pulled me away from her. "Chloe, you got to let it be."

Later that night, she seemed to become even more angry. As the house was clearing out, I found myself sitting alone in Grandmother's bedroom. It still didn't seem real. I examined her ring on my finger, and for a moment my hands looked like hers. Aunt Diane appeared in the doorway.

"Hi."

"Hi," she replied in a formal tone.

"You okay?"

"No, I'm not," she snapped.

"I know this isn't easy for any of us," I said, wiping my nose.

"I'm appalled at this entire night!"

"What are you talkin' about, Diane?"

"I'm talking about that circus of a wake!"

"What?" I was confused.

"Catholics don't participate in all this type of hoopla. People are in the other room laughing like this is a party. This was your doing, Chloe. I wanted to have Mama's body cremated right away, settle the business, and that would be the end. But no, we had to have a wake, and this nonsensical funeral. Where are all her papers? I know she used to hide money and valuables. Where is everything, Chloe?"

"I don't know what the hell you're talkin' about, Diane! And I hope you aren't accusing me of anything. I honored Grandmother. And those people in there are her friends, remembering the good times they shared with her. She was dedicated to her religion, her church, to charity, and her club. But you never came around, so I guess you wouldn't know that!"

"I had a different relationship with my mother than you did, Chloe."

"I should hope you did. She was your mother!"

"You don't understand. She made me hate my father."

"Whatever you're still holding against her or Granddaddy, you need to let it go. They're both dead! I'm not the enemy!"

Just then Eve came back in the room.

"What is goin' on?" she questioned.

"Nothing!" Diane stormed out.

I broke down crying again.

I was dreading this morning. Today would be the last day I'd ever see her again. I stood in front of Grandmother's dresser mirror, while Mother sat on the bed in the background, sniffling, fighting back her tears. I suddenly began to laugh.

"Praise the Lord, you found your laughter again," she said softly.

"I just thought about how Grandmother was always so prim and proper and buttoned up all fancy like Easter Sunday, even when it was a hundred degrees outside."

"Tell me about it. I'd be takin' Millie shoppin' and you know I hate the mall. Her feet would be squashed down in them li'l bitty fancy shoes of hers."

Fawn walked in. "What are y'all laughin' about?"

"How vain Grandmother was," I said, with a chuckle.

"Well, Millie. We gonna send you off right today. With all the laughter and love this family has shared with you." Mother put one arm around Fawn and the other around me and we headed out to say our final good-byes.

I imagined it was just like Grandmother would've wanted. A traditional Catholic funeral mass, except Aunt Billye Jean played a rousing "His Eye Is On the Sparrow" and Carol Jane sang it 'til the song cried. The lavender casket I picked out matched Grandmother's dress. Although Grandmother was scheduled to be cremated in about three hours, I had shown Diane what a special mother she had. I looked back at the church one last time as we exited, at the throngs of farewell wishers. At least I got to give her the proper homegoing she deserved.

Thora

CHANGE OF PLANS

MY HAND WAS on the the doorknob and I was just about to turn it when I heard my inner voice say: STEP AWAY FROM THE DOOR, THORA GOLD!

I had arrived at my scheduled appointment with the oncologist with ten minutes to spare. When it came to Thora Gold, everything was always in order. I played by the rules, stayed the course according to the plan. But why weren't the cards being dealt in my favor anymore? My hand was still on the doorknob, but I couldn't do it. I couldn't go in for some reason. It was like my feet were stuck in cement.

"Am I really the most beautiful little Davis girl in the world?" I heard a squeaky sweet voice ask from behind.

I turned around and there she was, all starched and shined like that same little brown porcelain doll wearing freshly pressed and done Shirley Temple curls.

"At least that's what Muh says," she sassed.

I wanted to reach out and touch her, but she wasn't real, was she?

"My name is Thora Louise Crouthers." She extended her delicate hand. I looked side to side, making sure no one was around, then reached out and shook her hand.

"Whenever I'm sick, Muh makes me something good to eat like chicken and dumplings or fried green tomatoes, or banana pudding, and I feel all better," she said with a giggle. "My favorite is when she makes fried butter and bread."

"Mine too." I smiled. "Muh was right. You are the most beautiful little girl in the world." Tears gathered in my eyes.

"C'mon, we gotta go!" A voice called out in the distance.

"I'm comin', Billye Jean. That's my mama, I gotta go! You wanna come?" She giggled and skipped down the long corridor in delight. I tried to follow her but she was gone.

I never made it to my appointment. Instead, I ended up in the mall parking lot. I hadn't been to a mall since shopping for Erin's senior prom. I walked into Macy's. My steps had obviously been ordered.

"May I help you?" the effervescent saleslady asked.

"Yes, you can!" I said confidently. "I'm looking for a new life!"

"Girl, tell me about it. I think I got just what you need!"

For the next three hours MiMi, my personal shopper for the day, showed me rack after rack of the latest fashions. I tried on so many designers my head was spinning. MiMi had even enlisted one of the stockroom workers to help us carry the shopping bags.

"Now, what are we doin' about the rest of your makeover, girl-friend?" I gave her a baffled look and before I could respond, she had whisked me off to the salon, where they flat ironed, curled, and teased me into a whole new look. However, my transformation wouldn't be complete without a stop at the makeup counter, where Jovan "beat that face" as he called it.

"Go 'head, girl, take a look!" MiMi proudly helped me out of the chair. I stepped in front of the mirror and a smile crept across my face. I liked what I saw. I even twirled around a few times. "Lookin' fabulous, Miss Thora. Your husband might marry you all over again!" she said.

"You think so?" I gushed.

"Girl, I know so!"

As I exited the mall I stopped in front of the large floor-to-ceiling mirrors near the doors again, admiring my transformation. "Yeah, I *am* the most beautiful little Davis girl in the world!"

Chloe

ESTRANGED

I THINK SHE WAS prepared to die. She had all of her important information neatly organized in a small metal box under her bed with a note addressed to me. It read simply: *Chloe, make sure your father is fair with Diane. Love, Grandmother.* Grandmother had saved over a hundred thousand dollars and I couldn't figure out how in the hell she had done it doing domestic work and serving school lunches most of her life.

"Would there be anything else today, Ms. Michaels?" the bank representative asked.

"No," Diane and I answered at the same time. She cut her eyes at me. The bank rep handed Daddy and Diane each an envelope. Inside, a check made out for $50,000.00.

We dropped Diane back off at her hotel, and later that night I was busy packing up Grandmother's belongings, sorting through what to keep and what to give to charity.

Things have been moving so fast since I got home, now almost three months ago. I still don't think I've had a chance to let Grandmother's death sink in. The same was true of my failed marriage and the perils of trying to divorce a ghost, who is at this point an even bigger mystery. Meanwhile, I've literally abandoned my business. Mother's finances are a mess, and my sisters have their own drama with all the fussing and bickering. Lord knows what else is going on in this family. It had all just been too much. I decided to lie down and take a nap. I could smell Grandmother's scent of lavender and gardenia in the sheets, which lulled me into a deep sleep.

Grandmother entered the room, all dressed up, but she looked younger and healthy again. She was smiling and wearing the lavender dress I had picked out for her. She sat down next to me and whispered softly and kissed me with invisible breath and I was comforted . . .

> *In the season of my silence*
> *In the hour of my twilight*
> *I have come, full bloom*
> *To drink of God's eye—the healing nectar*
> *Transformed/redressed, released from all distress*
> *I have come full bloom*

I rested my head on her shoulder . . .

> *So release me, lift your voice*
> *Sing the amazing of God's grace*
> *For I have finished the race*

She took my hand in hers . . .

> *Like time, love, sunshine, and God*
> *I too am infinite . . .*
> *"And like the sparrow"—I'll be watching you*
> *My children and my children's children's children . . .*

I opened my eyes. I wasn't scared or anything, but I could feel her spirit strong in the room. When Mother arrived, I told her about my dream right away. She just nodded like she knew already. "She's lettin' you know she's okay." Mother took a deep breath. "You are special,

Chloe, and I told you that as a li'l girl. We have to listen to our dreams and pay attention. They guide us, they teach us."

I shocked the hell outta Diane when I showed up at the hotel to pick her up the next morning to take her to the airport. She was clutching her bag tightly when she got in the car. The nerve of her actin' like I wanted her funky inheritance check or something. I couldn't hold my tongue any longer.

"I can't allow myself to hold on to the anger I've been feeling toward you since the night of the wake. Truth is, Grandmother won't let me." Diane closed the passenger door, looking like she was about to jump outta her skin at the mere mention of Grandmother's name.

"But love and the meaning of 'family' instilled in me by my mother also won't allow me to take the easy way out. You have been pushing me away since the day you got here. But I've been bending over backward to respect your feelings. Maybe you think I wanted her money, but for the record, Grandmother's money don't mean anything to me. I didn't even know she had that kind of money.

"She sacrificed everything for you and Daddy. If I had millions and that's what it would take to bring her back for five minutes, I'd hand it over. I'm not some friend of the family; I'm your niece, and I was her granddaughter. So if you're holding some ill feelings toward me about having stepped into the driver's seat, get over it!

"I would hate to see you become a bitter old woman who's angry. Angry at her dead mother and father, angry at her only blood niece, and distant and bitter with her only brother. My mother told me a long time ago that when it comes to family, you love them unconditionally, however they come."

I didn't even realize until I was done that we had never left the parking lot of the hotel. Diane looked at me with glassy eyes. She let out a wail that sounded inhuman. Then her eyes released a river of tears that she'd been holding back all her life.

I understood at that moment the message Grandmother was sending me, and I didn't even realize it until after I'd said all this. It wasn't about me. I was just the conduit. It wasn't about suddenly fixing the relationship between me and her. No, Diane needed to cleanse herself. She needed to get right with God. Mother says it's never too late to get right with Him.

That night Grandmother came to me again, and like before, I wasn't afraid. I was almost like I was expecting her.

"*I know you're worried about Diane, but you did the right thing,*" she said.

"*I don't want you to be mad. I just did what was in my heart to do,*" I replied.

"*I know and your blessing will be shown in his word. Remember that your good comes out when your thoughts, words, and the things you do are faith filled.*"

Then Grandmother kissed me with invisible breath, like the other time.

We had about an hour before the Catholic Charities truck came and the boxes were neatly packed and sitting by the front door. Fawn set the last one down and let out a sigh as she straightened her back. She picked up Grandmother's bible that was sitting on top, as she walked over and sat down on the couch next to me. Mother and Eve had given up a long time ago.

"Mother, I had another dream last night. Grandmother talked to me again, but I wasn't scared."

"You shouldn't be. I told you her spirit is sweet."

"What happened, Chloe?" Eve asked, leaning in.

"She said there was a blessing for me in his word," I said, suddenly strangely eyeing Grandmother's bible that was in a stack of books on Fawn's lap. Fawn picked up on what I had said instantly. "Hand that here, Fawn," I said, pointing to the Bible.

"Here, open it up," she said, gently setting it down on my lap.

I opened it and began to flip through the pages slowly. When I got to Psalm 23 there was a small envelope, with the words *Commerce Bank* written on it. I opened it and there was a tiny key and a note with "Safety deposit box #23, Millie Michaels and Chloe Michaels" written on it. Psalm 23 was Grandmother's favorite psalm in the Bible. It was the first prayer she ever taught me.

I sat nervously in the booth as I unlocked the safety deposit box. Praise the Lord was right. There were stacks of hundreds in neat rows. Grandmother must've been saving for each year I had lived to come up with this kinda cash. Fifty thousand dollars wasn't the Missouri Lotto, but it was nothing to balk at. How did that little lady do what she did?

I discreetly transferred the stacks of cash into my purse. Praise the Lord, Gucci made such a good and roomy bag. I kindly thanked the bank teller as I closed out our account.

As I got into the car with Mother, Fawn, and Eve, I couldn't help but get an adrenaline rush, like we were in that scene from *Set It Off* where Cleo and the crew made their fast getaway, and it was the taste of that first successful robbery that made them want to keep robbing banks.

It was still hard for me to fathom how Diane never thought Grandmother was good enough. No matter how many toilets Grandmother had scrubbed. How hard she scraped and scrounged to put Diane through Catholic elementary and high school and college. It was never enough. When Diane eventually went off to serve in the Third World missions, where she met her husband, I'm sure it was just another way of running away.

I don't feel sad for her anymore, though. No, Miss Millie Michaels was as strong as they come. I guess a mother will love you when no one else will. She did for her family what any good parent would and should do. And what most never can do, and that's make sure she left a little something for their pockets and a lotta something from her heart.

Ceci

WHO AM I?

I DON'T KNOW what it is but I just wasn't up for goin' to the club tonight. Humph, I could have me a drink right up in here or at my own house. Daddy called and said Satin was doin' all right. I'd be tellin' a big-ass lie if I said I wasn't concerned about my child, but ain't nothin' I can do about it now. Too much done happened, and after Mama jumped all on me, how am I s'posed to face her? She don't understand me.

I mightta talked to her before now about what I be thinkin' and feelin', but if it ain't about church or line dancin' what I'm gon say? Humph, whatever! I reached in my bag and pulled out my li'l foil envelop. Sexy Twain, my li'l young somethin' somethin', brought me by some good shit this time. I opened it and took a deep breath. Damn, why was Mama's words 'bout to mess wit me gettin' my buzz on?

This is my life not hers! I folded me over one of my business cards, scooped a li'l bit of powder on it, and put it up to my nose. *Sniiiiiiiif!* I was just about to get me one more hit when there was a knock on the breakroom door.

"Ceci, Mr. Gibson here!" Angie said.

Daddy? Aw shit! What the hell! I quickly folded up my stash and stuffed it in my bra. Before I opened the door, I checked my nose to make sure nothin' was on it.

"Hi, Daddy," I said, givin' him a kiss on the cheek. "You feelin' all right, Daddy?"

"Hey, Cecilia, can I sit down?" Daddy rubbed his hands together, pulled up his pants leg, and sat down. "Yeah, yeah, baby, I'm doin' pretty good. My pressure been pretty good lately." Daddy scratched his beard that was now fully silver. I could see his seventy-five years good in the wrinkles in his face. But Daddy so fair that his skin just more like white folks', and they don't age good at all.

"Listen, Cecilia, you know I normally don't come down to your job, but this time I needed to. I don't like what I'm seein' and most of the time I just keep my mouth shut, but I cain't this time." Daddy's eyes got narrow like little slits.

"If this is about me and Mama, I don't know what to say." I let out a puff of air.

"Cecilia, your mother's a good mother, more than that, she's a good person. She just try to be there for everybody and I done made some mistakes. I probably shoulda put my foot down more and maybe your drinkin' might not have gotten so outta hand!"

"Daddy!"

"Don't raise your voice, Cecilia," Daddy sternly warned.

"Drinkin' ain't got nothin' to do with Mama jumpin' on me."

"Damnit, Cecilia! Your mama needed to probably jump on you a long time ago. Now, I may not have been the best father, but I cain't sit back no more. I've lost a daughter, but I'm not losin' a wife! I don't want her gettin' sick or dyin' and her sugar's been up. It's time for you to be a grown woman. It's time for you to respect us better."

"But see, Daddy!"

"Be quiet, Cecilia! Now, Satin's pregnant, but that don't mean she can't finish school. Look at you, Cecilia! You didn't come from the slums. We tried to give you a good life. You got yourself in some of these situations. It's time to get your act together." Daddy had gotten so mad, he was turnin' red.

Damn! He ain't never talked to me like this before.

"I'm sorry I yelled at you," Daddy said, gettin' up outta his chair. "I just don't want your mama upset and sick like this. She made a lot of sacrifices for you." Tears was comin' up in Daddy's eyes. I ain't never seen my daddy cry. This shit got me real twisted, I ain't gon lie. Then

Daddy just walked out. I didn't even know what to say at that point. I reached in my bra and pulled out my stash. I just needed somethin' to make all this shit go away. I opened it up, but when I looked down at that shit, I just didn't even want none. I just folded it up and put it back in my bra.

SALVATION

I have known women
Dancing women/be-bop and shushu feet women who re-bop a
jitterbug real sweet/package a hukka-buck and sell it/hip-hoppin/
bop a boggie/woogie stompin' women/women holy rolling/dancing
w/jesus/two stepping w/the devil/rocking w/the wind women/
drumfeet bare and sturdy/dancing women dancing the wrinkles
out of their brows/bed and their head/making spirit rise/passion/
snatches a jellyroll and a boody-grin like an electric slide woman
who point ballet/a boogaloo/and dance the nutcracker between the
cracks-dancing women . . .

Joy Ann

NOSY

I MADE ME a hot cup of tea to unwind and was standin' in the kitchen lookin' out at the window when Chloe snuck up on me.

"Mother, what are you lookin' at?"

"Nothin' much. Just thinkin' about me and Billye Jean. We've come a long way in our relationship you know, but I think she can appreciate me for who I am now. We're very different in the sense that I'm more eccentric and she's always been the practical one, but the older we get, the more we both look and act like Muh."

"When I see you all, even Carol Jane, the three of y'all. It makes me appreciate my sisters. They're my rocks, no matter how much we argue and fight."

"I want my girls to stay close too. At least I know if somethin' happens to me, y'all got each other. I wish I had a big house for all my children to stay in," I said as I wistfully looked around the room.

"Would that be a blessing or a curse?" Chloe joked.

"Chloe, you're a mess." We both laughed.

I tried to shake off the twinge of melancholy that was creepin' up on me. Maybe my pensive body language gave my thoughts away.

"Mother, I know I'm here to get myself together, but I'm not incapable of handling anything else. And don't worry, I'll be fine still giving you some financial help. We just have to tighten our belts a bit until this Gregorry mess is over."

"Oh, Chloe, I wish I could do more for you. I wish I could've done more for *all* of my children. But you're in such a bad situation right now and I'm mad I don't have the money to help you. Sometimes I wonder if I failed."

"Mother, you didn't fail. Where's that kinda talk comin' from?"

"No, Chloe, I've always moved to the beat of my own drum. I can't help that. Been that way since I was a li'l ol' girl. Muh called me contrary. MaMaw would say, 'Just let the chile be who she is.' I've withstood a whole lot. I've tried to lead by example, being educated, pushin' my girls to go to school. Didn't I deserve to live my life like I wanted to?"

"Yes, and you're not through living yet."

"Sometimes, I feel like givin' up." I swallowed hard.

"Mother, it'll all be okay. I know you don't like that you had to give up your old place to be here. I'm sure you miss your extra room that was your studio."

"I really haven't been able to paint since I been here, Chloe," I said after a long pause, "I have to confess. I moved here because I got evicted."

"But how? You've been working, right? I know you don't make much, but I figured between your workshops and the extra I send, you had your bills covered. What about your retirement money from that full-time job you had at the elementary school years ago?" she asked.

"Chloe, I don't know. I just kept gettin' further and further behind on my rent. As far as that job, I didn't work there long enough to build up no pension. I get my Social Security, but that ain't that much. And I don't even look back at years ago. How was I going to save? I had to keep all the plates spinnin'. And now I'm just an old, carefree artist. That sure don't get you no 401(k) plan. Thankfully, my friend Salvatore who owns the house is a good person. God was right on time."

"Mother, you should've told me."

"I know, my baby, Miss Fix-It. Chile, I've been fightin' in this world a long time. So don't hold it against me for not wantin' to run and hide behind my children," I said, puttin' my arm around her.

"I'll be okay, Chloe. I'll be really okay once things are back to normal for you. I'm usually here by myself, but today it just worked on me and I couldn't hide it. I never expected to end up sixty-eight years old with no life insurance and livin' like a gypsy."

"But you used to have insurance, right?"

"Yes, but I let it lapse and never was able to get it back. I don't know, Chloe, I guess I always spent what I had, one 'cause I had to, and two 'cause I felt like you can't take money with you when you die." I kissed Chloe on her forehead and walked back over to the kitchen window and poured the hot water in my cup.

"I'll be fine." I winked at her, then hugged her again. I probably shouldn't have even had this kind of conversation with her. I guess I just got down on myself today, that's all.

The headlights from a truck in the next-door driveway caught my attention. "Chloe, come look. Ain't that a movin' truck?"

"Yeah, I think so," she said squintin', lookin' over my shoulder. "But it's dark outside."

"I know. Wonder why folks are movin' in the dead of night. Don't that seem strange to you, Chloe?" I said, putting my tea down and walking to the front door.

"Mother, stay out of them people's business."

"I'm just steppin' outside to get some fresh air."

"Stop being so nosy," she said, with her hands on her hips.

"I'm not nosy," I whispered back, openin' the door and exitin' the house. Chloe followed me. I eased my way over to the fence to get a better look.

"Hey there, neighbor!" A handsome, tanned man who looked to be in his late sixties with a heavy New Orleans accent approached us from the other side of the fence. He was wearing a T-shirt, work jeans, sandals, and a straw hat. "Evenin', I'm Alexandre Duprey. I'm movin' in," he said, reaching over the fence to offer his hand.

"Nice to meet you. I'm Joy Ann Michaels and this is my daughter Chloe." I hesitantly shook his hand. Chloe waved and offered a friendly smile. "Kinda strange to be movin' at night, isn't it?" I said, eyein' the man suspiciously.

"Not my cupa tea. I come up from Nawlins. The movers got a flat, and then that storm hit us about two hours out, now we behind about six hours. I'll try not to disturb you too much, Ms. Michaels."

"Oh no, she's fine. She's usually up late lookin' out of her window," Chloe joked. I nudged her hard.

"Anyway, Mr. Duprey, is it? What brings you to St. Louis?"

"Well, I lost my house in Katrina. I been fightin' with FEMA all this time. I'm a retired music professor. My daughter wanted me to move up here so I could be closer to my grandkids, but I think they just want to keep an eye on me. Seem like they started treatin' me like the child after my wife passed ten years ago," he chuckled.

"I know exactly what you mean, Mr. Duprey. I have three girls and sometimes I feel like I've lost all my power as the parent." We shared a nice laugh.

"Please, call me Alex. All my friends do," he said with a wink.

"Okay, Alex, I'm Joy Ann. Well, it's gettin' pretty late out here, I'mma head on in." Chloe and I waved good-bye and headed back into the house.

"You satisfied, woman?" Chloe teased.

"Look, I have to know what's goin' on where I live."

"Okay, whatever you say." She playfully swatted me on the arm.

"I look a mess tryin' to talk to anybody tonight, Chloe," I said, closin' my kitchen blinds and reheatin' my tea.

"Not according to your new neighbor from Nawlins," Chloe said, addin' a hint of Creole dialect. "I think Mr. Alexandre Duprey is a nice-looking older man and might be sweet on you, Mother," Chloe teased.

"Hush, girl! He just seems like a nice man. He had a nice smile too, but them probably ain't his teeth!"

"So what, those ain't your teeth either!" We laughed.

"Hush your mouth! I'm just checkin' things out 'cause you gotta be careful nowadays. Folks is crazy. That man could be a psycho!"

"Or a rich widower!"

"Chloe, even if he ain't some serial killer, I'm too old and ain't got time to be thinkin' about some white man who probably ain't got two nickels to rub together."

"You got a point 'cause ain't nothin' goin' on *but* the rent!"

Chloe and I shared a few more laughs before I hugged and kissed her and sent her off to bed. I sat on the couch and turned on the television, thinkin' about what she had just said. I wouldn't ever be thinkin' about nobody's white man, especially, an old one. Humph! I lay across the daybed, clicked on CNN, and started to doze off.

Chloe

GOIN' BACK TO CALI

MY PRAYERS, MOTHER'S prayers, all our prayers seem to have finally been answered . . .

I took Fawn's advice and contacted the lawyer from a newspaper article she had seen in Sunday's paper. A top divorce attorney was profiled for her knack for exposing the criminal acts of ex-husbands. Fawn even dialed the woman's office number, practically holding the phone up to my ear. Turns out her firm was too busy to take my case. Frankly, I didn't have a twenty-five-thousand-dollar retainer either.

However, after I poured my heart out over the phone about Gregorry taking my money and me losing the baby, the attorney felt so sorry for me she offered to refer me to another lawyer who used to clerk at her firm, and who now had her own firm. She didn't make any promises, but at that point, what did I have to lose?

The short of a really long story, Tina Matillo of Weinberg, Taub, and Matillo agreed to take my case. Fawn was so excited that I was firing my lawyer she came up with fifteen hundred dollars to help out my legal fund. You know she had to be excited, as tight as Fawn is on a dollar.

"Look, the main thing is that her address is in downtown Los Angeles, and she's got two Jewish names next to hers on the marquee! I just want you done with that tired, unprofessional hoodrat paralegal you paid all that money to. We don't want no more Tashanista or Quintonetta, or no name that's gonna have the judge laughing at you. It's time to show that weak-ass Negro you married you mean business!"

Fawn was going on and on for a good fifteen minutes before Mother told her to hush so we could all pray.

"Every eye closed and every head bowed. Heavenly Father, we are praying for a breakthrough," Mother said as the whole family held hands and stood in a circle in the middle of her living room after dinner. She wanted me to eat a good meal before getting on the plane.

"Yes, yes," Aunt Billye Jean nodded.

"Glory! Glory!" Carol Jane shouted.

"God, we're askin' that you encircle Chloe with your light and cover her with a shield of divine protection as she prepares to go back to California. We're not askin' for a crack in the door, we're askin' that the doors of justice be knocked down!"

"Glory! Glory!" Cousin Carol Jane shouted again, but this time she added a few jumps.

"Yes, Lord!" Aunt Billye Jean was always more reserved. She just stomped her foot one good time and balled her fist up and waved it to the ceiling.

"And Father God, we ask that wherever Gregorry is, he feel a resounding message that he can run, but he can't hide, and that's all I'm gonna say!" Fawn blurted out.

"Amen!" Eve smirked, giving her a hard nudge.

"Thank you, God, and bless Chloe on the highways and skyways. Amen!" Mother said, shaking her head.

I was wrapped in a cloak of light and had my invisible shield and sword of victory in tow, as Mother kissed me for the twentieth time, fighting back tears. I gave her my best confident face to keep her from worrying too much. Underneath, the fear seemed to swell inside me. I had left L.A. over three months ago, and although I missed my house, deep down I didn't want to have anything to do with that city or that life anymore.

"Chloe! Chloe!" My cousin Caroline's high-pitched almost squeal got my attention as soon as I exited baggage claim. I may not have been missing Cali, but I sure missed the weather. It was a breezy seventy-five, no humidity, and Caroline was waving from the sunroof of her Range Rover.

"Oh my God! You look as perfect and beautiful as ever, my little muffin!" Caroline was dressed in a flowy silk tunic and drawstring pants and wrapped in a bright orange cashmere wrap. Sparkly, jingly bracelets stacked each arm. The way she dressed reminded me of Mother. Her short blondish-highlighted hair was in loose curls that made her sun-tanned sugary cinnamon skin almost luminous.

Caroline's mother, Marie, was my mother's first cousin. Her mother was Aunt Elizabeth who married a preacher. Marie did the same. She's Fawn and Ceci's age so I've never spent much time around her. Cousin Marie and her husband, Rev. Doctor Elmore Cummings, as he referred to himself, were sort of traveling missionaries.

He didn't have a "real" church, according to Mother. As a family they traveled the country by car, and later by RV, in their very own mobile church. Caroline was sort of a flower child for the Lord, and apparently after Caroline finished college at Berkeley, she became a world traveler.

I'm not sure if Caroline has ever worked a traditional job, but she seems to know all sorts of interesting people, even some African and Middle Eastern royalty. Caroline's dating life is a bit of a scandal too—three marriages. One to a man the family refers to as "that low-life wretch." Another to Akbar, supposed Arab royalty. I remember Fawn saying something about having to loan Caroline money to get out of the Middle East in a hurry.

Her third husband was Ramone. Fawn said it was a total "lust thing." She married him about two years ago and that lasted a whopping two months. Fawn said Caroline told her that it was necessary because she got bored having sex all day. Plus, even though he was apparently fine as hell, his ass was broke and he didn't have a job.

About a year ago, Caroline was in Italy and met Fabrizzio, a wealthy art dealer, and it seems like she has struck gold on this one.

She's sworn off marriage, but Fabrizzio loves the ground she walks on and is her permanent "sponsor." They live in Portofino, Italy, New York, and San Francisco. She happened to be in the States and made a special drive down the coast just for me.

"I haven't seen you since I was in high school, Caroline, but you look the same, too!" I said, tossing my carry-on in the backseat.

"Please, I'm twenty-five pounds overweight, but, hello!" She snapped her fingers. "Baby, I'm still sexy, fabulous, happy, and loving life! Plus having a rich man doesn't hurt, hello!" she chirped. "You hungry? I hope you're hungry. Your timing is perfect. Fabi, that's what I call Fabrizzio for short, is in Italy and I was actually coming down to L.A. to look for a little beach house to rent for the spring.

"Fabi wanted me to look in Malibu and I was oh, hell no! I'll be done got pissed off and had to whip off in some rich beeyach's ass!" she said, zipping in and out of lanes. Caroline was yapping a mile a minute, and I couldn't get a word in edgewise.

By the time we arrived at my house in the Valley, I was on sensory overload thanks to Caroline. My ears were worn out and I was ready to devour the Thai takeout we had picked up on the way. Fawn warned me that Caroline was more than a cousin, she was an experience. She filled me in on everything from her South African safari to sunning on the French Rivera. I was actually so amused I had almost forgotten my current set of unfortunate circumstances. That is, until we pulled into the driveway and she shut off the engine.

It was dusk, and the house almost had that same eerie glow as it did the night Tracey and I were here.

"You okay, sweetums?" Caroline asked.

"I'm cool, I guess. I just feel like I don't belong here anymore," I said, opening the back door and grabbing my bag. "It's like my life has been put in this suspended animation mode. I just wish I had never taken that call from Gregorry. And what if he's watching us right now?"

"First of all, it's called 'over' for a reason. Honey, shit happens, I can testify to that. But you press on, you collect yourself, and you move the fuck on! What you need is a good spiritual shake-up in your soul. We got a little less than forty-eight hours here, so we're gonna do just that. And let me tell you, dumpling, if that punk-ass loser you married even thinks about steppin' up on this doorstep, oh hell no! I will whip his ass!" She jumped into a karate stance. We let out a rousing round of laughter as I inserted my key in the lock and opened the door.

The house was dark, and the sadness had settled in good like dust. There was a faint hint of burnt sage in the air. Caroline patted me on the back gently, then hugged me.

"First thing we gotta do is bring some life back into this old place!" She began to breeze through the house turning on all the lights. "That's better!" She called out from the guest room in the back. I looked around and all I could do was cry. I leaned against the wall and put my hands over my face. Caroline rushed back into the room when she heard my sobs.

"I don't know what's next for me and that's the scariest part of everything. I'm used to having a plan for my life, things mapped out. I don't know why God let this happened."

Caroline told me to let it all out and after a few minutes guided me over to the dining-room table where we sat down. She handed me a Kleenex from her purse.

"Okay, I wanted you to cry, get mad, say what you needed to say, even curse God, because, gumdrop, he always forgives his angels. Let me tell you something, when I married that first fool and came home and all my shit was gone, what! Ooh, and I don't mean a few items. I mean all my shit, including the Yellow Pages and the fucking toilet paper.

"What kind of sick mofo does that kind of shit! Everything gone, gone, gone!" She dramatically illustrated, throwing her hands in the air. "Honey, I wanted to kill myself. Literally! I had a fierce prescription from one of my fabulous doctor girlfriends for some sleeping pills and, girlie, I was gonna take myself right on outta here.

"My daddy was gone on to glory. 'Cause believe me if the Reverend Doctor had been alive, talk about some whip ass! At the time Mama was sick and on her way to join Daddy at heaven's pearly gates. Rest her soul," she said, making the sign of the cross. "Anyway, I didn't want to tell her what had happened 'cause she was on her deathbed. I had no one.

"As much as I love my family, I didn't feel comfortable just poppin' up asking for help. I wasn't about to call Billye Jean—she always thought Mama and Daddy were raving lunatics in some religious cult. Even Carol Jane looked at them funny. Joy Ann was always the only one in the family who understood Mama and the Reverend Doctor, probably because she's so creative and artsy, and such a beautiful free spirit.

"I wanted to tell Fawn, but as much as I love your sister, my cousin got a big mouth like Billye Jean does." We laughed. "I was embarrassed. That's why I understand so much when Fawn sent me that urgent e-mail the other day, told me you had to come back to L.A., and asked me to be here with you. I understood why you felt you had to keep all that madness to yourself.

"I had never felt so alone during that time. I swear, I was so hurt I cursed God, Daddy, even myself. I remember lying on the floor, 'cause remember he took the furniture. There I was splayed out, having just finished a bottle of amazing Australian shiraz, and was just about to take that handful of pills, and that's when it happened!"

Smack!

Caroline clapped her hands together so loudly I jumped. "I heard my daddy speak to me. I swear, clear as a bell. He said, 'Babydoll!' That's what he called me. He said, 'Babydoll, faith is the substance of things hoped for, the evidence of things not seen! With the faith of a mustard seed you can make it. You can hold on!'

"Now, you know I made a decision a long time ago not to follow religion in the traditional sense, but, baby, when all hell is breakin' loose, you go back to your roots. I opened up my grandmother Elizabeth's bible and I turned to Philippians 4:12–13 and I read, over and over, *'I know both how to be abased and I know how to abound: everywhere and in all things I am instructed both to be full and to be hungry, both to abound and to suffer need. I can do all things through Christ which strengthens me.'*

"I went to the hospital that next morning, looking fabulous of course, but nonetheless wearing the same outfit I'd had on the day before. I only had that and the clothes in my suitcase from my trip, but Mama would have snapped out of that coma and slapped me silly if I hadda been lookin' a mess.

"Anyway, I pulled on the last morsel of strength I had and promised my dying mama and my daddy that I would never let no man, no situation, nobody, or nothing ever cause me to give up. I owed that to not only them but my grandmother and our great-grandmother, MaMaw, who we've all been taught about." Caroline gave me a big hug, then proceeded to busy herself opening blinds and curtains, determined to bring some life back into this house.

That night, as I lay staring at the ceiling, fighting a bout of worry that was brewing in my gut, I wondered if Gregorry was lurking in the backyard or if he had tapped my phone lines. What if he was planning on burning down my house! All kinds of crazy things bounced around in my head. I took a deep breath and shut my eyes tightly.

When I reopened them, I looked over at Caroline who was on the other side of my massive California king bed snoring away, dressed in full nighttime regalia—a satin eye mask, face cream, her special neck and back pillow, and sleeping gloves to keep her hands moisturized. I thought about her words and having the faith of a mustard seed.

I sat up and turned on the lamp on my nightstand and opened the small travel bible Mother had tucked inside my purse. The page opened right on Psalm 30. I read silently, *"Weeping may endure for a night, but joy cometh in the morning."* I smiled. Mother thought she was slick. I turned off the light and lay back down, closing my eyes.

I didn't know exactly what the outcome of meeting with the lawyer would be, but God had certainly opened a door for me. I didn't even know how I would pay my mortgage in two months, but I had to trust that God would make a way for that, too.

Billye Jean

THE FISH IS JUMPIN'

I KNOW I'M RUNNIN' late, but this family know I fry catfish better than anybody else in the family, so they just gonna have to wait. We normally have fish on Friday, but Satin come tellin' her grandmama, no sooner than she popped that baby out, that she had a taste for fish. So fish it was. I figured I'd better go on 'head and make some spaghetti, too. Eve make some good coleslaw, but you cain't have fish and coleslaw without spaghetti.

I took my time loading up my van. I put the glass Corning dish of spaghetti on the floor in the backseat and the fish on the front seat to keep it from overheating on the drive over. I know I'm fussin' a lot about the fish, but the fish ain't really the problem. It's Arnaz. I'm worried, I ain't gonna lie. I'm used to him not comin' home until two or three in the morning—that's been his thing for the past year or so—but two days!?

I'm really okay if he don't come home ever. I don't care if he live someplace else, as long as he keeps givin' me his check, that's all that matters. I still sign his checks after all these years, because he don't know how.

I know Arnaz has been cheatin' on me many times before with them low-life women, especially after he got out of jail. I believe you got to honor marriage no matter what. He only recently, in the last ten years, started takin' vacations with me. And even then, it's only to go visit Thora and her family. I don't care. I don't wanna be bothered anyway. I done put his ass out before, but he won't leave. He worried the hell out of me each time. He worse than Junior.

I started up the car and wiped my face off with my sweat rag and took me a sip of ice water. It was hot, but I had my food packed up good. Takin' the streets was best. As I passed neighborhood after neighborhood on the north side of town I just couldn't help but think about the fact that over this way is where Arnaz always be hangin' out. He's done messed around with a lotta women over the years, but the main one he be messin' wit is that damn Korean woman.

I done had my run-in wit her, but it didn't do no good. One time me and Joy Ann was out and when we came back to the house, I found clothing in the back bedroom. At first I thought it was some of my grandkids' stuff.

"Billye Jean, this ain't no children's stuff," Joy Ann said, holdin' up some women's underwear and a dress. I couldn't deny it all no longer.

"Joy Ann," I said, ploppin' down on the edge of the bed, "Arnaz been cheatin' on me for a while now, maybe even years, with some Korean woman." All I could do was bury my face in my hands. That woman wanted me to know she had been to my house and slept in my bed. I just let it go. Joy Ann didn't and still don't agree, but I'm too old and too sick, plus Arnaz don't really throw it in my face.

I had a strange feelin' when I turned onto St. Louis Avenue. I slowly cruised down the street just in case I saw Arnaz's car. My eyes ain't as good as they used to be. Somethin' that look like Arnaz's car was up ahead and I'll be damned, it was his car! As I got closer, I squinted, 'cause it looked like somebody was in the passenger seat. *Ain't that somethin'! That wench sittin' up in my husband's truck!*

I don't know what done come over me, but I threw my van in park and jumped out. "Hey! Hey, you! C'mon you li'l benchleg hussie, you street walkin' strumpet! Get out so I can kick yo ass," I screamed, bangin' on the passenger window with my flip-flop and my fist.

"No, you get back!" That woman started jumpin' and shoutin' all over the place. I jiggled the car door handles, but the woman had locked them.

"Open the goddamn door!" I banged on the window harder.

"Arnaz get you fo this!" The woman pointed from the other side of the window in broken English.

I remembered I had my set of keys in my hand. I started flipping through the key ring to get to the truck key. "When I get this damn door open, I'm gonna kill yo rice-eatin' ass, and when I get to him, I'm gonna kill him too!"

As soon as I had swung the passenger door open, the Korean woman had scooted her li'l ass halfway out the other side. My heart was poundin' almost as hard as it was for me to catch my breath, and sweat was pourin' down my face. The world started to spin around me.

I reached out my right arm. I could see the woman was almost within my reach. I grabbed hold to the back of the woman's button-down shirt. "Your li'l ass thought you could . . ." and before I could finish my words, a sharp pain shot through my chest. My knees gave out and my chin partly hit the running board to the truck. My vision was blurry, but I could see the woman had shimmied outta her shirt and had gotten away. She was runnin' down the street with nothin' but a brassiere on at the top.

Lord, don't take me like this! The sun was beatin' down on my face and I couldn't get any air into my lungs. My chest felt like it was cavin' in, but I was still holdin' her shirt in my hand. I looked up and Arnaz was kneelin' down over me. Everythin' was fuzzy.

"Billye Jean, don't die, please don't die!" he begged.

Chloe

PACKED MY BAGS

I SAT QUIETLY in the vast conference room that overlooked down-town Los Angeles, tapping my foot lightly. The brass lettering across the back wall that spelled out Weinberg, Taub, and Matillo matched up to this small but powerful firm's sterling reputation in the practice of family law.

By the looks of Tina Matillo's buttoned-up Brooks Brothers attire and loafers, I could tell she was a no-nonsense type. Fawn would be ecstatic. You could tell by Ms. Matillo's confident walk that she was a woman who had encountered more than a few sexist moments in the chauvinistic, male-dominated world of law, but she wasn't going to let that break her stride.

Tina, a petite athletic woman with a short spiky haircut, was natu-rally pretty, sans heavy makeup, only wearing a pinkish gloss. Clearly she downplayed her beauty, another sign that she was strictly about the business of winning cases.

"Chloe, I'm Tina," she said, extending her hand.

"Tina, it's so nice to finally put the voice with the face." I wiped my clammy hands on the side of my pants and returned the gesture.

Tina dropped my file on the conference table and sat down across from me. The large swivel chair looked as if it would swallow her up. "Chloe, your case seems pretty straight ahead. Unfortunately, I think you've been a victim of the runaround, plain and simple. I don't want to spend time dwelling on another lawyer's error, but I give you my word that I can clean this up. I'm assuming after what you've been through in the past four going on five months, you just want to put this behind you."

My eyes welled up and I placed my hand over my forehead. "I'm sorry, I don't mean to cry like this," I said, pulling a tissue out of my purse and dabbing my eyes. "I've been angry for so many months and trying to find my way. It's like everything was taken from me, and all I was trying to do was build a life for myself. I don't even want the money back. I just want to be whole again, once and for all."

"Listen, you definitely have been through something very dramatic, but sometimes you have to look at the circumstances as steps or lessons to make you stronger. I'm taking a much smaller retainer than I normally would. This was one of those cases that I had a feeling I needed to take on."

My stash of money was just about tapped out, but I gladly slid a check for ten thousand dollars across the table and signed off on the retainer papers. She was my last hope for the freedom I had been clawing my way to. For the first time in this whole ordeal I could see the light at the end of the tunnel.

I let out a good hard cry in the ladies' restroom before getting on the elevator, and when the doors opened, I could see my cousin Caroline waving out of the sunroof of her car.

"Did it work out, Muffin?" Caroline asked, peering over her oversized shades.

"It's not quite over yet, but I do think God had his hand in getting me to this lawyer."

"Okay, first of all we are going to change the direction of all this talk. We speak in the positives! We speak in the affirmatives! No more *mights* or *maybes*! We are speaking it into existence! So tonight we dance!" Caroline turned up the music and we zipped and zigzagged our way onto the freeway with the wind whipping through our hair.

That night we not only danced, but with the help of Deborah, Tracey, Christy, and Deja, we had a good old-fashioned packing party. Deja was still amped as she pressed Play on the iPod.

"Girl, this is for that hatin'-ass busta you married!" She busted out the running man dance as Jill Scott's ode to haters, "Hate on Me," pumped through the speakers. Tracey joined in with the old-school cabbage patch and started to sing along. Caroline popped the cork on another bottle, and Deborah jumped up and showed them both out with the robot. I let my ponytail loose and swung my hair all over my head.

Caroline handed me a hairbrush to use as my microphone before grabbing another bottle and uncorking it. After she poured us another round, she left the room and returned with the cast iron skillet and my wedding photo album. We each grabbed a stack of pictures, sorting through all of them and pulling out all the ones with Gregorry, his father, and his uncle. Caroline lit a match and the bonfire was on!

We danced around the barbecue pit like Scouts at a campfire. By midnight the five of us had packed up most of the house and polished off three bottles of wine. Caroline had passed out on one end of the couch, I was on the other, and Deja was sprawled out on the floor with a pillow over her head. Deborah, Christy, and Tracey headed home. Tracey's babysitter had already called four times. We gave each other girlfriend smooches and big hugs.

"Christy, you know I love you as my friend, but thank you as my business partner for hangin' in there with me. I'll be back on track soon, 'cause, girl, you know I need to get back to work."

"Listen, Chloe, you've laid the foundation for our company. I've learned from the best, and that's been you. These past months have not only been an eye-opener for you but for me, too. I've had to step up to the plate and now people take me seriously in an industry that only catered to me because of my dad."

"Well, his juice got us in the game."

"Yeah, but I didn't want my father's life. Five horrible Hollywood divorces, rich but miserable. And, by the way, Deja has had your back and I think she's really ready to be promoted. All we want you to do is be happy again. Wherever that may be. Bloomberg-Michaels is just getting started, girlie! Who knows, maybe we need to talk about expanding to St. Louis; think about it," she said with a wink.

Christy zoomed off and her words were still ringing in my brain. I had decided to sell the house, because not only did I need the money, but when I made my new start, I wanted it to truly be fresh and new. Caroline set me up with one of her "fabulous" friends who was the top real estate guy in Los Angeles and he already had six potential buyers lined up. In the meantime, while Fabi was in Italy, she'd rent my place instead of the beach house. Relief was finally on the way.

I climbed over Deja, made my way back to my cozy spot on the couch, and turned off the light. Deja, in a drunken stupor, was still humming our new hater anthem. *"You cannot hate on me 'cause my mind is free, feel my destiny, so shall it be . . ."*

Carol Jane

NEW LIFE

WHERE OLD LIVES end a new one begins . . .

I held my new great-grandbaby in my arms and just for a li'l bit had a flash of when Cecilia came into this world. I was alone like this child. But just like Mama and Muh had prayed me up, I done prayed this girl up. Satin's gonna be all right. She ain't got no choice. I cain't help but wish it was all different, but that's like tellin' God you don't want the hand he done dealt you. Must be a reason.

We got our first baby boy in a long time, ain't this somethin'. Sage Davis Gibson. We got to keep the Davis name alive. We were all so proud when Thora named her son that. And so we carry on. We didn't have much time to be blessin' stomachs. Too much turmoil was goin' on, but when the time comes, Lord, we gonna have a good time baptizing this baby. Right now, right today, I just want to hold this li'l ol' boy and love him up good. We got to raise a man here.

It ain't gonna be easy, I know. Lord help us, we don't know nothin' about the daddy and I just refuse to call him Poo. I just ain't gonna do it. It takes a man to raise a man, I believe. I was surprised my husband, Lawrence, has been so attentive to me. Shoot, shocked, but I ain't gonna question and I definitely ain't gonna complain. He act like he kinda excited it's gonna be another man around here. I'm sure it ain't been easy all these years just being around me and all my family. I know women will drive you crazy.

"Granny, is the baby okay?" Satin said, wakin' up from a nap.

"This boy is just fine. He's strong, too. You gonna need him to be strong."

"I'm sorry about gettin' pregnant," she said, lookin' down.

"We past all that, Satin. Now you are a mother and there's responsibility you gotta think about. I was a young mother, and I didn't plan on things. I didn't want any of my children to go through that, but you cain't control some of the stuff that happens. I had to put it in God's hands, and I've put you in his hands."

"I'm sure ever'body in the family got somethin' to say."

"We are older and we know better, so even if somebody says somethin' it is for your benefit, you hear me? You have to learn from the wisdom your elders pass on. That's all I ever wanted you to understand."

"Granny, I just feel like I hate my mama."

"Satin, don't say that," I said, puttin' Sage in his crib. "Your mother didn't always do the things she does. Somewhere along the way she just took a detour. But when loved ones are weak and have a sickness, we just have to pray for them."

"I pray for her all the time, it don't do no good."

"That means you just have to pray a little harder." Satin was silent.

"Look, Satin, you done had this baby, but it's not the end of the world. Look at what I did! I went to college, your grandfather went to college. We got our education, and we made a life. You've got your whole life ahead of you. But now that you got this baby, what you do is up to you!"

"I'm not gonna be like her, Granny!"

"You know, I will give your mother credit. She got her education, and she'd give you whatever you want in the world. She's just scared right now."

"She didn't act so scared when she was knockin' me upside the head."

"Okay, so she doesn't have such a good way of expressin' her fear. But, baby, you've gotta think about the future. You cain't get a good job and provide for that baby without an education. You've got to go back to school, or get your high school equivalency, somethin'. Look at Aunt Billye Jean, back when she got pregnant at fourteen, there weren't nearly as many opportunities for black people as there are now. But what did she do? She got her GED, went to college, and then became a registered nurse. She had her mother and father, my mother, and the rest of our aunts to help her too. We love you. We want the best for you, baby."

"She did?"

"Yep!"

"I want my baby to not just have everythin', like clothes and stuff, but I want my baby to know that I love him. I don't wanna drink and be wild like Mama."

"You don't have to be like Cecilia, Satin, but she is your mother, and like I said, the best you can do is keep prayin' for her and succeed in life."

I put my arms around Satin and hugged her tightly. She held on to me good. After that, that chile couldn't stop tellin' me about all her plans for the baby and goin' back to school. I think she might be a good li'l mother, after all.

Chloe

VISIT WITH AN OLD FRIEND

LARONDA, MOOSE, CHINKY, and I were wrapping up an afternoon of going down high school memory lane, after I had returned to St. Louis.

"Well, we gotta go. Let me gather up all my kids. TJ, Tomika, and Tania, c'mon!" Moose rattled off their names like a tongue twister, and they must've known Mama don't take no mess. They all ran into the room and stopped at attention. "To the car. Now!"

"Shawnique and Shanae gone 'head out there wit them," Chinky commanded, checking her watch.

As the kids filed out in a single line, I turned to Moose and Chinky, impressed. "Y'all got them children in check big time," I said, clapping.

"You mean their *tribes* in check," LaRonda teased.

"You keep on talkin'. Don't think Marcel don't have plans for yo ass. Before y'all done you gonna have the damn St. Louis Rams up in here!" Moose slapped five with Chinky.

I suddenly felt out of place, like I was a foreigner. My childhood friends had grown up and become wives and mothers and I was this successful alien, who had failed in the world of matrimony, on an island alone. We said our good-byes, and I stuck around and helped LaRonda straighten up. She caught me staring off into space.

"Chloe, what's up with you?" LaRonda asked.

"Huh?"

"You seem a million miles away."

"No, girl. I'm just thinkin' about how happy all of y'all are. I have to confess—I'm not married anymore. I don't want to really talk about it, though."

"I'm sorry, Chloe, and you know me. I ain't never been one to pry. But just know I'mma pray for you 'cause your homegirl still got your back. And as far as your marriage, it'll come the right way next time. But please believe it ain't easy all the time."

"And Marcel just *came* into your life?" I asked.

"God *brought* him into my life. By the way, Marcel and Lance are real cool and he told Marcel he gave you his card that night at the St. Louis Room, but you haven't called." LaRonda looked at me and winked.

"It's way too soon. There's so much happening. Between my grandmother passing, my life being turned upside down, no, girl. I'm just trying to get divorced."

"Ain't nobody talkin' about marriage. It's just about talkin' to an old friend. Just go to dinner with him or drinks or whatever you in-the-mix people do!" She gave me a playful shove.

"Baby!" Marcel called out as he entered the house through the garage.

"Oh, Lord! Just be nice; I think Lance is with him. Me and Chloe are in the family room, baby!" she yelled back. "Just be nice!" she threatened in a motherly tone.

I checked Lance out better today. It was so dark in the club that night. Unlike most pro athletes, his jewelry was expensive, but not gaudy: a classic Cartier watch, no rings or necklaces with Jesus in diamonds, and a stylish diamond earring that looked to be just shy of two carats. I did actually like Mr. Lance's style, blingy-not-pimpy.

He had edge, but with a sterling background like his, I know his mother reminded him every day he was Dr. Milton James's son, and don't forget it. Still, I was shocked that ten years in the NBA hadn't corrupted him and turned him into some walking ghetto-fabulous-hip-hop fashion disaster.

Marcel and LaRonda conveniently left us downstairs, claiming they had to check on something in the nursery-to-be. There was an awkward silence.

"It's cool seeing old friends," I said, breaking the ice.

"So, what's been going on with you, Chloe? Married? Divorced? Kids?"

"Soon to be divorced, I hope."

"Sorry, I guess I put my foot in my mouth."

"No, it's cool. Other than the obvious drama. I've been busy building my public relations company. And you?"

"Widowed, no, and yes. In that order. I have a son. He's five now."

"Oh, that's right, I heard your wife passed. I'm sorry. Just one child, though. I'm impressed. Don't you ballplayers usually have all kinds of kids runnin' around," I said with cynicism in my voice.

"*Was* a ballplayer, as in retired. What's that supposed to mean? I was married when I had my son!"

"My bad. I guess I put my foot in my mouth this time. It's just that most of the ones I've known or worked with have kids they don't even know about."

"Hold up! I could put you in a box and stereotype you too. Career woman, ballbuster, Ms. Independent. Perhaps that's why your marriage didn't work!" Lance retorted.

"First of all I am not a ballbuster, and you have no idea the circumstances surrounding my marriage." I was furious, and this conversation was officially over. "Please, tell LaRonda I'll give her a call later." I collected my purse and keys and headed toward the door.

"Chloe," Lance said, following me. He gently touched my arm. I whipped around. "I'm sorry." Lance extended his hand. I accepted.

"No problem. Look, I'm sorry, a lot is going on and I'm just on edge. Just please tell LaRonda I had to go."

"Hey, just try not to let things get under your skin so much. I can say that because I've been through a lot and I never thought I'd be back in St. Louis either. As an olive branch, I'm just offering to take you out totally on the friendship tip."

I eased up on Lance. He was just a decent guy getting caught in the cross fire. "I'm not sure," I said uncomfortably. "I'm gonna go now." I made a quick exit. That was for the best. Maybe my anger toward Gregorry was turning me off from dating altogether. Oh God, I didn't want to be some bitter, broken woman!

Joy Ann

KEEPIN' COMPANY
(A MOTHER'S WISDOM)

"**M**ORNIN', JOY ANN!" My new neighbor, Alex, was sweatin' and workin' away, choppin' down tree branches.

"Alex, you better be careful out here before you hurt your back or somethin'!" I called out into the yard.

"I'm old, but built like steel, Joy Ann," he said with a laugh. "Salvatore must not have ever trimmed back these trees. They all hangin' on the power lines. I don't want y'all to have no problems."

"Well, how much do I owe you?"

"You don't owe me nothin'. This keeps me busy."

"I just made a fresh pot of coffee, you want some?"

I poured us two cups of coffee and carried it outside on a tray. Alex wiped his brow. I had never really looked at him before, but I could tell he had been a handsome man. Well, handsome for a white man. But I don't know if he's really white white. I think he's just Creole.

"You know, when I was livin' with my daughter they didn't understand that I needed to work outdoors. I had grown up huntin' and fishin' in the country."

"I try to tell my girls about how I used to camp and sleep in the woods when I was a Girl Scout," I said, taking a sip from my cup.

"Back then it was a great thing to be a Girl Scout. I was in an all-black troop and we traveled all over the country—Washington, D.C., California, New York."

"That is an amazing story, and you've got some good daughters, it seems. They must be proud of you and your work."

"My girls, they are wonderful, even when they make me mad. But right now I'm tryin' to figure out who Joy Ann is, I guess. They're gonna be okay. Even my baby girl, Chloe, who's goin' through somethin' bad right now. I would imagine they're very proud of my work." I smiled. "I just wish *I* was more proud of it right now."

"You ain't been able to paint?"

"Been thinkin' I should give up on it."

"You can't. It's what you do, ain't it?"

"Well, I don't have much room here, and I guess I just don't feel creative anymore. Probably gettin' too old." I smiled again.

"That's too bad 'cause you can't let what you do die. That's what keeps a person livin'."

"I always said that when I die I want to leave behind a legacy for my children and grandchildren. But shoot, if I died today, my kids won't be fightin' over how to divide the money, but over who's gonna pay the funeral bill. Lord, I swear, when did the roles reverse?"

"Joy Ann, I think you're much too hard on yourself, and one day we're gonna have to do somethin' about gettin' you that studio again." He gulped down the rest of his coffee. "That was some good coffee. I sure hope we can do it again." He tipped his hat. I felt myself kinda blush. "I'd better get back to choppin' these trees and leave you alone."

I refilled my cup and sat next to my easel and took my time dippin' my brush in my paint. I've been workin' on this piece, but it's just not coming together. Maybe I'd just try some abstract freestylin'. The trees are always good inspiration. Green would be a good color today.

Humph, Alex was worried about leavin' me alone. He don't know I don't mind the company. I've been by myself for too many years to count. Billye Jean says that's why I'm all caught up in my kids. I'd rather it be them than bad marriage. I done had two husbands, but I don't believe in sittin' on dust and that's just what I was doing. So I had to step out in the wind and let it blow that dust on away.

My girls probably think I meddle too much in their lives, but I'm a mother and that's what mothers do. Mothers and daughters have a special thing. Billye Jean didn't really get into her daughter 'til she was grown and married with children of her own. She still don't have the connection that I do with hers. She has literally spent all her time complainin' about money and that no-good man she been with all these years. When she wasn't stuck on stupid with Arnaz, she was babysittin' Junior's issues. She never *really* knew Thora until Thora started havin' kids. They are beautiful, too. Muh would be so proud.

Carol Jane, on the other hand, don't never complain. It's pitiful 'cause she's always on the prayer line when somebody needs it. And Lawrence ain't no kind of support. I cain't stand no weak man. Do I think about the fact that I haven't felt the warmth of a man's hands in all these years? Yes, I do, but I've accepted that maybe God had other plans for me.

So I may not have been so good with my money, or had the best jobs, or been able to buy a big home with expensive furniture. But I made sure my girls were loved and had a good education. That they had the freedom to dream. I'm so happy Fawn has a good husband because she was my delicate child. So sickly when she came into this world a month early.

Fawn was always book smart, but flighty. You know sometimes she'd be a li'l off the wall with her thinkin'. I just worry 'cause she holds so much inside and you just don't know when somethin' bad's gonna come out. I want her to take time for herself more. Sometimes when we give every piece of who we are out, we just end up bankrupt and runnin' on fumes. She used to talk to me more. I wish she would do that again.

Eve, well I faced it a long time ago. She's my child who has a daddy complex. Some women just need a man, plain and simple. The whole world stops when she gets one, too. She be mad at a man and take it out on her family. That's one child I've done plenty of praying for. Prayed so much my knees got calluses on 'em. I usta have to knock her in her mouth to make her shut up.

Me and that child butt heads so much. I think it's 'cause I wanted that baby the most, out of all of 'em. Not that I didn't want Chloe or Fawn, but I was so young with Fawn. And technically, Chloe was a mistake that came around years later. But Eve was right on time. Fawn and Chloe have pieces of me here and there, but Eve, shoot, that's my twin, folks say.

I was in labor twenty-two hours and she was a week overdue! Only one of my children who came out cryin' about everythin'. Cryin' 'cause I left her crazy daddy, cryin' when she got her period, cryin' *just* because. I used to think she hated me. I don't know why. I loved her with every piece of me. But one day, *one* day she'll see. It might be the day I die, but she'll see.

But no matter what, she's a good mother and when it's all said and done, she done raised that child Christina damn near by herself. That girl's gonna go far, too. She's a lot like Chloe. Whew, Chloe is one child who's always determined to do just what she wanted. I pray she slows down. She's seein' right now that a hard head makes a soft ass. Lord knows my heart cain't handle no more drama. She done got herself mixed up in somethin' real stupid. I have to just keep prayin' on each of 'em. Maybe *that's* what God intended.

Honestly, the scary thing is that my children are grown, and I am really alone! One day I know Eve will get a good man, and Chloe will marry again. So what exactly is that plan God has for me? I think about my sister's unhappiness, and Carol Jane, how she eats 'til she's sick! She wasn't meant to be that big. You can tell by them itty-bitty feet of hers. Her daughter, Ceci, binges on alcohol and drugs and she binges on whatever food she can get her hands on.

I swear they've lost their zeal and zest for life. I don't want to lose my zeal and zest for livin'!

SOLACE

I have known women
Healing women/spirit women/visionary women/women who beat a
dream coming true/peacekeeping women sunsipping/women who
light up dark corners and dingy hearts/women who put a move on
the fog with knees of harmony and smooth teeth/divas and doers/
righteous women of purpose substance with music/wordwalkers
between the foot of the mountain and the mouth of the sun/love
sowers and seed planting/women birthing and bridging/praying
women/standing ground women/traveling light good vibes and
laughing women who be merry with tears that turn crystal/I know
these women/these mothers and daughters and lovers and wives/
these sisters/grannies/queenies and hoochies/these women who
make women to make women/to make men/I know these women . . .

Chloe

MOMENT OF TRUTH

I SAID I WOULDN'T call, but I'm too weak, always when it comes to him. It's almost as if he's a part of me—like flesh and blood and breath. A girlfriend once explained the definition of "soul mate" to me.

She said it was having someone in your life who knows you almost as good as you know yourself. That one person who, no matter what, no matter how many children you go off and have, or how many times you get married, or how many times you walk out that door, that person's always going to be there for you, waiting with open arms. No excuses.

Maybe I feared calling so much because I knew just hearing his voice would pull me right back under his spell. Before we parted for what was supposed to be the "last time," Edward whispered in my ear, "I'm always going to be here for you, Chloe." I hope that offer still stands.

I pulled out my cell, but stopped myself as I remembered.

Twelve years! Twelve years of life in L.A., and eleven of them were consumed by Mr. Edward Gentry. I ain't gonna lie, in between there were a few unmentionables who rested their hats on my nightstand, but I never kept them around long. Plus, Edward was no saint himself,

I'm sure. He travels the world and lives between San Francisco and Los Angeles, two of the biggest cities in this country.

I'm sure he has plenty of other "other" women. However, I put in my time and when it was all said and done, I probably ended up in the number-one spot. It could be the perfect situation for some lucky woman. I sure *thought* it was. Edward is just the security any woman would kill to have—a filthy rich real estate developer who gave me carte blanche to shop 'til I dropped. I traveled to exclusive destinations, and I didn't have to deal with somebody breathing down my neck twenty-four hours a day.

Oh, and how can I forget? The best part—weekend retreats at five-star hotels, like the Four Seasons in Beverly Hills when he came to Los Angeles for two days a week. We'd been coming for years, and the entire hotel staff knew me. I usually planned a light business day when he was in town, and he gave me a pocket full of cash, and the okay to order room service to my heart's content. But I guess those are the perks that come with dating a man who will never commit to you because he has it all. What would he need you for?

A man who would rather keep you hidden away in a glass tower than marry you. A man who would rather keep you hidden in the shadows, dressed up and fancy for his own personal display case. Like something he's both proud of yet ashamed.

I ain't gonna lie. Edward had my heart on lockdown until a couple of months before I met Gregorry. I started to feel emotionally un-settled with our "thing." Maybe antsy is the better word. Just once I wanted us to try doing some things that normal couples do. Normal things like going out for pizza, holding hands while walking, or even getting dressed up and going out dancing.

Just once I'd have liked for him to spend the night at my house. Do you know that in all those years he never slept in my bed? It's a really comfortable mattress, expensive too. Hell, he bought it and doesn't even know it! Just once, I'd have liked us to rent a bunch of DVDs and hole up for an entire weekend at my place, order takeout, and take a long bath together, the works! But the reality is that Edward's not interested in doing stuff like that. I guess that's too normal.

Sometimes Edward could be just downright mean and cold. Those were the times I despised everything about him and his controlling way. It didn't matter what time of day Edward was on the phones maneuvering or negotiating the next big venture. I would try to talk to him about our relationship, but he never had time. Maybe my timing was all wrong. Maybe we were just wrong. Damn, why did I call him when I knew he was busy? I remember one time in particular.

"Edward, it's Chloe."

"Hey babe, I'm right in the middle—"

"It's really important," I said, cutting him off abruptly. "I never ask you to stop what you're doing, but I need to talk to you."

"Okay. Let me clear my line." A few seconds later, he clicked back on the line. "What's up, Chloe?"

It was hard finding my words. His controlled tone made me wonder if this was a stupid move. Edward does so much for me. Was I really in a position to walk away? But if I didn't do it now I may never do it. I didn't want to watch another twelve years go by, and be angry at myself and resent him for not taking control of my own life.

"Baby, I'm in the middle of a huge deal. You either got to speak up or I've gotta call you back."

"Edward, do you love me?"

"Chloe, where are you going with this?"

"Do you love me?" I stated firmly. He knew I was serious.

"Yes, I do, Chloe. You know that."

"Then say it."

"This is foolishness. I don't have time to play games with you with all the shit I've got on my plate!"

I said nothing.

"This isn't about hearing me say a bunch of words. Is it?"

"No, it isn't," I said flatly, holding the phone in silence.

"I'm not one of these young guys who's gonna feed you a bunch of talk, Chloe. I'm too old to dance around stuff and too busy to be a part of your melodrama."

Then I'd feel powerless once again. Like my father had reprimanded me and if I didn't get my act together I could forget about the dance, the phone, and hanging out with my friends after school.

The flip side of all that were the times when Edward and I, although separated by a fifteen-year age difference, were completely in sync. No one has ever cared for my well-being like him. He was my biggest champion and fan who, after Mother's fierce prayers encouraging me to step out on faith with my business, brought up the rear with the serious financial backing. No strings attached. Simply because . . .

We melted into each other's bodies and became one. Him: commanding, yet gentle and skilled. Me: meek, innocent, sensitive. Our lovemaking was sacred, intense, mental. The way he caressed my breasts, followed every curve of my body with his fingertips. The way I ran my hands down his lean torso, around his back, clinging to him as he pressed deeper and deeper inside of me.

He directed me when to turn over, how to sit on him just the right way so he could hit that spot. The one who shook my body like an earthquake and made me forget that he had pissed me off earlier when he rushed me off the phone. The one who sent me into eurphoric bliss and made me forget about the fact that he still, after all these years, wouldn't commit to me.

Simply because . . . "I believe in you, Chloe."

Maybe this was a stupid idea to think I could even call Edward, now, after the fallout. He'd give me the I-told-you-so speech for sure. What did I have to lose? I was already at the end of my rope. The reality is that if any one person, outside of my mother, knows the core of who Chloe Michaels is, I'd have to say it's Edward. As strange and crazy as that sounds. I did need him. His words could give me peace in my heart and mind. This call was long overdue.

It's after one in the morning on the West Coast, but I still keep track of his schedule. This is his night to be in L.A., so I know he'll answer, because he's a night owl. I dialed. After three rings, I took a breath and was prepared to hang up.

"Hey!" he answered and sounded happier and healthier than he had ever sounded before. Damn, his life was great without me.

"Hey there back," I replied. My heart sped up.

"What's goin' on there, married lady?"

"Hangin' in there." My body began to tremble all over.

"How's your mother?"

"She's good, good. How's your mom?"

"She's good, real good."

"Um, I'm visiting my mom now."

"Oh, you in St. Louis? That's good, real good."

There was a long gap of silence.

"Edward?"

"Yeah, babe."

"I just called . . ."

"Baby, I'm glad you called."

"No, stop! I just called, because I need you to tell me everything's gonna be all right."

"Chloe, what's going on?" Edward said in a panic.

"It didn't work." I broke into tears.

"Aw, Chloe. I'm sorry, baby."

"I, um, came home, and um . . ." A knot formed in my throat.

"It's okay, baby. It's okay," he reassured, gently.

"I lost, um," I blinked back my tears. "I lost a baby."

"I'm so sorry, baby."

"He took, um, everything."

"What are you talking about, Chloe?" Edward's voice instantly became firm and protective. "What did he do to you?"

"He stole my money . . ."

"We don't give a damn about money! Did the nigga hurt you? I need to know!"

"I got out before he could. Things are just bad . . ." I let out a hard cry, and for the first time Edward didn't rush me off the phone on his way to a meeting, or to take another call. I was the priority.

"Listen to me, Chloe. You cry, baby, and get it all out. That's what I'm here for. I told you I would never leave you. Do you hear me?"

"Yes," I weakly replied.

Edward never in a million years expected me to announce I was getting married that last time I saw him. I shocked myself. I think after that happening, Edward wasn't sure what I was going to say or do next. He took a deep breath and exhaled slowly.

"Look, in order to close this new deal, looks like I'll have to go back east in a couple of days. I don't think we should talk about this over the phone. I need to see you. On my return I'll stop through St. Louis. Why don't you meet me at the airport?"

"Okay."

Handling love has always been the hardest part of my adult life. None of the men I've ever met captured my heart and soul like Edward Gentry did though. I knew the moment I saw him, he was the one for me. The truth is a tough pill to swallow too. I got angry. I was tired of wishing and waiting and convincing myself that I could make him marry me, be the father of my child.

My clock was ticking and I just wanted out, but I needed something to seek refuge in. Gregorry appeared from nowhere and I thought he was what I had been wishing for. I made myself fall for Gregorry. I wanted what Edward said was the impossible dream. So I was going to show him that Chloe Michaels could be okay. That Chloe Michaels could make it without him. But had I really shown him?

Eve

COLLECTING THE PIECES

I was having that dream again. I hadn't had it in a while, but this time I'm swimming and I almost reach the top and I see someone standing there. I can't see the person's face, but I know it's a woman. She reaches her hand into the water and this time her hand isn't pushing me back down, but she's pulling me out. I break through the surface, gasping for air. I can see her clearly now. She is me. I climb out of the water and she takes me by the hand and we start to walk away, but as I look back in the sand I don't see any footprints. I turn to look ahead and I see the other me has disappeared, but she's left a trail of footprints that seem to go as far as the eye can see.

"I JUST DON'T UNDERSTAND your thinking sometimes, Eve. Did you even take time out to process what happened the other night? Did you?" I had been sitting on Dale's couch for the past fifteen minutes while he gave me the third degree.

"You know what, Dale. The only thing I know how to do is give from my heart," I meekly replied.

"Well, maybe you should start doing things with your brain and not your heart then."

"I'm really sorry your birthday was ruined, Dale," I sniffed as my eyes began to water. "Dale, can we just move on?"

"Piggly," he said, sitting down next to me and lifting my chin with his hand. "I mean, c'mon, what would possess you to think that Ceci, who's ghetto, and loud, and drinks too much, would be at the top of my birthday guest list? And even your mother? Please!" He snickered.

"I wasn't thinking they would be on the top of your list." My head was pounding. I rubbed my temple.

"You don't even have any control over your own family. How in the hell would you expect to have control over running a household?"

"Dale, I think that's hurtful."

"Hurtful, but true, Piggly!"

"Can we please get past this?" The more he called me "Piggly" the more I felt as though he was patronizing me.

"No, because I need you to understand what's really at stake. Obviously, after all these years you don't even know me!" *Blah . . . Blah . . . Blah.* Dale was on a roll. His words at that point began to run together.

"Dale, please!" I had had enough of him badgering me. "I have a father. I have heard you loud and clear and I'm not stupid," I said, standing up. "First of all, stop insulting my family. I made a mistake, and that was thinking that you were worthy of what I have to offer."

"You can't be serious?" He laughed.

"Oh, very! I don't need nobody tearing me down no more."

"You're not going to ever find anybody like me."

"Dale, I think you may be right about that last part. You are definitely one of a kind," I said, with a raised eyebrow.

"You got a baby daddy and you're strugglin' check to check. Where would you or your daughter be without me?" I was stunned at the level of arrogance Dale was displaying.

"We are gonna be just fine. My child is my blessing and she's strong because she comes from a strong woman, who came from a whole line of strong women!"

And then all I remember is feeling this intense heat shoot through my body. My hand flew into the air, and with all the strength I had in my body, I, in the words of Mother, "smacked the fire outta" that man. It hit me that it wasn't about me not knowing him, Dale didn't know me.

I had actually convinced myself that forty-four meant my life was over. I was a damn proud strugglin' single mother, and Dale had been tearing me down piece by piece over the years. Hell naw! I picked up my box of belongings and walked out the door. Dale didn't have to worry. For the first time in a long time I knew exactly what I was doing.

I think I finally understood the dream, too. Perhaps, I was the person always holding me back and pushing me back under the water. I was fighting against the current. It was time for me to let go and let God. And I was proud of how I had stood up to Dale. Fawn and Chloe had insisted on coming with me, but I needed to do this by myself. I needed to use Eve's voice to speak up. I have abandoned doing the things that make me happy for too long. Making my soaps and baskets make me happy. Fuck what Dale thinks. He said I was wasting my time with my "little hobby." Maybe so, but I felt like I was showing people what I could do.

I started my car and the gas light came on. I was almost on empty! But I'd be damned if I had to go back up in that house and ask Dale for shit. Hell, I'd make it. I always had. If Mother did it, so could I!

Chloe

BOBBY NASH

"HE JUST UP and had a heart attack . . ." That was all I heard before Fawn's voice trailed off. She tried to clear her throat, but her words trapped somewhere between a tear and disbelief.

"Fawn? What are you talkin' about?" I questioned, high-pitched.

"Chloe . . ." Fawn struggled, her voice cracking.

"What's wrong? Fawn!"

"It's Daddy . . ." she stammered.

"Wha, wha . . ." Now my words were getting stuck and I could feel my heart pounding in my ears. "Wha, wha, what happened?" I swallowed hard.

"It's Daddy. He's dead!"

"Wait a minute, which daddy?" I was breathing hard, and my chest was heaving up and down.

"Daddy! Daddy Bobby!" she screamed, crying hysterically.

After several minutes, I finally got her calm enough to tell me what happened.

"Eve rushed over to Daddy's house after Ursile called saying she couldn't wake him up. Eve called me when the ambulance arrived. By the time I got to the hospital, Daddy was gone . . ."

Mother and I were standing at the front entrance of Lake Funeral Home as the limo pulled up. I sat, stiff, expressionless. Fawn, Eve, Christina, Cliff, and Lola were all riding inside with Ursile and two of her sisters. Christina's flight had gotten in late last night. People were lined up everywhere to pay their respects. Some were holding bouquets of flowers, others large plants.

It was humid from an early morning downpour, typical for St. Louis this time of year. But that didn't stop the black folks from getting decked out to the nines. Some brothas had on full three-piece suits, and hats to match. The sistas had their stockings and high heels on, and some with hats on like the men.

"Well, Lake gonna get used to us comin' here, seems like just yesterday we were here for Millie. Lord, what's next," Mother said, sighing from the passenger seat. I looked over at her. I could see Mother fighting back the tears. "I can't believe I'm burying my first husband, Chloe." Her voice quivered.

"I know, this is surreal, Mother."

"Beyond surreal, chile. Lake's got him laid out in style. Look at all Bobby's buddies from the Post Office."

Christina made her way over to me and Mother. She was stylish in her black dress and pumps and had shocked us all by cutting off her shoulder-length tresses for a chic blunt cut, just below her ears.

"Hi, Gran!" She hugged and kissed Mother. "Aunt Chloe! Oh my God, I have so much to tell you!" She gave me a repeat of hugs and kisses.

"Go on, Christina, get back over there with your mama. Aunt Chloe ain't goin' nowhere. C'mon, I need to see about my girls," Mother said.

Mother and I followed closely behind Eve and Fawn and the rest of Bobby Nash's family as everyone made their way into the funeral home. I was alarmed by Fawn's unusually calm behavior and the blank stare on her face.

"You all have to be strong for your father," Mother said, kissing Eve's hand. She turned to Fawn. "Just let it out if you want to," she said, kissing Fawn's hand next.

"I'm fine, Mother," Fawn said, blinking several times.

The tension was thick inside. Mother and I sat in the pew across from Fawn, Eve, Christina, Cliff, and Lola who were seated with Ursile, Fawn and Eve's stepmother, and her family. Bobby's brother, his wife, their children, grandkids, and a gazillion other cousins filled up the rest of the rows.

Bobby's brother, John, who I had grown up calling Uncle Johnny, and his wife, Aunt Myrtle, along with Bobby's cousins, were excited to see me and Mother. Some of them hadn't seen me since I was a teenager. They seemed to be just as concerned about how Mother was holding up as they were about Ursile. I saw Ursile's sister, Thelma, shoot Mother a nasty look.

What made it even worse was when Carol Jane, Ceci, and Satin and the baby arrived, pushing Aunt Billye Jean in a wheelchair. Half of Bobby Nash's cousins rushed over to them. Aunt Billye Jean wasn't supposed to be out, overexerting herself. Against the doctor's orders, she had come to the funeral. She told Mother she "wasn't missing her brother's funeral." Carol Jane said the only way she'd bring her was if she got in that chair.

Mother's presence was always strong throughout Ursile and Bobby Nash's marriage. I'm sure that made Ursile feel threatened a lot. I remember once she and Ursile were on the phone arguing when I was about fourteen and I heard her tell Ursile, "If I wanted Bobby Nash back, I coulda had him years ago!" In their younger years, they had plenty of arguments.

Ursile was crazy to think Bobby Nash and Mother would stop being friends. Beyond having to raise two children, they were childhood friends, who became sweethearts. They probably were just too young to be trying to be married. Plus Aunt Billye Jean was Bobby Nash's buddy. He'd stop by regularly to check on her on his way home from work because he had to pass right by her house.

As everyone was settling in and the preacher approached the podium, Mother kept looking over at Fawn and Eve. I kept looking at my watch. Where was Daddy? Thank God he arrived minutes before the service began and slid in next to me, kissing me on the cheek. He put his arm around me and rubbed Mother's shoulder. Daddy looked over at Fawn and Eve and winked, sending his silent support.

Fawn hadn't really broken down yet, but you know Eve is more emotional. We were worried about Fawn, though. She's not as strong as everybody thinks. Anyway, I know my sister. She was hurting bad, and when it hits, it's gonna be hard.

The service seemed to go on forever. Ursile's pastor was reading scriptures I'd never heard or seen before in the Bible. Some of them sounded like he was making them up.

"Our house had holes on da top and when it rain, it rain on the inside and leak on the outside. You got folks they done bought homes in the hills, cain't visit 'em no more. They'ze gotta *alitude* but they came from the same place as us. Peoples that's gotsa *alitude* wit no *gralatude*," he said with a heavy southern drawl. I gave mother a questioning look, thinking to myself, I know this man did not just say the word *a-li-tude*.

He sounded like one of those uneducated, backwoods, self-ordained preachers you might catch on a cable access channel in the middle of the night.

I was still stuck on the word *alitude*. He had to have meant "attitude," and only God knows what that other word was. Mother rolled her eyes. I heard Carol Jane behind us say "Good Lord! What is this mess?" under her breath. Aunt Billye Jean chimed in, "Bobby Nash is turnin' over as we speak." She was never too good at whispering. I thought he was finished, but he wasn't.

"I, I, know a man, a man who was wit some apostals, amen. Folk like John tha Babas who live in da wiltaness. And God, He say, He say, 'Isiah!' " He gave an animated bug-eyed expression that was like one of those Bernie Mac coonin' faces he likes to make. "God tole him 'dis wha I won't ya ta do, git ova there, c'mon boy." He paused and I guess he was so filled with the spirit that he shouted, "Hallelujah!"

Mother kicked me in disgust. Meanwhile, he just kept jabbering about nonsense. I tried to listen harder, but I just gave myself a headache.

"He up in hebum an, an, an, He can make it all right," he continued. By now he was sweating so badly it was running all down the side of his shiny bald head and dripping on his suit jacket. He took a handkerchief and wiped his large round forehead. I couldn't figure out for the life of me what his eulogy was supposed to be about. Did he even know Bobby Nash?

Bobby Nash had never been a very religious man, and Ursile always hated that. He was raised Catholic, but hadn't set foot in anybody's church in years. Lake Funeral Home had buried just about everybody in Bobby Nash's family. Their families were as close as cousins. Ursile hated that too, because her brother was a mortician and she wanted him to handle the body.

Fawn asked to say a few words and Ursile said no. It was *her* right and Mother was furious, but she kept her mouth closed. Mother was no longer his wife, and how Ursile handled his funeral was none of her business. If you ask me, Ursile was just always bitter that she and Bobby Nash had never had any children of their own.

"Well, that was the worst funeral I've ever been to," Mother said through pursed lips. I couldn't figure out what a "good" funeral was. All I know is it was the *longest* funeral I had ever been to. It made me appreciate Grandmother being Catholic. I was happy to be out of that place and back in the car, headed over to Ursile and Bobby Nash's house for the repast. I was starving.

After Daddy hugged and kissed Fawn and Eve, he took off and told them he'd come by Mother's tomorrow to see them. I think the service got to him. Grandmother's funeral was still so fresh on all of us. At one point he leaned over and whispered to me, "When I die, don't do all this long drawn-out shit for me. Just cremate me and dump my ashes in the Mississippi!"

So there we sat, in the house Eve and Fawn spent so much of their lives in. A house that was now empty of the funny jokes Bobby Nash would tell and his robust, jovial laugh. However, Bobby Nash's spirit was strong. In fact, it was somewhat unsettling. I could feel it when I walked in. It was like he wasn't pleased with things. All of us were present with Eve and Fawn: Mother, Aunt Billye Jean, Carol Jane, Ceci, Satin, Sage, Christina, Cliff, and Lola. Ursile and her family didn't like it one bit either.

Fawn placed a ham on the counter and began slicing it slowly, and Eve was separating the bottles and cans from the rest of the garbage. Aunt Billye Jean was resting on the couch. Ceci was finishing up a slice of coconut cake, while Carol Jane laughed and reminisced about Bobby Nash with Uncle Johnny and Aunt Myrtle.

I was standing at the kitchen island, and just about to swallow a forkful of sweet potato pie, when all of a sudden I heard a barrage of screaming and hollering coming from upstairs. It was Mother and Ursile going at it full blast. I dropped my plate and gave Fawn a panicked look. We all stopped what we were doing and bolted upstairs. Ceci was hot on our trail.

"I ain't got to do nothin'!" Ursile shouted, pointing in Mother's face.

"I tried to be civil with you, Ursile, now get your hand outta my face," Mother said, squaring off with Ursile.

We all stumbled and slid into the master bedroom where they were midargument.

"Who the hell you think you are? I *am* Mrs. Bobby Elvin Nash, dammit!"

"Mother, what is going on?" Eve shouted.

"It's only right that Ursile give Bobby's only children something to remember him by. I was just askin' about his insurance policy," Mother said.

"None of yo damn business!" Ursile staggered slightly.

"She's drunk, Joy Ann!" Ceci snapped. "C'mon, don't upset yourself over her."

"You gonna have your day, Ursile. God don't like ugly, and Bobby would've never let his girls be treated like this."

"Mother, please not today. Let Daddy rest in peace," Fawn begged. "Plus everyone's upset, and, Ursile, you've had a little too much to drink." Fawn was trying to reason, but as she started to pull Mother out of the room Ursile lurched forward.

"He ain't yo daddy! I ain't givin' *you* nothin'!" Ursile said, pointing to Fawn.

Fawn's face exploded with tears and her body was so weak from the blow of words that she dropped to the floor. I went over to her to help her stand up. Mother's face went pale. I saw her ball up her fist. Ursile had just given herself a death wish right there on the spot.

"Don't you ever in your natural life fix your mouth to say those words again," Mother glared. Then all I saw was Ursile flying backward. She fell to the floor, holding the side of her face. Mother had given new meaning to the term "ass whoopin'." Ursile had suddenly sobered up, realizing what she had said, but the damage was done. She just kept mouthing, "I'm sorry. I'm so sorry, Fawn." By this time Carol Jane had made it upstairs out of breath. Cliff burst into the room right behind her and carried Fawn out. It took me, Eve, and Carol Jane to pull Mother out of the room.

Aunt Billye Jean was bracing herself on the wall at the bottom of the steps, holding her chest and shouting, "Where's my sister? Oh, Lord, what's happenin'?" Satin took the lead and got Christina and Lola out to the car. Uncle Johnny, Aunt Myrtle, and two of Bobby Nash's other male cousins crammed into the stairwell to clear up the action. The house had erupted into utter chaos.

Fawn

THE REAL NERVOUS BREAKDOWN

"**F**AWN, I KNOW you don't want to do this, but as y'all's mother, I'm putting my foot down."

"I just feel like an outsider, Mother," I said, holding the telephone receiver.

"You're mine, do you hear me!"

I objected, but Mother wasn't having it. She made all of us come to her house for a "family meeting." She even summoned Daddy Ray. But I didn't feel like I was part of anybody's family right now. I didn't want to see Eve and Chloe.

The truth . . .

I found out Daddy wasn't my biological father back when I was in college. I had come home for my first Christmas break and was in a car accident. I had had a crush on Michael Dooley all through high school and had finally matured and came into my own and Michael asked me to go out. Can you believe a car would hit us on the way to the damn party? After you got past all the blood, I only had a few cuts, bumps, and bruises.

When they rushed me to the hospital, the doctors thought I might need a blood transfusion, but neither Mother nor Daddy had my blood type. Well, that's when Mother decided it was time to come clean to me about it all. "Baby, your daddy is not your biological father." I frowned, confused and unsure where she was going with all this.

Mother went on to explain how she had gotten pregnant by an upperclassman when she went away to school. When she told him she was pregnant, he refused to claim me. "I started seeing Bobby Nash and he told me that he wanted to marry me and that you would be *our* baby. So he's *your* father and don't you ever let anybody make you think differently! He's as much your father as the blood flowing through your veins. Never forget that you are Bobby Nash's daughter."

I had no choice but to process what she had just told me after eighteen years of living, and then I got over it. I never felt shame about that or even dealt with it for that matter. Even when I eventually met my biological father. I didn't create the situation, but I have to live with it.

I swallowed hard and approached the front door to Mother's house. I could see Chloe and Eve through the brightly painted picture window sitting at Mother's kitchen table. The window was open. I felt that same weakness in my knees again, and I was suddenly unsure if I could go through with actually sitting in front of them talking about all of this. I thought about turning around, getting in my car, and leaving. Mother wasn't standing outside anymore. She had walked up to Salvatore's house. Eve and Chloe hadn't seen me yet. If I left, they would never know I had been here.

As I got closer, I could hear that Chloe and Eve were in the middle of an intense conversation. I leaned against the side of the house and listened through the window.

"Get over it! I've been mad about it for years. I found out when I was seventeen or eighteen. It was stupid how I found out, too." Eve chuckled with a half smile. "You know we can't sit in the house and not have an argument. One day Fawn said somethin' about how she was glad she didn't have fat ankles like Nash's, and that that was the only thing thing she got from her daddy's side. And that was it.

"I remember sittin' there baffled that my *own* sister was talking about our father's family like that, and that my *own* mother was agreeing. Now to this day both Fawn and Mother will both probably deny that happened. But you know Fawn is just like Mother. They are always opening their big mouths saying the wrong thing at the wrong time," Eve said angrily. "So then Fawn came right out and said 'Daddy's not my biological father.' Just like that!"

"No explanation? Oh, hell naw, I do not want to hear any more about this!" Chloe shockingly replied. I was seething as Eve just kept right on flapping off at the mouth. How dare Eve. How dare both of them.

"Mother and Fawn should've kept that drama to themselves. I was mad, still am. How do you live almost twenty years, then find something like that out?" Eve said.

I had had enough. I barreled through the front door like a maniac. Eve and Chloe whipped around in shock. "If y'all want to talk about me, please do it in my presence," I shouted. My eye makeup was smeared from crying. "Say it all to my face!" My voice teetered between hysteria and insanity.

"I'm sorry, Fawn, but there's just been a lot of anger and there still is, and it comes out!" Eve shouted, beginning to cry.

"What are you talkin' about? News flash, everything isn't about you! Right now I'm hurting," I blasted.

"Forgive me for being bitter right now, but to me if anybody should've had a heart attack and died, it should've been Donald Aikens, not Daddy!" Eve's words were venomous.

"You don't have a right to be mad or bitter!" I exclaimed, bursting into tears.

Just then Mother flung the front door open, "Stop it! Stop it! I want it to stop now!" She was so angry her face was beet red and her fists were balled up. Daddy was standing next to her. Behind him stood the infamous Donald Aikens.

"All of you come over here right now!" Mother demanded, instructing us to gather in the living-room area. Mother sat down slowly in the rocking chair; she flashed a steely look, before taking several deep breaths, speaking in soft even words.

"I wasn't sure I was even strong enough for this. So when I got up this morning I just fell to my knees. I asked God to give me strength for my children today. I'm dealing with my own grief about Bobby Nash's death, but if it hadn't been for him dying, this day may not have come.

"But I made up my mind after Ursile crossed me after the funeral I wouldn't take another day of your abuse, Eve, about your daddy. I won't stand another negative comment about Fawn's biological father," she said, looking over at Donald. "Donald knows what he did and he'll have to go to his grave with that guilt."

Mother stood up and commanded the attention of everyone in the room. "Now Bobby Nash loved both of you, Eve and Fawn, but he didn't sacrifice one damn thing for you. He was very selfish until he got older and realized what wonderful daughters he had. Some things he was just too late on. And Ray," she said, turning to Daddy, "you could never handle anything outside the insulated walls of your own damn world. You've never been able to give much more than a little bit.

"I want each and every person in this room today to know that I'm not ashamed of anything I've done as far as my girls are concerned," Mother said, looking around the room, zeroing in on Daddy Ray and Donald Aikens. "To see that I'm so far from that scared eighteen-year-old girl, pregnant and alone," she said, staring right at Donald. "I know that God brought the union of me and Bobby Nash and he served his purpose giving my baby his name and claiming her as his own.

"Ray and Bobby Nash may have had their shortcomings in the husband department, but they loved my girls, and a mother can't ask for much more. And this don't hardly make Ray a saint. 'Cause, Ray, you made it a point to constantly remind me that you was raisin' somebody else's kids. So if I wanna tell every last one of the men who have come in and outta my life to kiss my ass, I can.

"I have cleaned up enough of they shit. Bobby Nash has gone on and we cain't do nothin' about it. Eve, you think to this day that your daddy could do no wrong. Well, there's a whole lot you don't even know about your daddy. Ray, you and all your skeletons and secrets, sneakin' around with a woman half your age like some kind of playboy," Mother said. Daddy Ray's eyes went wide.

"You think I didn't know? I been knowin'. You don't get this old and go through as much hell I've been through to not be smart. But I bet when you get sick, you won't be goin' to *her*. 'Cause then she might know how old you *really* are." She rolled her eyes and turned to Donald. "I know, Donald, that it wasn't until you saw how successful Fawn had become that you suddenly wanted to reconcile and claim her. My mother always said the truth comes to light.

"None of us need to keep livin' lies. I've covered up and protected men long enough! Baby, the cleanup woman is officially retirin'. No more pickin' up other people's shit and taking the heat for each of your fathers' fuckups!" Mother stood solidly with her hands on her hips.

"Errum," Donald cleared his throat nervously. "Well, I, I just want to say that I made a terrible mistake. I would never try to be your father, Fawn, after all these years. Bobby Nash was, and even you, Ray. They were both clearly better men than me. Joy Ann, I just thank you for forgiving me. I'm gonna go now." Donald made a cowardly exit.

"Forgave, *not* forgot," Mother clarified with sternness.

"Look here, I'mma say my piece on this whole thing. I'm with Joy Ann. No more needs to be said about who somebody's father is. Bobby Nash loved both of his daughters. I've been lucky enough to be able to share in that love with him. We could all be better. Sometimes I wish I had been a better stepfather." Daddy's eyes filled up with tears. He cupped his hand over his mouth, took a deep breath, then walked over to me with open arms.

He hugged me real good "daddy style." Tears streamed down my face. I was an innocent little girl all over again. Eve slowly rose and walked over to us, and Daddy Ray put his other arm around her. The three of us stood hugging each other for a long time.

About an hour later, just me, Mother, Eve, and Chloe sat quietly at the table. I finally broke my silence. "I don't like to say it, but we all have different fathers," I said, suddenly digging deep and pulling out a confidence I had covered up and tucked away for fear it would unleash unbearable pain. A tightness formed in my jaws. "It's not something I'm proud about, but it's reality.

"I think as much as Daddy Ray cares about me and Eve, it will

313

never be the same as he feels for you, Chloe. I accept that. I don't expect him to pick up where Daddy left off, either, now that he's dead. I don't even think he's interested. But I do know that he loves and cares about both Eve and me, and our children. So whatever he does is a bonus and not an entitlement.

"As for me and my father experience, Eve, I loved Daddy and always thought of him as my true father and I always will. He was there for me and claimed me. And I love and care about Daddy Ray and appreciate our relationship. As for my biological father, it has taken me years to even become comfortable referring to him as *my* father, but that's who he is.

"I will never love him the way one loves a father, but he's been very nice to me and my family and I hope that one day you two will respect that." She paused and wiped her eyes. "The truth is I've had to get pieces of a daddy from three different places to make up a semblance of a whole! But that's life!" I had finally laid my foot down, big-sister style. I stood up and smoothed down my skirt. "Mother, I gotta go."

"You gonna be okay, baby? Do you wanna stay here tonight?" Mother asked.

"No, I'll be okay."

Mother put her arms around me and hugged me for a long time. "I love you, and I'm proud of you," she said.

"I love you too." Then I turned to Eve and Chloe and gave each of them a hug before walking out the door.

I thought I'd feel better since everything was out in the open, but a week later I didn't. I felt like the bond I had with my sisters had been cracked. Mother had been calling for the past few days and I just didn't have much to say. I knew Chloe was going through her own drama and I was hurting for her, but I couldn't be supportive like I wanted to.

Eve and I have always had a relationship as sisters that's hard to explain. I always feel a tremendous sense of jealousy from her, because

I'm married, have my family, and have a big house, all the superficial things. I can never call and talk to her about what I'm going through with Cliff. She always finds a way to make things about her. At the same time, she probably understands me better than anyone else in the family, even Mother.

We also have to grieve about Daddy in our own ways. My way is alone. I have enough social activities to plan for anyway. Plus, I've got some things I have to work through within myself. I know my feelings, no matter how brief, for Reverend Gibbs were wrong, but it comes from a deeper place. I dropped my membership to the church, anyway. Sure, I am worried about my marriage, and I miss my relationship with Mother. I wanna go to her, but I need her to listen and not judge.

I finally got fed up with it all after realizing that Cliff was been spending less and less time at home and more and more time on the golf course. My curiosity got the best of me and I decided to take a drive out to Pleasant Greens Golf Course and Country Club. When I got there, much to my shock, Cliff wasn't there and hadn't been for over a month. He was cold busted.

As I sped down Highway 40 my thoughts were racing, thinking about how I was going to confront him when he got home. That was all the evidence I needed. He was cheating, and his ass was gonna pay. I burst through the front door and was so mad I left the car idling in the driveway, the car door wide open, and my purse and a backseat full of groceries in the ninety-five-degree sun.

I ran up and down the stairs screaming Cliff's name like a madwoman. When I got to his study, I found he had left the computer on and his AOL mailbox was still up. I sat down and curiously started going through his recently deleted mail and saw that Cliff had been exchanging e-mails with a woman. There were a slew of messages from someone named "Bootylicious." The message read: *Cliffy, I'm glad I could be there for you. I hope you take me up on my offer. Muah!*

I was livid; clearly the Negro had gotten either too damn excited or was just plain stupid, but he left the evidence on the screen. I went into a rage and started ripping up and tearing down everything I could put my hands on in the study. I grabbed the cordless and dialed Mother's. Chloe answered.

"Where's Mother?" I panted. "I'm gonna kill his ass!"

"Fawn, wait a minute, she's not here; she went out with Eve to the casino. Tell me what's going on!"

"Didn't you hear me? I'm gonna kill him!"

"Calm down! I'm on my way over there," Chloe said, but it was too late. I was on a mission and I didn't have time for all this conversation. I dropped the phone and continued on my rampage. Oh, he's gonna cheat on me, on me? Then his ass won't have shit by the time I finish with him. I picked up the desk lamp and threw it across the room into his trophy case. Glass exploded and shattered everywhere.

"Fawn! What the hell is going on?" I spun around, enraged. Cliff was standing in the hallway, holding his golf bag and looking at me like I was crazy.

"I'm redecorating, motherfucker!" I shouted, charging him. He backed up and ran into the master bedroom. I reached into his golf-bag and pulled out his lucky nine iron.

"How could you do this to me!" I said, swinging the club wildly at the air. The chaise lounge was the only thing separating us.

"Fawn, calm down," Cliff pleaded, trying his best to duck.

"You're on the Internet making plans with some whore!" I swung it again.

"Put the club down so we can talk!" he shouted.

"I ain't puttin' shit down! How you gonna talk without no damn teeth? I'm about to knock all of 'em out!"

"Let me explain!"

"Fawn! Fawn!" I heard Chloe and Ceci's voices from downstairs.

"Don't come up here," I shouted, holding Cliff at bay with the club.

"Fawn, I'm here now and Ceci's with me. We're coming upstairs!" Chloe called out.

"Get out!" I refocused on my target and swung again.

"I just wanna explain!" Cliff was making a poor attempt to change my mind about killing him.

"Explain what, motherfucker? That you cheated on me with some bitch named Bootylicious right in my own house after I helped you through medical school!" He ran to the other side of the room. I was in hot pursuit. I swung again. *Crash!* There went the night table lamp. "Had your child!" *Bam!* There went the bookcase, and all the books went sprawling across the carpet. "Helped you build your stupid practice!"

"Hell no, she done lost it!" Ceci said as she and Chloe stumbled into the room. "Fawn, you gots to put that shit down," Ceci said.

"Let's be rational, Fawn," Chloe said, out of breath, leaning on Ceci. "Fawn, please stop!" Chloe shouted.

"This Negro ain't worth it, cuz!" Ceci tried to reason, stepping closer to me. I had paused, taking aim at my next target.

"Ceci, please help!" Cliff pleaded.

"Shut up, Cliff, and fuck being rational!" I said. I was confused. Too many people were in the room and talking. We were right in the middle of a domestic brawl. I heard plenty of stories about how people die in these type of situations.

"I'm calling Mother," Chloe said, pulling out her cell. "Eve, you gotta come quick! I'm at Fawn's house and she's done flipped! Calmly, get Mother and y'all get your asses over here!"

"That's right, just calm down, cuz. We gotta all think with a clear head," Ceci explained, holding her arms out.

"Screw all y'all. That's right, Fawn has flipped!" I took aim at the next target that was sure to advance her to the bonus round. Cliff's brand-new flat-screen television.

"Oh, no! Oh, no! Not my baby!" he cried.

"Aw, hells no! Not the flat-screen, Fawn!" Ceci shouted.

"That's right, Cliff, you love that damn TV more than me obviously!" *Smash!* With one clean stroke, I had destroyed it.

Cliff made a dive across the room and landed on top of me. Ceci came flying after him, and then as I struggled to break free of the bodies piled on top of me, I saw Chloe leaping over the overturned bookcase and snatching up the nine iron. Ceci got a good hold on Cliff and was pulling him off me.

"I'm not going to hurt her! I'm not going to hurt her!" Cliff shouted.

Chloe grabbed me, but I was so rage filled, my hundred and twenty pounds was giving her a run for her money.

"Fawn, stop! Calm down!" Chloe begged, as I collapsed into her arms and began weeping.

"I just don't understand. I have tried to do everything I could to be the perfect wife, to make a perfect home for you and our daughter, to support all your shit, and look what it got me!" I cried.

"Dammit, Fawn maybe all I needed was for you to just be my wife. My friend! Treat me with some respect!" Cliff said, pulling away from Ceci and pacing the room.

"What the hell do you think I've been doing for all these years? This has all been for you. What about me?" I stammered between more tears. Suddenly, my own words must have struck another nerve in me. I pulled away from Chloe and before she knew it, I had opened the night table drawer and pulled out a 9 mm. They all gasped in unison.

"Oh Jesus!" I hadn't heard Ceci call the Lord's name in I don't know when. This was sure to send her back to drinking. "Fawn, girl, this ain't worth goin' ta jail for the rest of yo life."

"Fawn, please, put the gun down! I been there. Please don't make a mistake," Chloe began to cry.

"I'll leave, Fawn. I'm sorry. I love you, just put . . ." Cliff lowered his head.

"I will kill yo ass before you just cheat on me and leave!" I said, training the gun on him, cutting him off.

"I'm sorry. I love you, just put . . ."

"Don't you say shit else, Cliff! You don't love me."

"Fawn, yes I do."

"How long you been screwin' her, Cliff?"

"I didn't sleep with her. I swear to God. I only talked to her and met her for dinner a few times. I swear to God! Please don't do this!" Tears were streaming down Cliff's face.

I was frozen with terror.

Just then I heard the front door slam and Mother's voice, "Fawn! It's Mother. I'm comin', baby!"

"We're upstairs in the bedroom, Mother!" Chloe yelled back.

By the time Mother reached the bedroom door she was panting and Eve was out of breath behind her. "God, don't let my baby do this!"

Eve was fear-stricken. "Fawn. Please don't do this." She fell up against the wall and began crying.

Mother started praying harder. "Lord, what is going on? I call on your spirit to bind Satan up. Bind him up and loose his hold on my family, God." Suddenly the strength of God filled her body and she began to walk toward me, holding her arms out. I was scared and confused. I put the gun down, following Mother's voice.

Ceci grabbed the gun and emptied the chamber. Mother rushed over to me and wrapped her arms around me and rocked me gently. "I'm not lettin' the devil destroy my family. Satan, I rebuke you!"

"I'm sorry, I tried, Mother. I tried!" I released a cry that I had been holding inside for so long I had forgotten what tears felt like. I had buried all my feelings in PTA meetings, and ballet, and shopping, and reupholstering furniture, and cocktail parties, and benefits. Somewhere in all that, I lost Fawn. Somewhere in all that, I forgot that I had a good man who loved me and a beautiful daughter.

"Baby, it's okay. I told you to stop tryin'. God wants you to be just like you are. You hear me?" Mother understood, finally.

Chloe

FREE YOURSELF

E SCADA WAS ONE of Edward's favorite designers on me. I had picked out the most perfect, flowery flounce skirt and a matching silk blouse. It's fitting me a little more snug since the last time I wore it, but what the hell. It's been almost a year since I've seen him and my stomach is doing a serious flip-flop.

I could see him up ahead. He must've had the same thing in mind because he always looked damn good in an Armani suit, never too fancy. Edward never drew attention to himself, but I always noticed the little things, like a fresh haircut or shave. He exited security and walked toward me. I sucked in my gut and adjusted my neck and shoulders so that my posture was straight. Seeing him made me realize just how much I've missed him. Damn, I hoped this was a good idea.

"Hey, there!" He threw his arms around me, then leaned in to kiss me. Edward and I never practiced public affection. I stiffened. Surprisingly, he kissed me on the lips. I blinked several times, not really sure of what had just happened. "You look good, baby."

"I'm glad you could stop through," I said, regaining composure. For some reason I wanted to cry, but I knew I couldn't do that in the middle of the airport.

We found a quiet spot in the food court. His layover was short, but for the first time Edward didn't seem rushed.

"Thank you for understanding all this."

"You mean a lot to me, Chloe, and you already know that. We've got a lot of history," he said, reaching across the table and putting his hand over mine. "And nothing is ever going to come between us. I don't care if you have ten kids!"

"I'm sorry, but I have to get some things off my chest once and for all about our relationship." I was pensive and fidgety.

"Chloe, baby, with everything you've got to deal with, this should be the furthest thing from your mind."

"But it's not. Please listen, Edward." I paused. "Do you realize we never spent one holiday or birthday together? We may have seen five movies together in eleven years. I've never met your family. That was very important to me. I wanted you to greet me with open arms so many times. You don't even know what my favorite color or song is." My eyes welled up.

"I didn't need to know that stuff. I know who *you* are and I know your heart. I know what you need—security, dependability, consistency. You can talk about everything else with your sisters or your girlfriends."

"But what about love? I didn't want to be in the shadows of your life anymore!"

"And I respected that," he said, lowering his head. "Part of caring about a person is accepting them for who they are. Go on."

"Edward, you've taught me so much. Hell, you helped me build my business."

"No, Chloe, you built your business. I did what any upstanding man should do. Cheer you on and support you."

He was making this so hard. I cleared my throat and started again. "Edward, I've shut myself off to a lot of my emotions because of the circumstances between us."

"Stop." Edward placed his hand gently over my mouth. "You are one of the best things that's happened in my life. I'm sorry that I couldn't have been your fantasy composite of a man. But you need to understand some things too. Things that I know more about because I'm older than you. Beauty fades, and the sex dries up. When somebody loves you, that means they're down for you when everything else is collapsing all around. That person is there like solid rock when bad shit happens, like death and sickness. That's love. That's more than a ring or some piece of paper. I can only give you what I have to give. I ain't never been no warm and fuzzy man. It ain't my style, but I love you and I'm gonna always make sure you have what you need."

"What did you want from me?" I asked.

"What I still want. I want you to be happy and I want you to have the best, and I'm going to always make sure of that."

I felt my heart drop. God, give me the strength. I took a deep breath and quickly let it out. I closed my eyes, and Edward kissed my lips again. Edward grabbed his briefcase and was just about to walk away when he stopped and turned back around.

"Oh, I almost forgot something." Edward reached into his suit jacket and pulled out an envelope. "I wanted you to take a look at this." He handed me the envelope and kissed me again, and whispered in my ear, "I'm always going to be here." He smiled. I smiled back.

I watched him clear security and fade into the distance. When he was out of sight, I opened the envelope. Oh Lord! It was a check for $100,000.00 and the note read: *Maybe this can help with starting over. Edward.*

Thora

GUESS WHO'S COMIN' TO DINNER

WHEN I WALKED into ICU, they still had Billye Jean hooked up to all these machines with tubes sticking everywhere, even after all these days.

"They don't know if she's gonna make it this time. This is her third heart attack. The doctor said she's too weak to have any surgery right now," Joy Ann announced in the family waiting room. So I waited.

I knew Joy Ann was gearing up to start some shit when she leaned over and whispered something into Carol Jane's ear. I overheard her as I was coming back into the waiting area from checking on Billye Jean. I paid her no mind and found me a seat in the family lounge.

"My sista is in that room dyin'." Joy Ann can be so dramatic sometimes. I ignored her, picking up a magazine to pass the time.

"We just gotta keep prayin' and thinkin' positive, Joy Ann." Carol Jane tried to shush her.

"I'm sicka holdin' my tongue, Carol Jane." Joy Ann just kept on mumbling.

"Thora, how long you gonna be in town?" Carol Jane asked.

"I told my job I'd try to get back after the weekend," I said, crossing my legs, flipping the page.

"Thora, I think we should talk," Joy Ann said.

"I'm goin' out for a cigarette, you wanna join me?" I said, putting the magazine down, reaching for my cigarettes that were in my purse.

"You know Chloe's gonna get you if she finds out, and don't go blaming it on me," I said, taking a long drag.

"That's okay, I got my spray in my purse," she said, pulling out a trial-size bottle of $1.99 body splash. We shared a laugh.

"Thora, I don't wanna see the same thing happen with you and Billye Jean that happened with Earl."

"It's not the same, and it's never gonna be the same!" I found myself raising my voice. Shouting and arguing is out of my character. I had to take another puff on my cigarette to defuse the tension knotting up in my neck.

I turned and started to walk away.

"Thora, wait! I'm sorry. I know this is a lot on you, too."

I stopped walking. "Do you remember the day Earl died and you called me?" I asked, with my back to Joy Ann. "I was in the middle of looking through wallpaper samples with David. And you said, 'Well, Thora, I know Earl's passing is hard for you, and you didn't always see eye to eye with Earl, but hopefully coming home to the funeral will help you bring closure to your pain.' Do you remember, Joy Ann?"

"Yes, I do, Thora. Billye Jean had told me you wouldn't be attending the funeral, but I just felt that you needed to be here. He was your father, Thora!"

"I was glad Earl died. He was about as significant to me as those wallpaper samples. You know why? Because Earl didn't know me. He didn't know what my aspirations and dreams were."

"Thora, he was askin' for you on his deathbed."

"Earl was a lifetime too late."

"Thora, any way you say it, it's still wrong, but I don't have to look at myself in the mirror and face that; you do."

"Joy Ann, how about *I* don't have to look in a mirror or anyplace else, because the scars from the glass ripping through my skin are still visible on my body." Tears were streaming down my face by now.

I took my hand and wiped the side of my face hard. "I'll live with certain things every day for the rest of my life."

"What about Junior?" she asked. I almost thought she was making a joke.

"What about him? He ran that day, and he ain't stopped running! He was never the big brother I needed. You all talk about me, but has Junior even been here to the hospital to see Billye Jean?"

"Junior is sick and in pain."

"Joy Ann, that's been the excuse we've all given him for all these years. Look, I love Billye Jean. I love her, and I'm proud I can finally say that out loud. Time has healed my wounds, Joy Ann." Suddenly, I couldn't hold back the buckets of tears I had been collecting for what felt like my entire life. She put her arms around me and we stood, locked in an embrace for a while before I pulled back.

"We needed this," she said, wiping her own tear-soaked face with the palms of her hands. "You know, I was so busy meddlin' I didn't get to tell you how much I like your hair and this whole new style you wearin'." She smiled, looking me up and down. I did a mini *America's Next Top Model* spin and gave a bashful smile. "Go on, girl!" she said, putting her arm around me.

I do believe that Joy Ann makes sense when she talks about how gettin' right with God is important. But I think in this case, God will make an exception.

Chloe

PLANS TO THE WIND

"**I**'M GLAD YOU decided to go out with me. I thought it was my breath," Lance said as we walked down Mother's walkway to his car.

"I'm sorry I was so short with you before. I guess the fact that I came home to deal with my own personal issues and have been confronted with so many other problems, and losing loved ones has gotten to me. I just feel like my life plan has been tossed out the window," I said.

"You know, Chloe, when my wife passed, I was lost. I had spent four years going through cancer treatment and she just couldn't fight it anymore. My son was a newborn; at the same time, that's when my father became ill. At that point, I stopped planning," he said, stopping to open my door on the passenger side. "When you get the reality check of death, you learn quickly to leave certain things like life and the inevitable up to the man upstairs." We shared a smile. "And you know what?"

"What?" I coyly replied.

"I may not know as much as I pretend to know, but I do know you need somebody to worry about *Chloe* for a change. Somebody to take care of you. Get in!" He ordered me inside the car and shut my door, then dashed to the other side, hopping into the driver's seat and starting the engine. "Also, I know this is hard for you high-powered types, but try *not* to be in control tonight. You've gotta learn to trust *the man*." I shut my mouth and we pulled off.

We passed the sign entering Lake St. Louis, a small town about forty-five miles outside of the St. Louis city limits. When we pulled into Lance's driveway, I saw that his massive home sat on the edge of a small lake. I was even more impressed when he opened the front door and turned on the lights. There were windows and space for days.

"It's beautiful, but where's your furniture?" I asked curiously.

"Yeah, I haven't really gotten around to that. Restructuring my father's company has kept me busy. When I sold my place in New Jersey, I sold all the furniture with it. I lived in that place for six years. I wanted to start fresh."

"I can relate to that!"

We decided to hang out in the one room that *was* finished—his den, complete with a plasma-screen television, state-of-the-art stereo system, DVD, surround sound, the works.

"Look at all this music!" I said, referring to his extensive CD collection.

"Told you I was a music connoisseur," he said with a laugh, walking over to the wall and pulling a CD from one of the shelves. "Want a glass of wine?"

"I'd love some wine," I said, sitting down on the floor and closing my eyes. The Commodore's classic, "Zoom," was both soothing and seductive. I was so into the music I didn't hear Lance reenter. He kneeled down behind me, handed me the glass, and began to massage my temples.

"Ooh, that feels so good. And this wine is great. How did you know to pick pinot noir?" I asked, taking slow sips.

"I'm fly like that!" We laughed. "No, seriously, I remembered from the club there was some red wine next to you. So I took a stab in the dark!"

"That fool I married didn't even know what kind of wine I liked. Let me correct that. He didn't *want* to know anything about me."

"Hey, tonight we ain't talkin' about all that negative stuff. I don't even have to know your business like that, to know that that dude had to be crazy."

We started groovin' to the song. "Man, I've spent so many years runnin' and hangin' out and doin' the jet-set thing, that nowadays, I just wanna keep it simple and spend time with my son and people I care about. Don't you feel that way?" he said, turning toward me.

"Yeah, yeah, sure," I said, not quite sure how to answer his question. I almost felt at a loss. I'd been home just trying to catch my breath and keep from having a nervous breakdown. I wanted to change the subject. "Hey, do you mind playin' that again?"

"Done. It's already on repeat." He stopped rubbing my temples and sat down in front of me. "Can I kiss you?"

And he did, passionately, taking me in his arms and caressing me gently. And with precise choreography he stretched me out on my back and slowly placed himself on top of me. He kissed me down my neck over my shoulders. My entire body was covered with chill bumps. The brotha went straight for my feet. When he got to the straps of my sandals, he untied them and slid them off. He kissed each of my toes. I didn't realize just how bad I needed the touch of a man.

My eyes surveyed his smooth skin that reminded me of chocolate mousse. I closed my eyes and ran my fingers through his thick, soft waves that slid between my fingertips. I smiled, escaping into the song's chorus. I let my hands explore Lance's six-three frame. Thank you, Jesus, this man was built. Oh yes, I had had some fine ones before, but this man's body was sculpted, molded, and toned to perfection. For a moment I felt slightly insecure of my rounded belly.

Suddenly, I felt the pressure of his rock-hard manhood through his cargo pants, and I panicked. "Lance! No!" I said, stopping. I pulled away and grabbed my glass of wine, downing it in one swallow.

"I'm sorry. Damn, I got caught up," he said, clasping his hands behind his head.

"Me too."

"Chloe, you're special and I don't want to blow it with you."

"Thanks. It's just that I'm nowhere near ready for anything like this."

We both sat quietly while the song faded and started up again, then Lance reached for me, pulling me close again. "Hey, I'm into slow, very slow."

"Thank you," I said, safely snuggled in his strong arms. Lance propped his back against the wall and I slid in between his legs and he held me for the rest of the night.

"Mornin'," Lance whispered.

I jumped up in a panic. I had fallen asleep on his floor. "Oh my God, Lance! You gotta get me back to my mom's!" I frantically searched for my purse.

"Erumm," Lance cleared his throat loudly. He was already holding my purse up. I let out a sigh and smiled.

I had Lance drop me off in front of Salvatore's. I wanted to get out and walk a bit.

"Hey, y'all movin'?" he said, pointing to the For Sale sign in front of Salvatore's yard, as he pulled slowly to the curb.

"This is new to me. Let me out here," I said, giving him a peck on the cheek. "Thank you again!" I winked.

"That's what good dudes are for." He winked back. "Maybe we can catch a movie sometime."

"Bet!" I said, jumping out, closing the passenger side door, a bit distracted by the sign.

I quickened my pace up the steps to Salvatore's door, and before I could knock he opened the door. He was headed out and looked like he was in a hurry.

"Mornin', Chloe," he said in a heavy Caribbean accent.

"Good morning, Salvatore. I see you're in a rush," I said, following him back down the front porch steps.

"I can manage a moment for you."

"Salvatore, how long has the house been on the market?" I asked. We mainly go to Mother's from the side street that led right to her end of the driveway so I hadn't seen the sign.

"I just decided 'bout a week ago. I'm gonna move back to my home where my family is in Jamaica. Being here is too hard on my wife and children. I told your mother already. I'm sorry," he said sadly, checking his watch. "I'm gonna be late. Do you need anything else?"

"No. Thank you. And good luck."

As Salvatore pulled off, I stood there with a perplexed look on my face.

Ceci

THE NEW MOON

"GIRL, YOU KNOW I'm trippin'! I cain't believe I'm up in here doin' yo hair, Thora!" Me and my cuzin crew was chillin', kickin' back like old times at the shop. *Shiiittt!* I did my best work after hours.

"Oh, please, Ceci. You act like I ain't never had my hair done before!" We all fell out laughin'. Thora had to laugh her own damn self. Thora was lettin' me get up in her head, finally. "I just wish you had let me do it the first time. How you gon come here with your hair done? They ain't do no hair, fo real tho, 'cause you need yo ends clipped. You lucky it's the new moon."

"You still old-fashioned like that?" Chloe asked.

"See, you young and don't know shit 'bout the new moon!"

"Yes, I do! Mother always talked about having to cut our hair on the new moon. I just don't remember exactly why."

"In other words, she don't have a clue!" Thora said, with Fawn chiming in.

"Break it down for baby sis, Ceci!" Eve said.

"Yep, nobody could get their hair cut until it was the new moon." I put a cigarette in between my lips and struck a match, inhaling, then blowin' a puff of smoke out. "Girl, my mama, y'all's mama, Billye Jean, all of 'em learned that superstitious stuff from MaMaw."

"Who learned it from her mother who was a slave living on a plantation right up in Joplin, Missouri. Hell, that stuff we learned growing

331

up was from the ancestors and I don't play around. That stuff ain't no joke!" Fawn's eyes went wide.

"Hello!" Eve high-fived her.

"I know I be talkin' shit, but I don't give a fuck. I believe that hoodoo shit. I remember watchin' MaMaw when me, Fawn, and Thora was little, shit, I was like two or three. She'd be mixin' up stuff in pots and shit. I ain't gonna lie, she scared the hell outta me sometimes. Chloe, you wasn't even thought about, Eve you might not have been born yet, but, don't y'all remember seein' MaMaw heal that one lady in her kitchen that summer we all drove up to her farm? It was right before she died."

"I was older than y'all so you *know* I remember," Thora said. "Her name was Miss B and she looked just like a cockatoo; well, her hair did. She would come over to get her hair grease that MaMaw made."

"Ooh, yeah and she fell on the floor in a seizure," Fawn recalled.

"That heifer was jumpin' around like a fish in some hot-ass grease!" I said, dumping the ash from my cigarette.

"MaMaw put a spoon in her mouth and started prayin' on her and the woman's body settled down. Next thing you know she was up on her feet like nothin' had happened and walkin' out the door with her grease in a tin coffee can. Then MaMaw burned some sage to get the leftover spirits out."

"That's where Mother and all of them get that burnin' sage stuff from! Anyway, it's the new moon, and if we don't hurry up, y'all gonna mess with me makin' some new money! So let me get to work." I picked up my trimmin' scissors and started carefully snippin' Thora's ends with my cigarette hangin' from my lips.

"Ceci, don't catch my hair on fire!" Thora warned.

"Girl, I'm a damn professional!" We all fell out laughin'.

When I was done clippin' Thora's hair, I placed the hair in a sandwich bag. "This is for good luck!" Thora, never being much of the sentimental type, gave me a hug. "C'mon, Thora, let's get this here hair blown out and whipped! I ain't got time to be snifflin' and cryin'!" We all broke out laughin' again.

"I'm really happy for the first time to be back in St. Louis, even though it's under these circumstances. For real, I actually miss being as connected to y'all. I feel like I'm missing out on everyone's lives," Thora said.

"Well, y'all know me so I'm just gon say it. Cuz, on a serious note, why it take 'til Billye Jean get sick for you to come around? We miss you." Ever'body nodded, agreein' with me. "I mean you know Ceci gonna always keep it real."

"Contrary to what our mothers—who are now old, busy-body ladies—spend their precious time cacklin' about, I'm not antifamily. My life just has to be stress-free at this point. Honestly, it's stressful here."

"She ain't lyin'!" I said.

"You're right, Thora, but what would we all do without this family?" Eve asked.

"Be sane!" Fawn blurted out, and we all cracked up.

"Seriously, y'all. Time flies and being here this time has changed my mind about some things. I do need to come back more often. My children need to get closer to you all. I've kept my life simple—"

"And secluded!" Eve interjected.

"Maybe." Thora took a deep breath and buried her face in her hands.

"Hold up, girl, whassup? You not okay," I said, droppin' the flat iron.

"Get her some tissue." Fawn motioned to Chloe. We all gathered around her.

"I have cancer, I think. They found a lump in my left breast. They did a biopsy," she wiped her face with the tissue.

"Take your time, Thora," I said, pattin' her on the back.

"I went for the follow-up appointment, but I changed my mind when I got there. The doctor called several times after that, but I didn't want to deal with any of it. David finally made me call back and the doctor said they want me to come in. There's a possibility they may want to do a mastectomy, or radiation or something. I'll have to face the music when I get back."

"Hold up, they talkin' 'bout cuttin' your breast off?" I ain't gonna lie. I was winded and messed up in the head. Thora had always been my big cousin who I looked up to 'cause she had her good life out there in Nevada. "This is some straight up mess. Thora, you got a good heart, and be tryin' to do the right thing, and here I am just out here kickin' it like I'm invincible or somethin'. Somebody like you don't drink or nothin' and done got this shit," I said, shakin' my head in disbelief.

"But you look fine," said Eve, who was just as stunned.

"I feel pretty good." Thora sniffed, wiping her nose. "And Ceci, don't be silly. It's nobody's fault that I have cancer, and feeling bad about me having it versus you or anyone else is just plain crazy. We deal with the cards we're dealt in life. I just want them to take care of it, and I don't want Billye Jean to know. That woman will have the whole family in an uproar. She's already one foot in the grave 'cause of Junior and Arnaz."

"Thora, you have to tell her. She's your mother! The family will pray for you. We can come be with you," Fawn said, pacin' the room.

"I don't believe this. Damn!" I said, shakin' my head. "I agree. You've gotta tell her."

"You're gonna fight this cancer thing, aren't you?" Chloe said with tears in her eyes.

"You're strong; you've gotta fight it!" Eve added.

"What's your plan?" Fawn asked.

"I'm gonna go in and whatever they have to do is fine. It's okay. I don't want anyone to worry. And Lord knows all of you have your own lives." Thora's eyes were watery again.

"I know I don't have much room to say a lot, but as the next to oldest of all of us, I'm puttin' the law down. We gonna stick together, pray together, and be there for you, and Billye Jean should know," I said.

"Okay, but I don't want her to know until she gets better and no matter what, I *will* be here for Billye Jean." Thora wiped her eyes again, and then we all joined hands. "But Ceci, I need one more thing from you."

"Cuz, you just say the word." I had to hold back my own emotions that were gettin' outta hand at that point.

"I need to find Junior." Thora was lookin' at me all serious and shit. Damn, I didn't know if she was really ready for that shit.

"You cool, Thora?"

"Yep." I could see how tense she was. I was tryin' like hell to slow down on my drinkin', but this kind of stuff will push some damn body. I done let go of that coke shit for the most part, but I'mma have ta get me somethin' to drink after this.

"Open the door, Archie!" I said, bangin' on the door. I had asked enough of my peoples in the streets where Junior was after we checked the shelter where he said he was 'posed ta be. I was actually kinda disappointed that he didn't get clean this time.

"You know what? Forget it, Ceci. I changed my mind. I don't want to see his ass." Thora was so mad she started pacin'. "He hasn't even been to the damn hospital! It's so typical."

"I'm comin'!" I heard somebody yell from inside the apartment.

"Naw, Thora, we done came all the way down to these damn projects, you ain't runnin' from family this time," I said, grabbin' her arm firmly. "Plus, you don't know nothin' 'bout these streets. I ain't lettin' you walk back by yo'self!"

"Who is it?" Archie opened the door and let out a puff of smoke. Archie had grown up with Thora and Junior, and he was nothin' but a straight crackhead.

"Go get Junior!" Thora demanded. I didn't have to say shit. Archie closed the door and we heard him soundin' all nervous and shit.

"Junior, Junior, yo sista Thora and 'nem is outside."

A few minutes later, Junior opened the door and stepped outside. He was tryin' to straighten out his clothes and pat down his hair. I just turned away. I couldn't stand lookin' at him like this.

"I didn't come here because I wanted to. I came here because you need to know Billye Jean is in the hospital. For once you need to get your shit together and go see about her. She might not make it this time. Please take me to the airport, Ceci. I can't stand the sight of this!" Thora threw her hands up in the air and turned to walk away.

"Thora, wait." Junior grabbed her by the arm. She was about to jerk away. Aw, naw! I couldn't handle breakin' up another damn fight in the family. They really workin' my nerves.

"I'm sorry. I'm tryin' this time, I really am. Where is she?"

"She's at the same hospital she's always at!"

"I'mma get myself cleaned up."

"Dammit, Junior, when are you gonna grow up and quit using drugs as an excuse? You didn't give a damn about Monique, so do this at least for your mother! I gotta go!"

After I dropped Thora at the airport, I thought about seein' Junior and how it tore Thora up. I opened my purse where I had me a brand-new bottle of Hennessy. I looked at it and then I thought about it. I just didn't have a taste for it tonight, after all.

STARTING OVER

I have known women/rivers of women
Blu/blk/tan/highyella/blu-vein women
Knitting hands/collecting eyes/ribbons/photographs/hairclippings
poems and stories/stringing pearls and parables/tears and smiles
Gathering picnic baskets/silk gloves/birthmarks/teacups and ashes/
pickin' the flowers/snatching the breathprints of women past/
writing a song called ... Women ... Rivers of Women!

Joy Ann

THE HEALING

To my girls: I see the manifestation of my dreams in each of you . . .

I WOKE UP EARLY this morning and burned some sage. I placed fresh lemon water on every windowsill in the house, and opened the Bible to Ecclesiastes: "To every *thing* there is a season, and a time to every purpose under heaven." Then I got down on my knees and prayed real hard.

Well, Lord, these past months have tested our faith in more ways than we expected. But you spared us once again. You promised that you would open up new territory for your faithful and diligent servants. New and greater territory! And you have, through three precious gifts, my daughters. Women who are lovin' women, fightin' women, soft women, prayin' women. Women who carry my legacy and the legacy of all the women who came before me. And Lord, I still got dreams and I know you ain't through with me yet. Thank you, Jesus! Amen.

When I was finished with my mornin' prayers, I made a hot cup of fresh mint tea, put on my heavy wool sweater, gathered my brush bucket and paints, and headed out into the yard. I set my easel up and placed a large framed canvas on it. I'd started working on this piece right before Chloe came home, but in the past few days I've found new inspiration, and it's on my heart to finish it.

I'm inspired by my three rising suns, and my sister, my cousin, mother, grandmother, aunts, and even the men who I've loved with every fiber in my body. This is for each of them. Even though the weather is kinda brisk, the sunshine got it feelin' just right. Too early for snow, but probably gonna be a long winter though. Sometimes you just get that feelin'.

My arthritis was actin' up so I put some of my Chinese oil on my hands and they feel all right now. I closed my eyes and inhaled deeply. I opened them and smiled, dippin' my brush in red, symbolizing our passion, heartbeat, and the blood flowin' through our veins. Next I dipped my brush in black. It symbolizes our heritage. I furiously mixed it with other colors on my palette to create shades of black, brown, and beige. We are reflections of our African and Native American roots.

The late autumn air shot a familiar chill up my back. I could feel in my spirit change was comin'. My eyes welled up with tears, and I began to cry as the strokes from my brush became more intense. My tears this mornin' were a joyful explosion of life come full circle. New life, old life, past life, future life. The fullness of life MaMaw always spoke of as she held my tiny hands when I was a li'l girl. I didn't understand, but she was tellin' me my gift would spring forth from my hands. I would bless others' lives with these hands.

"Good mornin', Joy Ann!" Alex called out from the other side of the fence.

"Good mornin', Alex!" I said, quickly wiping my tears.

"It's a good day!" he said, settin' up his work tools for the day.

"It's a blessed day!"

"Joy Ann, I don't wanna be too forthright, but I'm gonna go jam with some musicians down there at Blues Alley, nothin' too fancy, and I wanted to see if you'd like to join me."

I felt myself coverin' up a full-fledged blush. I do believe Mr. Duprey was askin' me out on a date. "Well, that sounds nice, but I have to see what day it is," I coyly replied.

"Wednesday night, maybe we could have dinner after. Like I said, not too fancy and I don't know how good we gonna play together, but just to dust off that gift you know, so I don't lose it. We gonna play a li'l blues and a li'l zydeco. Um, I understand if you cain't . . ."

"Yes, Mr. Duprey!" I said, cuttin' him off, still keepin' right on with my work. "I said I'd like to go, now I gots work to do. I'mma have to talk to you later."

"You just made an old man's day," he beamed, tippin' his hat.

I just smiled. Can you believe that Joy Ann Davis Michaels done messed around and got a date at sixty-eight. Now I didn't read too much into it 'cause a mouth will say anything, especially an old one. Ooh, I sure hope he ain't sickly. I ain't got no time for no old and sick man! Humph! I took a sip from my teacup and leaned back on my stool, takin' a better look at my work in progress. I smiled. I think I'mma call this piece *The Women Gather*. I smiled again, inhaled deeply. Yeah, somethin' was tellin' me I was definitely gonna conjure up a masterpiece.

Chloe
THE SIGN

"**C**HLOE, YOU HAVE more angels than you have enemies and you need to be about the business of housing joy, not pain, inside of you from now on," Mother said as she clenched her eyes tightly. "I'm speakin' to you in the spirit this mornin'. Don't burden yourself with God's business 'cause you don't have control over that." Mother spoke those reaffirming words to me right before I walked out the door.

When I woke up, I decided I had to get back to the Chloe basics and work off all my stress and calories. I couldn't believe nearly six months had passed. The runner's trail in Forest Park was a good start. It was the one place that reminded me of childhood innocence and peace. I took off at a slow and steady pace.

It had been a while and I had to find my rhythm. Life was about rhythm and pace. Push yourself too hard, you're bound to crash and burn. Go too fast, you're bound to miss the goodness it has to offer. This time away is showing me that it may be time for a fresh start. Fawn had a point. The cost of living is much cheaper here, and I could get more for my money.

As the sweat poured over my body, I felt my body begin to release the negativity and fear that had been clogging up my pores for weeks. I was drenched with sweat and my pulse was on overdrive. I looked up and had reached the five-mile mark. I slowed to a stop and shook my legs and arms out. I stood at the edge of the park and looked out over the blossoming vastness.

Watching the trees swaying, the grass bend, feeling the sun penetrating my skin, was a sweet release. Nature can withstand the freezing cold, floods, scorching heat and it still lives to see the next morning. Nature lets me know that I am always in a holy atmosphere, that God's spirit and energy pervades the world. People make life way too complicated. I suddenly felt a sense of clarity wash over me. I was renewed, revived, and refocused on what was important: happiness.

Eve and Fawn didn't know what I was talking about when I told them to meet me at the Art Museum right away, that we were having an emergency sister lunch. They were both somewhat uninterested until I announced I was treating. I ran all the way to the museum café and felt exhilarated by the time I got there.

"I have a surprise," I said, reaching into my purse. "I got my papers! They came this morning. Mother doesn't even know yet!" We all screamed so loud I thought our heads would fall off.

After we ordered, Eve picked up her water glass and tapped her spoon on the rim. "Ladies, I have an announcement too," Eve said excitedly.

"Oh Lord, you know we gotta watch those announcements in this family," Fawn joked.

"Shut up, Fawn! OK, I was waiting to tell y'all, but I think seeing firsthand everything that you do, Chloe, and thinking about all the things that we've been going through over these months, I decided to take some steps to get my life in order. It was time to 'shit or get off the pot.' Hello!"

"That's the new motto for me too," Fawn added.

"I got a catalog in the mail by accident from St. Louis University. But like Mother says, 'God don't make mistakes.' I've already enrolled.

I don't know how I'm gonna pay for it, but I've gotta go for my dream to own my own business. I may have to make and sell a whole lotta candles and soaps, but I'll do it!"

"Well, go on, girl!" Fawn cheered, as we both gave Eve a round of applause. Then Fawn said, "I guess I can pass on my good news too. Well, it's not really news 'cause I haven't done anything yet. But, since we're talkin' about goin' for our dreams, I've decided I want to open a bed-and-breakfast."

"Ooh, today is a good day!" I shrieked.

"I don't know where I'm gonna get the start-up money. I'll probably get a job and start saving, but I've always wanted my own hospitality business. And St. Louis doesn't have anything that's black owned like this. Maybe it will have a mini spa and even a store that could sell your stuff, Eve. I want to display Mother's art there, too."

"Wow, y'all, Mother's gonna be so proud," I said.

"You know, she's a big reason why I'm goin' back to school. I mean it's for me, but I want to make her proud. I love Mother. It's just taken me a while to understand her!"

We laughed.

"Maybe it's gettin' rid of Dale and focusing more on Christina that makes me see for myself. I think Daddy dying and all of us comin' to grips with the father stuff has helped us get here. I just want you all to know that I'm blessed to have sisters like you and I'm sorry if I every hurt you, Fawn. I think I always felt like at home I didn't have a place in this family. What I mean is, Fawn, you were book smart and fearless. Then you, Chloe, were the little go-getter. It was like I didn't fit. I was wrong, and God has shown me that. I know that even as much as you preach to me, Fawn, that you love me, and only want the best for me.

"I was so busy fighting everyone that I didn't see my own talent. After Christina was born, I started foolin' around with makin' my candles and stuff and had a knack for that. Maybe it's more than just a hobby. Maybe it'll turn into something. Whatever happens, I'm just happy I'm finally getting my life in order."

Fawn chimed in, "I just wanna say, we all come from Joy Ann and are all sisters in the supreme meaning of the word! This stuff with Cliff has put a lot into perspective for me. I decided to go to counseling with him and make my marriage work. He's a good man, and he has a good heart. He still is gonna get on my damn nerves probably, but when you love somebody, you stick it out come hell or high water, in no particular order.

"I know y'all be gettin' sick of me passin' on my big-sister wisdom and advice, but this time I've got some self-directed pearls of wisdom to follow myself. The operative word for me starting today is organize, organize, organize. I need to learn how to say N-O. Stop overloading my circuits. Stop trying to be a superwoman and do fifty different things.

"I'm also going to take a hiatus from some of my social group responsibilities. Those Negroes don't appreciate a person's hard work half the time. I'm going to start workin' out more. Honey, I'm closer to fifty than forty! I've been seeing in the magazines how women my age have bodies like Madonna's—tight and lean. That's what I'm gonna be—a lean, mean, sexy machine.

"But I will tell you both. It takes a strong belief in the Holy Spirit to tackle life's challenges. We've got to all start practicing humility and prayer. Joy Ann knows she taught us to pray. Okay! So I just want to say thank you, Chloe."

"For what, Fawn?"

"For bringin' *all* this insanity home with you from California," Eve interjected. We laughed.

"No, seriously, despite all the bad things that we had no control over—your divorce, Daddy and Grandmother passing away, Aunt Billye Jean getting sick—all this madness has somehow brought us closer as sisters. I wouldn't have made it these past months without you all, and without our family," Fawn said.

"All right!" We toasted.

"And one more thing! Chloe, as far as your love life, know that when one door closes, another always opens. So don't sweat it. Imagine if things would have gone on with that idiot another six months or a year. Even with Edward, if you had abandoned what you really wanted, just to live according to what he wants, you wouldn've been puttin' him before yourself. Take it slow and love yourself for a while."

My eyes welled up. "Hear, hear!" Eve said, lifting her glass, on the verge of tears herself. "To Chloe!"

"Y'all are really going to make me cry. I was going to wait until before I left to give you these. I've been carrying them around for days." I reached into my purse and pulled out two envelopes, addressed to each of them. "This is for you, Eve, and this is for you, Fawn." They looked at the envelopes strangely. "I know Grandmother would've wanted me to share a piece of her with you too. Hey, maybe it'll help with that tuition or go toward that down payment on your bed-and-breakfast."

They opened the envelopes to each find a check for ten thousand dollars. There was so much hootin' and hollerin' going on at that table the hostess came over to see if we were all right. Eve told her we were celebrating life. The woman was so tickled she told us to carry on. A nearby patron, who apparently felt our joy from across the room, was practically in tears. She motioned for the waiter to bring us a round of champagne on her.

For an instant, I closed my eyes, and when I opened them again, tears began to stream down my face. We were each other's heartbeat, each of us unable to survive without the other.

Billye Jean

GOT MY GROOVE BACK

I'M JUST GETTIN' out the hospital and the least Arnaz coulda done was finish pullin' up this floor. I know I ain't s'posed to be doin' no housework or nothin' but ain't nobody else here to help me. I ain't like Joy Ann, always tryin' to have folks over and her house just be junky, paint stuff everywhere. Oh no, it'll make me sicker up in here with a dirty house. I know I gotta lotta stuff, but at least I got a house and I know how to keep it clean. Not as clean as I used to. Since I got this bad heart I just be runnin' outta breath if I do too much movin' around. I done got to the point where I just have to go lay down.

I had started on the sunporch, and now I just gotta finish it. I made me a pad for the floor outta old towels and got comfortable on my knees. I yanked up a large square of the floorin'. Joy Ann would think I was crazy, but, shoot, I'm 'bout the only sane person in this family. I know I betta be feelin' betta by next week 'cause that's our annual fashion show at the church. I'm sure gonna miss Millie this time.

The last show was really beautiful. I bought myself a new outfit, too. But I swear you know folks ain't got no home trainin'. At the lunch after, Viola and Miss Vivian they just was grabbin' food from the buffet like they ain't have no home trainin' and talkin' loud, with they big behinds. It was just awful. Millie was there. We was so mad. It was a joint event with my parish and hers, St. Elizabeth's. I was the chair of the Ladies Mission and Hospitality Committee.

Arnaz ain't never around no way. I guess I like stayin' busy at the church and I gets bored around here. Doin' work is like keepin' company for me. I know I should be restin', but I can do that when I die. I decided to take a break and stood up to stretch my legs. I collected the scraps and tossed them into the garbage can.

I ain't never been afraid of no work though. That's the problem with most of the young folk today. They don't know nuthin' about gettin' they hands dirty, workin' hard for somethin'. They get stuff too easy. I kneeled back down next and started pulling up a new section. My sister asked me one time if I ever thought my life would end up like this. Shucks, I didn't think I'd be livin' *this* long.

"You seen my work shoes, Billye Jean?" Arnaz called out from the back bedroom.

Speak of the devil. Hell would freeze over and this linoleum would rot if I waited on him. Humph! He in the back gettin' dressed, talkin' 'bout he gotta go to work. Probably lyin' like always. I don't know and don't care no more.

"No!" I yelled back.

Arnaz shuffled into the kitchen, wearin' a gray workman's jumpsuit. Seventy-five was ridin' him hard. He all hunched over, with that stiff walk, and head so white he look a hundred. You can tell by them quick short steps, he was still tryin' to keep up a front. Probably for his woman!

"I cain't find my glasses. I'mma be late fa work," he mumbled.

"Yo lunch is in the pot in the refrigerator." I had just cooked some beans I had froze before the day I went to the hospital, and I fried a piece of chicken, and mixed it all together. Arnaz reached into the refrigerator.

"Yo work hat is on the washer in the basement." We been doin' this so long I don't even have to think about it. It was hard to believe we was husband and wife. We don't hardly speak to each other and there ain't no emotion.

"Arnaz," I said, lookin' up from my work. "I want you to look at that paper over there on the table before you go."

"I gots ta go, Billye Jean!"

"No, I think you need to look at that." I went back to pullin' up the square of floor I was workin' on. I saw him out the corner of my eye squintin' at the page.

I tore back a large corner of the floor, stopped for a moment, and caught my breath.

"Billye Jean, what is this shit?!"

"You see it in black and white, don't you?" I said, keepin' on workin'. "The pen is right there next to it. The way I see it, you ain't got no choice." I leaned back on my heels. "After this last brush with death I had to look at myself real good. I been stupid for a long time, but ain't nothin' smarter than an old fool wakin' up. See, 'cause you done had time to get smart. I done spent years worryin' about where you at, what you doin', and who you doin' it wit.

"I didn't even listen to my own children. I lost one. I'm lucky I didn't lose the otha one. So while she was here I had her take care of a li'l business for me. I got me a lawyer. I had him put that paper together. So you just betta go on and sign it 'fore things get real ugly for you, Arnaz. The people called from some credit company sayin' you and your lady friend are in some fraud trouble.

"Now, I ain't crazy; when you die, I got money comin' to me, but 'til then, in the meantime, this house don't belong to you no more. It belongs to Thora. You sign that paper and get on outta here, and I'mma keep prayin' for you just like I been doin' all these years. But now I'mma be prayin' that you don't suffer when yo time come 'cause Lord knows it's comin'."

I went right on back to work and Arnaz signed that paper.

"I'm gone. Don't wait up."

"I won't."

Then Arnaz was gone just like that. No good-bye kiss, no nothing. Fine by me, hell, he ain't really *been* here in too long to remember. I took a long swallow of my ice water, drainin' the glass. The ice jingled in the bottom of the glass. I think I'mma make me some sauerkraut and rib tips. They wanna tell me I cain't eat this or that.

Shoot, if this old fool ain't killed me, ain't no sauerkraut and rib tips gonna do it.

God must be keepin' me around for some reason. I think to right a lot of the wrongs from my past. It's ironic. I've always been known as the family hell-raiser, but if I don't do nothin' else, I'mma go through hell and back for my kids and my family.

Chloe

WIDE OPEN SPACES

"CLOSE YOUR EYES," Lance said, guiding me up a flight of stairs. "Boy, I have a blindfold on, what more do you want me to do?" I said, gingerly stepping up.

"I want you to close your eyes is what I want you to do!"

Before I could retort, Lance untied the blindfold and told me to open my eyes. I was still fussing.

"First, you want me to close my eyes, then you want me to open them, make up your mind. Oh my God!" I couldn't get another word out. I had opened my mouth to the most beautiful space I'd ever seen.

"You like it?" Lance said, pulling me over to a large picture window that overlooked a sprawling roof-top courtyard and garden. Beyond the roof was a picturesque view of the Mississippi River and the St. Louis Arch.

I looked around the large loftlike room that had several doors and a winding stairwell that connected to various other parts of the warehouse-looking building.

"I asked if you liked it, woman?"

"I love it! It's beautiful. What is it? Is it yours?"

"Oh, now you got a million questions. Yes, Chloe, I purchased the building. It's going to house my new offices and my foundation. And then I don't know what I'll do with the rest. Rent out office space or something. I gotta make sure I've got some income coming in or how else am I going to take care of you?" He cracked a smile.

For some strange reason my eyes welled up with tears.

"You okay?" Lance asked.

"I'm really, really great. Maybe better than I've been in a long time." I paused, wiped my eyes, and swallowed hard. "Lance, that night at your house you said you just wanted to keep things simple in your life at this point. I couldn't give you much of an answer when you asked if I agreed, because the words just weren't there. What I'm saying is, since I've been home this time, I'm seeing that life will pass you by if you let it."

"Yes, it will," he said, kissing me on the forehead. "Chloe, I'm not going to let good things pass me by anymore. I like you. I like you a whole lot and I wanna take care of you."

"Yeah, I've heard that before."

"You'd better let go of the past or else we aren't going to be able to work on our future," he said, kissing me again, this time on the lips. I smiled. "Let me take care of you. You are very special, Chloe Michaels."

"I like the way that sounds."

I pulled away and walked over to the large floor-to-ceiling window across the room. I stood there momentarily, looking out at the river below. Something about the water and the view was very eye opening and cathartic. "How much do you think you'll be renting that office space out for?" I asked.

"You interested or something?" he said with a laugh.

"Maybe, if the deal is right."

"Well, let me check with my partners. One minute." Lance walked away, disappearing behind a wall. A few seconds later he returned. "Looks like my associates think you're okay, and as long as you're clean and don't throw wild parties, they say you can be one of our first tenants!" I swatted him playfully.

My ideas were running wild. I was envisioning where I'd put my desk and I saw the perfect wall for one of Mother's paintings.

"By the way, I know someone who's looking for representation."

"Who? You know Bloomberg-Michaels has a reputation. We're very selective," I said, twisting my mouth.

"Lance James!"

"You? But don't you have a publicist already?"

"Did, but I fired them. So why are you worried about that? Do you want me as a client or not?"

"Yeah! But business is business. I don't mix it with the personal stuff," I stated firmly.

"First of all, Chloe Michaels, don't flatter yourself that much."

"Let me speak to my associates." I walked out of the room and seconds later returned. "Looks like your profile checks out and you will officially be the first client of Bloomberg-Michaels, Midwest!" I extended my hand and we shook on it. Then Lance playfully yanked me closer in a passionate embrace, followed by one of those kisses right out of the movies.

I said a silent prayer to myself . . .

> *Dear God,*
> *If all that drama and pain was needed to get me to this place of peace, then so be it. I'm putting you in control this time. Oh, and if Lance is the one, then, God, you did real good! Amen.*

Carol Jane

OH HAPPY DAY

IT WAS THE first Sunday and I wanted my family to celebrate in the blessin' and baptism of Sage Davis Gibson. Joy Ann and all her girls, and grandkids, and Billye Jean, even Lawrence, were all here with me on this glorious day. God is so good and awesome. I couldn't stop smilin'. The choir, mothers of the church, and missionary society were all in full regalia. There was gonna be some good singin' and prayin' up in here today.

Reverend Yancy called Billye Jean up for a special healin' prayer and I know she needed it. We all turnin' over some new leaves in our lives. I guess you ain't never too old for that. I'm glad she finally is gonna start livin' for herself and not Arnaz no more. I guess we all need to do a li'l bit of that. I see Joy Ann with her children and I ain't never been a person who put they mind on jealous thoughts. But I cain't help but be a bit sad.

Joy Ann got her girls, and no matter what, they stand by they mama and love her and honor her. That's what a child is s'pose to do, honor thy mother and thy father. I guess as hard as my life was, as deep as the pain goes, I loved my child. I still love her, but I know God wants me to let her go. I got to. I got to set her free so she can come back right.

I started writin' her a letter and put it in my bible, tellin' her the whole story of how she got here. But ain't no real need to hurt her like that. I just gotta help Satin be better and not hold her so tight. I think that's where I went wrong. I did get a message to Cecilia, asking her to come this mornin'. I gotta have faith that she'll change, what else can I do as a mother? The choir was lining up for the processional. I checked my watch once more before givin' up.

"You just knew I wasn't comin' didn't you, Mama?" Cecilia whispered, smilin' big as day, sliding into the pew next to me. Stanley was on the otha side of her. Satin, Sage, and Kamal Robert Johnson, also known as "Poo," rushed in, scooting into the row behind us. Praise God, he got a government name! I didn't even smell no liquor on Cecilia. Glory! Glory!

Reverend Yancy was finishin' up a rousin' sermon.

"I cried unto the Lord with my voice and he heard me out of his holy hill. Selah!" Pastor shouted. That man sho can preach. He was a large man, about six three, and at least two seventy-five. His rich, eloquent, baritone voice seemed to mesmerize the congregation. "Church, there is sweetness in the name of God. Church say amen!"

"Amen!" we all replied.

"So today I tell you like Second Corinthians, chapter thirteen, verse eleven. 'Put things in order, listen to God's appeal and agree with one another, live in peace; and the God of love and peace will be with you!' " Reverend Yancy stepped down from the pulpit with his arms outstretched.

The choir stood preparin' to sing their final selection and as the organist began to play, Reverend Yancy walked over to me and took me by the hand. "This is impromptu, but I feel like we need Sister Carol Jane Davis Gibson to bless us with her angelic voice. Church say amen!"

"Amen!" we all replied.

I grabbed the microphone and took a deep breath. "Before I sing, I just want to give a li'l testimony this mornin', if y'all don't mind. My family's been through a lot over the past several months. We've lost some loved ones, and praise God, the life of my cousin, Billye Jean, was spared. We've made some choices to clean up our lives," I said, winkin' at Ceci. "And we've put some old dogs to bed."

Joy Ann nodded and threw up her right hand. "Thank you, Jesus!" she shouted.

"So I say thank you, Heavenly Father, this mornin' for wakin' us up and bringin' us into your house today. Thank you for givin' us another chance to do your work. And like the scripture says, Thessalonians One, chapter five, *'Let us, who are of the day, be sober, puttin' on the breastplate of faith and love, and for a helmet, the hope of salvation.'* Hallelujah! Hashanuna Shana Na!" I had got so happy I was speakin' in tongues. When the spirit moves you, you can't be concerned about what it'll make you do. Mother Henrietta, who was the eldest member of the church, at one hundred and one, stood up and put her hand on one hip and the other hand shot straight up in the air. She began pacing back and forth, shouting, "Yes, Lord! Thank you, Lord!"

The organist played as I came in with that first verse of "I Surrender All." As the choir's chorus soared, tears were streamin' down my face. Cecilia stepped outta the pew, and so help me God, took my hand and joined me at the front of the church. Do Jesus! I changed my mind right there about tellin' her about anything from the past. Wasn't no need. Sometimes you gotta, like the old sayin' goes, let sleepin' dogs lie.

Chloe

THE HOUSE OF ESTROGEN

I REMEMBER THE DAY I walked into Mother's tiny house feeling like life was over for me. *Who would've thought that a temporary visit back home, and being confronted with so much conflict and sadness, would've resulted in such a joyous day?* I thought, smiling to myself as I drove Mother's car, leading the way after church back to Mother's. Fawn and Eve were following us in her car, and Carol Jane was behind them in the minivan, which carried Aunt Billye Jean, Satin, the baby, and Ceci.

I motioned for them to pull over as I slowed down, turning into the driveway in front of Salvatore's house. I parked the car and turned the ignition off. I could see Eve and Fawn in the rearview mirror with perplexed looks on their faces.

"Chloe, why are you parking here, baby?" Mother asked.

" 'Cause we're home. This is where I'm supposed to park." The car was silent. "I made a decision, Mother, that I'm gonna move back home."

"Chloe, what about your business?" she asked, wrinkles forming across her forehead.

"Mother, this is what I want to do. I'm tired of L.A. anyway. I was living, eating, and sleeping that job. The money is great, but I never had time to do anything but make a lot of it. Might be kind of nice to actually spend some of the money I've made. Plus, I'm going to open a satellite office here and rent space from my friend Lance."

"I think we should talk about this inside, Chloe," Mother said with a look of uncertainty on her face.

"Good idea. Here," I said, handing her a set of keys. "I think these belong to you."

Mother was speechless.

"Mother, these are yours. I bought it for you."

There was a look of shock frozen on her face for a whole five minutes, and then she burst into tears.

"Here," I said, jingling the keys in front of her face.

"Oh my God, Chloe. I can't believe you bought me this house. I love this house!"

We stood in the foyer of Mother's new freshly painted home. Salvatore had left us with an early housewarming gift. He framed the painting Mother had been working on for months.

"*The Women Gather*! I just finished it!" Mother was bursting with joy. We all stood back and admired it. The painting was in bright hues of purple, orange, red, yellow, and green, and the abstract women represented all different shades of black women, telling the story of a family of women congregating at the dinner table.

The house was completely empty now, except for a large dining table I had purchased especially for this room, large enough to seat ten—now Mother could have all the Sunday dinners her heart desired in style.

"What am I gonna do with all this space? This house has five bedrooms, Chloe."

"I don't know. I guess you'll just have to figure it out. Just stay out of the basement. Mr. Duprey fixed it up just for me." I smiled.

While everyone milled about the house, checking out its renovations, courtesy of Salvatore hiring Mr. Duprey, Mother pulled me into the large living-room area.

"Words can't express your mother's love and appreciation for you, Chloe. My pride illuminates like the sun in you. This is so humbling for me. Courage is the key to life, and you are an example for me and your sisters. And nerves don't hurt, which God knows you have. You are the sunshine in my life, shared by two other sun-risings and two star grandbabies," she said, taking a deep breath. "Lord, have mercy! I just know how to build my home on rocks, feathers, sticks, clouds, and rainbows. Now, you have helped me join a circle I never thought I'd reach . . . homeowner! But you gotta promise your mother somethin'. Okay?" she asked, taking me by the hand.

"Anything," I said.

"I just want you to let the sun in and you keep shinin' and laughin' in your life. All that you've endured is leading you to greater happiness."

I want my mother to have nice things from here on out. No matter what mistakes she's made or decisions she could've done better, for once she deserves not to worry. She deserves to have life a little easier. So, we've got that brand-new house just like she always promised when I was a little girl.

"Everybody, there's one more surprise and it's outside!"

The whole family followed me out to the backyard to the garage. Mr. Duprey was standing outside and hit the button, opening the garage door. As it rolled up, Mother's eyes went wide.

"This is your new studio, Joy Ann. Now you can paint all those masterpieces you be dreamin' 'bout!"

Mr. Duprey had transformed that old garage into Mother's very own art studio, set up with her easel and a display area and even a little café counter for making tea and coffee when she had guests. "God is so good," she said, letting loose tears of joy. "I didn't have one house, now I got a buncha houses!" We all laughed.

"I'mma be gettin' to work on fixin' up that one you was in, too. It keeps me busy."

"Alex, don't you wanna eat somethin' first?" Mother asked. I do believe she was blushing!

"Why don't you save me a plate!" He winked, tipping his hat.

And no sooner than I handed the new key over, Eve chimed in. "Chloe, I wouldn't ask if I really didn't need to, but do you think I could stay here just for a little while 'til I get on my feet since I'm going back to school now."

"You gotta ask Mother, this is *her* house."

"Well, Chloe, I'd really like for Eve to be here and Christina when she comes home."

"Fine!" I said, throwing up my hands. I knew Mother would be a nervous wreck worrying about where Eve would lay her head. "But it's just temporary, Eve!"

"Six months max—well, maybe a year, but not longer than that, promise!" Eve kissed me and eagerly rushed off to begin planning her new move.

Fawn just shook her head, "You know she ain't never gonna leave, right? Humph, well, I hope you make her pay rent!" she said, sucking her teeth.

We had our first official Sunday dinner in the new house and Mother was in her glory. Sitting around the dining-room table made me realize that it really doesn't matter how fancy the house is or what kind of structure we are in. What matters is love, breaking bread, mending spirits, and healing hearts. Family joining together in fellowship.

The true meaning of home can be found in its foundation. In spite of all the tears, the arguments, the celebrations, the smiles, the laughter, the pain, there is love, a love so deep it flows infinitely and endlessly through your veins. In the still of night I feel my ancestors' presence. I know their strength. It strengthens me. I know MaMaw, and Muh, and Grandmother are all sitting up there in heaven looking down smiling, proud that we are passing on the traditions passed on by the mothers, aunts, sisters, and daughters before.

And so the meal was served. As always, a feast had been prepared, fit for a king, but in the "house of estrogen," the queens always ruled.

The women gather
Like painted brides/a tapestry of

Eyes/hands/knees/hearts like open baskets
Pieces of their peace/fragments of their dreams
Snatches of their lives/with/their mothers, mothers
Rhythms/visions/breathprints/wrapped in their bosom
There, women gather
Dropping tongues in terra-cotta bowls
With their bibles and harms/bluz, boogie, herbs, oils, and curls
Seeing eyes and gospel pearls/heady laughter/lies and tears
Rolling like Jordan/prayers, rituals, and folktales
Stuffed between their teeth/a bloodline rich and mahogany
The women gather
Mothers, daughters, sisters, wives, and sweethearts
Grannies and aunt sister bell with their hellhounds and
Hollars/their children and men/lost lovers/lifted
Left/lost/forever and lasting with skeletons/secrets/gri-gri
And hush-hush folded in little bitty pieces
The women gather
Knitting hands/re-stitching their lives
Reconnecting the circle
Piecing the guilt to keep us warm
From generations for generations and generations to come . . .

ACKNOWLEDGMENTS

Very special thanks to Amy Schiffman, my agent, for your passion and expertise. Cheers to a bestseller and making movies!

Special thanks to my new editor, Laura Swerdloff, for your enthusiasm, direction, and support.

Many thanks to Stacey Creamer, Michael Palgon, David Drake, Ellen Folan, Jennifer Robbins, and the entire Broadway Books/Crown Publishing family.

Thanks to Charles Wartts, a brilliant scholar and one of the baddest freelance editors around. Thank you for challenging and strengthening me as a writer.

To Alan Haymon, as always, for your friendship, belief, and unflagging support.

Additional thanks to the following for their professional and personal support: My former editor, Janet Hill-Talbert, for opening the doors and for your friendship; Christian Nwachukwu Jr., my former associate editor, for your early support of this book; DL Warfield, my creative partner-in-crime; Patrik Henry Bass, for your professional advice, support, and most importantly, friendship; Lynn Whitfield; Sherry B., for your beautiful spirit, friendship, and love; Chandi Bailey; Tynisha Thompson; Marva Allen of Hue Man; Margena Christian, Clarence Waldron and the *Jet* family; *Ebony, Uptown* magazine; *Essence,* Curtis Bunn and the NBBC; Troy Johnson and the AALBC; and the black booksellers still hanging in there to keep the dream alive; finally, to Marie Dutton-Brown, my former agent, for the wisdom and knowledge that helped shape my career as a writer.

To the other women in my family for your prayers, love, and

strength during the evolution of this book: Sydney, GiGi, ShaRee, Angel, Joyce, Aunt Janet, Carla, Valerie, Passion, Doris (our acting matriarch), Mary Lou, Gloria, Jamina, Faith, Brenda, Gwen, Patricia, Lolita, Vivian, Mildred Lindsay, Kathi, Tudie, Sheryl, Linda, Frances, Susan, Tracey, Kim, Keylee, and Pat.

My circle of sisterfriends, "big sisters", and sorors who *always* have my back: Mamie, Tizzi, Dion, Crystal, LaShannon, Lajaun, Leah, Angie, Leslie, Africa, Lisa, Lesvia, Daphne, Kathleen, Crystal Gore, Dale, Allison, Pam, Dr. Pam, Sue, Carnetta (the fighter), Barbara Anne, and Wanda.

Finally, very special acknowledgment to Kelly for your friendship, courage, and strength as a woman, daughter, mother, and wife. And to my former attorney, Gina Castillo, my guardian angel, for fighting the good fight and giving me a fresh start.

ABOUT THE AUTHOR

Lyah Beth LeFlore, television producer and author, is one of today's most talented and respected creative forces. She's been featured in the *New York Times, Essence, Ebony, Jet,* and *Entertainment Weekly*; also on CNN and BET. Television producer credits include: *New York Undercover* (FOX), *Midnight Mac starring Bernie Mac* (HBO), and *Grown Ups* (UPN). She has worked at major networks and production companies such as Nickelodeon, Uptown Entertainment/Universal, Wolf Films/Universal, and Alan Haymon Productions. Her books include the coauthored, *Cosmopolitan Girls*; the *Essence* bestseller *Last Night A DJ Saved My Life*; and the *New York Times* bestseller and *Essence* bestseller, *I Got Your Back: A Father and Son Keep It Real About Love, Fatherhood, Family, and Friendship*—the nonfiction collaboration with Grammy Award father and son duo, Eddie and Gerald Levert. *I Got Your Back* was a 2008 Nominee/Finalist for the Essence Literary Awards and the NAACP Image Awards. In 2008, LeFlore also wrote the CD liner notes for the O'Jays' *The Essential O'Jays: Giving the People What They Want* and multiplatinum artist Usher's *Here I Stand*. In addition to LeFlore's third novel, *Wildflowers*, she will also expand her fan base in fall 2009 to include young readers with her hot new teen series *The Come Up*, illustrated by DL Warfield (Simon Pulse/Simon & Schuster). The first book of the series is *The World Is Mine*.

LeFlore, 39, is a native of St. Louis, Missouri, and holds a B.A. in Communications Media from Stephens College. In May 2005 she became the youngest member of the Stephens College Board of Trustees and only the second African American to be appointed to the Board in the college's history. She is also a member of the Alpha Kappa Alpha Sorority Incorporated. For more information, go to www.lyah bethleflore.com.